MW01138949

Picking on Retards

Scott Carpenter

AuthorHouse™
1663 Liberty Drive
Bloomington, IN 47403
www.authorhouse.com
Phone: 1-800-839-8640

This book is a work of fiction. Places, events, and situations in this story are purely fictional. Any resemblance to actual persons, living or dead, is coincidental.

First published by AuthorHouse 4/19/2010

ISBN: 978-1-4520-0891-2 (e)
ISBN: 978-1-4520-0743-4 (sc)

Library of Congress Control Number: 2010904667

Printed in the United States of America
Bloomington, Indiana

This book is printed on acid-free paper.

To Uncle Frank,
who has always had my back,
whether it's words or music.

Picking On Retards

Prologue

We are most shaped by the things that we are ashamed of.

I'm pretty certain of that.

The thought occurred to me one night a few weeks ago while I was sitting at the door in Gazonga's, watching a new stripper do the chicken walk. All new strippers do the chicken walk. It is a combination of nervousness, high heels, and the alcohol that they have to drink to work up the courage to dance naked in front of strangers. When they walk around the stage, they stretch their legs out in front of them extra far and bring their body up to the leg. They think they are being sexy and alluring, but it really resembles a chicken strutting in a barnyard, hence, the chicken walk.

But the chicken walk was not what brought on the thoughts of shame and its effect on shaping man. It was the presence of the club's new deejay, my old friend, Ethan. The club's new owner, a former regular who just happened to have hit the lottery a few years back, had hired him as a favor to me. Ethan had trouble finding work due to his… disability, so I was always keeping an eye out for a job he could handle. When Ricky, our old deejay, got fired for smoking crack in the deejay booth, I called the owner and asked him to give Ethan a shot.

"Lenny, we had to fire Ricky," I said, holding a napkin to my bleeding knuckle.

Ricky hadn't taken his firing well and took a swing at Devlynn, the manager. When I busted him in the mouth for swinging at her I cut my knuckle on his front tooth. The tooth itself was lying on the floor in front of the bar, all pearly on one end and bloody on the other. I explained to Lenny what had happened and he thought we had done the right thing.

"So, do we have anyone to deejay? Any applications?" Lenny asked.

"Well, yeah. Ever since you fixed this place up we have had no problem getting people to work here. We have a big stack of apps in the back."

"Then pick somebody and put 'em to work. I trust your judgment."

That was true. Lenny did trust my judgment and that of Devlynn. We were all old friends. But it was more than that. Lenny was too busy to come down and put things in order himself. Gazonga's was a toy for him. Lenny Kapowski was the master of a small media empire, and he couldn't be taking time out to handle every little thing at a little hometown strip club. After all, he'd only bought the place to keep the former owner from closing it and putting us out of work. We were a profitable business, but when you deal with the kinds of numbers that Lenny was used to dealing in, our profits were negligible.

"I have a guy in mind," I began tentatively. "But I'm not sure if you'd want him."

"Why? What's wrong with him?"

"Well, he could do the job, no problem. But he's a little slow," I answered honestly.

"How slow?"

"Not that bad, really. But he isn't the sharpest knife in the drawer," I said, trying to decide if I should let him know who it was I was talking about. Then I just said it. "It's Ethan. Ethan Miles."

Lenny didn't say anything for a few moments.

"Lenny? Still there?"

"Teeth?" came the reply. "You want to hire Teeth?"

I didn't like it when people called him that, but I wanted to get Ethan the job, so I didn't say anything about it. Besides, I knew Lenny didn't mean anything by it. *Teeth* was a name they used to taunt Ethan with in high school. Not only was he retarded, but he had these really horrible teeth, all snaggly and yellowed. Hearing Lenny call Ethan that had been like a knife in my heart. It reminded me of when everyone used to pick on Ethan and I hated it.

"Yeah. I want to hire Ethan," I said, acting like nothing Lenny said had bothered me. "I think he could do the job. There aren't a lot of places that would give him a chance, but I really think he might be good at this."

Lenny was silent for another stretch of seconds.

"As long as you can let him down easy if he can't handle the job, I see no problem with it," Lenny said with a sigh. "Get him in there."

So I did.

I called Ethan's mother, Linda, and asked if she thought he could do it. When she gave the go ahead, I went and got him. He still lived with her, and probably would until one of the two died. Ethan was moderately functional, but he would always need someone to look out for him. When it wasn't his mother looking out for him it was me.

Ethan caught on to the procedure fairly quickly. Quickly for Ethan, anyway. I showed him how to turn the gear on and how to arrange the girls' music into sets. I showed him how to work the microphone and the faders and how to keep track of which girl wanted what songs. Other than a few minor mistakes, he did really well that first night. That is, once I could get him focused on his job and not simply staring at the naked women he was working with.

I was proud of him, almost like a father to a son.

And that's what got me thinking.

I realized that I was the person that I had become because of Ethan. And I like who I am. I know myself very well. I hold honor above all else. I'm a strong person in mind and body, and I realize that the duty of the strong is to help those who are weak. I know that I am a good man. I hate to see someone picked on or called names because they are different, because they are weaker.

What does any of this have to do with shame shaping us as human beings?

Well, Ethan Miles is one of my oldest friends. But I used to pick on Ethan, too.

And I'm the sonofabitch who named him Teeth.

Chapter One

1. Big Men on Campus

False modesty be damned. I was the star of the high school football team in the 1988-1989 season. My senior year.

Sure, we had other guys who stood out in their positions, but I was the only guy who played Iron Man Football. I was on the field for nearly every play that year. I played running back and defensive end, leading the conference in rushing yards and sacks. I set records for those positions that year, both of which still stand. I was really good, if I do say so myself. I had the strength *and* the speed.

The school day started at five in the morning for those of us on the Mims High School football team. While everyone else lazed in their beds, we were in the gym, hammering our muscles into armor and weapons, testing our pain thresholds. We would lift massive amounts of weight until we'd puke, gargle and rinse at the drinking fountain, and then lift some more. The entire team gave two hours in the gym every morning before school. It was dedication like that that got us to the championship that year.

I was a big guy, but I was not the biggest on the team by a long shot. We had two monsters on the offensive line, Chewy and Shorty. Or Mitchell Gumm and Mike Short, respectively. I was six one; they were both easily six five. Shorty was over three hundred pounds, Chewy was close behind. Their nicknames might seem pretty obvious, Shorty for a guy named Short, Chewy for a guy named Gumm. But in Gumm's case, it had another meaning. The guy looked like a smaller version of Chewbacca. He had a dark brown beard and a really long mullet haircut that hung out beneath his helmet in back. But in the shower was where he really got the name. Chewy looked like a flesh colored scuba suit that had been stuffed with bowling balls and then wrapped in brown pipe cleaners. The guy was like the missing link, thick and curling hair everywhere. He reminded me of the Bigfoot in the old Six Million Dollar Man shows. Chewy was the guy that had the full beard and hairy chest even in seventh grade.

Shorty looked like a teenage Joe Don Baker back in the *Walking Tall* days. Where other kids were tall or muscular, Shorty was just plain big. He was a walking mountain.

They both would have been considered big by even natural standards, but it was common knowledge that Chewy and Shorty were shooting steroids. Well... common knowledge among the inner circle of players. Had Coach Rollins known about it they would have been off the team in a heartbeat, but the rest of us never said anything. Hell, we were winning. Why fuck up a good system?

Chewy and Shorty had something else in common as well. They were both dumber than a box of shit. Not to propagate a stereotype, but they were your typical big and stupid goons. Good thing for them they had Derek Skyler to guide them.

Skyler was the hot shit quarterback. God's gift to Midwestern high school football and teenage girls everywhere. He had talent in spades, but the guy was an incorrigible prick. I couldn't stand him, but we were a team. You always stand by your team. That is the law. I hung out with him when it was expected, but I really could do without his arrogant bullshit. The whole team was arrogant, but Skyler made us look humble.

Every member of the first string had a nickname except for Derek. He told us all to call him Sky King, but no one, other than Chewy and Shorty, ever did. You don't get to pick your own nickname. It's given to you by the team. If you don't like the name you're given, that's just your tough luck. The trouble was, Derek was a fucking crybaby. He was unanimously given the name Showboat, but he didn't like that one. For anyone else it wouldn't have mattered, but Derek Skyler always got his own way.

Always.

After two days of being called Showboat against his wishes, Derek went to Coach Rollins and whined until the coach came out and asked us to lay off the name. We tried to come up with a name that suited his showy, attention grabbing style, but nothing else seemed right. When he suggested Sky King we laughed it off. None of us wanted to participate in his ego stroke. So, in the end, no nickname.

My nickname was Butcher, on account of the way that I carved my opponents into just so much meat. I'm really a nice guy, but on the football field I made every hit with the intent to kill. Whether I was crushing a quarterback or busting through a defensive line for a big run, I brought the "A" game. I loved the look of fear in the quarterback's eyes when he saw me closing on him. Whenever I knew I had the sack I would yell, "Meat!" right before slamming the poor kid into the ground. As a running back, I used to drag three or four defenders with me on almost every play. Whenever Coach Rollins needed a first down, the ball was in my hands.

The only guy on the team who liked to hit as much as I did was my best friend, Jerome Kent, the tight end. I called him JK, but his team name was Hammerhead. He had great hands and never dropped a pass his entire high school career, but he was also my favorite blocker. I think it was just that being friends for so long, he knew what I was going to do and moved accordingly. JK knew what move I would make and when, then he would put himself between the defender and me. We were a hell of a pair.

Coach Larry Rollins was like a second father to us. The man would not put up with any bullshit whatsoever. When he said to do something, you had damn well better do it. When you did well, he would let you know. When you fucked up, he would ream your ass. But he always did it eloquently and with perfect grammar. Coach Rollins was an English teacher first, a football coach second. We all loved him and feared him in equal parts. That's a sign of a good coach, I think.

As is customary, the seniors ruled the school. And the twelfth grade varsity football players ruled the seniors. We were the top of the food chain at MHS. The crowds in the halls would part like the Red Sea when we passed. Especially on Fridays. We would wear our purple and green jerseys to class on game days, and everyone afforded us a little more space in the halls than usual. It is the closest thing to being a god that I have ever experienced. Not only were we worshipped by the student body; a winning football team is worshipped by the whole town.

And boy, were we winning. By the second week of September we were 3-0, our closest game being 56 to 7. The Central High Jaguars scored against our third string after the coach took most of the first and second string players out. That year, until the championship game, no one else even scored against us. We were a machine.

Saturday's morning paper boosted our egos even more during football season. With headlines like *Mustangs Mangle Mavericks* or *MHS v. DHS= KIA*, it is no wonder we thought the sun rose and set on our collective ass. Bill Morgan was the local sportswriter and he loved us, being a former Mustang himself. Every story was a glowing account of white knights fighting against the forces of darkness. We were the Superbowl, the World Series and the Second Coming all rolled into one.

Individually we all reaped our share of praise as well. My favorite headline was *Butcher Blake Steals Show.* I'm not immune to an ego stroke every now and then. That game I ran a hundred ninety yards with four touchdowns and six sacks. Plus, I forced two fumbles that were run back for touchdowns. I did, in fact, steal the show that night. I still have the story saved in a scrapbook. As well as all the great words that Mr. Morgan bestowed on me, there was a picture of me dragging the other team down the field, with a caption that read: *'Ron "The Butcher" Blake powers through a clutch of defenders in Friday nights 70-0 route of the DeMille Lions'.*

I liked that. Who wouldn't?

We had it made and we knew it. All the girls wanted us, all the guys wanted to be us. Certain fast food restaurants gave us free food and drinks. The college scouts were calling several of us every day or two, telling us how great we were and how bright the future could be if we would just go to *(fill in the blank).*

The Mims High School Mustangs football players were masters of all that we surveyed. Those of us who were seniors were the elite of the elite. We were gods among mortals.

I think that's why Derek Skyler got so pissed off when the little retarded guy with the bad teeth didn't get out of our way fast enough.

2. Meeting Teeth

September 16, 1988. Friday.

I remember this like it was yesterday.

There were five of us, all seniors, walking down the hall in the English department. Derek Skyler was in the middle with Chewy and Shorty to his right, JK and me to his left. We moved through the corridor, shoulder to shoulder, like a big, royal purple wall. That was us, the Purple People Eaters, as Bill Morgan liked to call us.

(Why they chose royal purple with lime green letters and numbers for our school colors I will never know.)

The five of us took up the entire hallway, leaving the other, lesser inhabitants of the school to squeeze against the wall to let us pass. We had just got out of an afternoon pep rally and the five of us were making our way to Coach Rollins' class, still buzzing on the school- wide outpouring of hero worship.

In our defense, the people we were forcing against the walls were only too happy to make way for us. We were their champions, the gladiators who would defend their honor later that night against the evil and insidious King High School Aztecs. They fawned over us even as we looked down on them with contempt and disdain. On the rare occasion when someone didn't get out of the way all we would do is stare them down. At that point they just about broke their necks in clearing a path for their betters.

But this time it was different. The hall crowd had parted for us just like was expected, but all was not right. The crowd opened to reveal not the Path of Heroes, but a small shambling shape. The guy was barely over five feet tall and slightly hunched, with a gait that suggested his pelvis might have been twisted in some way. He had his head down and moved intently, staring at the floor, swinging his right leg a little. It looked like he was trying to catch up with himself. Under his left arm was a stack of books and in his right hand he carried a purple and green *Mims High School Mustangs* duffel bag, packed to the point of bursting. The little guy was wearing a *Thundercats* t-shirt, as well as a *Thundercats* baseball cap, brown corduroy pants, and a pair of old, beat-up *K-mart Special* tennis shoes. Reddish blonde hair jutted out around the edges of his cap at weird angles.

The entire wall of Purple People Eaters stopped and stared, but to no avail. The little bastard was all wound up and heading in our direction with the single-mindedness of a guided missile. As he walked his right arm, with the duffel bag, was cranking back and forth, as if it was necessary in order for him to achieve forward motion. The crowd against the walls grew deathly silent and I could hear the little guy's breathing and the flopping of the loose rubber sole of his left shoe as he approached us, every step deliberate.

Apparently, he didn't notice anything different, didn't note the silence around him, because he kept coming at us. Barrel-assing down, as my dad might say.

On cue, the five of us puffed up and put on the war faces. There was no way we could let this little runt of a guy get away with fronting us out. Skyler pumped up his chest and raised his arms slightly away from his sides, in order to simulate a set of wide lateral muscles. The rest of us really had those wide muscles. We were five giant peacocks, putting on a show.

But our show didn't impress *Mr. Thundercats*. He couldn't even be bothered to look up and see the wall of impending doom before him. He crashed face first into Skyler's chest, knocking our quarterback a step or two in the wrong direction. The little guy bounced back a step and then tried to come forward again, on the same track.

"I'm quite sorry. Excuse me," the little guy said curtly, his words short and clipped, as if he couldn't be bothered to slow down and acknowledge his rightful superiors.

Skyler quickly stepped back up into formation and blocked the runt's progress.

"Excuse me please," the little guy said again, attempting to squeeze between Chewy and Skyler. "I have to get to class. I'm in high school."

Chewy gave him a little shove, keeping him in front of the line. "Who the fuck do you think you are?"

The little guy brought himself up as straight as he could manage and raised his face to greet Chewy. There was a look of pure, naïve innocence under the brim of that *Thundercats* hat. The guy had blue eyes, wide and open like you see on *Precious Moments* figurines. He had a huge smile that ate up the lower half of his face. It was a smile that was completely unselfconscious of the fact that his teeth were a mess. They were yellow and crooked with large bits of what appeared to be chocolate cookie in the gaps and nooks between snaggles.

The little guy dropped his duffel bag to the floor unceremoniously and stretched out his hand for Chewy to shake. Chewy just looked at the hand and then back into the little guy's face.

"My name is Ethan Gabriel Miles. Pleased to make your acquaintance, sir."

Chewy cast a hateful glare directly into those lamb's eyes.

We all waited breathlessly to see if Chewy was going to smash the little guy into the floor, like he did the last guy who had pissed him off. And it didn't take much to piss Chewy off, what with the steroids coursing through his system. I didn't realize why at the time, but I really didn't want to see the little dude get hurt. That's why I did what I did next. I thought I was defusing the situation with humor, but instead I exacerbated the problem with one word.

"Teeth!" I said, with a small laugh.

Everyone else laughed with me, and at the little guy, who only looked confused. His hand was still sticking out to Chewy, but he was looking at me.

"No, E-than," he said, pronouncing his name slowly, thinking I had misheard him. A few people against the wall laughed, until we glared toward them.

Chewy slapped Ethan's hand away, hard.

"Hey, Butcher. The retard here thinks that you're fucking stupid," Skyler announced, reaching out and knocking the stack of books from beneath Ethan's left arm. "You think you're smarter than us, Teeth?"

Ethan Gabriel Miles still looked innocent, but now he also looked scared. He might have been retarded, but he had sense enough to know that he was in trouble. He backed away from Skyler and started to retrieve his books.

"Leave 'em down there, Teeth. We ain't done with you," Skyler threatened, stepping toward Ethan.

Ethan cowered a little, but continued trying to pick up his books. He was panicked and had no idea how to get out of the situation. "I need my books! I'm in high school!"

"He's in high school!" Shorty taunted, laughing, as he kicked some of Ethan's books down the hall. I was laughing, too. In fact, I was so inspired that I grabbed the duffel bag that Ethan had dropped and pulled it to me.

"No!" Ethan yelled, ignoring his books and leaping for the bag as it dangled from my fingers. "That's mine!"

I pushed him away easily and unzipped the bag. It was light, even though it was packed full. Full of stuffed animals.

"Leave it alone! Leave it alone!" he yelled, trying to grab the bag from me by the straps. I jerked it out of his reach.

I guess Chewy took the lunge that Ethan made for me as aggression and he stepped in and pushed him hard in the chest, sending him sprawling. Ethan hit the linoleum floor and slid on his back about ten feet. Chewy had really let him have it. And he wasn't done.

Chewy was standing over Ethan in a split second, clenching and unclenching his fists. He was going to pound on this little retarded guy. I was willing to fuck with him a bit, but I didn't want to see the guy get hurt. I stepped up.

"Chewy, wait!" I yelled.

Chewy stopped and turned his head to me without turning away from Ethan.

"He's mine," I said. I had an idea. It wasn't nice, but it was a lot better than leaving the little guy to Chewy. I reached into the bag and plucked a small teddy bear from the top of the pile. The bag held about twenty stuffed toys. "Let me handle this."

Chewy nodded and backed away. "All yours, Butcher."

I stood over the kid on the floor and looked down at him. At that very moment, on top of feeling sorry for him, I hated him. I hated that he was weak. I felt that he deserved to be made to crawl.

I threw the teddy bear into his face a little harder than I had meant to. It didn't hurt him, physically, but Ethan's eyes began to tear up. The tears made me even madder. I reached into the bag and grabbed another stuffed toy, tossing it in my hands a little. Just showing off for the guys. I blasted Ethan in the face again.

What kind of fucking punk brought his toys to school, anyway? You stupid and weak piece of shit, I thought. I grabbed another stuffed animal and slammed it into Ethan's face again, but this time he had gotten his hands up in time to deflect some of the blow. That, too, pissed me off. How dare he defend himself against me?

"Move your hands!" I ordered.

Ethan didn't move his hands. He might be retarded, but he's no dummy.

"Move your fucking hands!" I screamed angrily, my voice dripping with hate. "Now!"

I knew that I had scared him badly then, because he spread his hands away from his eyes and looked at me. He was too terrified not to do what I said. I responded to his terror with a stuffed Garfield toy to the face. Ethan had gotten his hands closed over his face in time and the Garfield bounced harmlessly to the floor. I reached back into the bag.

"BLAKE!" I heard from behind me. Ice ran through my veins. "STOP RIGHT THERE!"

I dropped the bag to the floor, a dose of my own terror flowing up my spine. I knew that voice very well and it scared the shit out of me. It went against every instinct I had, but I turned to confront the man who had called me down.

Coach Rollins was stomping angrily towards me. I was in the middle of the hall alone, the rest of the Purple People Eaters had taken up residence against the wall with the peasants. I had been so inflamed by my own savagery that I hadn't even noticed everyone slipping away from me. JK was looking at me with horror. Skyler, Chewy, and Shorty had gleaming looks of approval. Of course, they weren't about to implicate themselves with me, no matter how righteous they thought my actions were.

"What the fuck do you think you're doing?" Coach hissed at me. The look of anger on his face was fighting for space with a look of disappointment. I know my own face was slack and wounded looking. I was instantly ashamed of myself. But I wasn't sure if I was ashamed of what I had done, or if I was ashamed of getting caught.

Right then the bell rang.

"Get to class, all of you. Now," Coach ordered, and everyone began slipping out of the hall and into the classrooms. My four teammates ducked into Coach Rollins' classroom with a look of relief. Glad they weren't me.

Coach Rollins dropped to his knees and helped Ethan up and helped him collect his books and stuffed animals. "You okay, son?"

Ethan was crying in torrents now, his chest heaving with sobs, but he was nodding affirmatively.

Coach Rollins pushed me up against the lockers, hard.

"I'm going to walk this boy to his class," he whispered, getting right in my face, a snarling edge to his voice. "Then I am going to Principal Greenwood's office where your fucking ass will be waiting for me. Am I clear, Blake?"

"Yes, Coach," I said, sounding small. I felt small, too. I was six foot one and about two hundred and sixty pounds, but I felt like I was about three inches tall.

"Get out of my sight!" Coach hissed in my face.

3. Taken Out to the Woodshed

Principal Greenwood's office was very intimidating to me that day.

The large portrait of President Reagan that hung on the wall behind his desk stared down at me disapprovingly. The student assistants and the ladies who worked in the outer office cast looks at me that made me think they knew what a shit heel I had been. I was sure that everyone knew what I had done already and they were going to ostracize me. I couldn't argue that I didn't deserve it, either.

Now, I realize that no one in that office knew what was really going on, and that the portrait was not chastising me. I know now that it was a stabbing pain in my conscience that made me feel that way. But at the time, I had no way of recognizing the feeling. A conscience is a foreign concept to someone who is always being babied and having someone cater to every whim.

I was Butcher Blake. I wasn't used to being in trouble. Everything I had ever done wrong in high school had been happily smoothed over or covered up entirely. I was, for all intents and purposes, above the law.

But I also knew that this time I had really fucked up.

The thoughts going through my head were entirely selfish, I admit. I felt small and ashamed of my behavior, but that didn't bother me nearly as much as contemplating my punishment. Coach Rollins wasn't just being his ordinary blustery self; he was livid. The anger that we saw on the football field every day was nothing compared to the rage that burned in his eyes when he had looked at me and ordered me to the principal's office.

I knew I was looking at a minimum three-day suspension. How much worse it could get I wasn't brave enough to guess. Principal Greenwood was a huge supporter of the athletics program at Mims, but I had stepped way over the line. I knew that if he let me slide on this one, that retards parents would have his ass. For the first time in my life I had the feeling that I was actually going to be held accountable for my actions. And I did not like the feeling one bit.

The moment I was dreading, and hoping for at the same time, came all too soon. Principal Greenwood breezed into his office; Coach Rollins on him like a pit bull.

"I don't care! He's off the team!" Coach Rollins roared, shutting the office door behind him. He shot me a look that I took to be pure hatred. If everyone in the office didn't know what I was there for when I came in, they sure as Hell did now. I would have bet President Reagan knew, too.

Principal Greenwood remained calm and casually took a seat behind his desk. Coach Rollins stayed on his feet, stalking the walk in front of Greenwood's desk like a lion in a cage. Every time he walked close to me I cringed a bit, waiting for Coach to hit me. Truth be known, I was almost hoping Coach would hit me. I could handle being hit a lot better than I was handling being looked down upon.

"Have a seat, Larry," Principal Greenwood said, motioning to the chair closest to me. "Let's talk this out."

"I can't sit down! I'm too pissed!" Coach Rollins spat, the veins in his neck bulging. "And there is nothing to talk about. Blake is off my goddamned team! I don't coach punks who pull this kind of shit."

I looked away, at the wall. I couldn't look at Coach Rollins. Someone that I respected more than anyone else in the world thinking I was a piece of shit was just too much for me.

"Larry… sit down. Now," Principal Greenwood ordered firmly.

Coach Rollins snorted, but he got himself under control and sat in the chair next to me. I got the impression that having his boss there was the only thing keeping Coach from outright pummeling me. I was a big strong kid, but that's just it. I was a kid. Coach Rollins was a strong, strong man. If he decided to beat the shit out of me I had no way of really defending myself. The way I felt about what I had done, I doubted if I would even lift my hands in the attempt.

"When you can get yourself together we can discuss this reasonably. Not one word until you can do that. Understood?" Principal Greenwood asked.

Coach Rollins just shot an angry look at the principal.

"Understood?" Principal Greenwood said more concretely, less a question than a command.

"Yes," Coach Rollins sighed, rocking back and forth in his chair. "Understood."

The three of us sat there in silence for a long moment. I felt their eyes on me, but I couldn't look at either of them. Finally, Principal Greenwood broke the silence.

"Ronald, tell me exactly what happened."

So I did. And it sounded even more pathetic being spoken than it had felt in doing it. In my own words, we came across as the biggest assholes I could imagine. None bigger than me, though. Every explanation I attempted to give as to what happened and why I did it, sounded like I was trying to excuse myself. I didn't mean it that way, but I just did not have the capacity to truly exhibit remorse. I was pretty new at even feeling it. Expressing it was a long way off. I left out the parts about what the other guy's had done. I was busted; I was going to take the heat by myself.

That was me. Always thinking of the team.

Coach interrupted me about the time I got to the part about throwing the second stuffed toy in Ethan's face.

"Tell me, Butcher. What do you get from picking on that little kid? You're a big guy. Don't you feel big enough?"

I couldn't explain that I had only done it to keep the other guys from kicking his ass. Not only did I not want to get them in trouble, it was a piss poor excuse. I terrorized and humiliated a retarded kid for his own good? That one didn't even sound plausible to me, even though that was actually what had happened. But it also wasn't *entirely* what had happened. I was leaving out the part about how much I enjoyed doing it and about how much I hated him for being weak and small. That part I couldn't even really admit to myself yet. I had always thought I was a good guy, but if I accepted that as a true part of me, I knew that that couldn't be so. I couldn't be a good guy.

I tried to rationalize things in my mind a lot back then. I thought that if Ethan had just taken a different hallway to his class that day then none of it would have happened. If he had followed school protocol and got out of the way, then it wouldn't have happened. Every rationalization I came up with somehow made it Ethan's fault that we brutalized him. That I brutalized him.

"Well, answer me, Blake? What did you get out of it?" Coach Rollins asked again.

"Nothing," I said quietly. I had a man-sized body and child's voice.

"Bullshit! You had to have gotten something out of it. It made you feel good, didn't it?"

"No."

"Sure it did! That's why you did it. It made you feel like a big man!"

Principal Greenwood noted Coach Rollins' agitation and interjected, "Larry, watch yourself. Keep it civil."

Coach Rollins stopped and looked away from me, struggling to get his anger back under control. I followed suit and looked away from him. After a few seconds of tense silence Coach spoke, but calmer this time.

"So, let me get this straight. You terrorized and humiliated that boy for no goddamned reason? None at all?"

I kept my head turned to the wall.

"Look at me, Blake! Look at me and tell me why you did it!" Coach demanded.

I didn't want to look, but it wasn't a request. I turned my head and looked at the Coach, a tear slipping down my cheek. "I'm sorry."

"Sorry for what? You got caught and now you're going to cry about it?" Coach asked angrily. I thought I saw him soften a little, but I wasn't going to bet on it. "Why are you sorry now?"

"I'm sorry that I did that to him. I'm sorry that I made you hate me. I'm just sorry that it happened," I said, fighting to keep any more tears from falling. Butcher Blake simply could not cry.

"It didn't '*just happen*', Blake. You did it! You made it happen," Coach replied pointedly. "He was walking down the hall minding his own business and you took it upon yourself to crush him."

"I know. I'm sorry," I said, defeated. "I wish I could take it back, but I can't."

Principal Greenwood watched silently, curiously. Coach Rollins was staring at me, but I couldn't read him. He seemed to be looking through me, searching to find something worth looking at.

"Can I talk to you out in the hall for a minute?" Coach Rollins asked Principal Greenwood.

Wordlessly, the two men got up and walked out of the office, leaving me to stew in my own self-loathing. At the time I was very appreciative for the minute alone, but the longer they were out of the office, the more nervous I got. I knew full well that my future was in the balance of whatever they decided to do with me. Although they were probably out of the office for less than five minutes, it seemed like an eternity before they finally walked back in. Principal Greenwood walked around the desk again and reclaimed his seat; Coach Rollins leaned against the wall beside the chair he had vacated.

"Here's what we're going to do," Principal Greenwood began, steepling his fingers in front of his mouth. "You are going to remain on the team. You will not be suspended from school."

I was shocked. They weren't going to do anything to me for this? I can't say I was entirely pleased, either. My first brush with guilt had awakened something inside of me, and I realized that I could not be allowed to get away with what I did. I was actually a little angry when I thought about them letting me off the hook.

"However, we have a deal that you will have to agree to for that to happen," Coach Rollins added. I remained silent.

"Ethan Miles is going to be your responsibility," Principal Greenwood finished.

"What do you mean 'my responsibility'?" I asked.

"What he means is, if anything else happens to Ethan Miles, you are off of this team," Coach Rollins said, leaning close to me, his voice serious. Ominous.

I thought about it. How was I going to keep anything from happening to him? I wasn't around him all the time. Were they going to hold me accountable for things that happened when I wasn't there? I had to ask. "What if something happens when I'm not around?"

"That's your problem. The deal is, no one messes with Ethan without you sticking up for him. Or, you get a five-day suspension and kicked off the team, right now," Coach Rollins said, spelling it out for me.

"We are going to arrange for you to have extra time between classes to walk Mr. Miles to his locker and to his classes. You will leave your class a few minutes early and be waiting for him when he leaves his class," Principal Greenwood informed.

"Also, you will be giving him a ride to and from school. Every day," Coach Rollins said intently, watching my face for a reaction. "He is your responsibility in every way, as far as this school is concerned. You will be excused early from weightlifting in the morning to go get him and bring him to school, and you will be required to take him home before after-school practices."

"Do we have an agreement?" Principal Greenwood asked.

"Yes," I answered, still unsure of how this deal was going to work.

Coach Rollins opened the office door. "Then get to class."

I walked out of the principal's office feeling like I had dodged a bullet, only to be hit by another.

Chapter Two

1. Shirking My Duties

You would think that after dodging that bullet I would have left well enough alone.

Nope.

All I had to do was to meet Ethan at his last class and run him home, then come back for practice and my babysitting was done for the day. Instead, I blew it off and just went out to the football field. I hurriedly got dressed in my practice uniform and hit the field for some calisthenics, I guess figuring that I was untouchable once I hit the field.

And I was. For a little while.

The guys had busted my balls for a while when I got back to class after I made the deal with Coach Rollins and Principal Greenwood. I told them what was going on, the whole thing. Except for the part about crying and feeling bad about how I behaved. I still had a reputation to maintain for the team. They gave me a bunch of shit, but they were all really happy that I was still going to be on the team. Skyler was a little bit more obnoxious than the rest of the guys.

"So, you're really going to baby-sit that fucking retard?" he asked, sort of calling me out. Almost daring me to defy the coach.

"I have no choice," I told him, shaking my head and letting his dare go unaccepted. "It's better than being off the team. This is our year!"

I said that last part with some added excitement, as much to change the subject as to justify my reasons for accepting the deal. It worked. The guys all gave a rousing chorus of "Hell yeah!"

For some reason, though, I just couldn't bring myself to stop and pick up Ethan from his classroom. I knew I had agreed to do it, but there was something inside of me that still felt that punishment was something for other people. I had to get to practice. I couldn't be carting around retards and still be on my game. I needed to get my scrimmaging in and get ready to get on the bus. We always did a light practice before a road game and I thought that Coach Rollins would understand.

I was wrong.

We were running through some plays when I noticed Principal Greenwood standing in front of the bleachers talking to Coach Rollins. Ethan was sitting forlornly behind them, in the stands. The ball was snapped and Skyler tried to make the hand off to me, which I dropped. Coach Rollins yelling at me had drawn my attention away from the matter at hand.

"Blake! Get your ass over here! Now!" he bellowed from the sideline.

I trotted over to the line.

"Did you think I was fucking around when I told you to take care of this boy?"

"No, I…"

"I don't want to hear it. Get your keys and take him home."

"But the game…" I stammered.

"Get your keys and take him home now, Blake! Don't even change. Just go. You've made that boy stay after school long enough, don't you think?"

"Yes, Coach."

I ran off the field and to the locker room, grabbing my keys and my wallet. Had to carry my license, even though any cop who pulled me over was probably going to let me go anyway. Butcher Blake didn't need identification. And hell, I was in uniform and full pads. I was pretty sure they would recognize me. I did take off the helmet and leave it in my locker, though.

As I approached Ethan on the bleachers he recoiled, fear screaming behind his eyes.

"I'm not going to hurt you," I said, unsure of how convincing I could make it sound. As far as Ethan knew I was nothing but a raging monster, I couldn't blame him for not trusting me.

"Ethan, it's all right. He is going to drive you home. He will be nice to you," Principal Greenwood assured the scared kid.

My heart actually hurt, seeing the terror that I had inspired in this small boy. I had inspired fear in football players all over the state for the last two years, but this was different. A quarterback knew I was coming for him and that I wanted to take his head off. Defensive linemen knew that I would try to run them over. It was part of the game. But this kid only knew that I hated him. For no reason at all, I hated him.

"Ethan, I called your mother and told her what happened. She said it was okay if he brought you home. Ronald will not hurt you. I promise," the principal added.

Oh great, I thought. I'm going to have to drive this kid home *and* deal with his mother. She is going to rip my ass and I'll just have to take it. I would have really rather not have had to meet her. But, I guess it should have been expected. They really couldn't let me give rides to a retarded kid I had picked on without his mother knowing about the situation. I was surprised she would have said yes to that. I would have thought that she would have wanted me kept as far away from her son as possible.

I had an idea. Stepping closer to Ethan I extended my hand. "I'm Ron Blake."

Ethan still looked scared, but he stood up, straightening as best he could and shook my hand. "My name is Ethan Gabriel Miles. Pleased to make your acquaintance, sir."

Ethan looked anything but pleased, yet still he remembered his manners. I knew that he would from how he had acted in the hallway when he had offered his hand to Chewy. I could tell that he had been taught to always be polite.

"Can I give you a ride home, Ethan? I promise not to hurt you," I said calmly, hoping none of the team could hear me.

He nodded slightly and then reached down to grab his bag of stuffed toys.

Principal Greenwood walked with us to my car. "Don't just drop him and come back here. Take him to the door."

I nodded resignedly. No way out of meeting his mother, I figured.

Ethan's eyes lit up when we got to the parking lot and he saw my car. In high school I drove a black 1977 Pontiac Trans Am with gold details and T-tops. It wasn't my car of choice, but it was in good shape and got me from point A to point B.

Ethan loved it, though. He was excited as all Hell.

"Ooooh! SmokeyandtheBandit! SmokeyandtheBandit! SmokeyandtheBandit!" he said breathlessly, shaking his palsied fists close to his body.

If he had been a dog he would have been pissing on himself, he was so pumped. I wasn't sure that he didn't. The fear seemed to be gone in his joy at getting to ride in "the Bandit's" car.

I unlocked the door and allowed Ethan to work his way into the passenger seat. Everything he did, every move he made was awkward, due to his physical limitations. Once he was settled and had his duffel bag securely in his lap I shut the door.

Before I could walk around and get in the drivers side, Principal Greenwood stopped me. "Don't mess this up, Blake. You are on thin ice as it is. Skipping out on him like that was a stupid thing to do."

"I won't mess this up," was all I said.

Principal Greenwood just gave me a scolding glare as I slipped behind the wheel.

2. Substitute Short Bus

I turned the key in the ignition and revved the engine a little more than necessary, sending Ethan into minor palpitations.

"Where do you live?" I asked. Ethan had to think for a minute, but then I saw the light bulb come on over his head.

"1725 N. Polk Street," Ethan said mechanically. I got the impression that he had been forced to recite that address many times to get it into his head.

"Hold on," I warned, dropping the shifter into drive and stomping on the gas. With a little chirp of rubber on asphalt we shot out of the parking lot and onto the road. In the rearview mirror I saw Principal Greenwood shaking his head as he walked away. We were on our way, Smokey and the Retard.

I slid around the corner at the end of the block and headed for Polk Street.

Maybe it was just being in the Trans Am, but something had definitely changed in Ethan. You wouldn't have believed that I had just pounded him in the face with stuffed animals a few hours before. There was no real fear anymore. Maybe he just believed so much in what Principal Greenwood said. That I wouldn't hurt him. I did see a change come over Ethan when he was told that his mother said it was okay if I took him home. That had to be it. He just trusted his mother completely.

"You like music?" I asked.

Ethan nodded absently; content to ride in quiet awe. He still couldn't get over the car. He had braced himself between the console and the passenger side door, holding on for dear life, even though I was no longer speeding or burning out.

With a flip of my fingers from the shifter I pushed the cassette into the stereo and turned the volume up a little louder than it had to be. Ethan might have been content to ride in silence, but it was driving me up the wall. I have never handled awkward silences well, so the best way to deal with it seemed to be to annihilate silence. Worked for me.

The cassette was Pink Floyd. I never really liked Pink Floyd, but I listened to them a lot because they were "cool". In school, all the cool people listened to Pink Floyd, so I did, too. I had no idea what music I truly liked. My music purchases went strictly according to what everyone else was listening to. *Dark Side of the Moon* rarely left my tape player.

I drove methodically toward Polk Street, trying to think of something to say. What do you say to a retarded person? I had no idea.

'So Ethan, what do you do for fun? Drool?'

I didn't think so.

I found myself looking over at him while I drove. He was on the edge of his seat, white knuckles holding him in place, his *Mims High School Mustangs* duffel bag clutched firmly between his palsied knees. The *Thundercats* cap had slid crookedly on his head. Those awful, jagged teeth jutted out of his smile, dirty and stained. He had become entirely unselfconscious again, lost in the pure joy of riding in my car.

Tires squealing, I took a corner a little too sharp sending Ethan thumping into the door panel, hard. His head hit the window with a second thump.

"Sorry about that," I apologized, mostly sincere. "I thought you had a good grip."

I looked over at Ethan and his smile had grown bigger.

"Do that again! Do that again!" he cackled ecstatically.

I wasn't sure too many blows to the head could be good for the kid, but it really seemed to make him happy, so I figured 'What the fuck?' and took another corner on two wheels, fish-tailing the Trans Am as I straightened out onto Polk Street.

"You like that?"

"Yeah!" Ethan giggled.

I slowed down and checked the houses for addresses. I was on the 1500 block. For the last two blocks of our ride Ethan was begging me to do it again.

"There are no more corners," I tried to explain. We went through the intersection onto the 1600 block and Ethan pointed out the window.

"Uh-huh! There's one right there!" he yelled turning back to watch the intersection drop behind us. "You missed it!"

"We're not turning anymore," I said, laughing softly. "I have to take you home and get back to catch the bus."

"No! Turn more! Turn more!"

"I can't. I have to get you home and get back so I can make the game tonight," I said, seeing the dejection cross his face.

As we pulled onto the 1700 block of Polk he eyeballed the corner at the intersection hopefully, but said nothing. I found the house and slid effortlessly into a parking space right behind an old junked out 1973 Impala.

Ethan seemed to have a little trouble getting himself squared away and out of the car. He would have managed nicely if he had just sat the duffel bag down, but he wouldn't drop it. It reminded me of when they say monkeys won't let go of a piece of food, even though with it in their fist they can't pull their hand out of a hole. That was Ethan. For all the headway he was making in trying to get turned in the seat of my car he might as well have been a turtle on his back. I got out of the car and ran around the other side to help him.

It was kind of funny, but I didn't want to laugh at him. He was so frustrated with trying to maintain his belongings and open the door that I could see a semblance of anger cross his face briefly. When I opened the door he wasn't quite ready for it and he fell out of the car a little bit, catching himself before he hit the curb. I helped him up.

"You okay there, buddy?" I asked, making sure he was stable on his feet.

"Yes, thank you very much..." Ethan said, trailing off as if searching his mind for something. "What's your name again?"

"Just call me Butcher. Everyone does," I answered.

"Thank you very much, Butchie," Ethan said, smiling his big retarded smile.

"No, not Butchie. It's Butcher. Butch-er."

"That's what I said," Ethan grinned. I let it go. Let him call me whatever he wanted, I didn't care.

"Well, let's get you in the house," I said, putting an arm around Ethan and moving him away from the door so I could close it. I walked with him up the walk to his house.

It was a nice enough house. Nothing special. A little on the small side, but well kept. Black shutters and white siding, it looked like any number of houses in town. It looked like it could use a new roof soon, but other than that it seemed to be in good shape.

As we stepped onto the small front porch slab and under the aluminum awning, the front door opened. Behind the glass of the screen door stood who I presumed to be Ethan's mother. And she was hot! At the time I wasn't familiar with the term MILF, but I was familiar with the concept immediately. She had the same reddish blonde hair that Ethan had, just kept much nicer. It was over her shoulders in a long, but business like cut. There was a very shapely figure hidden under the navy business suit she wore, the long legs sticking out underneath the skirt giving away a little more of this perception. Her face would have been movie star beautiful a couple of years ago, but she was still exceptionally pretty, even under the icy look she was giving me.

Opening the door, she stepped out onto the porch with us and held the door open. "Ethan, go in the house and make some Quik."

"Quik! Yay!" Ethan cheered, somewhat less excitedly than when he saw my car. He turned to me, "Bye, Butchie!"

"Bye Ethan. I'll see you Monday."

Ethan didn't look back. He moved into the house with the same head- down, determined locomotion that made him run into Chewy in the first place. That left me alone on the porch with his mother.

Shit.

Oh well, I guess it was time to take the rest of my medicine. I waited for her to say something. And I waited for what seemed a very long time. She looked me up and down, taking my measure. I felt a little silly and self-conscious, standing there in my football uniform. Finally, she said something.

"So, you're Ronald Blake." It wasn't a question.

"Yes, ma'am."

She was quiet again for some time. She kept looking me in the eye, but I couldn't maintain her gaze. I looked away, only to look back and find her still staring into my face. It was very disconcerting. Talk about awkward silences! Where was Pink Floyd when you needed them?

"Principal Greenwood said that you are going to be watching out for Ethan. Taking him to school and bringing him home. Everyday. Is that so?"

"Yes, ma'am," I answered, feeling like I should have a sloppy hat or something to wring nervously in my hands. She wasn't a very big woman, and I was a giant for a high school kid, but I still felt small beneath her perusal.

"See that you do, Ronald," she said, the edge on her voice softening a bit. "Ethan is all I have. He doesn't deserve to be treated like he was."

"I know. He doesn't. And I promise, I will take care of him," I told her, knowing right then as I made the promise, that it was something I would hold true. Not just because it was the only thing keeping me on the team, but also because it was the right thing to do.

"Thank you," she said. I just nodded. I had victimized her son and she was thanking me? Not what I expected. "You'll pick him up on Monday morning then?"

"Yeah. Yes. Coach is letting me go from practice early so I can come and get Ethan."

"What time?"

"I'll be here at 6:45. Is that enough time?"

"6:45 is fine. Ethan will be ready."

I stood there on the porch waiting for something to be said, or to be dismissed. I didn't know what to do.

"Have a good game tonight, Butcher. All of us old Mustangs fans are rooting for you," she said, stepping back into the house and closing the door.

I stood there staring at the closed door for a second, before turning to walk back to my car.

3. Trial By Fire

I got back to the practice field just in time to run into the locker room and change clothes before running out to the bus. I was the last one onboard.

Coach Rollins sat in his traditional spot, the front seat, right behind the driver. I didn't intend to say anything to him as I passed, but he stopped me, pulling me down to whisper into my ear.

"Don't go back on your word, Butcher," he whispered. "A man whose word means nothing *is* nothing."

I nodded and he let go of my arm so I could take my seat and get the team underway. JK had a seat saved for me in the back of the bus, where the coolest of the cool rode. The cheerleaders would follow in a van. The school administrators had learned their lesson years ago about allowing the cheerleaders to ride in the bus with the players. Every cheerleader on the 1978 squad ended up pregnant; so from that point on, separate vehicles. I came back in such a hurry that I didn't even get to kiss my girlfriend before we loaded up. It was more superstition than tradition. I always felt that if I didn't kiss her before we got on the bus that we might lose. Well, it was time to test that theory. I just didn't see Coach letting me slow us down even more so I could run back to the van and steal a kiss.

My girlfriend at the time was Tabitha Butler. She was the head cheerleader, but honestly more by default than by degree of talent. She rode her older sister's coattails onto the squad back when she was a sophomore, and now that her sister had graduated, she assumed her former position. Tabby didn't have the talent that her older sister Tiara had displayed, but she was smoking hot, so it didn't really matter. She was kind of a bitch, too. But, as I said, she was smoking hot and that didn't matter, either.

I was hoping for a nice quiet ride where I could reflect on my situation from the day. Come to peace with what I did. I hadn't really had a chance to do that yet. Of course, it was too much to ask. The ribbing started the second my ass hit the seat.

"You know, you better not let Tabby see your new girlfriend. Skipping out on practice to see her," Skyler said, smiling, but not for real. It was a malicious dig. I didn't think Skyler actually had a problem with me. It was just his way. Some people are just assholes.

I rolled my eyes and shrugged it off. I knew that I couldn't say anything without making it worse.

"Did you at least get a goodnight kiss?" Shorty teased. They were all laughing, except the underclassmen, who knew better. JK even had a smile on his face.

"You kidding? He couldn't get around those fucking teeth!" Skyler chimed in again, bringing juvenile peals of laughter.

"You never know, guys. Teeth might have some pretty good pussy," Chewy threw in, which was pretty clever for him. When it came to intelligence, Chewy calling Ethan a retard was almost like the pot calling the kettle black. Almost.

"Yuk it up, fucksticks. It was worth it," I said, trying to force a good- natured smile. "Teeth's mom is a hot piece of ass. I think she kinda dug me."

They all laughed, with me instead of at me.

"You fucking wish, Blake!" Skyler said with a smirk.

And that was the last that was said about it during the ride. The topic easily switched from Ethan to pussy and there was no looking back.

Apparently, my playing suffered no ill effects from the events of the day, or from not getting my pre-bus ride kiss. We killed the King Aztecs. So much for my bruised conscience and my kissing superstition.

From the second we took the field we knew the game was ours. The Aztecs knew it, too. They were standing around looking intimidated, fearful. I think they were simply hoping not to get hurt too badly. The final score was 56-0. We had something to prove after allowing the Central High Jaguars to score against us the week before. I had four rushing touchdowns and three sacks.

Maybe picking on retards was good for my game.

The rest of the night went according to tradition. The bus ride back home, a stop at the school for the victory dance, and then back to Tabby's house for some victory sex. For the night I allowed myself to be the football hero and to forget about being a monster.

Chapter Three

1. Personal Best

In accordance with tradition, there was no practice on Monday.

Whenever we won on Friday night the coach always gave us the following Monday off as a reward. But, like I said, we were a dedicated team, so I still had to be at the gym at five in the morning to workout with the rest of the guys. It wasn't mandatory... but it kind of was. Coach Rollins usually showed up at six and worked out with us a little bit.

I was doing bench presses with JK, Shorty, and Chewy when Coach Rollins made his way over to us. We were going for our maximum lifts and trying to outdo each other. I knew I stood no chance of keeping up with the Goon Squad, as Shorty and Chewy called themselves. Not only were they both much bigger than I was, I didn't have the added benefit of shooting steroids. However, they did offer frequently. Shorty said he knew a guy who could get us anything we wanted. We always turned him down and he would laugh it off. No big deal. When he and Chewy were pressing between four hundred fifty and five hundred pounds, and JK and I were still struggling with three hundred fifty, they would make the offer again. And again. In the best interests of the team, of course. It couldn't have possibly been that Shorty was getting a kickback from his dealer, could it?

In the middle of my lift, three hundred sixty, a personal best at the time, I heard another voice cheering me on and I knew that Coach Rollins had joined the group. I was straining, my face red and engorged, eyes squeezed into tight little slits and teeth clenched. JK, Shorty and Chewy stood over me, Chewy spotting me, and they yelled encouragement. I wasn't going to make it. My arms, which had felt so strong just seconds before I pulled the bar off of the stand, were wobbling and threatening to give out. I felt like if I had to I could hold the bar where it was, slightly above my chest, for several minutes, but there was no way I was going to be able to push it any higher. I had hit my peak and I had nothing left. And then I heard Coach Rollin's voice.

"Don't you fucking quit, Blake! You got it! Just push!" he yelled.

I redoubled my efforts. Of course, from the miniscule space that the bar actually moved you couldn't really tell I was working any harder. I couldn't do it, I knew, but I was willing to give it all I had for Coach Rollins. He had a way of getting more out of all of us.

I let out a huge, tense grunt and tried to push harder. The bar went up about an inch.

"Come on, Butcher! Push!" Chewy shouted. He brought his hands down to the bar and lightly rested his fingers underneath it, not lifting, but ready if I needed help.

"Gumm, get your hands off that bar! He's got it!" Coach Rollins scolded Chewy, who jerked his hands away like the bar was hot. Then back to me, "Lift it, you pussy! Are you going to let that little bit of weight stop you?"

I screamed and the bar surged up about four inches, but I hit some kind of invisible force field and stopped dead. Then it began to slowly slip back down. Some of my other teammates, noticing what I was attempting, began to gather around the bench.

"Butch-er! Butch-er!" they chanted, almost like back up singers to Coach Rollin's lead.

The pain was intense. I wanted Chewy to grab that bar and lift it off of me, but not nearly as much as I wanted to lift it. I pushed harder and gained back some of the ground that I had lost when I hit the stopper.

"PUSH IT UP THERE, YOU MAGGOT!" Coach Rollins yelled, getting down closer to my face. "DON'T YOU FUCKING DARE QUIT!"

With another little grunt/scream I pushed, the muscles in my chest feeling like they were about to tear. My triceps were bulging with the effort, and they were only secondary muscles in this lift. The bar began to rise steadily. Slow and painful, but steady.

"THERE YOU GO! ALL YOU! ALL YOU!" Coach Rollins was bellowing. The chant of "Butch-er! Butch-er!" grew louder.

Somewhere I found a reserve of strength and I gave it everything I had. I was either going to push that damn bar all the way up or I was going to collapse and let them pull it off of me. I was not going to let that "little bit of weight" beat me. I made the most horrifying sound, guttural and bestial, and I locked my elbows, straight up. Chewy immediately grabbed the bar and guided it back to the stand and I let the weight fall with the loud clang of iron striking iron.

A small cheer went up. A smattering of 'Good job, Butcher' and 'Nice lift', and then everyone went back to their own workouts. Myself, I just lay there on the bench, panting and feeling the blood rushing out of my head. I looked up when I felt a soft, backhanded slap against my shoulder.

"I knew you could do it," Coach Rollins said with an approving smile. Then he hooked his thumb toward the clock on the wall above the gym door. It was half past six. "You better shower up quick and go get the kid."

I nodded and rose shakily to my feet as Coach walked away. Chewy and Shorty were laughing as I walked into the locker room. I heard JK say, "Hey, he doesn't have a choice. Back off."

Maybe it was my own inflated sense of self-esteem, due in part to the new plateau I had just reached, but I had had it. I wheeled around and marched right back to Shorty and Chewy.

"The only reason I am stuck having to do this is because I didn't narc everyone out. I took one for the team," I said, keeping my voice low so that Coach Rollins didn't hear.

Both of the hulking brutes grew instantly quiet, taking in my seriousness. I have a little furrow between my eyes that deepens when I am serious. They knew I wasn't happy about the constant teasing I was getting. They knew that the only reason I was in trouble was because I had taken all the heat myself and kept them clean. Chewy and Shorty both seemed to understand where I was coming from.

Then they looked at each other and laughed again.

"Nobody's stopping you, man," Chewy smirked. "Go get your pet retard."

I shook my head and walked into the locker room, realizing that I had just fucked up really bad. I let them know that their razzing was bothering me.

Now it would never end.

2. Ethan's Keeper

I pulled up in front of Ethan's house at ten to seven.

He was standing on the porch, dressed much the same way as the day before and carrying his bag of toys. His mother stood beside him, dressed for business with a small, worn looking briefcase at her feet, and she looked at me with a mild scolding gaze.

"If you can't be on time maybe we should just forget this deal and put Ethan back on the school bus," she said, her lips pursed.

"I'm sorry, I got hung up at the gym," I apologized, expecting my excuse about the gym to be sufficient. Anything Butcher Blake needed to keep his game up was usually all right with the rest of the town.

She wasn't impressed, I could tell.

"Hi, Butchie!" Ethan said happily, looking past me and out at my car beside the curb.

"Hi, buddy," I smiled. Surprisingly to me, the smile didn't feel totally false. "Ready to go?"

"Yes!" he answered, then he turned to kiss his mother. "Bye Mom! I'm going to ride in the SmokeyandtheBandit!"

She kissed her son back and smiled in spite of herself. "Bye Ethan. Have a good day at school."

"I will. I go to high school!" Ethan replied proudly.

"We're running a little late, but we'll make it, ma'am," I said, hoping to placate her. "And if we don't they will take care of it at school I'm sure."

"Well, that's great," she said, picking up her briefcase and walking to the curb with us. "Now if my boss doesn't fucking fire me everything will be all right. I have to be in at seven."

"I'm sorry," I said again as I helped Ethan into the passenger seat.

"Just be on time from now on or I'll have to put him on the bus. I can't afford to lose this job." She turned on the heel of her sensible shoe and walked to the car parked in front of mine at the curb. Ethan waved to his mother one final time before she got into the junk Impala and drove away in a hurry.

"Can we go real fast, Butchie?" Ethan asked, a hopeful gleam in his eye.

"Yeah, I think we're going to have to," I answered, turning the key and bringing the beast to life. I watched Ethan's face as my engine roared and smiled at his reaction. "Hold on."

I hit the gas and we leapt away from the curb. We slid around corners all the way back to school, bringing Ethan to rolling peals of laughter. He didn't stop giggling until we were securely in a parking space.

There was still some of the usual rabble hanging out in the parking lot getting in a few more cigarettes before having to run to class or a few extra kisses and gropes from their sweetie to hold them until after first period. They all stopped and stared at me as I got out of the car and went to the passenger side to help Ethan. No one said anything. I was just a curiosity to them. They had to be wondering what the hell I was doing with that retarded kid in my car. Those who didn't know the deal, that is. As far as I knew only Coach Rollins, Principal Greenwood, and a few members of the football team knew that there was any kind of deal. All the rest of the school knew was that I had picked on Ethan last Friday. And of course, as it usually works, I was sure the story had been blown out of proportion. I wouldn't have been surprised to hear the rumor that I had beaten Ethan to a bloody pulp. We'd had the weekend for the story to grow. Hell, I wouldn't have been surprised if someone hadn't been told that I had killed the poor kid.

"Good morning. Good morning," Ethan said nodding and smiling to everyone who stood looking at us. Always polite, was Ethan. No one said anything back. No one even acknowledged him. They just stared, their eyes following us into the school.

"Butchie, why won't anybody be nice to me?" Ethan asked, a hurt and questioning look in his eyes. "I'm being polite, right?"

"Yes. You're doing fine," I answered, feeling a new stab of guilt for my actions of the previous week. "It's not your fault. Some people are just dickheads."

"Like you were?"

"Yeah," I laughed. "Like I was."

Ethan smiled at that and hugged me with his free arm. "You're my friend, Butchie."

I didn't want to push him away, but I didn't want him hugging me either. I was already being stared at; I didn't need a public display of affection from a retard killing my reputation any further.

"I'm your friend, Ethan," I said in a low voice, gently separating him from me and trying to hide my embarrassment. I made a quick look around to see who was watching. Of course, everyone was watching. Fucking great. "We're running late. Let's get you to class."

The halls were abuzz with manic activity with only seconds before the first bell was to ring. The kids were all frantically trying to get to class. A loud, cacophonous din reverberated from the narrow walls of the corridor. Several teachers were standing in the halls right outside of their classrooms, urging everyone to hurry up. It was the standard Monday morning chaos at Mims High.

As Ethan and I walked down the middle of the hall, the noise died. It was gradual, but when the full silence finally fell, it came down like a brick. According to custom, the crowd parted as I walked. They all moved against the walls and stared. But this time they were staring in curiosity instead of awe. Time was moving slowly around us, like we were underwater in one of those tubes at Sea World. Even some of the teachers stopped and cast curious looks as I walked with Ethan.

The faces along the walls were watching me with a look I hadn't seen before. I think it was doubt. They were looking at me like a fallen hero. Their eyes held a touch of pity. It was just too much. I whirled on one of the kids closest to me.

"What?" I shouted. He cringed.

"Nothing! Nothing!" the boy said, sufficiently intimidated.

"Is there a problem?" I asked a boy on the other side of the hall, looking down into his face.

"No! No problem!" he replied, stumbling over himself to get away from me.

"Then quit your goddamned gawking and get to class!" I bellowed.

That's when the teachers came out of their trance and started herding the students along again. The hall once again exploded in noise and motion.

"Come on, Ethan. Let's get moving," I said, tugging on his sleeve.

The bell rang just as we turned into the math hall, where Ethan's first class of the day was located. Mere seconds after the bell sounded, the hall was empty, except for Ethan and me. Even in the wide-open hallway I had to slow my pace not to walk ahead of Ethan. I was used to taking long strides and walking fast, but I had to hang back with my charge.

Ethan was limping along, his twisted hip locomotion looking like it was all he could do to keep up with my already slowed pace. So I slowed some more. I could see the strain on his face from trying to keep up with me.

"We're almost there," I said, putting a hand on Ethan's shoulder. "Don't kill yourself, we'll make it."

"We're late, Butchie! The bell rang!" Ethan said, still going assholes and elbows to get to class. "We can't be late!"

At the end of the hall I saw the teacher step out of Ethan's classroom. Mrs. Rickman was a severe looking middle-aged woman who shaved her eyebrows off and drew them back on, but too big, too high, and the wrong color. She always looked surprised with her earthy brown eyebrows pointing at her blonde-gray hair with the gray-brown roots. Mrs. Rickman was a mix of a Vulcan and a German dominatrix, in a button-down suit. Her attitude was so sour I'd have been willing to bet she douched with pickle juice.

"Mr. Miles, care to join us today?" she snipped.

"I'm sorry!" Ethan howled as he doubled his pace, loping like a wounded dog. I reached out a hand and slowed him. He fought me, but I got him to slow down a bit. "I'm sorry!"

"Slow down, Ethan. You're already late," I said, trying to calm him. He had a slight look of panic on his face.

"The bell rang! I can't be late! I'm in high school!" Ethan said as he started to run. I increased my speed to my normal walking pace and stayed alongside him as he ran.

Mrs. Rickman cast a disapproving glare at Ethan as he came to a stop in front of her. "I'm sorry, Mrs. Rickman!"

"Take your seat, Ethan," she said with a calm, icy voice. Ethan hurried into the classroom and sat down.

"It's my fault, Mrs. Rickman. Ethan is late because I was supposed to pick him up and I lost track of time in the gym," I explained.

Mrs. Rickman almost sneered, turned on her heel and walked into the room. "Mr. Blake, there are more important things in life than football."

"Like eyebrows?" I said under my breath as I walked away.

Mrs. Rickman turned back to me sharply. "Excuse me?"

Her face was rigid and the furrow between her painted eyebrows was deepening before my eyes.

"I didn't say anything," I replied, voice dripping with innocence.

How's that for luck, I thought. Two people completely unimpressed with my work ethic for my sport. I'd never experienced that before and I had just had it happen twice in one day. Within a few minutes of each other even.

I didn't let it bother me. Mrs. Rickman was wrong, I knew. There was nothing in life more important than football.

3. Outcast

The rest of the day was more of the same.

I would get out of my class early to go and pick Ethan up from his class and then we would walk the halls like some freak exhibit, everyone staring. The only ones who ever said anything were the other members of the football team. They were the only ones who had the right, or the balls. It's kind of like picking on a brother. You might bust his balls, but no one else had better give it a try. Not to mention the fact that I scared the living shit out of the other kids.

I would stare back when I found another student with overactive eyeballs, boring my gaze into them until they looked away. It usually didn't take long. I can be quite intimidating when I want to.

It wasn't really their fault, I realized. Seeing Butcher Blake walk through the halls babysitting a shambling retard was something they thought they would never see. Even so, I wasn't enjoying the bug-in-a-jar aspect of my deal with the Coach. Someone staring was nothing new. But this wasn't someone staring in awe of a football hero. It was almost pity, and I didn't like it. I couldn't take it. It was driving me up the wall. It never occurred to me until much later that it was the same thing Ethan dealt with everyday.

When lunchtime came I had to hurry to the opposite end of the school and up to the second floor to get Ethan and then hurry back. My class before lunch was right next to the cafeteria. I used to meet the guys in the entry to the cafeteria and we would go through the line as a group. We had our own personal tables. Everyone knew that to sit at one of the football team's tables meant death. I had a routine that was convenient and worked very well for me. Picking Ethan up from class was a pain in the ass.

Even leaving class early to get him made me late for meeting the guys. Mr. Fewell, my English teacher, made me wait to go after Ethan until shortly before the bell. He said that I didn't have to be in such a hurry. It was only lunch next. I found his attitude a bit cavalier, considering that lunch was my favorite subject.

I got to Ethan's class seconds after the bell rang. A line of slow kids came filing from the doorway; all of them with the same glassy, dumbfounded look. Of course, Ethan was the last one in the line, right behind a tall, skinny girl with pop bottle glasses and reddish blond pigtails. He was looking down and smiling his silly, bad-toothed smile. I could tell he was checking out her ass.

'What a little pervert', I thought. And the thought made me smile.

The girl made her way out of the classroom and headed down the hall to the stairs. Ethan was hanging back and taking in the view. I don't think he even realized I was there.

"See something you like there, Ethan?" I asked, teasing.

That snapped him right back to reality. His eyes were guilty as he turned to me. "I wasn't looking at her butt! Honest!"

I had to laugh. "Ready for lunch?"

"Yes," he said, glad in not having me call him on his wandering eye.

"Well, let's hurry. I have to meet the guys."

That morning I told Ethan not to be in such a hurry. By lunchtime I was almost dragging his slow ass to the cafeteria. He was whining as I tugged him down the hallway a little quicker.

"Butchie! Slow down! Slow down! My legs are slow legs!"

I caught a quick glimpse of his face and it looked like he was in real pain, so I stopped.

"Are you all right?" I asked.

A tear slid down his cheek as he nodded. "Yes."

"Then why are you crying?"

"It hurts to run. I got slow legs."

Once again, I felt horrible. It was becoming the standard. "I'm sorry Ethan. We'll slow down."

I let Ethan set the pace the rest of the way to the cafeteria. The way his pelvis moved made me think of a human trying to move like a sidewinder rattlesnake. Trying to do that too fast was bound to hurt like a sonofabitch.

We got to the cafeteria with plenty of time to eat, but it had severely cut into my social time. I could see our table across the room, all the guys halfway done with their food and having a good time. The seat beside JK, my seat, was empty. But I still had this long line to wait in to get my food. It was moving fairly quickly, but not quickly enough for my tastes.

Ethan didn't seem to mind, though. He was once again behind his sweetheart from the slow class. And he was once again ogling her ass. There was nothing suave about it, either. His jaw hung down, the edges of his lips curled in a smile, and his eyes were wide, glued to the view. There wasn't much to see as far as I was concerned, though. The girl was a beanpole in baggy, ill-fitting clothes. She had no shape at all. Unless you thought straight was a shape. But she sure did the trick for Ethan.

I leaned up and whispered in his ear, "Ethan, are you checking out her ass again?"

The smile faded from his face and he pursed his lips tightly, shaking his head in small, quick shakes. The rest of the time in line I caught him stealing glances down at the girl's butt when he thought I wasn't looking.

A few minutes later we had our trays and were heading to the table. That's when I realized that we were going to have a problem. There was no way the other guys were going to let Ethan sit at any of the football tables. There was a strict rule. Players only. No exceptions. Some of the guys caught hell from their girlfriends for not eating lunch with them, but that was just the way it was. I had no such problem. Tabby sat at the cheerleader's table.

"What's up, guys?" I said, setting my tray at the space in front of my empty chair. My seat was on the corner of the long table. There were four chairs on each side and the ends of the table were pretty wide. Wide enough to put another chair in the space and let Ethan sit on the end, beside me.

No one said anything as I went to the table next to ours and brought over one of the empty chairs. In fact, the table had gotten instantly quiet.

"Have a seat, Ethan," I said, pointing to the chair. He was a little apprehensive. It wasn't hard to tell that something was wrong. Everyone was glaring at him. He didn't move. He just stood there holding his tray and looking lost.

"Come on, Ethan. Sit down. It's all right," I assured him. And I honestly thought that it would be. Surely the guys had to understand the situation I was in. If they wanted me to stay on the team and keep running those touchdowns and sacking those quarterbacks, they were going to have to make allowances for my new circumstances.

Or so I thought.

Chewy reached out a huge, meaty arm and grabbed the back of Ethan's chair, and flung it roughly away from the table. "No fucking way, retard! Go sit somewhere else!"

I heard Skyler laugh, followed by the rest of the table. Everyone else except for JK.

For once, I didn't have to think about what was expected of me. About what I should do. I immediately picked up my tray and stepped back from the table.

"Come on, Ethan. We'll go sit somewhere else," I said, casting the evil eye at Chewy and Skyler.

"Aw, come on, Butcher. You can sit here. Just not the retard," Skyler said.

I didn't say anything; I just turned and led Ethan to an empty table on the other side of the cafeteria. No sooner did I get seated and get Ethan settled than I saw JK come walking over to us carrying his tray.

"Hey, can anyone sit here?" JK asked with a smile.

"Sure. If you don't mind being an outcast," I said, returning the smile. "Have a seat."

JK sat down and turned to Ethan. "Hi, I'm JK. They call me…"

"Hammerhead!" Ethan interrupted. "Because you bust through the defense like a hammer. You have the most catches for a tight end at Mims. Ever."

JK smiled and nodded with approval. "Hell yeah, little man. You know the deal."

Ethan held up his MHS duffel bag. "I'm a Mustangs fan. I go to high school."

JK didn't seem to know what to say, so he just kept smiling.

"JK, this is Ethan," I said, finishing the introduction. Ethan looked mortified that he had been caught up in his excitement and not finished the introduction properly.

"Pleased to meet you," Ethan said, sticking out his hand. JK shook it.

"Yeah," JK said with a nod of his head. Ethan took that as his cue to devour the food on his tray, diving in like he hadn't eaten in days.

"So what the fuck is up with those guys?" I asked JK. "They know what I gotta do."

"Yeah, they know. They don't blame you at all," JK replied.

"Could have fucking fooled me! I've been worm shit since this started."

"They really don't blame you, Butcher," JK said, motioning towards Ethan with his head. Ethan was in the middle of chowing down on a nice gravy-covered slab of Salisbury steak and didn't notice.

That made perfect sense. Of course it was Ethan's fault. The retard bit was just an act. He was really some mastermind trying to get me away from the team.

"Well, I have no choice. Fuck them." I said, digging into my own Salisbury steak.

I never really liked the guys on the team. None of them. They were pricks. Skyler was a whiny little bitch. Chewy and Shorty were bullies. Their bullshit had even started rubbing off on me. That's what started the whole problem in the first place. A few of the other guys were okay, I guess. But the offensive players were the main ones I had to deal with. JK was my only real friend on the team.

I probably would have just quit if it weren't for three things. I loved playing football. I was good at it and I loved it. Second, I felt like I had a future with football. College scouts were always coming to our games and talking to me. Even in my sophomore and junior years. A few pro scouts had made themselves known as well.

And lastly, my dad would have had a fit.

I was living my dad's athletic dreams for him. He had knocked my mom up in high school and had never been able to carry on with his football career. Ever since I was a little kid he had me out throwing the football or working on strength and speed. I wasn't as much his son as I was his redemption. I was going to have to make it to the NFL so that he could feel like his dreams were crushed for a good reason.

There were a lot of good things about being a high school football star, don't get me wrong. But all in all, I could have done without the bullshit. Being on the team with JK was one of the saving points. Getting to have a hot cheerleader girlfriend like Tabitha Butler was another. The adoration of the entire town was pretty cool, too.

You have to take the good with the bad.

We ate our lunch and talked, ignoring the cold stares from the player's table. I noticed also that Tabitha and all of the other cheerleaders were giving us some nasty looks. JK and I eating at a separate table with a commoner was a huge breach of protocol. What did they want from me? It wasn't like I didn't wish things were still the same. Maybe it wasn't an ideal situation, being on a team with so many people I didn't like, but it was comfortable. Maybe they weren't friends, but they were teammates, and that counts. If I could have gone back in time I wouldn't have done anything to Ethan. And not just because it was wrong. I would have rather just kept everything nice and comfortable.

Once our trays were empty it was almost time to head back to class. Ethan and I had to leave a little early so that I could get him to his class and get to mine on time. This situation was a real pain in the ass. Not only was I running from one end of the school to the other, I couldn't meet Tabby and make out between classes, as was our routine.

Ethan stood up and hung the straps of his duffel bag around his neck, the bulging stuffed animals riding like Quasimodo's hump, and he picked up his tray and books. He didn't have the coordination to carry his tray and his books in one hand, hence the duffel bag around the neck. JK and I followed behind him, going to put our trays on the conveyor belt that took them back to the kitchen to be washed. Ethan was a little ways ahead of us, twisting his way among the aisles of tables and chairs, concentrating hard not to drop anything or bump into anyone, and not letting his duffel bag swing off of his shoulders.

And that's when I saw it coming.

There is almost a sixth sense that you get when you work in a security position. You can read body language very well. I have it honed to a sharp edge now, having been a bouncer for so many years and working security at concerts and such. But back then it was a new reaction.

The guy was a fairly small kid named Mike something or other. When I saw his eyes as Ethan passed, I knew he was going to do something to him. I didn't know what, but it was coming. There was nothing overt. Mike Something was lying in wait like a predator, camouflaging himself in his natural surroundings.

Ethan walked by him, untouched. It looked like I had been wrong and that the kid was going to let Ethan go on his way. But right at the last second, Mike's hand shot out and snagged the duffel bag, giving it a sharp tug, and effectively clotheslining Ethan from behind. The straps were pulled tight across his throat and I heard a horrible gagging sound that was quickly strangled off. Ethan's books and his tray tumbled from his hands, the papers folded inside the books scattering everywhere and the tray and silverware clattering on the floor.

I handed my tray to JK and headed for the scene of the crime.

Mike Something and his buddies were laughing their fool asses off , mocking Ethan's gagging sound and having a grand old time. Until I grabbed little Mikey by the throat. He made a pretty realistic duplication of Ethan's gag as I jerked him to his feet.

"You're going to fucking pick his shit up!" I hissed into Mike's face.

Without argument, Mike Something dropped to his knees and began gathering the scattered papers. Ethan had been doing it, but I told him to stop. "Let Mike get it. He wants to help. Don't you, Mike?"

Mike coughed a little, clearing my grip out of his throat and said, "Yeah, I'll get it."

Mike handed the books and papers back to Ethan and then scooped the tray and silverware up. When he tried to hand it back to Ethan I stopped him. I turned and took the trays from JK and handed them to Mike, stacking them on top of Ethan's tray. "You can take these to the conveyor for us."

"Okay, I'll do it." Mike was terrified, but unlike the last time I terrorized someone I didn't feel bad about it. He started to walk away with the trays.

"Don't you think you should apologize?" I asked, a hint of menace in my tone.

Mike spun on his heel and hurried back to face me. Looking me right in the face he almost cried, "I'm sorry Butcher! It won't..."

I interrupted him rudely, pointing at Ethan, "Not to me, dipshit! Apologize to him!"

Mike had a stunned look in his eyes as he turned to Ethan, who had tears welling in his eyes.

"Go ahead," I ordered.

"I... I'm... I'm sorry," Mike stammered, and then looked at me for approval.

"His name is Ethan," I said.

"I'm really sorry, Ethan," Mike said humbly. "I'm sorry."

Ethan didn't say anything; he just looked back and forth between Mike and me.

"Get the fuck out of here," I said to Mike, low enough so that Mr. Hall, the lunchroom monitor, didn't hear. Mike hurried to the conveyor with our trays, glad to have been excused.

"You okay?" I asked Ethan as he walked out of the cafeteria with JK and I. He nodded, wiping his eyes.

"Well, we better get to class," I said to JK. "Catch you on the flip-flop."

I started to walk with Ethan the opposite direction of JK when he called back to me. "Can you give me a ride home after school?" JK asked. "My car wouldn't start this morning."

"Yeah, no problem. I have to take Ethan home first, though."

"That's cool. I ain't in no hurry, I just don't want to be walking all the way across town."

"Just meet me in the parking lot."

JK nodded from down the hall, flashed the devil horn salute, and walked away.

4. Ass Men

The last minutes of the day found me standing outside of another one of Ethan's classrooms, waiting for the final bell.

One thing I had noticed was that even though all the classes were in different rooms, all the kids were the same. All the slow kids were together. I also noticed that Ethan made sure to follow the same girl out of the room every time, his eyes always glued to her ass.

She turned and headed the opposite way than we were going. She was headed to the front of the school to catch her ride on the short bus and we were going to the back of the school to the student parking lot. Ethan stopped and stared as she walked away, a look of what passed for lasciviousness in a simpleton written all over his face.

"Ethan," I called, trying to get his attention. He didn't hear me. I called his name a couple more times and he still didn't acknowledge me. Finally, I grabbed his shoulder and shook it. "Ethan!"

He turned and looked at me, a dreamy smile on his face.

"Looking at her butt again?" I teased, smiling.

Ethan turned beet red, embarrassment rising up his face like a thermometer in a cartoon.

"Uh... No... I... No..." he stumbled.

I just laughed. "It's okay. I'm kind of an Ass Man myself."

Ethan let slip a shy smile and dropped his face away from me, giggling self-consciously. "I think she's got a pretty butt."

"Nothing wrong with that," I said, holding up my hand for Ethan to slap me a high five, which he did awkwardly.

We started for the parking lot.

"So, what's her name?" I asked.

"Miranda Lewis," Ethan answered, almost in a sing-song tone. It was like just saying her name made him happy.

"Well, why don't you ask her out?"

Ethan didn't say anything, and when I looked over at him, he wasn't smiling anymore.

"What's wrong?" I asked.

"I can't ask her out. She wouldn't go out with me."

"Why not?"

"Cause... Because I'm... you know," Ethan said, searching for his words. I didn't let him finish.

"I bet if you asked her to the movies she would go with you," I said, offering hope.

"Really?"

"Hell yeah."

"Then I might do that," Ethan said through a crooked-toothed smile.

JK was leaning against my car when we got out to the parking lot, talking to Tabitha in her little white Cabriolet convertible.

"Hey baby," I said to Tabby as I leaned down to kiss her. "I missed you today."

She kissed me back, but there was no feeling in it.

"What's wrong?"

Tabitha looked at Ethan quickly and then back at me. "I want my boyfriend back."

"I'm still right here," I said with my typical football hero winning smile.

"I didn't get to see you all day," she whined, pouting. Her bottom lip was sticking out to an exaggerated degree and she cast her best sad puppy dog eyes up at me. "I had to carry my own books."

"Oh, poor baby," I said, mocking her pout as I leaned in to kiss her again. "I'm sorry. I can't help it."

"I know," she said, resigned to the fact, but not liking it in the least.

"I'll call you when I get home. Maybe we can go out and do something tonight," I said, trying to placate her. 'Do something' for us generally meant finding some place to have sex. That was pretty much all we did, occasionally working a date in somewhere between orgasms.

"Well," she said, a teasing lilt in her voice, "If we go to my house right now there will be no one home for the next thirty minutes or so."

I wanted to go. I really did. I mean I *really* wanted to go.

But I couldn't.

"I can't," I sighed. "I have to take these guys home."

Tabby looked disappointed and then disgusted. She cast a baleful glare at Ethan, and to a lesser degree at JK. "Fine!"

Tabitha shifted into first and chirped her tires on the asphalt, almost running over my toes as she pulled away.

"You need to drop that bitch," JK said with a smirk.

"Well, I would. But you know how it is."

JK just nodded and then shrugged. "But still..."

"I know," I sighed.

JK got in the backseat of the Trans Am. No small feat for a large man. I helped Ethan into the front seat. He was already getting better at it and didn't seem as awkward as he got comfortable.

As I slid behind the wheel Ethan asked me a question, his tone very serious.

"Butchie, does your girlfriend have a pretty butt, too?"

"Yeah," I laughed and nudged him with my elbow. "Yeah, she does."

I turned the key, pumped the accelerator and watched Ethan smile as it roared.

And, of course, I gave Ethan the kind of ride that he loved so much, squealing my tires around every corner on my way to his house. JK was getting a kick out of watching Ethan's delight as I fishtailed the rear end of my car before straightening it out and streaking on my way. I could see him smiling in the rearview mirror.

I slowed to a calm stop in front of Ethan's house and got out to help him climb from the seat. JK waited in the car, but jumped up into the front seat Ethan had just vacated. As I got Ethan to the front door, it opened and his mother came out to greet him with a hug.

"Hi, Mom!" Ethan trilled, grabbing around her waist, inordinately happy to see her it seemed.

"Hi, Ethan!" she said, laughing a little.

"Hello, Mrs. Miles," I said politely.

"Hello, Butchie," she said. Now even his mom was calling me Butchie! It was polite enough, but she was so hard to read.

"Any trouble today?" she asked.

"No, not really," I replied honestly.

"Nothing happened in the lunchroom that I should know about?" she questioned, hoping to get something out of me. They must have called her at work.

"Well, there was one little thing, now that you mention it," I said. I had already dismissed the situation in my mind. It was nothing. "But I took care of it."

"That's what I heard," Mrs. Miles smiled. "Thank you."

"I was glad to do it."

Her smile made me feel good. Much better than I had felt since Friday when all the shit got started.

Ethan's mom turned to him. "So, did you learn anything good in school today?"

Ethan thought for a second, coming up blank. Then suddenly he perked up and smiled a huge smile. "I did learn something good!"

"What was that?" she asked.

"Butchie said I'm an Ass Man!" Ethan declared happily.

My blood ran cold. Mrs. Miles shot another of her patented disapproving looks at me.

"Oh, he did, did he?" She was talking to Ethan, but glaring at me. She sent Ethan into the house.

"Care to explain?" she asked, hands on her hips.

So I did.

She didn't seem too upset once I put the Ass Man comment into context. She knew the girl and wasn't surprised. Apparently Ethan had been holding a crush on Miranda Lewis for a long, long time.

"I need to go. I have a friend in the car waiting for a ride home," I said, making to leave.

"Well, thank you for looking out for him today, Butchie," she said.

"You're welcome, Mrs. Miles. I was glad to do it."

She stuck out her hand. "Call me Linda. Please. I'm not *that* much older than you."

I reached out and shook her hand. "Okay. Linda."

Linda turned to walk back in the house and I watched her go. I noticed the way that her business skirt hugged her hips and her butt.

Yes, I thought, Ethan and I are definitely Ass Men.

Chapter Four

1. Judgment at Sharky's

JK was pretty impressed with Linda Miles.

"Damn, man! No wonder you haven't seemed to mind taking Ethan home! His mom is one fine piece of ass."

"That she is," I agreed.

I couldn't help but smile as I cranked the engine over and we pulled away from the curb in front of Ethan's house. With JK's endorsement, in the eyes of the team I would be absolved of my guilt for breaking protocol and sitting with Ethan. They would allow me to step beyond the expected behavior if it meant that I was getting laid by a hot older woman. They still might not be happy about it, but rules are rules.

"Do you have to be right home?" I asked.

"Naw, I got all day. Why?"

"Wanna stop in and see the guys at Sharky's?"

JK knew exactly what I intended, and he all was for it. "Yeah, stop in. I have something to tell them."

Sharky's Pizza was downtown, right off the courthouse square, and it was the place to be if you were an upperclassman at Mims. Sophomores and freshmen were taking their well being into their own hands should they come through the door at the wrong time, because the juniors and seniors ruled the place. The pizza wasn't very good and the drinks were fairly expensive, but Sharky gave us a place where we could hang out and not get harassed by the police for it. Cruising the local strip had become too much of a hassle for the most part and there wasn't really any place else to go. Every once in a while some well-meaning person would open a place where teens could hang out, but that never lasted. Someone in the community would have a fit and get the place closed down because their kid came home drunk or high. The fact that it probably didn't happen at the place in question seemed to be irrelevant.

Due to the lack of good hangouts, the upperclassmen tended to guard our territory pretty diligently. The underclassmen needed a place to go too, but that wasn't our problem. When we were freshmen and sophomore pukes we made due with what we had, they could do the same. Besides, it gave them something to look forward to.

Skyler's car was parked on the street, right in front of the door to Sharky's. I never thought that a high school student had any business driving a brand new Jaguar, but that's exactly what he had. His father went out and bought him a brand new XJ6, black with a tan interior. Even though Chewy and Shorty were ever present around Skyler, to my knowledge neither one of them had ever been allowed to ride in the Jag. Skyler only let girls ride in the car. He always made Chewy ride with Shorty in his old pick-up truck. They would just follow Skyler wherever he went. Very sad.

As expected, Shorty's pick-up was parked right behind Skyler's Jag.

And also as expected, Sharky's was pretty raucous.

The top song on the jukebox was AC/DC's *Back in Black*, and it was beating its way through the walls and out onto the street as JK and I walked to the door. JK loved the song, but I suspect it was only because he was black. He liked Black Sabbath, too. Go figure.

We stepped through the door into the cacophony inside. Video games beeped and whooped behind the frontal noise of the music and the high school kids yelling. I realize now that Sharky must have been a saint to put up with us on a daily basis. The noise was ungodly.

Something was immediately different.

No one came to greet us or acknowledged us when we entered. Typically, whenever we entered Sharky's, it was like on *Cheers* when Norm or Cliff walked in. It was like coming home.

But not that time.

That time we were both looked at as intruders. And it wasn't just Skyler, Chewy and Shorty who looked at us that way. It wasn't just the other members of the team who milled about.

It was everyone.

Everyone who looked at us seemed to know that we were pariahs. I had just forced myself to read *The Scarlet Letter* in American Literature class and I equated the way they all looked at us, me in particular, with how Hester Prynne must have felt. I was sure they all saw a big red T, for *traitor*, on my chest. If it had been the Old West, the piano would have stopped playing and everyone would have turned to look. But as it was, the jukebox kept blasting and the Ms. Pac-Man game kept wokka-wokka-ing.

JK led the way to the team table and I followed him through the light smoke and the pungent aroma of burnt pizza. It was a common smell there. Quite often Sharky would lose track of what he was doing while hitting on one of the high school girls and forget that he had a pizza burning in the oven.

Skyler was at the center of attention as always, holding court. Chewy and Shorty hemmed him in on the sides, laughing at all of his lame jokes. The team table was really two six-person tables slid together. As we stepped up to the table, all the talking stopped. All but two of the guys at the table were on the team. JK and I stood there at the foot of the table and stared at the two until they took the hint and got up. We slid into their vacated chairs.

"What's up, Skyler?" I said coolly, waiting to see how this was going to play out. He regarded me with iciness.

"Butcher," Skyler nodded, giving the barest of acknowledgments. The rest of the team sat waiting for his approval to engage JK or myself.

We sat wordlessly for a few long seconds, staring each other down.

"So," Skyler began, exhaling for effect. "Finished with Teeth for the day? Have time for your friends now?"

"Let me ask you a question, Skyler? What would you rather I do? Get kicked off the team?"

"Rollins wouldn't really kick you off the team," he replied condescendingly. "He knows we need you if we're going to keep winning. He wouldn't sacrifice that for some fucking retard."

"You weren't there in the office when he made me the deal. I'm not still on the team because of Coach Rollins. Principal Greenwood talked him into keeping me. Coach wanted me gone."

"Bullshit!" Skyler spat, looking around the table to see how everyone else reacted. They all remained expressionless. It was the safest way.

"No, it's true. He was fucking pissed at me," I told them all. "This deal is the only way I can still play. The only way."

"Besides," JK chimed in with a conspiratorial glance around the table. "Have you seen Teeth's mom? Shit! She's hot."

"She is, huh?" Skyler asked, intrigued. "How hot?"

"Smoking hot!" JK said with a laugh. "I can't blame the Butcher here for trying to get next to that."

JK was playing it perfectly. I could see the interest on all of their faces. Sure, we all had girlfriends and a steady stream of female companionship, but this was different. JK was insinuating that I had something going with a real, honest to God, woman. And that was all that was needed.

"You fucking her?" Skyler asked, getting to the heart of the matter.

Truth be told, I wasn't always the pillar of propriety that I am today. The idea of cheating on a girlfriend wasn't always something that bothered me. I liked Tabitha

Butler a lot, but cheating on her was not out of bounds. I answered Skyler honestly.

"No." Skyler gave a knowing nod, but then I added a lascivious, "Not yet."

"You're going to be fucking this retards mom?" he asked skeptically.

"It's just a matter of time," I replied.

Skyler seemed to be weighing his thoughts. Finally he got a sly smile. "Cool. Just do me a favor?"

"What's that?"

"When you're banging her, slip it in her ass and make her call you Skyler."

Everybody roared with laughter, high school humor being what it is.

Just like that, I was back in fashion.

2. The Vicious Circle

Almost exactly a half hour later I was walking in the front door of my house and being called directly to the telephone by my mother.

"This is the third time she's called in twenty minutes," my mother said, her hand over the mouthpiece of the receiver, and quite perturbed. I shrugged an apology and took the phone.

"Hey baby, what's up?" I said smoothly. I was guessing that Tabby's parents were going to be out for a while and she was calling me to come over for a little romance.

"Don't you fucking 'Hey baby' me, asshole!" Tabitha shrieked into the phone.

Hmm. I was wrong.

Before I could ask anything else I was on the ropes and she was working me like a speedbag.

"So, I hear you're fucking that retards mom! What is wrong with you? You have me, what more could you want? I can't believe you're fucking some old bitch! I bet she looks exactly like her retard fucking kid! I hate you! You are such an asshole! I thought you loved me! How could you do this to me? You'll be sorry! I can have any guy I want! You'll see! I loved you! And you treat me like this? I hate you! You piece of shit! How could you? How could you?"

For my part of the conversation, I punctuated Tabby's tirade with the occasional, "Uh… uh…"

My mother stood beside me in the front hall as I tried to interject my brilliant "Uh… uh…" argument. I finally decided to shut up and just let her go. Rail away, crazy lady. When she finally started to wind down I tried to say my piece.

"Tab, it's not true. I don't know who told you that, but it's not true," I explained futilely. She was in no frame of mind to listen. And what argument did I really have. I had in fact insinuated to the guys at Sharky's that I was going to be fucking Ethan's mother. It wasn't the smartest move in the world. I should have figured that it would have gotten back to my girlfriend.

"Everybody is telling me that! Every time I hang up the phone someone else calls to tell me that they heard it, too!"

"Do you have to believe everything you hear? What if someone is just trying to break us up?" I asked. My mom walked away, back into the kitchen to finish cooking supper. She was shaking her head as she left.

The line went silent. I was waiting for a click and then a dial tone, but then Tabby finally spoke up. "What's going on, Ronnie?"

I could tell she was still mad, but she was letting me at least say something. Maybe I had broken through.

"Nothing's going on. Really."

"Then why am I hearing this?"

Time to say the right thing, make it all better.

"Because you're hot. Every guy wants a shot at you and they can't have you while you're with me," I said, playing up to her substantial ego. Every woman likes to hear that they look good. But Tabitha Butler lived and died by it.

Tabby got quiet again. I was waiting to hear what she'd say when I heard something else in the background. I wasn't sure, but it sounded like there was someone there with her, whispering.

"That's bullshit!" she finally shouted. "I'm hearing it from everyone, Ronnie! Everyone!"

"You know how fast rumors spread, Tab," I reasoned, keeping my tone calm. "Just because someone repeats a lie a hundred times, that doesn't make it true."

"I have it from some very reliable sources and..." she started, but I cut her off.

"From who? Who is telling you this?"

"I'm not telling you who."

"After all we've been through and you're just going to take someone else's word over mine? That's not right, Tab!" I said.

"Everybody is saying it, Ronnie! Why would everyone be trying to break us up? Why would everyone be telling me this shit?" she demanded, a hint of hurt and anger seeping from her voice.

It was time to say the right thing again.

"Because they know you're dumb enough to believe it."

'Well, that certainly fucking wasn't the right thing', I realized too late.

Tabby got quiet again. And I heard the voice in the background again. A male voice.

"Oh! So now I'm stupid! Is that it? Well, I'll…" she began to rage at me.

"Who's over there?" I asked. That stopped her cold.

"No one's over here!"

"I heard a guy's voice. Who is it, Tab?"

"I don't know what you're talking about. There's no one here but me," she lied.

"Who the fuck is it?" I demanded this time. She didn't say anything. "I see. You're going to call me up to accuse me of cheating while you have another guy at your house! Nice! Very nice!"

"Hey, don't you turn this around on me!" she yelled. "I've been faithful to you!"

"And so have I," I lied. I had had a few small indiscretions. But I had been *mostly* faithful to Tabitha. There had been several occasions where I had been faithful to her. Hey, I was in demand. How could I keep it all for one girl all the time? What I was upset about, I guess, is that I was getting busted for something I didn't do, after all the bad things I had actually done. It didn't seem fair.

After another long moment of silence, and more words from the disembodied voice, she spoke again. "Ronnie?"

"Yes?"

"We're through," Tabitha said emotionlessly.

I said nothing.

"Did you hear me?" she asked.

"Yeah, I heard ya."

"Well?"

"Well, what?" I asked, a little brusque.

This time, it was her turn to be silent.

"Fine! We're through!" I shouted, dropping the receiver back in the cradle.

Almost as soon as I hung up, the phone rang. I picked it up.

"Hello. Blake's." I said.

"Don't you fucking hang up on me, you sonofabitch!" Tabitha yelled before slamming her receiver down and hanging up on me.

Fuck her, I thought, as I dropped the phone back into its cradle once again. There were dozens of girls, just at school alone, who would kill their own parents for a chance to be with me. So she could get any guy she wanted? Yeah, so what? I could get any girl I wanted. Not a problem at all.

Of course, I did kind of like Tabitha. A lot, actually. But still, fuck her. I was Butcher Blake, King of the Grid Iron.

In just the time it had taken me to run JK home and go to my house, the anonymous members of the vicious circle had shredded my relationship with my girlfriend. It could have been anyone who was there at Sharky's. I'd probably never know who had run and tattled on me. So many people mingled and eavesdropped on conversations in that place that it sure wouldn't take long for the story to get around. Part of the danger of being a high school celebrity is that your business is everyone's business. If I found out who it was that told on me, I was going to beat the shit out of them.

I wasn't heartbroken that Tabitha and I were over, but it was the principle of the thing.

3. Chromosome Donors

In the kitchen my mom was setting places at the table and humming a little tune, trying to appear innocent, as if she hadn't been listening in on my conversation.

"Me and Tabby are through," I announced.

My mom never looked up, she just kept setting the table. "Well, you can always get another girl."

"Yeah, I know. I was just informing you."

"I never really liked her anyway," she said. And that was no surprise.

"You've never liked any of my girlfriends," I said with a small chuckle.

"Well, you've never had any good ones."

"You think you can pick a better girl for me, why don't you just go ahead?" I teased.

"I could pick a better girl for you by throwing a dart down a crowded hallway," she said, popping me on the shoulder with her wooden spoon. "Go call your dad and tell him dinner is ready."

I reached down and snagged a piping hot green bean from the serving bowl and popped it into my mouth as I left the room, heading for the sound of the television. I knew Dad would be camped out in front of the tube, shoes off and socked feet up in the recliner, smoking his pipe. He had a routine after work, and it never changed.

"Hey Pop, time for dinner," I said, tapping him on the arm to draw his attention away from Rebecca Wayne, the co-anchor on the channel 8 news. Dad had a thing for Rebecca Wayne for years. I think it started back when they did the promo spots that had all of the news personalities from the station saying, "We love being 8!" He always had some lewd comment ready for when Rebecca Wayne's spots would run.

"I took the trash out for you this morning," he said, in lieu of *'Hello, son'* or *'Be right there. Thanks'*.

"Yeah, I'm sorry about that. I was running late this morning," I answered, knowing it wasn't good enough. I couldn't tell him why I was late. If he found out that I was being punished and having to pick up Ethan every day, he would have went apeshit. There was no *damn* way he was going to let that *damn* school jeopardize my *damn* future over something like picking on a retarded kid. I didn't want my dad involved in the situation. It was bad enough as it was.

"Sorry don't feed the bulldog, pal. We don't ask you to do very much around here. The least you could do is the little that we ask," he said condescendingly.

"I know. I won't forget next week," I promised.

"See that you don't," he said, forcing the recliner down with his feet and standing up. "And I wanted you to come home and cut the grass after school today, but no, you didn't feel the need to come home and do anything. It's not going to be much longer until there is snow on the ground. Mowing the grass a few more times won't kill you."

"Sorry about that, too. I had to take JK home after school," I explained, knowing he didn't like JK, but not wanting to mention Ethan.

"That's just great! I bust my ass all day, then come home and have to mow the grass so you can hang out with your nigger friend," he said disgustedly.

I'd had enough.

"Mom," I yelled into the kitchen. "Dad is being a dick again."

My mom didn't like that my dad was forcing his racist views on me and she always called him on it. She sighed and then yelled back from the kitchen, "Ron, quit being a dick and come and eat."

Dad got up and walked quietly to the table, accepting my mother's rebuke as always. He wasn't happy with me, for many reasons, but he said nothing as we took seats around the kitchen table. My dad wasn't really a bad guy. I know that sounds strange to say about a hateful racist. The nature of being a racist makes it seem like one would be the classic 'bad guy'. I understood where all of his racist feelings and ideas came from. He learned it from my grandfather, another not so bad guy. It's just how they were. Grandpa was so racist that it pissed him off to see black people win on game shows. He thought they were cheating or being allowed to win.

Being racist wasn't entirely their fault, though. They came from a different time, as I was told quite often. Grandpa grew up in a world where it was just the way things had always been. You didn't address a black man as in, *'Excuse me, sir'*, it was always as *'Boy'* or even *'Hey, nigger'*. My dad was a teenager in the Sixties, right in the midst of all the race riots and civil unrest. I had never witnessed the things that they had seen in their lives. And they had never had a woman like my mother as they were forming their opinions about the world. I'm quite sure that without my mom's intervention I would have grown up just as racist as Dad and Grandpa.

Honestly, the only reason my dad could stand me at all was my skill at football. He had been a bit of a scrub on his high school team, but to him, those were the glory days. And he loved those glory days. (Football was all we ever talked about, except for when I forgot my chores.) Dad was re-living his youth vicariously through me. I had all the things that he had wanted for himself in high school. He was a second stringer; I was the star of the team. He always wanted to date the head cheerleader; I had dated all the cheerleaders. Better yet, the head cheerleader was my steady girlfriend. Until a few minutes ago, anyway. In some ways he was proud of me, in others he was frustrated. To him I wasn't taking full advantage of my star status. I wasn't doing things the way *he* would have done them in my position.

In all fairness, though, the only reason I was so good at football was because of my dad. He had started working with me right about the time I was entering kindergarten, long before I even had any clue as to what was going on. By the time I signed up for youth league football I had the knowledge equivalent of the average high school player. I knew tons of plays, how to read a defense and an offense, and hundreds of little tricks that no one tells you about. I remember berating my youth league coach when I was eleven years old for his "piss poor clock management". I *knew* the game. And I knew it well. Every Saturday at my house we watched college football all day. Every Sunday, it was the pros. Forever and ever, amen.

When we sat down at the table with Mom, our plates were already full and our meat was cut into bite-sized portions. She always did that for us. In fact, until I went to college I had never cut a steak for myself. I reached down and picked up a piece of steak and popped it into my mouth.

"Hey, wait for the blessing!" my dad hissed. He was a deeply religious bigot. He began, "Our Father…"

Usually when Dad bowed his head to pray, Mom and I made funny faces at each other, trying to make the other one laugh. He never knew. My mom was very against religion of any sort and Dad was an old school fire and brimstone kind of guy. A Southern Baptist living in a northern state. To know my parents was to be shocked not only that they had ever gotten together in the first place, but also that they had stayed together.

"…in the Holy name of Jesus. Amen," my dad finished. And in the next breath, "So, you're playing Rice this Friday. They're tough."

Mom rolled her eyes at the football talk.

"Yeah, they are," I agreed. "We'll kill them."

The Rice Trojans were a very good team. They were undefeated, too. But they hadn't played us yet.

We always liked playing the Trojans. It gave us an excuse to staple condoms to poster board and write, "THE TROJANS HAVE A HOLE IN THEIR DEFENSE!" That was always fun.

"Don't ever sell a team short," Dad admonished. "The second you do some last place team will jump up and bite you on the ass."

"Rice has only played punks. They aren't as good as their record indicates," I said. Then as an afterthought, "And we're playing at home. No one will beat us at home."

"Maybe. But it's early in the season. You guys go and rest on your laurels and someone is going to come along and hand you your heads."

"Can we talk about something else for a change?" Mom interjected with a reserved sigh.

Dad and I just looked at each other and then back at Mom. Neither of us could think of one thing to say to the other. What else was there to talk about? No one wanted to hear how the contracting business was going. No one wanted to hear what recipe my mom had learned at the beauty shop, or what book was inspiring her this week. My whole life at the time was all about football, so that couldn't be a change of subject.

We ate in silence for several long minutes, everyone trying to think of something to say. It got really uncomfortable and awkward. Way too uncomfortable and awkward for a group of people who were supposed to be a family, who lived under the same roof, and shared the same bathroom. I realized even then that it was pathetic that we had nothing to talk to each other about. I only had one other thing that I could talk about, even though

I didn't really feel like it. But at least it was current events related.

"Me and Tabby broke up," I said, turning toward my dad. Mom already knew, but hey, it was *something* to talk about.

"The hot little cheerleader? Why?" Dad asked incredulously, earning a reproachful gaze from Mom.

I told them the parts of the story I was comfortable with telling them. All the stuff about Ethan and my intention to have sex with his mother I conveniently left out. Some unknown, unnamable person, or persons, had told her that I was cheating on her. I left it at that.

"Well, there are plenty of other fish in the sea," Mom philosophized.

"Yeah," I agreed. And then Dad joined me. "But who wants to screw a fish. Ba dum bum!" we said in unison, laughing.

Mom shook her head, resigned to the fact that she was living with a couple of uncouth, uncivilized pigs. She took a couple more bites of her food and a drink of wine.

"So," she sighed. "How do the Steelers look this year?"

Chapter Five

1. Girl Trouble

The next morning found Ethan and myself sitting in my car in the school parking lot with time to spare.

After being so late the first day I made a special point of getting out of the gym early enough to get Ethan. I got my full workout in, I just had to cut out all the rests between sets. It was a bitch, but I pulled it off. I got a quick shower and jumped in my car, forcing my rubber arms up onto the steering wheel. The fatigue was set in really deep. It was partly due to the iron man workout and partly due to not sleeping so good the night before.

Breaking up with Tabitha was bothering me more than I wanted to admit. And knowing that my little act of showing off for the team was what caused it didn't make me feel any better. We broke up over absolutely nothing. Still, I couldn't go to Tab and say what had really happened. She wouldn't have been any happier with that than she would have been if I had actually been screwing Ethan's mom. I tossed and turned all night, either trying to think of a way to get out of my predicament with Tab, or thinking about which lucky girl was next in line for the Butcher. After dating the head cheerleader, everything else was a step down. I was debating on who would be the least of a step down.

Karla Fredricks was a pretty girl, and she was really nice, but Stacy Lampley would look really great with my car. The rest of the cheerleaders had steady boyfriends on the team. My other options were to go after either the wrestling cheerleaders or the basketball cheerleaders. I could possibly get involved with a girl from the volleyball team or the track team, but only as a last resort. They had a measure of status, but it was just more appropriate that I stay with a cheerleader. It never even occurred to me that I could have dated just a regular girl from the Debate Club or something like that. Maybe I had to babysit a retarded kid, and maybe my hot girlfriend had dumped me, but I was still Butcher Blake. That rep still had to count for something.

Ethan sat quietly beside me in the front seat, listening to AC/DC on the radio, while I sat there and weighed my options. Karla and Stacy sat two rows ahead of us, lounging on the hood of Karla's Dodge Dart. Some of the other cheerleaders were milling around her car. It was a morning tradition, of sorts.

"Can we go inside, Butchie?" Ethan asked me, obviously bored.

"Not yet. Wait for the first bell. Then we'll go in." I answered him mechanically, never pulling my eyes from my prey. This was an important decision.

If Tabitha was a ten, then Karla was an eight. Not a huge step down, but a step down nonetheless. Stacy was about a nine. Karla was a nice, sweet girl. Stacy was kind of a bitch. Karla was more independent. I wouldn't have as much control over her as I might over Stacy.

Maybe I could have them both at the same time, I began to wonder. They were really close friends and they were cheerleaders. I had read Penthouse Forum for a couple of years, so I knew that it happened like that all the time. Two cheerleaders and the football star? Of course they would double-team me! I was pretty sure I could date them both. Hell, it would never hurt to ask. I put it on my To Do List for the day.

About the time I made my decision to go for the deuce, Skyler's Jag pulled into the spot beside my car. I looked across Ethan and nodded a greeting to Skyler and he nodded back, throwing me a huge shit-eating grin. He leaned back in the seat and I got a good look at his passenger.

That motherfucker!

Sitting beside Derek Skyler, proud as could be, was Tabitha. I had to give her credit, though. She at least had the decency to look semi-uncomfortable at allowing Skyler to taunt me with her presence in his car. My jaw clenched and unclenched, my brow furrowing deeply in anger. Fucking Skyler had run right out of Sharky's after I left and told Tabitha what I had insinuated. I never should have given him that ammunition. I should have known he would use it against me. I just sat there next to Ethan, seething.

Skyler got out of the Jag, and like the perfect gentleman, went around to the passenger side and opened the door for Tabitha. He made a show of offering his hand to her as he helped her from the car. When she stepped out of the car Ethan saw her and began waving madly.

"Hey Butchie! There's your girlfriend!" Ethan cried happily. "See her? See her?"

"Yeah, I see her," I grumbled.

Skyler shut the passenger door and walked Tabitha around to the front of the Jag, where he placed a very aggressive and intense liplock on her. Ethan gasped.

"Uh-oh, Butchie! He's kissing your girlfriend!" Ethan shouted.

"I see that, Ethan!" I snapped. "I see it."

"Hey! Stop that!" Ethan yelled inside the car. "That's Butchie's girlfriend! Stop that!"

Even with the windows up Skyler heard Ethan's yelling and he began to put on more of a show for my benefit. His hands snaked around Tabitha's waist and slipped down to firmly cup the cheeks of her ass. I could see her body tense when he did that. I got the impression that she was all right with kissing him in front of me, but the pawing session was a little more than she was comfortable with. Skyler didn't heed her body language and just continued to knead her buttocks as he pressed his body against hers.

"Butchie, I think that boy is an Ass Man, too!" Ethan said. Then back to Skyler, "Hey, stop that!"

The first bell rang and all the kids in the parking lot began to move toward the school, including Skyler and Tabitha.

"Come on, Ethan. Time to go to school," I said, shutting off the ignition with an extra little pump of fuel, letting the engine roar to a dying gasp.

"Butchie, you should beat that boy up," Ethan said as he struggled out of the car, dragging his duffel bag behind him.

"No, that's okay."

"If he touched Miranda's butt like that I would beat him up," Ethan said, thrusting his chest out.

"Well, that's fine, Ethan," I began to explain. "But it doesn't matter because Tabitha isn't my girlfriend anymore. We broke up."

"Oh," Ethan said, losing his indignant look and setting his heart on getting to class. He dropped it just like that.

Once we got into the school, we could tell immediately that things had changed. The other students still looked at us curiously, but they didn't gawk like they did the day before. We actually came close to blending in. Mike Burt, our second string center, gave me a nod as I passed him in the hall.

Apparently he was still okay with me.

Ethan and I made our way to his classroom with no one bothering us. They pretty much ignored us. As soon as we turned into the hall where Ethan's classroom was I saw Miranda Lewis, towering over just about everyone around her. Ethan saw her, too. I could tell because his face lit up.

"So, are you going to ask her out?" I asked Ethan. He instantly turned red.

"No!" he shouted way too loudly, drawing stares from everyone in the hall.

"Oh come on! Why not?"

"Butchie, I can't do that!" Ethan said, monitoring the volume of his voice more carefully this time.

I was enjoying teasing Ethan a little bit, but I was also kind of wanting to see him take the big step and ask her out.

"I know you like her," I said, nudging him in the ribs with my elbow and leaning down to whisper into his ear. "Ask her to the game on Friday. I know you go to the games anyway. You can sit with her."

Ethan had a panicked look on his face. Pure fear. He was sweating and looked very pale, his breathing was short.

"What's wrong?" I asked, very concerned. He went from being happy to looking like death warmed over in just a few seconds. "You okay, Ethan?"

"I can't... I can't do it..." he gasped, his face turning purple. "I... can't..."

"That's okay, buddy. You don't have to ask her out. I was just playing around." I felt horrible. I sent the poor kid into a panic attack just by teasing him about a girl. He didn't panic when I was throwing his stuffed toys in his face, but this tall, geeky girl set him off. I stopped him in the hall so he could gather himself.

Ethan slowly began to get back under control. His color came back and he got his breathing back to normal.

"Okay?" I asked.

Ethan nodded.

"All right. Let's go," I said, taking his arm and leading him to class. I was a little freaked out myself. I didn't expect him to have a spaz attack over a little bit of light teasing about a girl.

Mrs. Rickman was waiting beside the classroom door as we approached, looking just as severe as ever.

"See, I knew you could make it on time if you put your mind to it."

"Ha, yeah," I said jovially. Then under my breath, "Bitch."

Ethan heard me call his teacher a bitch and he let out a giggle.

"I'll pick you up after class," I told Ethan as he went into the room, but he didn't hear me. He was following Miranda.

"Have a nice day, Mrs. Rickman," I said with a huge smile. I felt her eyes boring into my back as I walked away.

2. Babysitting and Practice

I spent Wednesday and Thursday acting like it didn't bother me whenever someone asked me about Tabitha and Skyler being together.

It was a strange feeling. I recognized that I really didn't care, but for some reason it still burned my ass to see them together. I would have to say that it damaged my ego much more than it affected my heart. Had Skyler not made all the effort to show everyone that he was now with Tabitha I probably wouldn't have minded much at all. It was more about what the school thought of me instead of what I felt about the situation. Throwing it in my face was starting to piss me off, but I kept myself in check. One thing I didn't need was any more trouble.

Thursday after school I hurried to get Ethan and run him home so I could get back for practice. Thursday practices were the longest because it was our last chance to really work on things before the game on Friday, and we always had a team meeting afterwards. Sometimes the meeting was a calm talk about what we could expect. Other times it was a chance for Coach Rollins to rant. I had no idea what to expect this time.

I was anxious to get back to practice and burn off some of the aggression that had been building up all week. I had Ethan hanging on for dear life as I skidded around every corner and jostled him around the inside of the car. He would laugh until I heard the thump of his body banging into the door panel or the console between the seats, then it was a loud grunt, but right back to laughing as soon as I came to another corner to fishtail around.

I slowed down as I got closer to his house. I didn't want his mother knowing I had been driving all crazy again with her son in my car. Turned out that it didn't matter because she wasn't home anyway. I looked up and down the street, searching for her piece of shit car and I didn't see it.

"Damn it," I cursed under my breath as I shut off the ignition and got out of the car. If she wasn't home I was going to have to keep Ethan with me at practice. Not exactly what I wanted to do.

I helped Ethan from the car and we made our way to his front porch. I knew she wasn't home, but I had to try.

I knocked on the door and even tried to open it, but it was locked. Ethan, of course, wasn't allowed to have a key. He had told me that he kept losing his keys, and his mom said he couldn't have another one.

"Have a seat, I can wait a few minutes," I instructed Ethan, and we both sat down on the porch step. "I hope your mom hurries up and gets here. I have to get back to practice."

"Yeah," Ethan nodded emphatically. "And the *Thundercats* are on, too."

We sat in silence for a few minutes. Ethan looked incredibly uncomfortable without talking, until finally he couldn't take it any longer. "Butchie, how much is a hundred dimes?"

"Ten dollars," I answered flatly. "Ten dimes to a dollar."

"Well, that's it. I'm going to start collecting dimes."

"You do that," I replied, wanting to pace instead of sit and wait.

After ten minutes I decided that I couldn't wait any longer. I had to get back. But I couldn't just leave Ethan here alone on the front step. With a quick scavenger hunt through my car I came up with a pen and a napkin and left Ethan's mom a note telling her that her son was with me at the school.

"Come on, Ethan. You have to go back to practice with me," I ordered, coming to my feet.

Ethan didn't move.

"Come on," I ordered again, and again he didn't move.

I walked a couple of feet down the walk and turned around. "Are you coming?"

"I'm not allowed to."

"Well, I can't leave you here and I can't stay, so you have to," I said, walking back to him.

Ethan wouldn't move or even look up at me. A tug on his arm got a response, though. He started screaming his head off. "I want my mom! I WANT MY MOM!"

I let go of his arm.

"Ethan she's not here. And I have to leave. And you have to come with me," I said, leaning down into his face. "So, get off your ass and get back in my car. Now!"

When I raised my voice Ethan whimpered a bit, but he stood up and got in my car, and we went back to the school. The team was already on the field when I pulled back into the lot. I quickly dropped Ethan off on the bleachers and told him to wait there while I went into the locker room and put on my practice gear.

"Hurry your ass up, Blake!" Coach Rollins called out to me from the field.

After all the years of dressing for games I got pretty quick at putting on my pads and getting into my uniform. I made it out onto the field after only a few more plays. Coach Rollins jerked his head backwards, indicating Ethan on the bleachers and gave me a questioning look.

"His mom wasn't home. I waited a few minutes and then just made him come back with me," I answered to his satisfaction.

"Get out there on defense," Coach commanded.

Mr. Buck, the biology teacher/defensive coach, stood on the end of the field barking orders. The first string defense was lining up against our second string offense to work on this one specific play that Rice was very good at.

"Look where they're lined up," he shouted.

The quarterback was in the shotgun with the running back to his left. I caught on quickly that this was a stretch play. The center snapped the ball long to the quarterback and they immediately began running forward and toward the left sideline. The entire offensive line moved with them. If you ask me, I think our second stringers pulled the play off better than Rice's first string could have.

With the line in such a huge sweeping motion I couldn't find a way to break it, so I had to go around and hope I was fast enough.

I wasn't.

We spent almost a half hour working on that play and we never stopped them. We tried to match up with them in as many different ways as we could think of and nothing worked. There just seemed to be no way that we could defeat the Rice stretch play.

It could have been that the play was just so good that there was no stopping it, but that wasn't it. Any play can be stopped. It's just a matter of knowing how. More likely it was the fact that my mind wasn't on the task at hand.

Ethan did as I said and sat patiently on the bleachers as I practiced. I kept checking up on him. Every once in a while I would look up and see a couple of kids who were near him. I couldn't tell if they were messing with him or just talking to him, but I was distracted from the play just enough to mess it up.

"Blake, get the lead out of your ass and get around that line or they are going to eat us up in short yardage tomorrow night!" Mr. Buck bellowed in frustration at me as I flubbed the last attempt.

"I'm working on it!" I hissed under my breath, knowing better than to say anything. I took my place at the line again, but before we could run the play I heard Coach Rollins' whistle.

"Hustle in, men!" Coach Rollins yelled out. We all hustled in as commanded. "Take a knee."

We all dropped to one knee and looked up at Coach. Mr. Buck and Mr. Walls, the woodshop teacher/offensive coach, stepped in behind Coach Rollins.

"As you all know, we have the Rice Trojans here tomorrow night. On our own field," Coach Rollins began. "I just have one thing to say. THEY DO NOT WIN ON OUR FIELD!"

That was greeted with a chorus of assent.

"Blake!" Coach Rollins called out.

"Yes Coach!" I shouted as we were instructed to do during these meetings/pep talks.

"Thompson, their quarterback, is the only one they've got with the wheels to pull that play off. You're the only one with the wheels to stop him. I want you to stop him."

"I will!" I shouted, greeted by another chorus of ascent from my teammates.

"Skyler!" Rollins called out again.

"Yes Coach!" Skyler shouted back.

"Take your time in the pocket tomorrow. These guys can't touch you. We're going to establish the run early, and then I want you going deep. Give your receivers the time to get there."

"I will!" Skyler shouted, and we all cheered again.

"Offensive line!"

"Yes Coach!" all the offensive linemen shouted out.

"My quarterback DOES NOT get touched tomorrow night! Understood?"

"Yes Coach!"

That's when I saw the kids picking on Ethan. I happened to glance into the stands and saw that they were now definitely not just talking to him. They were kicking his duffel bag around and flicking his ears with their fingers.

"Defensive line!" Coach Rollins roared.

"Yes Coach!" Everyone shouted back.

Everyone except for me.

I was on my way to the bleachers to intercede on Ethan's behalf again. When I got to within about twenty yards or so I could tell that one of the kids was Mike Something again. I had no idea who the other kid was or why they would be hanging around at practice.

"Blake! Get your ass back here!" Mr. Buck shouted behind me as I headed into the bleachers. I heard a few scattered laughs from the players, but Coach Rollins shushed them. I heard him quiet Mr. Buck as well.

Mike Something and the other kid saw me in time and took off running. I was hoping to catch them both and slam them together until they either cried or passed out. I probably could have caught them, but it wasn't necessary to run after them. The school wasn't that big. I would see them sooner or later. I turned and came back and took a knee.

In the locker room I heard all about it.

"Don't mess with Butcher's girlfriend! He'll kick your ass!" someone said.

"Damn, I can't believe he left Tabitha Butler for Teeth!" someone else teased. Of course, all the teasing came from the other side of the wall of lockers. No one said anything to my face or when they thought I could hear.

I walked around the lockers just in time to see and hear Brent Patton, our kicker, doing his impression of Ethan and me making out. He was doing a parody voice of a retarded person and saying, "Kiss me, Butcher! I love you!" He had his eyes closed and was making what passed for a mongoloid facial impression. A few people were laughing at him as I came around the corner, but they stopped when they saw me.

As soon as Patton realized how quiet it had gotten he stopped the impression and opened his eyes. Eyes that immediately took on a look of pure terror when he saw me standing right in front of him.

I didn't say anything, I just glared down into his face.

"I… um… I'm sorry, Butcher," Patton groveled, standing there shivering wet in just a towel.

Those of us on the football team had big, wide lockers. The ones everyone else had were only about five feet tall and about six inches wide. I suddenly thought that one of those skinny lockers would be a nice place for Patton to live for a few minutes. I picked one without a lock on it and opened the door.

"Get in," I ordered.

"Butcher, I won't fit in there. I can't…" Patton stammered.

"GET IN!"

In a rush of fear, Patton stepped up to the locker and slid his right leg inside. He was right. He was a little too thick to fit in the locker.

That is, without some help.

It took some pushing and shoving, but I eventually got him jammed in the skinny little locker pretty tightly and shut the door.

"None of you had better let this little bastard out, either," I warned.

I got dressed quickly and left to take Ethan home. I figured someone would let Patton out when I was gone.

I was wrong.

I found out later that the janitors let him out of the locker at around nine o'clock that night.

3. The Epiphany and the Evolution

When I got Ethan home the lights in the house were on and the door was open, but his mom's car was nowhere in sight.

Before I could get Ethan out of the car Linda was out of the house and walking toward us, a look of concern on her face.

"I am so sorry! My car broke down at work and I had to wait on a ride home," she explained.

"Don't worry about it. I think he enjoyed watching us practice," I said, dismissing her apology. It was no big deal.

"Boys were picking on me and Butchie chased them away!" Ethan told his mother excitedly. She looked at me for confirmation and I nodded.

"It was nothing. I went after them and they ran. Just a couple of punks," I shrugged.

"Well, maybe it was nothing, but thank you just the same," Linda said. "Ethan, go in the house. Supper is about ready. It's tuna mac and peas."

Ethan smiled, lowered his head and went for the door instantly, never looking back. "Bye Butchie!"

"Well, that was fast," I commented with a smirk after Ethan disappeared into the house. "Dropped me like a bad habit."

"He loves tuna mac and peas," she smiled. "But, you're his hero."

I wasn't sure I had heard her right. I was his hero? That didn't seem right. It wasn't that long ago that I had tormented him to tears. How could I go from villain to hero so fast? I didn't know what to say to Linda, but she seemed to read my mind.

"He doesn't remember things the way that we do. A lot of times he won't remember people he meets unless he sees them everyday," she said. "He's better now than he used to be because he works at remembering people, but he still forgets a lot.

"I think he remembers you because of how you treated him at first. But he doesn't remember what you did to him. Now he just knows you as Butchie, his best friend."

I was stunned.

The kid thought I was his hero and his best friend. Who knew? I felt sorry for him and tried to treat him well, but I never thought of him as anything more than a burden or a punishment. The idea that he saw me as his best friend told me a lot about Ethan. When he wasn't with his mother, he was totally alone in this world. I felt worse about what I'd done to him originally, but better for being someone that he looked up to and thought of as a friend. I still find it strange that the most complex relationship that I have ever had with a person could come from someone so… simple.

"Are you okay?" Linda asked me. I didn't realize that I had stood there in silence for so long.

"Hmm? Oh, yeah. I'm fine," I replied. "I just had no idea… you know… that… you know…"

Linda nodded knowingly. "Yes, I know. You see him now."

I nodded. That was it. She hit the nail right on the head.

"At first, you only saw his handicap. His differences," she began. "Then you saw his similarities and that made you pity him. But now you really see *him*."

That was probably the single greatest epiphany in my life. Something that should have just been common sense struck me like a bolt out of the blue. Ethan wasn't a retard or a burden or a punching bag for anyone who cared to take a swing. He was just a person. No more and no less. I realized that there was a big difference in treating him well and actually treating him like a real person.

After a long uncomfortable silence, Linda spoke up. "You can still pick him up at the same time. I have a ride coming to get me in the morning."

"If you'd like I'll take a look at your car. I know a thing or two and I might be able to help," I offered.

"Thank you, that's very nice," Linda said with a smile. "But I won't have the money to fix it until a week from Friday. You can look at it then if you want."

"It's a deal," I said, sticking out my hand and we shook on it. "I'll see you in the morning."

"In the morning," Linda nodded. She looked at me as if she were thinking of how to say something. I waited to see what she had to say. Or if she was going to say it.

"Could I ask you a favor, Ronald?" she inquired nervously. "You can say no and I won't be offended?"

"Sure, go ahead."

"Okay. Well..." Linda stammered, looking very girlish. "I don't get to date very often. You know, with taking care of Ethan and all. We have no family around here and I don't... well, we're pretty much on our own."

I nodded, listening with interest and wondering what she was getting at. It sounded like she was asking me out. I knew it! She wanted me. I guess it wasn't just high school girls who wanted a piece of the Butcher.

"There's this party on Saturday that I've been invited to..." she continued, looking even more nervous. "...And I was wondering if you... you would...."

Here it comes. This really hot older woman is going to ask me out! She wants me! She wants me bad!

"...If you would keep an eye on Ethan for me on Saturday night. I've been asked out by this really cute guy at work and I would love to go, but you know, I can't leave Ethan alone."

Well, sonofabitch.

I must have had a really strange look on my face, the shock showing through. Linda mistook it for a negative response. Her body seemed to sag in disappointment.

"I'm sorry. I really had no right to ask that of you," she said, embarrassed. "You don't have to worry about that."

"No, no. That's fine," I corrected quickly. I didn't want her to know what I had been thinking. It wasn't a rejection if I kept it to myself. "I'd be happy to keep an eye on Ethan. I'm not doing anything Saturday night."

"Really?" Linda asked, excited. "You'd do that?"

"Sure, why not? Ethan is no problem. And everyone needs a night out once in a while."

"Thank you!" Linda squealed, lunging forward and giving me a big kiss on the cheek and a hug. "You don't know how badly I need this!"

Actually, I thought I did.

"I haven't been on a date since Ethan's dad left. Ten years ago," she said.

Hmm, I guess I didn't. Ten years? Damn!

"Well, you can break your streak. Go out and have fun. I'll take care of Ethan. We can watch movies or something. It'll be cool."

"Ronald, I appreciate this so much!" she gushed. "Thank you, thank you, thank you!"

I smiled at her giddiness. "What time should I be here?"

"Charles said he would pick me up at six, so I guess anytime before that would be fine."

"I'll be here at five thirty."

"That will be good. I'll make sure I have plenty of good stuff for you guys to munch on and lots of pop."

"That's fine. I'll be there," I said, turning to head to my car. "I'll see you tomorrow."

She nodded. "Thanks again. This means a lot to me."

"Not a problem."

As an afterthought, when I was about half way back to my car, I turned around and called back after her, just as she was going into the house. "Linda!"

She stopped and leaned out of the doorway. "Yes?"

"Call me if you need a ride anywhere or if you need me to go get something for you," I said.

"Thank you, Ronald. I just might have to do that."

"Okay. Goodnight," I said, turning back to the car.

"Goodnight."

When I got to the car and pulled away from the curb I noticed that she was still watching me. She was absolutely beautiful in the dying September light and she was looking at me with something akin to love. Admiration? Respect?

Whatever it was, I took it as a compliment. She seemed to be seeing me as a man, not an immature high school boy. I was no longer the evil bastard who bullied and abused her son, but I was a respectable and noble person who had grown out of his prejudices and childish impulses. From just her look I got the impression that she saw a dignified man who had evolved far beyond his egocentric, selfish depths.

Hmmmmm.

Maybe I *would* get a chance to bone her.

4. Killing the Trojans

Friday night was another highlight in the promising career of Butcher Blake.

We got off to a slow start. They held us to a field goal on our first possession, more through their own good play than anything we did wrong. Rice was a pretty good team after all. Part of the reason we didn't get the touchdown was that I was stopped on third and short and it really pissed me off. I stayed on the field with the defense and took it out on the Trojans offense. They received their kick off and started their possession at their own forty-yard line, but in three plays we had driven them back to the ten and forced them to punt it away.

The first play out of the gate was their famous stretch play and I made them eat it. I crushed Thompson and dropped him for a ten-yard loss. They tried it again on their second play and I got him for eleven yards that time. I think I hurt him a little because he missed the snap on the next play, only recovering the fumble a fraction of a second before we all piled on him.

I scored four of our eight touchdowns and ended the game with seven sacks, including the sack that ended Thompson's season. He was attempting the stretch play again and I nailed him. It was a clean hit, but he fell in a bad way, his knee and ankle folded under his weight. Even above the crash of the pads hitting I could hear the snapping and popping of Thompson's leg. It is a sickening sound that you just can't forget.

Right after the hit I backed off and let the coaches and trainer get to him, and when I looked over at the sideline I saw Skyler leading a bunch of the Mustangs in cheering Thompson's injury. I turned my back on them and waited for play to resume. I no longer saw the point in gloating over a guy's injury.

After I took out their quarterback they never recovered. That was right at the opening of the second quarter and the rest of the game we just toyed with them. The back-up quarterback couldn't pull off the stretch play at all and he didn't have an arm to speak of. It was a parade of interceptions and crushed running backs. The final score came out 59-0, but the game wasn't really even that close.

I looked up into the stands and saw my dad talking to the scout from Notre Dame. Dad was all smiles, shmoozing the guy and waving to me. I wanted to break off from the team and go up and see what was being said, but that wasn't allowed. We had to wait to be released by Coach Rollins, and that only came after our game recap speech.

I ducked into the locker room knowing that Dad would tell me everything.

At least twice.

I hurried to my locker and started shedding my uniform and pads. I wanted to hit the showers and get to the victory dance in the gym. I was unattached again and the pussy would be falling out of the sky for the Hero of the Night. My dad wanted me to capitalize on my status, and capitalize I would. I didn't know who it would be, but some lucky girl was going to the Butcher Block that night.

Thankfully, Coach Rollins only gave us a quick "Way to go, see ya Tuesday" and headed into his office and shut the door.

As I was getting dressed after the shower JK approached with a huge smile.

"Guess what we're doing tomorrow night?" he asked.

"What are we doing tomorrow night?"

"We're going to a party. With college girls!"

I was intrigued. "Where?"

"Some guy my brother knows has a house in the country with a big pole barn. He hired Barry's band to play the party, so they said we could come."

"Cool," I said casually. I was excited about the prospect of college chicks, but I wasn't showing it. "Sounds like a good time."

"Hell yeah! College chicks like to fuck!" JK said, making pumping motions in the air with his hips.

"What a coincidence! So do I!" I laughed.

JK walked off with a forearm bash and went to finish getting dressed.

I was stoked about our first college party, but there was something eating at me. I felt like I was forgetting something and it bothered me all night, all through the dance. The only time it didn't bother me was when I was nailing Stacy Lampley in the back of Karla Fredrick's Dodge Dart out in the parking lot.

As soon as we were finished, Stacy and I got out of the car and went our separate ways. I went back to the dance to hang with my friends and she went back to hang with hers. It was just a one-time thing and we both knew it. No big deal. We probably wouldn't even talk in the halls on Monday.

I was driving home after the dance and trying to think of what it was that I could be forgetting. I just felt like I had something I was supposed to do on Saturday.

"Oh well," I sighed. If it were important I would remember it.

I had a party to attend. Beer to drink and chicks to nail.

What could be more important than that?

Chapter Six

1. That Thing That I Forgot

All day Saturday I was the epitome of young, dumb, and full of come.

Sure, I had just had sex the night before with Stacy Lampley, but I was ready to go again as if I hadn't been laid in years. I used all that pent up sexual energy to my advantage and leaped into my chores with reckless abandon, catching up on a whole month of things I had been putting off.

My dad would be pleased when he got home from work and saw that everything he had asked was done. Maybe shocked was a better word than pleased, though. It really wasn't that bad, doing all the chores, considering that Dad gave me a big allowance so that I wouldn't have to work and could concentrate on football. He owned his own successful contracting business and he made a lot of money, which gave him the means to ensure my future in the way he saw fit. How many high school kids get a hundred bucks a week in allowance? Not very damn many, I'm sure.

I grabbed a quick shower after cleaning out the garage and was waiting for JK to pick me up when the phone rang. I was going to hang out with JK until we went to the party at eight o'clock that night. Drink a little beer and get primed and ready for the party. I had made big plans and I was ready to dip my wick into some college chicks. The anxiety was too great to pace around my house alone waiting to go out to the party. I had to get out of there.

Besides, I didn't really want to be there when my dad got home. I knew that he wouldn't appreciate what I had done. Cleaning the garage wasn't even part of what I was supposed to do, I just did a little extra. Granted, I had only done it so that thinking about how much pussy I was going to get that night didn't drive me nuts, but the fact is, I still went above and beyond the call. As much as my dad supported me in my football endeavors, he really was never much of a father to me. Coach Rollins was actually more of a father than my dad was. Dad was just the guy who gave me his name and bitched at me constantly. Any way I could avoid him was good enough for me. As long as he kept the C-note coming every week and left me alone, we'd get along.

I had been on the porch when the phone rang and went back inside to answer it, passing my mom who was on the couch watching a cooking show and taking notes on a recipe she would never make. I snatched the phone up on the fourth ring, right before the answering machine kicked in.

"Blake's," I said automatically.

"Ronald?"

"Do you want Big Ron or Little Ron?" I asked, hating that I was known to anyone as Little Ron.

"Butchie? Is that you?" Linda Miles asked. I finally recognized her voice. Now I was humiliated, having called myself Little Ron in front of her. What really sucked was that I was considerably bigger than Big Ron. To me, Little Ron always sounded like a cutesy nickname for Big Ron's penis. After growing up with that I swore that if I ever had a son he could be named anything but Ronald Blake III.

"This is Butchie. Er, I mean Butcher. Hi, Linda," I said, glad that she couldn't see the red in my cheeks. Little Ron. Fuck! I couldn't believe I had said that to her. "I didn't recognize you over the phone at first."

"Same here. You sound much older over the phone," Linda said. "Anyway, I was calling to tell you that I didn't get a chance to get out, what with having no car available, and well… I didn't have a chance to get any snacks or rent any videos for you boys tonight. I wanted to see if it would be okay if I just left the money here and you could take Ethan and go pick out something after I leave for my date."

I went silent on my end of the phone. Suddenly I remembered what I had been forgetting the night before. Damn it! I wasn't going to get to nail the college chicks after all! Sonofabitch!

"Butchie? Will that be okay?"

"Um, yeah," I said, snapping back to the conversation. "That will be fine. No problem at all."

"Are you sure?" she asked.

"Absolutely. I can't wait. It will be fun," I said, excitement in my tone. To cover up that I had forgotten about her and Ethan I told a little white lie. "I've been looking forward to this."

"That's great. So has Ethan," Linda said, and I could hear in her voice that she was touched by what I had said.

"All right. Then I'll see you at five thirty," I said, mentally kicking myself. I hated the fact that I was going to have to miss the party of my high school life so that I could babysit Ethan. Sure, I was a little bit honored that Ethan considered me his hero, but spending a Saturday night watching movies with a retard just didn't compare to partying with college girls. But I had given my word. Like Coach Rollins said: A man whose word means nothing *is* nothing.

"Five thirty. See you then," I said.

"Thanks again, Butchie. Bye bye."

"You're quite welcome. Bye." I hung the handset back in the cradle. Before I had time to think, I heard JK's horn. It played *Celebration* by Kool and the Gang.

After telling my mom I was leaving and that I would be home late, I stepped onto the porch and saw that my dad was pulling into the driveway as JK came up the front walk. I saw the look of disgust on my dad's face as he got out of his truck.

JK knew that my dad was racist and that he didn't like him. He used to avoid coming to my house until my mom had a talk with him and told him that it was okay and just to ignore my dad. Instead, JK had done her one better. He knew that my mom wouldn't let anything happen, so he began antagonizing my dad. JK was always polite, but he also always found just the right thing to say to set my old man off.

"Evenin' Massa Blake," JK said to my father in his best minstrel show voice. I stifled a small laugh, but my dad remained stone faced.

"Jerome, there is no reason for you to keep coming over here," Dad said, deadpan. "I've told you, we don't have any fried chicken or watermelon."

JK just laughed at it like it was a friendly little joke, instead of the insult that it was. That pissed my dad off more than anything. "You so funny, Massa Blake! Lawd yes!"

My dad shot an angry glance at me, letting me know again that he didn't approve of my *nigger* friend. To staunch the bleeding, I chimed in with some news that Dad would appreciate. "I caught up on all my chores. I even cleaned out the garage."

Nothing. Not a nod, not a thank you. Nothing.

It was exactly what I expected, but it did serve to distract Dad from JK's presence for a second.

"Well, I'm outta here. I told mom I'd be back late," I said, heading to JK's car. Dad waved his hand dismissively.

JK couldn't resist a parting shot. "Come on, Butcher. Let's go bang some white girls."

I didn't have to look back to know what my dad's reaction was.

2. Plan B

When I explained my problem to JK, he instantly came up with the simplest solution.

We would take Ethan to the party with us.

It wasn't what I would have thought of as a Plan A, but as a Plan B it seemed like the way to go. I didn't think that Linda would really go for it, though. I could have been wrong and she might have been totally fine with it, happy that we were going to take Ethan out and expose him to more people, more social interaction, safe in the knowledge that he would be with me. I just couldn't take the chance of asking. If she said that we couldn't take him, then I would be blowing my chances of going. In turn, she would be more likely to check up on us, thereby busting us. I decided that it would be easier to get forgiveness than permission.

Ethan answered the door for us when we got to the Miles house and let us in, hugging me like we were long lost friends who hadn't seen each other in years. "Butchie!"

I gently pushed him away after a short time, unable to handle the awkwardness of such a public display of affection, even in semi-private. "Hi, Ethan. You remember JK?"

Ethan leaned over and looked around my left side. "Yes. Hammerhead!"

"Just call me JK, Ethan. Okay?" JK said, stretching out his hand to shake.

"All right. JK," Ethan agreed.

I wondered why it was that easy for JK. I had asked Ethan to call me Butcher, instead of Butchie, but he wouldn't do it. Oh well.

"Ethan, bring them in and close the door," Linda said, coming from the bedroom and putting in her earrings. Her dress hung loosely in the front, clearly open in the back. "Where are your manners?"

"I'm sorry," Ethan said to his mother. Then to JK and I separately, "I'm sorry. I'm sorry."

"It's okay, Ethan. Just finish the social action, okay?" Linda said.

"Okay," Ethan replied, going into his mental checklist. He thought for a second and then asked, "May I take your coats?"

"Ethan... is that right?" Linda questioned patiently.

Ethan looked lost for a second and then smiled his big, toothy grin.

"No," he laughed. "They aren't wearing coats!"

Linda waited for a few seconds to see if Ethan was going to remember what to do and then she helped him. "Ask them to come in and have a seat. Then see if they would like something to drink."

Ethan's eyes lit up, suddenly remembering that he had known that. Linda smiled, seeing that he now knew what he was supposed to do and she ducked back into the bedroom. "Out in a second, guys."

Eventually, Ethan got us squared away, seating us in the small living room and bringing us each a can of soda. He looked to be very pleased with himself as he finished his greeting procedure. Then just as quickly, he forgot all about us and went back to watching World Championship Wrestling on the Superstation. It was like turning a switch. Ethan was doing all he could to be the perfect host, and then suddenly it was like we weren't even there. I turned to JK and laughed silently. That's when I heard Linda call out from her bedroom.

"Butchie, could you come in here for a second?" came the lilting question.

JK smiled and raised his eyebrows as I rose from the couch and went into Linda's bedroom with an even bigger smile on my face.

I stepped through the doorway and Linda had just let her hair fall around her shoulders after clasping a necklace behind her head. She ran her hand around her neck, making sure that no hair was stuck under the thin gold chain. There was a pearl pendant hanging from the necklace, resting between her breasts. Not that I was looking at her breasts, mind you.

Yeah, right.

The dress, I knew when I saw it, was the famous Little Black Dress that chicks always talk about. This one was sleeveless and came to just above her knee, hugging her form like a body stocking. Suddenly my pants grew a bit tighter.

"Will you zip me up?" Linda asked, turning around.

I took her turning her back to me as my opportunity to adjust myself inside my pants and keep things as concealed as possible. "Sure."

"I would have had Ethan do it, but he always pinches me in the zipper. He can't help it."

I pulled out the material of the dress just above her buttocks and grasped the zipper pull and slowly slid it up, careful not to pinch her. The dress came to a final close just above her bra strap.

"Well, what do you think?" Linda asked, turning slowly as I backed away from her to take in the full effect.

"You're hot!"

"Really? Oh my God!" She looked embarrassed, yet pleased with my response.

"Hell yeah. Your date is a lucky man," I said, putting my hands in the front pockets of jeans, hoping to disguise any suspicious protrusions.

"Thank you, Butchie. That is sweet of you to say."

Linda turned off the lamp on her dresser and ushered me back into the living room.

A few minutes later her date showed up, flowers and a small teddy bear in hand. I thought it was a nice touch and decided to try it at some point in the future. All I had ever brought to a date was beer and a hard-on.

Linda introduced us to her date, a tall, somewhat geeky looking guy. He seemed nice enough, though. He had already met Ethan and said hello to him. Ethan ignored him, too engrossed in the wrestling moves of Chief Wahoo McDaniel to acknowledge the man.

"Charles Whitman, this is Butch… uh, Ronald Blake and Jerome Kent. They play for the Mustangs. They're friends of Ethan's."

"Pleased to meet the both of you," Charles said, shaking hands firmly with us. When someone squeezes my hand too tightly during a handshake it makes me think they are compensating for something. I wondered if Charles was intimidated by our size, being that he was such a thin and frail looking guy.

"Likewise," JK and I said almost in perfect unison.

Linda excused herself to put the finishing touches on her make-up and that left Charles with us to make small talk.

"So, Charles Whitman, huh?" I asked.

"Yes."

"Named after the mass murderer?"

"Who? I don't know... well... " Charles seemed taken aback.

"He's the guy who shot all those people at the University of Texas back in the Sixties."

"No. No relation."

The rest of the small talk didn't get much better than that, but at least I don't think I offended him any further. Being compared to a mass murderer wasn't his idea of a good time, I guess.

Linda came out of the bedroom and the feeling was as if we had been saved by the bell.

"Well, I think I'm ready to go," she announced.

Charles stood up a bit straighter. I got the impression that he was dating a woman who was far better looking than he ever expected to get.

Linda came over and gave me a quick, friendly hug, whispering in my ear, "Thanks again. I need this."

"Just have fun," I whispered.

"Hopefully I'll be home late," she whispered again, conspiratorially. "Very late."

"No problem. Ethan will be fine with me."

Linda straightened up and laced her arm through Charles's arm. "Shall we?"

"Again gentlemen, it was nice meeting you. Goodbye, Ethan," Charles said as he walked his hottie out the front door. Again, Ethan ignored him. I learned that night, and it was proven again and again over time, that when wrestling or *Thundercats* was on, Ethan was in another world.

I watched them conspicuously from the front window as Charles opened the door for Linda and helped her into the car before getting into the driver's side.

'*That smooth motherfucker*', I thought. I never would have been that polite with a girl. Hell, I usually honked the horn and they would come running out of the house. As it turned out I learned a few helpful tips from the tall geek Linda went out with.

As soon as they drove away I grabbed the remote control from the coffee table and clicked the television off.

"Ethan, put on your shoes. We're going out."

3. Stalking the Prey

To kill some of the time before the party, we went to the grocery and video stores.

We weren't going to watch the movies or eat the snacks, but we had to buy them anyway, simply so the alibi would hold up if we were questioned. At the video store I picked up *Willy Wonka and the Choclate Factory* because Ethan said it was one of his favorites. I figured that we would let him watch a little bit of it while we arranged the house to look like we had been there all night. I opened up the bags of chips and dumped about half of each bag in the garbage disposal. I poured a few cans of soda down the sink and left the cans on the table. Ethan said that his favorite board game was *Sorry!*, so we set it up and played about half a game, leaving the board and pieces in place. I felt confident that as long as we were home before Linda, she would have no reason to think that we had gone anywhere besides the store runs.

At about eight o'clock we loaded into JK's car and headed out to the party. Ethan was upset that we weren't driving Smokeyandthebandit, but he got over it once we told him that we were on our way to a party. A real *high school* party, I told him. That made him happy. I told him not to tell anybody, even his mom, or we wouldn't be able to go out like that anymore. Ethan looked a bit troubled by the idea of keeping something from his mother, but he said he would.

The music was plainly audible while still several hundred yards from the property. We pulled into the impromptu parking lot that someone had made on the lawn, cars parked haphazardly in all directions. If the cops showed up we would all be busted before we could get our cars out. I could recognize the sound of the band, having heard JK's brother in rehearsal with them many times. I wasn't much of a punk lover, but live music is always better than records and I was digging their groove.

There were people everywhere, wandering around among the cars carrying cups of beer and smoking cigarettes. Only a few of them did I recognize from school. Most were older, having graduated the year before. The large sliding doors of the pole barn were thrown wide open and the band stood inside, against the back wall, rocking out like they were in a packed stadium instead of being ignored by pretty much everyone. The bass player was tall and gangly with a high-rise mohawk haircut, dyed black and tipped in neon pink. I knew him only vaguely. He never spoke to us when JK and I would go to their practices. I assumed he was just really reserved. Apparently that was only for when he wasn't on a stage. He was slampunking his bass like it had fucked his girlfriend.

Barry finished a quick fill across his tom-toms and then nodded to us from behind his drum kit when he saw us walk up to the barn. Then he motioned his head to his left, pointing us to the kegs, and we stepped inside the barn, making our way immediately to the land of beer.

Ethan was almost glued to my shoulder. If I stopped too suddenly he was going to run right into me. He was squinting as if in pain, cringing every time that Barry crashed a cymbal. I began to think that maybe bringing him wasn't going to be any better than missing the party. If I couldn't get him to give me at least a little space I was never going to get laid. My only hope was that he would be fine hanging with JK if I got the chance to sneak away and get my wick wet. And I most definitely planned on sneaking away and getting my wick wet.

JK and I paid our five dollars each to the guy manning the kegs and were given red plastic cups full of, mostly, foam. But underage drinkers can't be choosers, so we took our alcoholic froth and slipped deeper into the barn.

"Ethan, want a sip of beer?" I asked. I didn't really think that alcohol was good for him, and I didn't want any harm to come to him, but I have to admit that I was a little interested to see what would happen if we got a retarded guy drunk. "It's good."

"No!" Ethan shouted, right about the time that band stopped playing. Everyone turned to look at us. "I am not allowed to have beer, Butchie!"

"Yeah, Butchie," I heard from behind me. "Teeth isn't allowed to have beer."

I heard a chorus of laughter as I turned around. Skyler was standing behind me, his arm around Tabitha, Chewy and Shorty flanking him. They all cackled maliciously.

"Butchie!" Chewy catcalled, laughing. "He called him Butchie!"

Well, that was that. From now on I would be Butchie to everyone. They would never let it drop.

"Hey Skyler. Syphilis cleared up yet?" I asked.

Skyler didn't answer my little jibe. He had other fish to fry. "What the fuck are you doing bringing that fucking retard out here?"

I could tell he was already pretty drunk, so what was best for everyone was just to ignore him. "Have a nice night, Skyler."

I grabbed Ethan's elbow and led him away, happy to see that Skyler and the Goon Squad didn't follow.

The singer for the band grabbed the microphone as the band filed off the small homemade stage. "We're going to take a little break, grab a brew and get back up here in a few minutes. We're Baloney Pony and the Spank Meats! Thanks for partying with us!"

The band headed for the keg, all except for the bass player. He was pulled aside by this semi-cute, but very severe looking girl and they were having some kind of argument. It started getting pretty heated and they walked out the back door of the pole barn where the bitching got going in earnest.

Ethan, JK and I stood there in the freshly silent pole barn, looking around for people we knew. Aside from Skyler and his boys, there weren't many. Barry approached us after he got his beer.

"Glad you could make it, little brother," he said to JK.

"Hell yeah, wouldn't miss it. There's some hot ass out here."

"If you like white bitches," Barry sneered.

"Well, if you want to meet black girls, play black music. A sista don't want to hear this punk rock shit."

The exchange from out back got louder, the girl sounding like a chainsaw on speed once she got going. I nodded my head toward the sound of the argument. "Your boy going to be okay?"

"Yeah. He'll be cool," Barry said calmly. "Norm said he's going to break up with Judith tonight so that he can concentrate on the band. She's probably not taking it very well."

Barry excused himself and went to hang out with the rest of his band.

I put my back against the wall and began to take inventory. I was looking for anyone who I would want to have sex with. Stacy Lampley was standing just outside the door. I put her on the list, but only as a last resort. After all, I'd already had her. Karla Fredricks was with her, of course. The two were virtually inseparable. Doing Stacy again wouldn't be too bad if I could get that three-way action I had meant to ask about with Karla. So, I figured that was a possibility. I had a fifty/fifty chance, the way I saw it. I could ask and they might say no. But then again, they might say yes.

There were quite a few pretty girls there that I didn't recognize. As far as I was concerned they were all fair game. I wasn't looking at them as people. I was stalking them like a lion hunting on the African savannah. The only ones off limits were the ones who were already there with a guy. The rest were clustered in little giggling groups.

I spotted one that I was interested in.

She was tall and blonde, standing amid a group of less attractive girls. I had to try to break her from the herd. "JK, keep an eye on Ethan for me. I'm going in."

"Go, Butcher!" JK cheered, slapping me on the back.

Low to the ground, I moved in for the kill.

4. A Good Night Gone Bad

The girl's name was Brenda and she was a cheerleader at DeMille.

Like everyone else in the area she knew who I was as soon as I approached her. A little small talk and a few compliments and the next thing you know, she was on her way out to JK's car with me. Back in the late 80's many of us were still blissfully unaware of the dangers of AIDS, so we slept around indiscriminately. Why should we worry? Only fags got AIDS, right? Back then, I thought nothing of having sex with a girl I had only known for twenty minutes or so.

As soon as we were finished we pulled our pants back on, I took her number, and promised to call her. Which, of course, I never did. She didn't go to my school anyway. The chances of running into her again weren't that high. But, seeing as how I was trying out the new gentleman routine that I saw when Charles picked Linda up, I decided that the least I could do was walk her back to the party.

No sooner had we gotten out of the car than we heard the sounds of an argument and a girl screaming. I ran toward the sound, twisting through the tangle of parked cars in the yard, out toward the road where the noise was coming from. Brenda followed close behind me. I heard loud, braying laughter mingled with the arguing the closer I got.

The argument was coming from Skyler's Jag. I saw Chewy and Shorty standing outside the car and laughing their idiot asses off as a girl slapped and hit at Skyler. Inside the car was a blur of motion as Skyler defended his face from the onslaught of blonde hair and fingernails. The passenger door suddenly flew open and the girl screamed again before flying backwards out of the car, hitting her head against the driver's door of the car next to the Jag with a solid thunk. I could see that the girl was naked from the waist down, wearing nothing but a purple and green Mims Mustangs sweatshirt.

"ASSHOLE!" the girl screamed, throwing the hair out of her face. Then I could see that it was Tabitha. "YOU FUCKING ASSHOLE!"

Skyler leaned over the passenger seat and pulled the door closed before stomping on the accelerator and throwing bits of the yard behind him. Chewy and Shorty ran to the truck and followed suit, fishtailing out onto the county road. Tabitha stood up, angry and ranting, but still trying to stretch her sweatshirt down far enough to cover herself. It wasn't working, so I took off my shirt and gave it to her.

"Tab, put this on," I said, tapping her on the shoulder. She spun on me, enraged. Her ranting stopped when she saw me.

"Ronnie!" she screamed, throwing her arms around my neck. She began to cry.

I noticed that more people had started to gather around us, attracted by the sounds of the scuffle. "Tab, put my shirt on. Everyone is looking at your ass."

She hid behind me and slipped the shirt over her head, wearing it like a short dress.

"What happened?" I asked as she threw her arms around my neck again.

"That mother fucker!" she snarled, her anger showing through the tears.

"What happened, Tab?"

She didn't say anything for a long time. She just stood there with her arms around my neck, crying softly against my bare chest. I remembered Brenda and looked around for her, but she was nowhere to be seen, so I just held Tabitha until her crying began to wind down.

"We went to the car… to be alone," she said, I assumed not wanting to tell me that she went out there to intentionally have sex with Skyler. "We had sex, but as soon as he got off, he told me to get out of his car."

That didn't surprise me one bit coming from Derek Skyler.

"I told him 'no' and he tried to push me out the door, so I slapped him. He kept pushing me against the door, trying to get it open so he could push me out. He bent my finger backwards. I think he broke it."

Tabitha held her finger up. It looked fine to me, but that didn't mean that it wasn't broken.

"That's when he pushed me out. He took off with my pants and shoes," she said through sniffles. "And my panties."

"Come on. Me and JK will take you home," I said, stuffing her in the crook of my arm and guiding her toward JK's car. I got her into the backseat and she sat there quietly crying while I went back into the party to collect JK and Ethan.

The band had started back up, playing a decent cover of the Sex Pistols *Pretty Vacant*. I was never much of a Sex Pistols fan, but it sounded just as shitty as the original version, so I guess that was pretty good. I came across the expanse of yard leading up to the pole barn and I came across JK. He was standing outside the barn doors talking to a couple guys from the team and Carl Cattrell, one of the guys who was on the team last year, before he graduated. Carl should have been away at college, but he suffered a serious injury late in the season the year before and lost his scholarships. No one wanted to take a chance on a potential star with a bum knee.

Looking around, Ethan was nowhere in sight. I picked up my pace a little as I approached the group. "JK, where's Ethan?"

JK turned around and looked, as if he expected to see Ethan standing right behind him. "Oh shit! I lost him!"

I didn't say anything; I just went looking for Ethan. JK broke off his conversation and went looking for him in the opposite direction. There was no telling who was picking on Ethan. I felt a little better knowing that Skyler and the Goon Squad were gone, but that was no guarantee that someone wasn't mistreating Ethan. I made my way through the slam dancing throng and looked around in the barn.

Nothing.

The barn was full of people and I couldn't see Ethan through the crowd. I nudged my way through the press of bodies, using my running back skills to make it through the slam dancing mass in front of the stage. I put a couple of the more aggressive "dancers" on the concrete floor when they came at me. No one got angry, though. They probably just thought I was a really good dancer.

I scanned the room from the other side of the stage, still not seeing Ethan. I wasn't at the point of panic, but I knew that if I didn't find him it was going to be my ass. Between Linda Miles and Coach Rollins I don't know which one would have kicked my ass harder.

Just as I was getting ready to give up on my search of the barn and head outside to look some more, I saw the edges of light coming around the sides of a door in the far corner. I went straight to the door and opened it, looking in.

There was Ethan, sitting around a table that was made out of a huge discarded spool from the power company. He was sitting with two guys, one of them a short chubby guy with long hair and glasses, wearing a Motorhead t-shirt, and the other one an anorexic looking little weirdo with spiky hair, wearing a gaudy Hawaiian shirt. The spiky haired guy was holding a lighter to the bowl of a ceramic cobra shaped bong that Ethan had his mouth fastened to.

"Go Teeth! S-s-s-s-s-s-smoke," the chubby guy said, joined in the sibilance of the word *smoke* by the spiky haired guy.

Ethan was hitting the bong like a pro, I had to give him that. But on the other hand, I had no idea of what might happen to him if he got high. I mean, he was already pretty fucked up. He didn't need any more fucked up on top of his natural state.

"What the fuck are you doing?" I demanded of the two guys. They were both pretty cooked, as was Ethan. I could tell once he looked up from the bong. His eyes were bloodshot slits.

"Hey Butchie!" Ethan yelled, way too loudly. He tried to hand the cobra bong to me. "S-s-s-s-smoke, Butchie."

The two guys laughed at Ethan's usage of their term and at the fact that Ethan was flicking his tongue like a snake and hissing.

I took the bong from Ethan and sat it back on the spool table. "Ethan, come on, we're going home."

I really thought the two guys deserved an ass kicking, but I just wanted to get Ethan out of there.

"Butchie, I want to stay here with my friends," Ethan begged, putting his arm around the chubby longhaired guy.

"No Ethan, we have to go now," I said more forcefully.

Ethan dropped his argument and got up from the table, walking to my side. The chubby guy clapped him on the shoulder. "See ya around, Teeth."

I pushed the guy down into his chair, hard. "His name is Ethan!"

I dragged Ethan out of the room as he waved to his new "friends".

As quickly as I could, I found JK and told him that we needed to go home, and that we needed to drop Tabitha off at her house. The night had gone from a pretty good night into a complete mess in just a few minutes. The party I had been looking forward to all day was a total bust, as far as I was concerned.

Of course, I did get laid. There was that.

5. The Long Ride Home

As it turned out, all of our preparations before leaving were for naught. Our stay at the party was painfully short, so we had nothing to worry about concerning Linda's possible early return from her date. We made it back to her house several hours before she did.

The ride home was interesting, to say the least. A fair word of warning, if I may. Never, ever, get a retard high. Ethan didn't handle it well. Not well at all. Think of everything that can happen to you when you smoke pot, and then amplify it in your mind. Then, imagine that you know absolutely nothing of what to expect. Ethan freaked out a little.

I rode in the backseat with Tabitha and let Ethan ride up front with JK. I was still a bit pissed at Tab about how she had broken up with me, but she was in a bad spot and I wasn't enjoying her misery. I restrained myself from saying, "That's what you get", even though that is exactly what I was thinking. I just put my arm around her and pulled her in close to me. She was silent all the way to her house, every so often releasing a quiet sob.

Ethan, on the other hand, was anything but quiet. I had explained to Ethan that the stuff that his two "friends" had him smoke was illegal and that he couldn't do it anymore or he could go to jail. It didn't bother him when I told him, but the typical smoker's paranoia set in with him on the ride home. At one point JK passed a cop coming the other way down the road and Ethan went crazy in the front seat.

"BUTCHIE! BUTCHIE!" he cried.

"What is it, Ethan?" I asked, somewhat alarmed by his panicked tone.

"That policeman! He looked at me! He knows I smoked the eagle stuff!"

"Eagle stuff?"

"Yes. In the snake. The eagle stuff!"

"What eagle stuff?" I asked, not following.

"You said the stuff I smoked with my friends was a eagle's stuff! And the cop knows! I don't want to go to jail!" Ethan shouted.

JK and I began laughing; finally catching on to what he was trying to say.

"No, it's not *a eagle's stuff*," JK explained, smiling. "He said 'illegal stuff'. It means against the law. Ill-egal. See?"

"Am I going to go to jail, Butchie?" Ethan asked, fearfully.

I shot a glance out the back window and saw the cop speeding down the road and heading away from us. "No, you're not going to jail. We're going to get you home and you'll be fine. Those two assholes should have never let you smoke that shit. It's not your fault."

Hearing that he hadn't done something bad, at least on purpose, calmed Ethan down considerably. A few seconds later I heard the sounds of lip smacking coming from the front seat. Ethan was popping his tongue against the roof of his mouth. "Butchie, I'm thirsty."

"I know. We'll get you something to drink when we get you home."

"I'm really thirsty, though." Ethan began smacking louder and looking into the backseat at me while making horrible faces, like he'd eaten something that tasted bad.

"It's called cottonmouth. You get it when you smoke that stuff," I explained. I was making sure not to use words like pot or weed. Anything that would let him know exactly what he smoked. I didn't want him blurting out, "Pot makes me thirsty" to his mother.

JK pulled the car up in front of Tabitha's house, way out in Rambling Hills. It was the richer than thou section of town and I was surprised every time they let me in, much less JK. The whole place was lily white. I half expected a series of alarms and klaxons to go off. Maybe a synthetic voice calling out, "WARNING! BLACK MAN IN THE PERIMETER!"

At the end of Dennings Drive, JK turned slowly onto Cindy Lane and found Tabitha's house. I had him turn out the headlights before he pulled into the driveway. It was still fairly early, but I thought that if Tabitha could get into the house without her parents seeing her it would be better for all. If she wanted to tell them what happened, that was fine, but I didn't want to invite any trouble if it wasn't necessary.

Helping Tab out of the car, I put my arm around her and walked her to the door. She began sobbing louder the closer we came. We were almost to the front step when her dad came out of the front door, seething.

"What the hell did you do to my daughter, Blake?" he said through clenched teeth.

Before I could even react, he put both hands against my chest and pushed me. I was considerably bigger than he was, and it didn't move me, but I stepped back in deference. I wasn't there for trouble. I knew I could have kicked her dad's ass if we got into a serious physical altercation, but his anger was understandable, just misplaced. Seeing his little girl coming home crying with no pants on upset him, like it would anyone.

"Daddy! Stop!" Tab cried, pulling away from me and stepping between her father and me. "Ronnie didn't do anything to me. He helped me."

Mr. Butler stepped back then, still regarding me coolly.

"Wait here," Tabitha said, kissing me on the cheek. "I'll get dressed and give you your shirt back."

"What happened?" Mr. Butler called after Tabitha as she ran into the house. "What happened? What happ..."

The door closed and he turned to me. "What happened, Ronald?"

As much as I hated Skyler I didn't want to name him and get him in trouble. He was a total prick and deserved any punishment he may get, but I was still thinking of the team. After all, when you spend your entire life having '*there is no I in team*' drilled into you, it's hard to let it go. "I think you should just talk to Tabitha. I saw her in trouble and brought her home. That's all."

It only took her a few seconds and then Tab came back outside wearing a pair of shorts and a different shirt. Her mother followed her, but stopped at the door.

Tabitha bounded off the front step, handed my shirt to me, and I pulled it over my head. She gave me a huge hug and a kiss on the cheek. "Thank you, Ronnie."

"Are you going to be okay?" I asked. She nodded.

Mr. Butler extended his hand to me. "I'm sorry about pushing you, Ronald. Thank you for helping Tabby."

"No apology necessary, Mr. Butler. I understand completely," I said, shaking his hand.

"I know you guys broke up, and when I saw you bring her up the front walk, crying, I thought the worst."

"It's okay. Really."

I excused myself and got back in the car. As JK pulled away I watched Tabitha and her dad going back into the house. She waved to me and I waved back.

"Butchie?"

"Yes, Ethan?"

"I'm still thirsty."

I sighed. "I know."

"And I'm hungry, too. Real hungry!"

"That's called having the munchies. You get that from smoking that stuff, too."

"Butchie?"

"What?"

"I don't like this. It feels funny."

I let out a small laugh. "Well, good. Now, don't ever smoke it again. Don't smoke anything ever again. Okay?"

"I won't. I promise."

When we got Ethan home, after allowing him a few minutes of satisfying his cottonmouth and munchies, I had him take a shower and change clothes. He reeked of pot. I put his clothes in the washer, all the while making a plan to tell Linda that he spilled something on them if I needed to explain to her why I was washing Ethan's clothes.

Shortly after Ethan got out of the shower he put on his pajamas and went to bed. He didn't look tired, I think he just wanted the familiar comfort of his bed. No longer needing the subterfuge, JK and I straightened up the house, put away the *Sorry!* game and settled in to watch some television until Linda got home. We put it on MTV and watched videos all night. For any of you who might be too young to remember this far back, MTV used to play music videos all the time. Not just in the wee hours of the night or intermittently between crappy reality shows.

Linda finally made it home at a little after three in the morning, laughing and stumbling a bit. She kissed Charles goodnight and thanked him for the date before closing the door and walking on wobbly legs into the living room with us.

"Looks like you had fun," I said.

"Oh, I did!" she giggled drunkenly. "It was wonderful! I haven't had a night like that in… well, ever!"

"Good. I'm glad you had a good time."

"How was Ethan?" she asked.

"Fine. We had a good time. Wore him out, I think," I said with a small laugh.

Linda kicked her heels off haphazardly and immediately seemed to become much more stable.

"That's great!" she said, trying to reach behind her and unzip her dress, unsuccessfully. "Could you help me with this?"

Linda walked over in front of me and turned around. I grabbed the zipper pull and drew it down slowly, exposing her bare back. Despite the sex I had at the party, I felt the stirrings begin again. Luckily, I was sitting.

We made a bit of small talk and then Linda walked us to the door, oblivious to the fact that her dress was on the verge of falling off and that JK and I were staring at it, willing it to fall.

With a few more thank you's from Linda we left and headed home, ready to put the night behind us.

Chapter Seven

1. The Lure of the Path of Least Resistance

Monday morning in the gym was a bit of a tense situation.

Derek Skyler had no idea how close he was to getting himself hurt really badly. You would think that the guy would have *some* sense of decency, regardless of how small and atrophied it may be. But he didn't. None at all.

I was working on the hip flexor machine when he approached me. For once he was alone, his goons over by themselves bench pressing the equivalent of small cars. "Hey, Butcher! How's it going?"

I nodded and grunted, consumed with the fire in my hips and upper thighs as I pushed myself harder than normal. I was angry, and even though I knew better, I was taking it out on my body. I had to lighten up or I was going to hurt myself. I stopped the exercise and slipped off of the machine, forcing myself to remain calm. Damn! I wanted to hit him!

"You know you're our guy," he began, laying the groundwork for something he probably shouldn't say. "I just want to make sure that you aren't mad at me for fucking your girl."

I roared in my head, struggling to keep a passive face. In a life with very little self-denial up to that point, it was a strain not to lash out and put Skyler on the ground with one big punch. I knew I could do it. Of course, then Chewy and Shorty would gang up on me. And the team would fall apart and we would lose the championship that we had all been working for since we were freshmen. I thought of the team and that bought me around.

I stretched my thighs and my lower back. "Don't worry about it, Skyler. She's not my girl."

"Well, technically, I know. But I heard you took her home, so I wasn't sure. I figured maybe you two were back together. Everyone said you looked all cozy when you left the party."

"No, we're not. I was just doing the decent thing and giving her a ride home after you threw her out of your car. Which was really big of you, by the way."

Skyler had a look of pure satisfaction cross his face. "You are mad, aren't you? I knew it!"

"I'm not mad," I lied, trying to stay cool. "That was just a shitty thing to do."

"A bitch is just a bitch," Skyler said, leaning in closer to me. "I just wanted to make sure that what happened wasn't going to be a problem on the field. I don't want some cooze coming between us and a perfect season, if you know what I'm saying."

My fists clenched uncontrollably for a second, and then I reined in my anger. "It's not going to be a problem on the field."

"You sure?"

"I'm absolutely sure. This is our fucking year," I said. I even meant it. "I'm not going to let this bring the team down."

"Good. I feel better about it now," Skyler sighed.

That's just great. I'm glad I alleviated your conscience, asshole.

I thought that, but didn't say it. I wanted to punch him, but didn't do it. I hated myself for placating him, even for the good of the team, when I should have been smashing his face in. There was no reason why I should have let him get away with what he did to Tabitha, not to mention what he did in breaking us up in the first place.

Skyler didn't say anything else; he just turned and walked over to where Chewy and Shorty were doing their Incredible Hulk impressions. There is a limit to how strong a person should be. That limit is at what you can do naturally. Chewy and Shorty were just complete steroid monsters. A high school student should not have a slab of muscle in his arm the size of a side of beef. How they were getting by with it I didn't know. It seemed completely obvious to me, so I knew that Coach Rollins had to know that something was up. Still, nothing was ever said about it.

I looked around the gym, thoroughly disgusted with most everyone in the room. Primarily it was Skyler that I hated, but there were others. Our whole team was made up of bullies and misogynists. The worst part was that I couldn't even really differentiate myself from the rest in the grand scheme of things. I wanted to look down on all of them, but my inner voice kept calling out to me, *"Hello, pot? This is the kettle. Yoooou're blaaaa-ack!"*

After all, none of the guys I was sitting in judgment over had beaten down a retarded kid. I did it. Whatever my reasons at the time, I did it. Chewy and Shorty might have been nothing more than chortling henchmen for Skyler, dishing out beatings whenever and wherever their fearless leader commanded, but I had taken the initiative in humiliating Ethan. And for what? These guys? The pricks in the gym? The high and mighty Mims High School Mustangs football team?

Other than JK, the rest of the guys had pretty much separated themselves from me. I was a pariah, of sorts, due to my commitment to Ethan. I didn't go out and hang with the guys like I used to, either. Not because they wouldn't have me, I just didn't really want to. I was still a member of the team, but I was no longer a part of the team.

My conscience was pulling me apart. On the one hand I wanted to stand up for Tab, yet I let it go for the good of the team. I wanted to completely separate myself from the other players, but I was a member of the top high school football team in the state. I wanted to bang every girl that crossed my path, but I wanted to be a better person, too.

And finally, what it all came down to, I wanted good things for Ethan, but I didn't want to have to deal with him.

I was no better, really, then the guys I hated.

It was a strange feeling, looking around that gym. Even though I knew how wrong I had been when I picked on Ethan, I still longed for the way things were before. Even though I knew I was a piece of shit for what I did and how I thought back then, some part of me still wished that I could have went back to being happily oblivious.

I was in an emotional no man's land, reminiscing fondly about something I now hated being in the first place.

Shrugging, I climbed onto the bench of the leg press machine and went to work, nostalgic for the time a few weeks before when life was easy and thinking was optional.

2. Heartbreaker

Later that day I had it out with Tab.

Somehow she had gotten it in her head that all was forgiven and that we were a "couple" again. Things couldn't have been further from the truth. I felt sorry for her that night and took her home out of concern for her, but I wasn't about to simply forget about the fact that she dumped me for that piece of shit, Derek Skyler.

As you might imagine, things did not go well.

All during school Tab was making eyes at me in the hall. She dropped little thank you notes with x's and o's and hearts over the i's through the vents in my locker door. She was "soooooo sorry!!!!" for treating me so badly and breaking up with me. The thing that threw me was when she wrote at the end of the last note, "This time it will be different." That brought it home to me that she was truly thinking we were back together.

When I pulled up in front of my house after dropping Ethan off after school, Tab was waiting there for me, sitting on the front steps with two bottles of Coke. I got out of the car and approached her warily. I knew what was coming and I didn't want it to happen. There were things that were going to be said that I didn't want to hear and I didn't want to have to say. Mean things. Hurtful things.

True things.

She was sitting on the top step, almost eye to eye with me as I stood on the front walk. "Hey there, Hero."

She handed me the unopened bottle of Coke and I took it. "It was nothing, Tab."

"Have a seat," she said, patting beside her on the step. "We need to talk."

Aw, fuck no! I don't want to talk… is what I thought.

"Yeah, we do," is what I said.

I walked up the steps and took a seat beside her, but not too close. I saw my mom looking out the window in the front door and then shake her head and walk away.

"I just want to make sure that… uh… everything that happened before can be… uh, you know… uh… left in the past now that we're… uh… back together," she stammered.

"Tab," I sighed. Damn, I didn't want to say what I had to say. I didn't want to hurt her. "Tab, I…"

"If we're going to make this work again we have to get all of the bad things in our past behind us…"

"Wait, I think…"

"…Because if we don't make our peace with what happened right now there is no hope for us…"

"Tabitha, there isn't…"

"And I really want to make this work between us. We are good together."

I quit trying to say anything and sat in silence for a few seconds. I was considering her words and thinking that it might not be so bad if we were to get back together. For one thing, she was right. We were good together. Of course, we had been living a lie. It was good in her eyes because she didn't know that I was constantly cheating on her. So that point was quickly abandoned. If we were truly good together I wouldn't have felt the need to cheat on her. Especially not every single chance I got, like I had been doing.

For another thing, she was the head cheerleader and I was the star football player. Wasn't that just too cute for words? Everyone expected us to be together. The thing was, I didn't care about that anymore. I wasn't quite so worried about what was expected of me. So that wasn't a good reason to do it.

On the other hand, I could come up with three reasons, right off the top of my head, why we shouldn't be together. Number one, if she left me once she would do it again. Two, Skyler would have a field day knowing that he had stolen my girl and then I had taken her back after he had his way with her. Maybe that wasn't a great reason, but it was definitely on my mind. Third, and most important, I didn't want her back.

"Well, what are you thinking about?" she asked me. Apparently I had been quiet longer than I realized.

"Tab. Tabby. Tabitha," I sighed, stalling, knowing I was going to hurt her and hating it. "We're not… we're not getting back together."

"But I thought… after Saturday night…" Tab said, her eyes almost instantly beginning to tear up.

"I still care about you. I do. That's why I took you home and took care of you Saturday night. But that doesn't mean that we can get back together."

"Why not? Can't you forgive me for what I did? Is it too horrible?" she cried, the tears coming in earnest now.

Fuck.

I hated seeing her cry.

"I'm sorry I didn't believe you! I'm sorry I had sex with Skyler!" she pleaded.

"Tabby, no. We can't be together. I'm sorry," I said.

"You had sex with Stacy Lampley and that girl from the party! I don't see why it is such a big deal that I was with someone else!"

It seemed like she was getting angry, more than hurt. I wasn't surprised that she knew about Stacy, and she had seen me with the girl from the party. I couldn't throw it in her face that we couldn't be together because she had slept with someone else. Damn! That would have been a good excuse.

"That's not it," I lied. It was certainly part of it. Double standard or not, it did make a difference to me. But probably only because it was Skyler she had been with.

"The fact that we could be broken up so easily should tell you that we weren't meant to be together," I reasoned.

"Damn it, Ronnie! I said I was sorry for that!"

"I know. I forgive you. But that's not it, either."

"Well, then why?" She wiped a tear away as it trailed to the edge of her jaw line.

I had to tell her. I had to give her the whole truth. And I knew she was going to hate me.

"When Skyler and all those other people called you and said that I was cheating on you, I wasn't."

"I know that, baby! I'm sorry I didn't believe you."

"Let me finish," I said, taking a deep breath. "I wasn't cheating on you then… but, I had before."

Her expression didn't change. She sat there on my porch steps, impassive. I didn't think I was getting through to her. That maybe she was blocking me out.

So I added, "A lot."

I only thought she was crying before. When I said those last two words, the water works really started flowing.

"No. Ronnie. No" she said, shaking her head. "We had something special."

"I'm sorry," I said. It was my turn to apologize. "I wish I hadn't done it, but I did."

Tab stood up and went down to the sidewalk, her arms hugging herself across her chest and rocking slightly. She stood there for quite a few minutes, silent. And then, "Okay."

"No, it's not okay. I'm sorry."

"I mean it's okay, as in that I don't care. We can still be together. I forgive you," Tab said, sounding very small..

"Tabitha. Listen to me," I ordered, speaking firmly. "No. We can't be together anymore. We're not right for each other and we should just end it here. We can be friends, but we're through as a couple."

Letting out a low, pained wail, Tab grabbed her purse and her bottle of Coke and hurried off toward her car. She was crying profusely, snot beginning to bubble in her nose and she was sniffling it back.

I jumped from the porch step and ran to catch her before she could get in her car. I called for her to wait, but she didn't. She couldn't get away from me fast enough. I didn't think she could see to drive with so many tears in her eyes.

I caught her before she could get in her car. I placed my hand against her car door and wouldn't let her open it. "Tab, you need to calm down before you drive."

That's when she hit me in the face with her bottle of Coke. And it hurt! For those who might not remember, Coke used to come in glass bottles, not the plastic ones like they do now. She hit me right above the eye. "Get the fuck away from me! Get away!"

I wrapped her up in my arms and hugged her tightly to me. Partly because she needed it and partly to keep her from hitting me again. "Tab, settle down. It will be okay."

She cried hard, her head pressed against my chest, soaking my shirt.

About that time my dad came pulling his truck into the driveway. He smiled when he got out and saw me standing in the street with my arms around that "hot little cheerleader" again.

"Hey, you two! Get a room!" he joked, laughing to himself and heading into the house.

Eventually, Tabitha's crying slowed down and she stepped away from me. She had a very angry look on her face, her jaw set.

"Tab, I want you to be happy. I want you to find a great guy. Someone who treats you right. Someone who won't cheat on you. Someone who won't fuck you and then throw you out of the car with no pants on."

That didn't even sound right to me when it came out. She hit me again.

"Ow! Stop it! That hurts!" I yelled.

"Good!" She hit me again for good measure and I took the bottle out of her hand.

"It's all about you, isn't it? The Great Butcher Blake," Tabitha said nastily. "The rest of us are just bit players in The Butcher Blake Show."

I didn't know what to say to that. I wanted to protest or say something to make her take it back. I couldn't.

She was right.

But that was the old Butcher Blake. I was turning over a new leaf. Breaking her heart was part of that process, sadly.

"Move your hand!" she snarled, trying to pull her car door open.

Reluctantly, I moved my hand and let her open the door. She slipped inside, tossing her purse forcefully into the passenger seat, and firing up the engine.

"Tab, I really am sorry," I said futilely.

"Fuck you!"

Tabitha sped off down the street, angry and hurting. Somehow I felt a little better knowing that she was mad, as well as hurt. If it would make things easier on her she could hate me all she wanted.

I was fine with that.

3. Damned If I Do…

Life was getting very confusing, and never more so than it did the following Wednesday morning.

That was the day I beat the hell out of Mike Something.

Ethan was just walking down the hall, minding his own business, when out of nowhere that little prick came up and pushed him down. The mistake little Mikey made was that he didn't know I was in the hall, only a few feet from Ethan. Mike tried to run, but being fast was my job. I caught him after just enough steps to reach top speed and I tackled him, driving his scrawny body into the wall.

Mike's torso seemed to cave in under the force of my body plowing him down, his breath rushing out of him in one long push. I felt his ribs break and I wondered about his skull. I heard a resonant thud when we went against the wall and I assumed it was his head meeting the tile.

When we hit the ground, Mike tried to kick me in the crotch as I stood up. He wasn't as out of it as I would have thought, apparently. That changed with a few well-placed kicks and a couple of punches to the face. I knocked him out cold. They had to call the paramedics to come and get him.

Ethan was jumping up and down and shouting, "Yay, Butchie!" Then he proceeded to tell everyone in the hall that I was his best friend. Seconds later I was swarmed with teachers.

As it turned out, performing the duty that I was charged with, protecting Ethan, got me hauled down into Principal Greenwood's office.

The school's hands were tied in a lot of ways. They couldn't just let me off the hook after beating down another student to the point that he required medical attention. But, they couldn't very well kick me out of school or punish me in any meaningful way, considering that they had told me to make sure that no one messed with Ethan. Could they? I didn't think so. How was I supposed to keep people from picking on Ethan if I didn't have any authority to do so? All I had was brute force, and I could use it well.

"Just what were you trying to accomplish, Blake?" Principal Greenwood asked me angrily. "Beating up on such a small kid."

"He pushed Ethan down!" I shouted, pleading my case.

"That may be, but you can't just go around beating people up!"

"What was I supposed to do? You said that if anything else happened to Ethan for the rest of the season that I was off the team! I had no choice!"

Principal Greenwood sat heavily down in his chair and we waited in silence for Coach Rollins, who was being called out of his English class. I knew that Principal Greenwood was only worried about what he would tell Mike Something's parents when they came breathing down his neck. They would scream that it was preferential treatment for a football player if nothing were done to me for hurting their son. Never mind that their son was a horrible little bastard who enjoyed picking on someone weaker than he was.

And, while it was true that I was getting preferential treatment, it wasn't because I was a football player per se. It was purely because I was doing what they had encouraged me to do. I was protecting Ethan, and doing it in the best way I knew how.

Coach Rollins came into the office and had a seat next to me. It reminded me of the exact day a few weeks before when I had been in the office for picking on Ethan myself.

"What's going on?" Coach Rollins asked. I said nothing at first, letting Principal Greenwood fill him in.

After the principal told Coach Rollins the entire story, Coach turned to me and said, "Paramedics? Jesus, Blake!"

"Coach! I had no choice!" I whined, feeling defeated.

Coach Rollins turned back to Principal Greenwood. "What can we do?"

"I'm afraid there's nothing we can do. He'll have to be suspended. And that includes missing Friday's game." Principal Greenwood hated to say that, I could tell. He didn't want to suspend me. He knew what a prick Mike Something was. He knew I was only doing what I was told to do.

"That is just unacceptable!" Coach Rollins bellowed. "You have to figure something out."

"Larry, I just don't know what I can do. We have to suspend him. The rules are very clear on this."

"Who's going to take care of Ethan if you kick me out?" I asked.

"Yeah! Who?" Coach Rollins asked the principal.

Principal Greenwood sighed. "I guess he'll just have to cope while you're gone. I'm sorry. I have no choice, Ronald."

The next ten minutes was nothing but Coach Rollins trying everything he could to get Principal Greenwood to see his way around booting me out of school. He played the guilt card as a last ditch effort, pointing out again that none of this would have happened if I hadn't been told to protect that "poor little retarded kid".

Despite Coach Rollins protests, I was suspended for three days. I would get zeroes in all my classes and I would miss playing the Hamilton Comets on the road. But there was no point in fighting it. Rules were rules.

I took my discipline slip and drove myself home, just in time for lunch with my dad.

4. Reinstated

"They did what?"

My dad was surprised when he came home for lunch and I was sitting at the kitchen table having a sandwich. He went from surprised to angry when I told him what had happened to get me kicked out. The only thing I could think to do was to tell him the whole story. Explaining about my situation of looking after Ethan was the only way I could justify what I did to Mike Something, so my hand was forced. I didn't want to tell my dad about that at all, but, as was the case with many things that day, I had no choice.

Dad didn't even eat his lunch. He threw his sandwiches and chips in the trash and grabbed his keys off of the counter immediately. "Come on."

"Where are we going?" I asked, although I thought I knew.

"We're going to that goddamned school and getting you reinstated, that's where," he snapped. Dad was livid. There was no way he could let them mess with his dream of me playing in the NFL. I didn't think we should go, but I didn't try to argue, either. I knew it would be pointless. "Get in my truck."

Less than an hour after I was suspended I was back in Principal Greenwood's office. But this time I was standing back and watching my dad roll all over the man.

"I don't know who the fuck you think you are, but having my son protecting some fucking retard as a condition of being on the team is bad enough. Kicking him out of school for doing what you told him to do is fucking bullshit!"

Dad looked like he was going to hit Principal Greenwood, who kept saying, "I had no choice! I had no choice!"

"Don't give me that shit! You had a choice," Dad argued. "You made a choice when you decided to coerce my son into babysitting the halfwit. Now you need to make the right choice in accepting your responsibility in what happened because of your actions."

I wanted to crawl into the woodwork and disappear. Taking my three-day vacation wouldn't have bothered me all that much. I wanted to take my medicine and come back to school, hoping that the beating I had dished out to Mike Something had the right effect of scaring everyone away from picking on Ethan. Dad just was not going to let that happen. As far as he was concerned, I wasn't going anywhere.

"Mr. Blake, I don't think you understand," Principal Greenwood interjected finally, when my dad's tirade slowed down. "Your son sent a young man to the hospital today. How am I supposed to explain to that boy's parents that the person who hurt their son is getting away with no punishment? What would you do?"

"I'll tell you how you explain it! You fucking tell them that their son was picking on a retarded kid when he got his ass kicked!"

"Sir, there may be a lawsuit in this. And not against the school. Against your son. Against you. This is very serious."

"Let them fucking sue me! No one will give them a fucking dime when they find out that my son was protecting a little fucking retard from getting fucking beat up!" Dad was using his favorite word with impunity since my mother wasn't around. She didn't like the word 'fuck', so he avoided saying it around her, but today he had all the excuse he could ever hope for.

My dad raged at Principal Greenwood for close to a half hour, finally wearing him down. The principal slumped behind his desk, giving up completely. "Okay, okay! I'll see what I can do."

"You'll do better than that! My boy will be out on that football field practicing tonight or I'll have your ass! The deal you made with Ronald was entering into a verbal contract with a minor. You had no right to do that without going through either me or my wife. And this is the first we have heard of any of this." Dad was leaning across Principal Greenwood's desk, looking him right in the eye. "I want that suspension lifted RIGHT NOW!"

Principal Greenwood took off his glasses and massaged the bridge of his nose with his thumb and forefinger. "I have to punish him in some way, Mr. Blake. I'll lift the suspension, but we have to come up with a punishment. I just can't let this go."

That didn't make Dad happy, but he accepted it. He and Principal Greenwood sat down and worked out what my punishment would be. They eventually agreed that I should come in to the school on three consecutive Saturday mornings and assist the janitorial staff in their weekend clean up and maintenance. Without pay, of course.

I had to be at the school at seven in the morning that Saturday, following an away game, which meant no victory dance, no after party, and no pussy for me. I was going to have to go right home after the game and get to sleep if I was going to have any chance of making it in for my punishment.

It wasn't my idea of fun, but I did get to stay in school and not miss any games.

I realized right then that the old adage was true.

No good deed ever goes unpunished.

5. Punching Mr. Something

Fifteen minutes into practice that afternoon I was summoned back into Principal Greenwood's office.

I had just broken through the line and lightly sacked our second string quarterback when the girl from the office showed up and gave a note to Coach Rollins, who immediately yelled at me. "Blake, get your ass over here!"

The girl was a student assistant and she looked a little intimidated while I was walking with her back to the principal's office. She kept her eyes turned away from me and walked silently through the deserted halls, all the way to the outer office.

That's where I could hear the yelling.

From behind Principal Greenwood's door I could hear a blistering barrage of rage, much worse than the one my dad administered earlier.

"Just knock and go in. Principal Greenwood is expecting you," the girl said, looking happy that she didn't have to go in herself.

I rapped on the door three solid knocks and opened it when the raging voice halted. "Principal Greenwood?"

"Yes, Ronald, come in," he said, motioning me into the office. The air was hot with expended anger. "Your father is on his way here."

"This is the boy?" the man before Principal Greenwood's desk asked angrily. "This is the boy who beat my son up?"

"You must be Mike's dad," I said.

"Yes, I am," the man said, looking angrier. "Good guess. Or how many other kids did you beat up lately?"

"I was defending a friend of mine against your son. Mike started it."

"Well, I'm going to fucking finish it!"

I didn't expect what came next, but Mike Something's dad punched me in the face. Principal Greenwood was taken by surprise as well and he couldn't get around his desk in time to stop it. The blow landed and didn't hurt in the slightest. Mike's dad wasn't much bigger than his son. I punched him back, landing a solid blow to his glass jaw and dropping him like a stone.

Principal Greenwood and I stood there in the new silence of the office, looks of 'Oh, shit!' on our faces. Mike's dad went down even easier than Mike did.

"Uh oh," I said, looking at Principal Greenwood to gauge his reaction.

"It's okay, Ronald. He hit you first."

My dad knocked on the door and entered the office a few seconds later, just as Mike's dad was coming around. "What happened?"

"Dad, this is Mike's father. He just punched me and I knocked his ass out!" I yelled into Mr. Something's face.

Principal Greenwood had come around the desk by then and was helping Mike's dad to his feet and simultaneously pushing me gently away, insinuating himself between the two of us.

"Are you okay?" Dad asked and I nodded.

"He hits like a girl," I sneered.

"I'm fucking suing you! All of you!" Mr. Something screamed in hate and frustration. "I'm going to own this school when I'm done!"

Principal Greenwood stayed between us and urged Mike's old man to have a seat and talk things out, but he was having none of it.

"There is nothing to talk about! I am suing your asses!" he bellowed. Mike's father went right back to raging the way he was before I entered the office, except this time he was doing it with a swollen jaw. He was going to sue the school for a million billion dollars, he was going to sue my dad and Dad would be working for the rest of his life just to pay him. He threatened to hire some guys to beat me up. Mike's dad was rolling with it, making every threat and intimidation he could think of. His lawyer would have us all living on the street, as far as he was concerned.

There came another knock on the door then and he got quiet as it opened. Linda and Ethan stood in the doorway, looking very serious.

"I've heard what you've been saying, sir. And I can only hope that you get a lot of money out of this school and this young man and his father," Linda began, stepping boldly up to Mr. Something. "Because you are going to need it to pay me when I sue you for your son's attack on my child!"

I looked up at Principal Greenwood and he said, "I took the liberty of calling Mrs. Miles before I sent for you. I thought she might have something to add to the discussion."

"Oh, I have a lot to add! A lot!" Linda said, bumping Mike's dad with her chest and knocking him down into the chair that he had just refused from Principal Greenwood. "My child is not a punching bag for your bullying little prick of a son! Today was not the first time that we have had trouble with your boy picking on my son, either! It's just the first time that something has been done about it! I'm glad that Ronald kicked your kid's ass! He had it coming for all the things he has done to my son!

"So, you go right ahead and sue the school and sue these two gentlemen. When you're done I am going to sue you for everything you get from them and more!"

Mike's dad kept looking from Linda to Ethan, Linda to Ethan.

"Yes, Ethan is mentally disabled," Linda said snidely. "Your son has spent this whole school year picking on a mentally disabled boy. You must be so proud!"

That ended the confrontation. Mike's dad fell silent for several long seconds and then he apologized for his son's behavior. He wasn't happy about his son being beaten up, but he wasn't cool with his boy picking on a retarded kid, either.

"Mike's injuries didn't seem that severe. Do you have insurance, Mr. Something?" Principal Greenwood asked.

"Yes. Yes, I do," he answered quietly.

"Then I would like to make a recommendation, if I may."

Mike's father nodded his assent.

"I propose that you let the insurance fix your son's injuries, let time heal his wounded pride, and leave everything else to the school to settle. I have already established a suitable punishment for Ronald Blake and I think this matter would best be used as a learning experience. Don't you think?"

Mike's dad stood up from the chair that Linda had pushed him into and made to leave the room. He seemed dazed. "Okay."

He was almost out the door when he turned and came back to face Ethan, who was standing obliviously in the corner.

"I'm sorry for what my son did to you. I didn't teach him to be like that."

Ethan, I could tell, had no idea what he was talking about. Mike hadn't really hurt him today and it had just rolled off of his back after the incident settled down.

Mr. Something walked out the door, the rest of us silent as he left.

As mad as I was at Mike's dad when I came into the office and he hit me, I respected him at that moment. I realized that he was only doing what he thought was right to protect his son. And unlike my own father, he had shown concern for Ethan, the center of the whole incident. My dad had come in to protect me as well, but that was really only to protect my future in football. I realized that it had nothing to do with protecting me, personally, at all.

Out in the hall I introduced my dad to Linda and Ethan. Dad didn't exactly snub them, but he was a little cold. He shook their hands, smiled and said that he was pleased to meet them. It just wasn't sincere and I think all of us except for Ethan knew it. Dad was deeply offended that I, his future NFL star, was being shackled with a drooling idiot child in what was the make or break season of my high school career.

"Get back out to practice now, Ronnie," Dad said, clapping me on the shoulder. "You've got Hamilton on Friday and they're a tough team."

With that, Dad set off down the hall and toward the rear parking lot.

"Thanks for sticking up for me," I said to Linda.

"Thank you for sticking up for Ethan," she said with a smile and a kiss on the cheek.

"Hey, I gotta watch out for my best friend, right?" I said, clapping Ethan on the shoulder much the same way my dad had just done to me.

"Bye, Butchie!" Ethan said.

"Bye, Ethan," I replied. "I'll see you in the morning, buddy."

I headed back out to practice, although I would have just as soon gotten dressed and went home.

I had had enough fun for one day.

6. Smashing the Comets

Friday night we rode into Hamilton High School in our big purple and green bus and rode out a few hours later with another win under our belts.

The Comets actually had aspects of a good game, but we still beat them 62-0. However, I only scored one of our nine touchdowns this time. They had geared their defense toward stopping me, so they brought up another man to stop the run and they blitzed a lot. All this really did was open up our receivers much more than usual and Skyler just picked their secondary apart. Most of my offensive game was spent providing pass protection. In fact, the only reason I had a touchdown at all was because I insisted that Skyler give me a shot at it.

On our first possession in the fourth quarter I blasted through the defensive line and dragged three Comets into the end zone with me. It was on first down from the nineteen, after I sacked their quarterback and recovered his fumble, so I figured I had earned a chance to score. Besides, if I got stopped we had three more plays to get the next first down or score. Coach Rollins ended up yelling at me over it, though. He said it was a stupid play; risking myself against that run coverage when we had receivers who were open for miles and making it look easy.

I had to agree, it was a dumb thing to do. But my ego demanded it. And I didn't get hurt, so I didn't see the big deal with it.

After the game we got back on the bus and rode home, where I parted company with the team. They went to victory parties and drank beer and had sex.

I went home and went to sleep.

Six a.m. comes awfully early on a Saturday.

Chapter Eight

1. Big Ron's Lecture

I was sitting on the edge of the bed, wide awake and stretching when my alarm went off at six.

I've always been a morning person, even now when I work all night at the bar. It doesn't matter how late I am up, I always rouse myself out of bed fairly early. I guess I feel that if I stay in bed I miss a large part of the day. Besides, I'll sleep when I'm dead.

I switched off the alarm as soon as it puked out its first annoying beep/buzz/honk. The fact that it sounded so ungodly awful was the reason I chose that particular alarm. I couldn't trust a clock radio to wake me up, I'd just groove unconsciously to the music and sleep right through it.

In a flash my clothes found their way onto my body and I was headed downstairs to grab a bite to eat and have a cup of coffee. I stopped at my closed bedroom door for a second and paid homage to my Walter Payton poster. I always wanted to be the white Walter Payton, but it was hopeless. I was fast, but I was only 'white guy' fast. I was more like the white John Riggins.

Dad was in the kitchen, sitting in the dark and drinking coffee and smoking a cigarette, his typical breakfast.

"Morning," I grunted through a sleep-addled throat. Dad just returned the grunt, no words.

Automatically, I moved around the kitchen, throwing Grape Nuts into a bowl with a splash of milk and then tossing them into the microwave. While I waited for the Grape Nuts to heat up and absorb the milk I poured a cup of coffee and dropped in two spoons of creamer and two of sugar. I had cut it back from when I first started drinking coffee where I had a splash of coffee in my sugar milk. Retrieving my cereal from the beeping microwave I sat down at the table across from my dad and dug in. For several long minutes I ate and Dad smoked in silence. We never had much to say to one another.

Except about football.

"You fucked up last night," Dad said, exhaling a stream of blue smoke.

"No, I didn't." I knew I did, but I wasn't about to admit it. He was talking about my touchdown run.

"That run was bullshit, Ronnie. You're going to get hurt and blow your ride if you keep that shit up," he said.

"Football is a risky game. If I'm going to play then I had better play to the best of my ability. Right?"

"You know what the hell I'm talking about! Don't be a smart ass!" Dad said, leaning across the table toward me. "That was stupid to run the ball against that defense!

They were waiting on you! You had two receivers and a tight end wide open in the end zone!"

I let out a huge sigh. He was right, just as Coach Rollins had been when he reamed my ass out over it the night before. But I would be damned if I was going to give him the satisfaction. "It's not a big deal. I came through the line clean, I didn't get hurt. I don't see what the problem is!"

"The problem is that taking stupid risks like that is going to end up making you work at a fucking factory instead of playing in the NFL! Wise up, dumb ass!" Dad said, getting really angry now.

"You ever think that maybe pulling off risky plays like that might be what would get me to the NFL?" I said in my best know-it-all tone.

"Get hurt now and see just how many college scouts will take a chance on you! No one from a school worth fucking going to, that's for damn sure!"

"Jesus Christ! I just wanted to score! That's all!" I said, raising my voice in exasperation. "They weren't going to hurt me. I run through defenses like a bull in a china shop!"

"You watch your mouth! I won't have you taking the Lord's name in vain! Not while you're in my house!" Dad bellowed, scooting back from the table as if he were going to come over it at me. "And the fact that you're good isn't the point. A bad hit could still end your career before you even get started. This is too important to be fucking around with now."

"Well, if I get hurt I guess I'll just have to do something else." I was scraping the last bits of Grape Nuts out of the bowl as I walked to the sink to rinse it out. If you don't rinse out a bowl that had Grape Nuts in it you might as well throw it away. They turn to concrete when they dry out.

Dad stood and grabbed my shoulder and spun me around to face him. "Like what? What are you going to do that would be as rewarding as a career in the NFL? Playing football for millions of dollars? Having your poster on every kid's wall, like Walter Payton? You want to punch a clock for a fucking living?"

I just stood there looking at my dad, trying not to give anything away.

"Look around. We have a few nice things, sure. But do you have any idea how hard I've had to work to have these things? I bust my ass and barely keep everything afloat. It's a hard damn living these days and it's only going to get harder.

"You've got a way out that very few people in this world ever get, and you don't even care! If I had your talent you can bet your ass that I wouldn't be hanging fucking drywall or building garages for a living! Son, you've got big things ahead of you, but you can't fuck them up. Right now is the time to be smart. Play smart! If you're going to have a better future than what I've ended up with than you have to be smart! No more of those fucked up glory plays, okay?"

I just nodded and he let go of my shoulder. I put the bowl in the sink and ran the water into it, hoping that the time that my Grape Nuts were air drying during my dad's speech hadn't already cemented them to the bowl. Grabbing my keys I headed toward the door. I still had plenty of time before I had to leave, but I decided that

I would rather cruise around in my car to kill the time rather than stay home and get more lecturing.

"See ya later," I called back on my way out the door.

"Wait!" Dad called from the kitchen. I could hear him coming to the front of the house. He leaned around the door. "Don't forget that the scout from Penn State is coming by Monday evening. You better start thinking about what you want to ask him. And how you want to answer him."

"Okay. Bye," I said noncommittally. I really didn't care. I would either pass or fail any of these meetings with scouts on my own. I wasn't going to be a robot, spewing out prefabricated answers for all occasions. I shut the door just as my dad said goodbye.

For the next twenty minutes or so I drove around in my car, seething about what my dad had said. What the hell did he mean "better future than what I ended up with"? I was out of line, and I can admit that now, but I knew what he meant. I just took it wrong because it was my dad saying it. I took it to mean that my mother and I were like an albatross around his neck. We were holding him back and his life was ruined because of his responsibilities to us. What he really meant was that he wanted what was best for me and that he wanted me to have an easier way to make it than he had.

But hell, I was a teenager. I couldn't let a little thing like honesty get in the way of my righteous indignation.

2. Hard Work Sucks

I knew it was going to be a shitty day just seconds after I met the guys I would be working with.

Randy and Hub were two serious rednecks. Nascar watchin', PBR drinkin', mullet wearin', sister fuckin' rednecks. (To be fair, though, the mullet was in style at the time. The funny part is that I saw Randy in early 2001 and he still had the same haircut.) And they were absolutely not impressed with my skills on the football field. All they saw me as was the new guy they could boss around and force to do the dirtiest jobs. They knew the deal and knew that I had no choice other than to be their punk, so they took full advantage of the situation.

Randy was in charge, and he made damn sure that I knew it. I knew because he told me every few minutes, plus I could tell because he wore the cleaner cover-alls. Hub's cover-alls were stained, dirt on the knees, food on the chest. Randy's cover-alls were pressed and fit his wiry frame perfectly. Hub's cover-alls were packed to bursting with his ample belly, and they were a little too short for him as well. There is nothing quite as unsightly as a bulging camel toe on a fat man.

"Hear tell you fucked up, boy?" Randy said. I thought it might be a question, but I wasn't exactly sure, so I just nodded. Randy using the word *boy* sounded strange to me. He wasn't that much older than I was. Maybe a couple years at the most. Hub, on the other hand, appeared to be in his mid to late thirties. I figured it must suck to have a kid for a boss.

"That's all right," Hub said, clapping me on the shoulder. "We glad for the help. We gonna put your ass right to work."

"That's the idea," I said. I was looking to sweep a few floors, empty a few trashcans and get this punishment over with.

Randy had other ideas.

"You know, we don't usually have time to get everything done, what with me and Hub being the only ones working," he began, looking at me like a slave he had just bought at auction. "Since we got you for the day we're going to do a little extra. You ever run a buffer?"

"No," I said, shaking my head. I wasn't even sure what the hell it was.

"Well, you gonna learn today." Hub laughed and Randy followed. I remained stone.

"Cheer up, Big Boy!" Randy said, patting me on the chest and looking up at me. "Hard work ain't gonna kill ya."

Before I got my shot at the floor buffer I had the grand opportunity to do everything I had previously expected. The three of us went down each hall together, emptying trashcans and sweeping each classroom with our big, wide dust brooms. Then we'd line up in the hall at one end and sweep the hallway. With three of us we were able to do it in one pass. Randy may have been disappointed if I had told him that it wasn't really hard work, so I kept my mouth shut. No sense in egging on a little hillbilly on a power trip and inspiring him to make me work harder.

After a few hours we had the classrooms and the halls swept and cleaned out. I started thinking that maybe I would get to go home early. I figured that even if they had me run the floor buffer it couldn't possibly take very long. What I didn't take into consideration was that we had to mop every damn inch of the floor. And we still had all the bathrooms to do, mopping and re-supplying.

'Lovely', I thought. It was exactly how I wanted to spend my Saturday. I knew I was looking at the full eight hours.

The broom closet was down by the gym and I heard a lot of noise coming from inside when we went to put the dust brooms away and get out the mops, buckets, liquid soap, toilet paper and paper towels. Shoes squeaking on the floor, intermittent thumps, and grunts of effort sounded from behind the closed doors.

"What's going on in there? I thought we were the only ones in the school today?" I asked.

"Volleyball practice," Hub said, a slight smile crossing his face. It was creepy. Not so much *horror movie* creepy, but more like *scary uncle* creepy. "The girls are in here every Saturday. We gotta wait till they's done so we can clean the locker room."

Hub looked like he wanted to tell me something, then he saw Randy coming out of the broom closet and thought better of it. Randy put his key in the lock and twisted, then gave a tug on the handle to make sure the door was locked.

"Take Football Star here and get him started on moppin' the bathrooms," Randy ordered Hub. "You can take a break when you get the first floor done, then we'll all head upstairs."

Hub looked a little upset at that. He started tapping his watch. "But… uh…"

Randy looked at his own watch and nodded. "Okay, get Big Boy started and then you meet me back here in twenty minutes."

Hub smiled really big and elbowed me softly in the ribs. "Come on, let's get this shit detail over with."

Hub gave me the quick rundown on what was expected in cleaning and re-stocking the bathrooms, but his mind seemed to be somewhere else. For the next twenty minutes he would work for a few minutes and then check his watch. Work and check the watch. Work and check the watch. Finally, he tapped the watch with a triumphant smile and set his mop in the bucket and leaned the handle against the wall.

"Keep workin', man. I gotta meet Randy and I be right back."

Hub took off out of the bathroom like his ass was on fire and I heard the soles of his shoes smacking down the hallway. He was really beating feet to get to Randy. Something was obviously going on, but I didn't care what it was. I just wanted to get finished and go home.

While Hub was gone I dove into the work, emptying the trashcans and re-stocking as fast I could so I could get to the mopping and get it over with. That was the day I learned a truth that still holds today. Women's public restrooms are far nastier than men's. Granted, a man might dribble a bit of piss on the floor in front of a urinal or toilet, but women take the cake. The bloody pad stuck to the inside of one of the stall doors in the girl's room showed me that.

I've got a strong stomach, but I felt my gorge rising as I reached out with a massive handful of paper towels and peeled the soiled manhole cover from the door. Wow, what a powerful stink! It smelled like a bucket of dead anchovies that had been left out in the sun for a few days.

"Sick bitch!" I hissed, dropping the stenchwad into the trash.

I finished one bathroom and went on to the next before Hub came back, flushed and sweating.

"You okay," I asked, concerned that the fat bastard might drop dead right there on the floor.

"Hmm? Oh… yeah. I'm fine. Fine as wine," Hub said, mopping sweat from his brow and going back to work.

True to his word, Randy met up with us after our break and we went upstairs and knocked out the four bathrooms on the second floor in no time. Then Hub and Randy whipped out the floor buffer and gave me the overview of how to run it.

"You put your wax here. Flip this switch. And hold the fuck on," Hub said, patting the machine. I watched him fill the wax reservoir, then I flipped the switch and took hold of the handles.

I realized immediately what I did wrong. I wasn't supposed to take hold of the handles. I was supposed to "hold the fuck on".

The floor buffer jerked out of my hands and began to spin violently. Hub ducked out of the way and scrambled to where the cord met the wall and yanked the plug. The whirling buffer instantly began to slow.

"Goddamn! I said 'hold the fuck on' and I meant 'HOLD THE FUCK ON!' Jumpin' Jesus Criminetly!"

Randy just laughed.

After unwrapping the cord from around the buffer Hub plugged it back in and grabbed my wrists, placing my hands firmly on the handles.

"This time," he said slowly, "Hold… the fuck… on. Okay?"

I nodded and he flipped the switch for me. The buffer lunged away from me and attempted to go back into its spin, but I held the fuck on, as instructed. The buffer was self-propelled and had a mind of its own. It was my job to force the damn thing to go where I wanted it to go.

Randy and Hub stood a few feet behind me, watching me wrestle the buffer and telling me when I wasn't getting a spot as good as they liked.

'Assholes', I thought.

But I said nothing and just fought the buffer all over the school. We went down every hallway on the first floor, took the buffer to the service elevator and did the second floor, then came back and did the large foyer before putting the damn thing away and calling it a day.

My muscles were sore and my back hurt like hell. I walked out of the school with Randy and Hub, stretching my back and hearing it pop.

"Whoa, what's the matter?" Randy cackled. "Hard work too much for you, Football Star?"

"I'm fine," I said coldly, not willing to admit that hard work was, in fact, too much for me. "Just got a catch in my back from the game last night."

"Probably when you pulled that stupid fuckin' run up the middle with the Comets showin' blitz!" Hub said with a cackle of his own.

Our cars were all parked side by side in the faculty lot, so I got to enjoy their company all the way out to the Trans Am. I just kept my mouth shut and let them cackle away. I slipped into my car, fired up the engine and just sat there for a few seconds letting it warm up.

Randy came over to my side of the car and made the universal motion of 'roll down your window'. I did and he leaned down to face me.

"This machine sounds fuckin' swee-eet!" Randy gushed.

"Thanks, man," I said coolly.

Hub joined us and for the next twenty to thirty minutes we talked muscle cars. I had to bullshit my way through a lot of it. While I drove a mean machine, I didn't know nearly as much about it as Randy did. I popped the hood and let him have a look at the engine. He exhaled a breathless laundry list of the prime features of my engine.

After a while he lowered my hood, we said our goodbyes and I slid back into my car. I was getting ready to roll up the window and drive away when Randy called out to me. "Hey Butcher!"

I turned my head to him.

"You did a good job today. Thanks."

I nodded. "See ya next Saturday."

With a quick wave I set out for home, ready to let my weary bones rest.

3. Another Saturday Night with Ethan

No one was home when I got back from the school, but my mom had left a note by the phone saying to call Linda Miles.

I caught a whiff of my body odor and debated with myself briefly about calling her back after I got a shower. As my grandmother would have said, I was a bit ripe. To say that I stank to high heaven was more accurate, though. The mix of sweat and cleaning agents hung around me in a cloud that was almost palpable. My own stench was making my eyes water. I desperately needed a shower and I decided that I would call Linda back once I had hosed off the grime and the stink.

I pulled off my damp shirt and headed to the stairs just as the phone rang. With a fluid turn I spun on my heel and lifted the receiver from the cradle. "Hello. Blake's."

"Ronald! I'm glad I finally caught you!" came the harried voice from the receiver. It was Linda.

"Hey, what's up?"

"Well… um… Charlie asked me out tonight," she began, and I didn't really need to hear the rest. But I listened patiently. "And… I have been calling around all day to find someone to stay with Ethan. I hate to impose on you… but if you're not busy… um…"

I could tell she was really bothered about asking me to stay with Ethan and I saw no reason to make her stammer out her request. "I'm not doing anything tonight. I can stay with Ethan."

"Really? Thank you so much!" she cried, relief streaming through the phone. "I can pay you a little if you want."

"No, that's not necessary. It's not a problem at all. I like spending time with Ethan."

"Are you sure? I've been calling on you a lot lately. I hate to do that."

"Yeah, I'm sure," I said, realizing that I really was sure. I actually did enjoy spending time with Ethan. It surprised the hell out of me. "When do you need me to come over?"

"Um… well… Charlie will be here in about an hour. Can you be here by then?"

"Sure. I just have to jump in the shower and I'll be right over."

"Thank you! This means a lot to me. I promise I will make it up to you. What would you like?" Linda said, innocently enough.

Hmmm. What would I like? Naked pictures? A blowjob?

"You could come over for dinner this week," she offered, obviously not reading my mind. "I make a great spaghetti and meatballs."

"Yeah, that would be good. I'll take you up on that," I said, disappointed in reality.

"Okay, it's a deal! See you in a little bit. Bye," Linda said, hanging up after I returned her goodbye.

Oh well. I liked spaghetti and meatballs. Hell, maybe she'd be willing to compromise? Hold the meatballs and give me some spaghetti and naked pictures? Nah, probably not.

I showered quickly, ignoring the urge to soak under the hot spray, and I headed to Linda's house.

Ethan was waiting at the door for me as I made my way up the front walk. He was bouncing on his heels like an excited Chihuahua behind the glass of the storm door. He threw open the door and called out to me. "BUTCHIE!"

"Hey Ethan! Good to see you!" I said, stepping into the house.

Ethan threw his arms around me, his joy bursting from every pore in his body. No one had ever reacted to me that way before. It was as if there was no one in the world Ethan would have rather seen right then than me. I found it quite humbling and strange all at the same time. To feel so important in someone else's life is a scary and wonderful thing, but I had no emotional basis to guide those thoughts. So it was really just kind of uncomfortable.

Eventually Ethan let go of me and we moved further into the living room. As expected, professional wrestling was on TV and Ethan went back to watching it, sitting down on the floor and rejoining the glass of Quik and the Oreo's that he had abandoned to let me in. I stood there just inside the room, watching absently as Ole Anderson put the hurt on some no name wrestler, and waited for Linda to appear.

Soon enough she did.

Linda obviously didn't hear me come in because when she walked back into the living room she let out a small scream and hurriedly ducked into her bedroom. She had apparently been in the back of the house, perhaps the laundry room looking for a shirt. I surmised that when she walked through the living room in nothing but a pair of tight fitting Calvin Klein jeans and a white bra. When she noticed I was standing there she panicked and ran.

Hearing Linda's tiny scream, Ethan cried out, "Mom! Butchie's here!"

"Thanks Ethan!" Linda called back sarcastically from behind her bedroom door. I was smiling ear to ear.

It took her quite a while to come out of her bedroom. I figured she found the shirt she wanted to wear in her closet almost immediately and then stayed in her room to let her embarrassment die down.

When she finally came out, fully dressed, I was sitting on the couch, pretending to be engrossed in the wrestling match on the screen. I had the decency to say nothing about what I had seen, but her face was still a little red.

"I'm… uh… sorry," Linda said, growing redder. "I didn't think you'd get here so quickly and I didn't hear you come in. I'm…"

"Don't worry about it," I said dismissively. "It's not a big deal. You were covered, right?"

"Well, yeah. But…"

"And it's not like I've never seen a woman in a bra before."

That made her even redder. It wasn't my intention, but she sure was cute when she was embarrassed.

"You really look great! Nice and fit!" I was talking and couldn't seem to shut up. She looked away, trying to hide her face.

"I have to admit, I enjoyed the view."

Damn, shut up, Butcher!

With a nervous laugh she said, "Okay… can we just stop talking about it now."

I had my mouth open, ready to spout off with another gem about how great she looked nearly naked, but with that I slammed my lips closed.

"So… can I get you something to drink?" Linda offered, motioning with her head toward the kitchen.

I lifted myself from the couch and joined Linda in the kitchen as she was getting me a glass from the cabinet above the sink and filling it with ice. "How's Coke?"

"Sounds great. Thanks."

"I can't tell you enough how much I appreciate you staying with Ethan," Linda said, popping the cap off of a sixteen-ounce returnable and pouring it over the crackling ice. "Charlie appreciates it, too."

I bet he fucking does, I thought nastily.

"We were going to take Ethan out with us again, but Charlie thinks we should spend more time alone before we bring my son fully into the relationship. You know, to make sure things are solid with us before Ethan has a chance to get attached to Charlie."

I nodded, agreeing that it made sense. If Ethan grew to love Charlie and then something happened and Linda quit seeing Charlie, it would be a crushing blow to her son.

"We took him out with us the other night. Out to dinner. Charlie seemed a little uncomfortable."

"Are you okay?" I asked. Something seemed off.

Linda sighed, looking like she had something to say. Then she shook her head. "I'm sure it's nothing. I just want this to work out *so* bad! I've been alone for a long time."

"And you're worried that Charlie won't want to be with you because of Ethan?"

"Well… yeah. That's usually how it works out."

"You can't just sit home forever hoping that the right guy will show up. Charlie might not be the one, but you won't know unless you try," I said, sounding wiser than I felt.

About that time the doorbell rang.

Linda flushed and said, "There's Charlie! How do I look?" She gave a little spin.

"Well, do you really want to get into *that* again?" I asked, smiling.

"Um... no!" Linda said, the familiar redness appearing at her cheeks again. Linda hurried off to let Charlie in and I followed her to the door. Ethan was standing in the living room, but not going to the door like he did for me.

This time Charlie stayed on the porch as Linda got her things together. She threw on her jacket and grabbed her purse before turning to Ethan. "Ethan, you listen to Ronald tonight and do what he says. Okay?"

Ethan nodded. "Okay."

"I don't think we'll be late, but if we are I'll call," she then said to me.

"Don't worry about it. Just have fun," I said with a wave.

"Okay, thanks!" Linda said, stepping out the door and taking Charlie's arm.

I stood there at the door, watching the two of them move down the front walk. Linda's ass was perfect in the tight jeans, her swaying curves hypnotizing me. I stared as each taut buttock seemed to dance with every step. I didn't even realize that Ethan had moved up and was standing beside me.

"Hey Butchie!"

"What Ethan?" I said, not looking away from the wondrous sight before me.

"You're staring at my mom's butt!" Ethan said, an amused lilt in his voice.

I turned to him quickly. "Uh… um… No, I'm not."

Ethan laughed. "It's okay. I'm an Ass Man, too. Remember?"

4. Calling Miranda Lewis

During the second game of Candyland Ethan came up with a serious question.

"Butchie, what's a date?"

"Well, that's where a boy asks a girl to go out and do something fun with him," I answered. "A good standard date is dinner and a movie."

Ethan seemed to be thinking hard for a second. "That's what I thought it was. Can I go on a date?"

"Anyone can go on a date. All you have to do is ask a girl out and see if she says yes. And you have to have some money."

"Oh," Ethan said dejectedly. "I don't have very much money."

"A date doesn't have to cost a lot of money. How much have you got?"

Ethan ran into his bedroom and came back out carrying a neon green plastic piggy bank. From the sound of it I could tell there was a lot of empty room inside for his coins to rattle. "This is all I have."

I had some money on me, and I was feeling generous. I figured a little date would be good for Ethan. "You want to call that girl you like from school?"

Ethan grew red in the face, but he was smiling. "Yes. I want to call Miranda Lewis and ask her out on a date."

"I'll tell you what," I began, taking out my wallet and making sure I had enough cash. "You give Miranda a call and ask her for a date, and if she can go I will give you enough money to take her out."

"Really?" Ethan asked, wide-eyed.

"Yes, really," I laughed. "Do you know her number?"

Ethan ran into the living room and came back with a little black address book. With the pages inches from his eyes he pored over the book, seeking out Miranda's phone number. Ethan had a bit of trouble dialing the number, though. He couldn't remember it long enough to dial it. He had to keep looking back and see where he was, and then he would forget his place and have to hang up and start over.

"What's the matter, Ethan? Nervous?" I asked, giving him a light punch on the arm. He nodded his head vigorously, his jaw hanging down dumbly.

"You know her pretty good, right?"

Ethan continued nodding.

"Then don't be nervous. Just call her and talk to her. Easy as that!"

Ethan must have relaxed a bit because he got the number dialed correctly on the very next try. I heard the first ring coming from the earpiece and Ethan began to breathe harder.

"Just relax," I said.

Then the second ring.

He held his breath.

Just as the third ring started he slammed the phone down into the cradle.

"What the hell was that?" I asked, palms out and pointing at the phone.

"I can't do it! What if she says no?" Ethan whined.

"What if she is going to say yes, but you don't have the guts to ask her?"

Ethan picked up the phone again, put it to his ear, and then set it back down quickly, like it was hot.

"If you would rather sit around here playing games and watching wrestling, then fine! We can do that," I said, picking up the phone and holding it out to Ethan. "But if you want to be a man and show some guts, you take this phone and call Miranda."

Ethan looked at the phone with great anticipation and great trepidation.

"Do you think she likes you?" I asked.

Ethan paused in thought and then nodded. "I think so."

"Then call her. Don't be a pussy!"

Ethan snickered childishly at my dirty word. "You said 'pussy'!"

I let my face grow stern, trying not to laugh at Ethan's reaction to my bad language. "Are you going to call her or not?"

Ethan took the phone and concentrated on the number in the book as he dialed it.

"Remember to be polite," I said, and Ethan shushed me with a finger to his lips and a few waves of his hand.

After two rings the phone was answered and I half expected Ethan to slam the phone down again, but he didn't. He spoke clearly into the mouthpiece. "Hello. This is Ethan Gabriel Miles and I am calling for Miranda Lewis. Is she in please?"

I put my ear close to the receiver and I could hear a female voice say, "Yes, just a second."

Ethan turned to me and gave me an enthusiastic thumbs up and a huge smile. I gave him the thumbs up back. I mouthed, "Be cool."

He started to breathe harder and I whispered to him, "Relax. Relax."

From the other end I heard, "Hello, this is Miranda."

And Ethan went to stone, eyes wide like a deer in the headlights.

From the phone, "Hello? Hello?"

"Talk to her!" I whispered frantically. "Talk to her, Ethan!"

Again, from the phone, "Is anyone there? Hello?"

I did the only thing I could think to do. It seemed a little mean, but I felt like I had to do something. I popped Ethan in the forehead with an open hand smack. "Talk to her!"

It worked.

"Um… Hello, Miranda. Um… Ummm… This is Ethan Gabriel Miles…" Ethan stammered.

"Hi Ethan!" came the bubbly reply from the phone. "What do you want?"

"I… um… I…"

"Spit it out!" I whispered harshly. "Ask her! Just do it!"

Ethan took a deep breath and spewed the words into the phone in one long breath. "Miranda… I wanted to know if you would like to go out with me to watch dinner and eat a movie."

Eat a movie?

Miranda caught it, too. I heard from the phone, "Do you mean eat dinner and watch a movie?"

Ethan was stricken with a look of panic and he tried to slam the receiver down on the cradle. I caught his hand and wouldn't let him do it. I brought the receiver back to his ear and mouth, looking him in the eye and nodding.

He nodded into the phone.

"Ethan, she can't hear you nod! You have to talk to her!"

"Yes! That's what I meant! Would you like to eat dinner and watch a movie with me?"

"I would love to!" came the giggling reply from the phone. The giggling cut off abruptly. "Wait a second, Ethan. My sister wants to talk to your mom."

Ethan handed me the phone. I guess I had to pass for his mother.

"Linda, this is Francine," came the new voice on the phone.

"Francine, I'm not Linda. I'm Butch… er… Ronald Blake. I'm keeping an eye on Ethan while Linda is out."

"Oh. Well, who are you exactly, Mr. Blake?" Francine asked, somewhat snootily.

"I'm a friend of Ethan's from school. Linda asked me to stay with him tonight because she had a date."

"Don't you think it is a little late to call up and ask for a date?"

"Not really," I replied. She was quiet for a long time.

"All right. Well, here's the deal, Ronald," Francine began, laying it out for me. "If my sister is going to go out with Ethan and Linda is not there then I have to go with her. Am I correct in thinking that you will be driving them on their date?"

"Yes, you are correct. I was planning on driving them for dinner and a movie."

"Well, I'll be coming, too."

"Like a double date?" I asked.

"Yes and no. It's not really a date… but you will have to pay for everything."

What the hell? Who did this bitch think she was?

I looked at Ethan's happy, hopeful face.

"Okay. Fair enough." I said.

"Where will we be going?"

"I kind of thought we would let them decide that. You know, seeing as how it is *their* date and all," I said, a little snottier than I intended.

"Agreed," Francine said curtly. "You can pick us up in one hour. Don't be late."

"We…" I began.

Click. Dial tone. That bitch hung up on me!

"…Won't."

Oh yes. This certainly was going to be a *lovely* fucking evening.

5. Ethan's First Date

Francine was nasty, spiteful, condescending, arrogant, rude, self-righteous, and mean.

Plus, she had a moustache.

In the history of the Wingman, this had to be up there with the all-time 'take-one-for-the-team' sacrifices.

I had to be eligible for the Wingman Hall of Fame after this date.

I had helped Ethan get ready for his first date in the hour that Francine had so graciously given us. He wanted to wear his favorite *Thundercats* t-shirt and his pajama bottoms, but I talked him into wearing a nice pullover sweater and some black slacks that he had in his closet. With a little help Ethan wetted down his hair and got his unruly cowlick mostly under control. When I told Ethan that he should brush his teeth he argued with me that it wasn't bedtime. I convinced him when I said that Miranda wouldn't want to kiss a guy with food in his teeth.

All in all, Ethan cleaned up pretty good.

We pulled up in front of Miranda's house with a bit of time to spare, so I put the car in park and gave Ethan some pointers. He was really nervous.

"You okay?" I asked, noticing how pale he had gotten.

"I'm o… No," Ethan said, clasping his hand over his mouth and fumbling with my door handle. He got the door open just in the nick of time as he sprayed puke all over the curb. It was over quickly, in one mighty hurl, and Ethan leaned back into the car, his eyes red and watery. "I'm okay now."

"Well, so much for brushing your teeth," I sighed, looking through my console for a piece of gum or something. I used to always keep a pack of Big Red gum in my console in case I got pulled over after drinking. Fortunately, I had a stick for Ethan. "Chew this."

Ethan popped the cinnamon gum into his mouth and instantly started waving his hand in front of his mouth. "Hot! Hot! Hot! Hot!"

"Shut up and chew it! You have to get rid of that puke breath before we go up there."

Ethan shut up and chewed the gum.

"Now, when we go up here, just be yourself," I counseled. "Miranda already likes you or she wouldn't have agreed to go out with you, so you can just be like you always are around her. Okay?"

Ethan chewed vigorously and nodded in time with his rapidly masticating jaws.

"When she talks, listen to her. Open doors for her. Pull out her chair. Just be nice."

Ethan gave me a closed mouth smile and nodded again. I pulled the car up several feet, putting some distance between us and the puke on the curb. "Well, let's go get the girls."

Standing on the Lewis's front porch I rang the bell and waited. Ethan didn't seem very nervous at all now. The vomiting must have helped.

Soon enough the door opened and I laid eyes on Francine.

Oh sweet baby Jesus.

To say she wasn't my type was the understatement of 1988.

I expected, judging from what I had seen of Miranda, to find someone similar in build and features. Just less… retarded looking. Miranda was tall and skinny. Francine was short and chubby. Miranda had reddish blonde hair. Francine had dark hair. (All the better to show off her moustache.) Miranda looked like a taller, geekier Nicole

Kidman. Francine looked like a stumpier and slightly less hairy Fidel Castro.

I swallowed hard. "You must be Francine."

Francine just cocked one eyebrow at me, as if to say, 'I'm not impressed with you'. "Ronald?"

"Yes. I'm Ronald. Just call me Ron. Or Butcher."

"O-kay. Ron, it is," Francine said, stepping aside and motioning Ethan and I into the house. "What the hell is Butcher? A nickname?"

"Yeah. It's what my teammates call me on the football team. I play for the Mims Mustangs."

"Football is a Neanderthal sport, played by dolts and watched by even bigger dolts."

"Uh… yeah… well…" I stammered, unaccustomed to not being worshipped as a football god, or being greeted by such rudeness. "Is Miranda ready? We need to get going if we're going to make it to dinner and get to the movie in time."

As if on cue Miranda appeared at the top of the stairs and slumped her lanky frame to the bottom. "Ethan! Hi!"

"Hi Miranda," Ethan said shyly.

A moment of silence grew awkward, so I clapped my hands and said, "Well, let's get this show on the road. You two can decide where to eat in the car."

Thankfully, Miranda and Ethan decided on the same place instantly. They came to their decision by discussing which fast food burger joint was giving out the best toys in their kids meals.

The four of us made our way inside and up to the counter and I let everyone order and I paid for it. The guy behind the counter was the longhaired chubby guy that had gotten Ethan smoking that cobra bong at the party.

"Teeth! How's it going, man?" the chubby guy said happily. It was obvious to me that Ethan didn't remember the guy.

"His name is Ethan," I said menacingly, leaning over the counter. I flicked the guy's nametag with my fingers. "Remember that, Leonard!"

The guy put his hands up in supplication. "Relax Conan! I didn't mean nothing by it."

We took our tray to a table and Ethan and Miranda sat together, alternately eating and playing with their toys together. I ate slowly, chewing every bite deliberately and sipping my milkshake with utter leisure. By keeping my mouth full I didn't have to say anything, so Francine could just talk and talk. And talk.

She railed on how unfair the wages were that fast food restaurants paid their female managers as compared to what they paid men. She gave me her ten-minute hunk on how the food we were all eating was so unhealthy. The only time she said anything that sounded even remotely positive was when she was talking about school.

Francine was a freshman at Vanderbilt, majoring in Women's Studies. Her professor had opened her mind to how the patriarchal society had oppressed women. She thought Andrea Dworkin was the be all end all of gender discussion.

"All heterosexual sex is rape, so don't even think you'll be getting lucky at the end of this date," she told me flatly.

If I were truly lucky I wouldn't be on this fucking date with you, I thought. But I said nothing. I just let her ramble.

Back in the car, Ethan and Miranda in the backseat, we headed for the multiplex. The two people who were actually enjoying the date wanted to see Halloween 4: The Return of Michael Myers. I was all for it. When we looked up the running times it was the shortest movie on the marquee. Whatever would get me out of there the fastest.

In the rearview mirror I caught a glimpse of Miranda leaning over and kissing Ethan on the cheek. She put her head on his shoulder. Ethan sat like a slab of stone, a look of panic on his face. We were almost to the theater when Ethan worked up the nerve to make his move. He started to put his arm around Miranda.

Unfortunately for Ethan, Francine noticed the movement in the backseat and whirled around angrily.

"HANDS!" she bellowed.

Ethan shot bolt upright and Miranda slid across the backseat and up against the side of the car, away from Ethan.

"That was really nice of you," I whispered. "You scared the shit out of both of them."

"I didn't agree to let Miranda date him so he could paw her in the backseat of some high school jocks *pussy wagon*," Francine said with a tone of finality.

I didn't speak again until we were on the way home from the movies.

During the movie, Miranda and Ethan sneaked their hands below Francine's line of sight and held hands during the scary parts. Miranda tried to steal another kiss, but Francine was on guard and she grabbed her sister's head and turned it roughly back toward the screen.

"Watch the movie!" Francine hissed.

Then she turned back to me and whispered about how slasher films were just another example of women being used as objects. "A woman who has sex with a man is seen as a whore, and therefore punished by death. It's like that in all these movies. There is always the gratuitous female nudity. The killer is always a man, always the one in a position of power."

Blah, blah, blah, blah, and blah.

I could have argued that the men who have sex with the women are usually killed, too. I could have argued that the victor in a slasher film was usually a woman who defeated the killer. I had no rebuttal against the gratuitous female nudity, other than to say that I really enjoyed it.

I decided that it was best just to keep my mouth shut. I leaned on my armrest and hid my face in my hand for most of the movie. Her prattling to me was only punctuated by her loud rebukes of Ethan and Miranda, and her threats to sit between them if they didn't behave.

In the car on the way home it was more of the same. Miranda was still the aggressor, but Francine felt obliged to defend her sister's honor. Ethan was a nervous wreck from all of Francine's shouting. His first date was ruined, and I surmised, may have turned him off from ever dating again.

I had to do something.

A slight detour was in order, so I hung a left into Fillmore Johnson Park. I knew it well. Certain parts of the park were notorious as gay hangouts, so the football team liked to come down and beat up on fags when we were bored. I'm not proud of it, but yes, I did it one time, too. The players would come down on a Saturday night, one of the guys would let a fag pick him up and then everyone beat the shit out of the guy when they got him alone. It was essentially a free beating you could dish out. Most of the guys in the park were married and were not about to report it to the police. They'd just take the ass kickings as a matter of course. I always thought it would be incredibly funny if they picked up a really tough gay guy one night and he beat the shit out of all of them.

Without thinking about it too much, I decided that I was going to do my job as Ethan's wingman and run interference with Francine. If I had taken the time to think about it I am sure that I never would have done it.

"What do you think you're doing?" Francine asked in an accusatory tone.

"I have something I need to say to you and I don't want to say it in front of Ethan and Miranda," I whispered. I had no idea what it was I was going to say to her, but as I saw it, I had about thirty seconds to come up with something.

I parked the car and got out, walked over to the passenger side and let Francine out. At first she didn't move, but with a little gentle coaxing she climbed out of the car. I motioned to the front of the car and she walked with me. I had left the car running and the radio on for Ethan and Miranda. Not just so they could hear it, but so that they couldn't hear us.

"Francine, you're a smart and strong woman," I began, playing to her ego. "You know what you want and you aren't afraid to say so."

She was a little taken aback by that, apparently unaccustomed to compliments from male oppressors.

"You really need to lighten up on Miranda and Ethan. They're good kids. Nothing is going to happen. They want to kiss and hold hands. That's all. It's perfectly natural," I said, trying to sound like the voice of reason. "They just want to be like other kids their age."

Francine kept peering around me and through the windshield, making sure that Ethan and Miranda stayed on their respective sides of the backseat.

"Miranda is just a child, mentally," Francine argued. "I have to look out for her."

"Of course you do. And I have to look out for Ethan. Mentally he is a child, too. But physically they are teenagers and they have natural drives. They are going to grow up. Nothing you or I can do about that. They're good kids and they're not going to just jump each others bones just because you allow them to kiss each other."

Francine appeared to be swayed, but she shook that off and glared into the backseat again. It wasn't working.

Back to working her ego like a speedbag.

"You're an incredibly intelligent woman. A very strong woman, self assured..." I was losing her. I could see her mind shifting gears away from what I was saying. No choice. I had to do it. "...And I find that very attractive."

What the fuck was I saying!

Shock washed over Francine's face in the streetlight's glow. "You do?"

"Yeah, I do. Very much."

Suddenly everything changed. Her expression, her body language. Everything.

"You're not just saying that?" she asked, a hopeful look in her eyes.

"No, no. I'm not," I lied. "All I ever get are these bubbly little airhead high school girls. You're a self-aware, fully realized woman. And that is so fucking hot!"

Without preamble, Francine grabbed my hand and led me into a nearby copse of trees, away from the streetlights and away from Ethan and Miranda. I had no idea what to expect.

It was my turn to be shocked when she pressed my back against a tree, dropped to her knees and tore my jeans open. The girl was simply voracious. She attacked my dick like an Ethiopian on a cheeseburger. (And thank God I didn't feel the moustache!) My knees buckled and I had to hold onto the tree to stay on my feet. This man-hating, female empowering, fight the evil patriarchy chick was gobbling my knob with the enthusiasm of a two-dollar whore.

When it was over, and it was over all too soon for my tastes, Francine stood up, wiped her mouth and calmly said, "Take me home please, Ronald."

Breathless and wordless, I nodded my head and zipped up delicately, then followed Francine back to my car. The windows were steamed up when we got there. Francine gave a couple quick knocks on the window before she opened the door. Ethan and Miranda broke off their rather chaste embrace as Francine and I slid into the front seats.

Dueling emotions roiled through my guts. On the one hand, I had just allowed myself to have sexual contact with a woman I found truly repugnant in virtually every way. On the other hand, I had just gotten the best blowjob of my life, before or since. I suppose it was a matter of feeling cheap and being okay with it that had me so confused. In the end I would have to say that if you ever have a chance to receive a grudge suck from a self-loathing feminist, you should go for it.

When we dropped the girls off at their house, Francine insisted on Ethan and I not walking them to the door. Ethan got a quick goodnight kiss and I got a cold look. Which was fine with me.

Ethan sat in the backseat, his face pressed against the rear side glass, and he watched Miranda walk away.

"Did you have fun, Ethan?" I asked with a nervous smile, still recovering from my ordeal.

"Yes I did!" he exclaimed.

"Good. Good."

"I touched her butt! With my hand!"

"That's nice," I sighed absently. "Want to get up here in the front seat now?"

"Umm… no," he said after some thought.

"No?" I asked, incredulous. Ethan always wanted to ride in front. "Why not?"

"I can't move very good," Ethan replied, his tone sounding slightly embarrassed.

"What's wrong?"

"This!" Ethan cried.

I turned on the dome light to look back and see what "this" was.

Ethan was pointing at his crotch where a rather impressive bulge stretched his pants out in a tent. "It won't go down."

I turned out the dome light and headed back to Ethan's house, trying not to laugh. "Don't worry. It will go down. Just wait."

6. Everybody Loves Darlene

It didn't go down.

I have no idea what the problem was, and I didn't want to know, but it was weird. We were back at his house for forty minutes and Ethan's dick was still sticking out, leading him by a good margin. Ethan was worried about it, and that may have had something to do with it.

"Butchie! Why won't it go down?" he cried, pacing in front of the television. I sat there with my head in my hands, trying to avoid looking at him. And trying not to laugh.

"I don't know, Ethan. Just relax," I advised, not knowing what else to say. When it first seemed to be a problem I suggested that he go in his bedroom and take care of it himself. He had no idea what I was talking about, and I didn't feel like giving him a lesson. At the forty minute point, and with his mother's return growing ever closer, I had to do something.

I called JK.

When he answered the phone I could hear some kind of party going on. A bunch of people were singing along to Marvin Gaye's *Sexual Healing* and laughing at each other.

"JK, I need your help!" I said, sounding like it was more of an emergency than it was.

"What? What do you need?" JK asked, concerned.

"Who is that girl in your neighborhood that you said would give a blowjob for a pack of cigarettes?"

"You ain't that fucking desperate are you?" JK said with a laugh.

"Not me. Ethan," I said, then explained the situation.

"Damn! Damn!" JK cackled. "Why don't you tell him to jack off?"

"I suggested it, but he doesn't know what that is. And I'm not about to teach him!"

More laughter.

"Bring him over here and I'll take you down to Darlene's house. She'll take care of him."

"I'm on my way."

"Oh! Don't forget the smokes," JK reminded.

"What kind?"

"Don't matter. She'll smoke anything. Literally."

A few minutes later I had Ethan in the car and we were on the way to the convenience store for the cigarettes and then to JK's house. Ethan was freaking out a little bit more than he was at home. You would have thought I was taking him to the emergency room for a medical trauma rather than just to get his dick sucked. "Don't worry, Ethan. We're going to fix you all up."

JK was waiting in front of his house when we pulled up and he trotted out to the car, stifling his laughter for Ethan's sake. I got out of the car and let him in the backseat behind me. Ethan was in no position to be leaning forward or moving around very much. "Just turn right at the corner and come back down Clark. She lives almost directly behind me."

We pulled up in front of Darlene's house and JK and I helped Ethan out of the car.

"How ya doing there, Ethan?" I asked.

"I'm scared, Butchie! It won't go down!" he whined.

"Don't be scared. You'll be okay in a minute." I kept my voice calm and soothing, trying to take the edge off of his panic. I looked at JK. "What if she's not home?"

"It's Saturday night. She's home. We might even have to wait in line."

"No shit?" I was shocked.

"It's happened before. She's a popular girl in this neighborhood," JK said with a huge grin.

"Yeah, I bet."

We half dragged Ethan around the back of the house. He tried to walk with us, but that would have been difficult for him even in the best of times.

"Let's stand him up here," JK said, guiding us toward a large central air unit beneath a window. There was a dim light on inside the room. "She's home. Told ya."

JK and I lifted Ethan up on top of the central air unit, placing his feet roughly in the existing footprints on top of it.

"What are you doing, Butchie?" Ethan sounded even more scared.

"Relax, Ethan. We're taking care of you. Just do what JK says. Okay?" I said.

Ethan nodded resolutely, placing his trust in me.

With a quick look in the window we could see the girl I presumed was Darlene. She was wearing a thigh length kimono-like robe, her dark hair pulled back into a long ponytail. JK held out his hand to me and I placed the cigarettes in it. He handed them to Ethan.

"Ethan, I'm going to knock on this window. When the girl comes to the window just hand her the cigarettes and she'll do the rest. Just let her do what she's going to do. All right?" JK instructed.

"All right," Ethan replied, breathing heavy, fear in his eyes.

"Trust me, you're going to like this. Don't be scared," JK said with a wicked smile. Ethan nodded and JK rapped on the glass three times sharply. The two of us ducked around the corner of the house and left Ethan alone at the window.

I peeked around the corner when I heard the window slide open and I saw Ethan give the cigarettes to Darlene with a shaking hand. Darlene took them inside the house and then reached out and took Ethan by the hips, moving him closer to the window. I thought he was going to tumble from the central air unit the way she was manhandling him, but Ethan kept his feet underneath him. Darlene's hands then grabbed the button and zipper of his slacks and tugged them open. The last thing I saw before decency demanded that I look away was Ethan's panic stricken face.

JK and I were beside ourselves trying to laugh quietly when we wanted to roar and roll around on the ground. The whole situation was beyond absurd, therefore hilarious.

And that was before the sounds started.

It was a cavalcade of animal noises that drifted around the house to our ears. It sounded like kittens mewling, mixed with a moose grunting, mixed with a dog panting. I could have sworn I even heard a dolphin.

"Oh, Butchie!" Ethan called out in the midst of his animal impersonations. I had my hand pressed to my mouth and was doubled over with my arms across my aching belly. "BUTCHIE!"

I could only imagine Darlene's confusion at hearing Ethan calling out the name Butchie, and I laughed harder. JK was on the ground, one hand on his belly, one holding him up on his knees. His head was turned into his shoulder and tears trailed down his face.

"BUTCHIE! BUTCHIE!" the call came again.

And then we heard the crash. Our laughter died instantly and we rushed around the side of the house.

Apparently, at the point of orgasm Ethan fell backwards off of the central air unit and fell into a tangle of folded aluminum lawn chairs.

"Oh… Buuuuu-tchie…" Ethan groaned quietly.

Darlene was in the window, looking less than pleased. "Get him the fuck out of here! My parents are home!"

She slid the window closed harshly as JK and I helped Ethan up from the twisted wreckage of metal and nylon. I picked Ethan's leg up and slid the lawn chair from around it. "Ethan, zip your pants up and let's get out of here!"

Ethan did as I asked and we made our way quickly back to my car. I was laughing again, but not as boisterously as before. JK, on the other hand, was having trouble walking from laughing so hard. We got in the car and were pulling away when the porchlight came on at Darlene's house and massively large man stepped out onto the porch. His body language said that he was very, very angry.

I dropped JK off at his house before heading back to Ethan's. "Thanks, man! You saved the day!"

"Aw, shit! You ain't gotta thank me! I gotta thank you. That was the funniest shit I ever saw in my life!" JK replied, hands on his left side.

He turned and made his way slowly back to his house as we drove away. When we were almost home, Ethan finally spoke for the first time since we picked him up. "Butchie?"

"Yeah?"

"When can we go see the cigarette lady again?"

I turned up the radio so he wouldn't get offended at me chuckling.

7. The End of the Night

Once I got Ethan home I had to clean him up. He had leaves in his hair from where he fell and there was mud on his pants. Those had to go into the washer and hopefully be finished before Linda got home.

Ethan was tired and I gladly sent him off to bed. Then I went to the couch and collapsed, flipping through channels expressionlessly. *The Longest Yard*, possibly the greatest football movie ever made, was on and I stopped there. I don't remember exactly how far I got into it, but I do remember Linda coming in and waking me up somewhere around one thirty in the morning.

"Hey," I groaned, coming around slowly. "How was your date?"

That's when I noticed that she had been crying. Linda turned away from me.

Apparently not so good.

"What's wrong?" I asked, rising from the couch and almost tumbling. I was awake, but my leg was still asleep. "What happened?"

Linda walked into the kitchen. "It's nothing. Don't worry about it."

"Did Charles do something to you? I can go kick his ass if you want."

"No, Ronald. No… It's nothing. Really," she said, sounding very unconvincing. "What did you and Ethan do tonight?"

Linda got a glass of water out of the tap and sipped it slowly, looking out the window over the sink, and keeping her back to me. I let her change the subject.

"Well, we went out for dinner and went to a movie," I replied, trying to decide how much to tell her about the girls. I figured she would find out soon enough anyway. "Ethan called Miranda and asked her to go with us."

Linda turned around quickly. "Oh! His first date!"

I nodded.

"Damn it! I missed his first date!" She sounded hurt, not angry at all. "I wish I would have known."

I explained everything to her about how Ethan had asked me about dating and I gave her the details of the date. Minus the stop in the park and the visit to Darlene's bedroom window. I didn't bad mouth Francine, either. Honestly, after the knee-buckling experience in the park I had nothing bad to say about her anyway. She really didn't seem so bad at that point.

"We had a great time. Now what about you? Something's wrong," I needled.

"You don't need to worry about it. Seriously. It's... adult stuff."

"Ah... sex," I said, seeing redness creep into her cheeks.

"Yeah. Sex."

"Well, since it's personal, I won't bother you about it. I just wanted to make sure he didn't do anything."

Linda smiled a thank you to me and then went quiet for a long, awkward moment. I decided to take my leave.

"Well then, goodni..." I started.

"It was bad! Really bad!" Linda blurted out, interrupting my goodbye. "I don't know what's wrong!"

I was sorry I asked. I didn't want to hear about Charlie's inadequacy or any freaky deviancies he may or may not have had. But I knew that Linda was going to tell me anyway.

"We've been dating for a little while now and I thought it would be okay to take things further."

I nodded. "Mm-hmm."

"Well, it was nice. It had been so long, and it really felt nice to be with someone again. But as soon as it was over Charlie just became really cold toward me."

Linda sat her glass down and leaned against the counter, folding her arms across her chest. Almost as if she were trying to protect her heart.

"Maybe I'm just reading things into it that aren't there because I want this to work out so badly?" she asked, looking up at me with tears rimming her eyes. "Maybe it was nothing."

"I don't know," I said honestly. Maybe it was nothing, maybe it was exactly what she feared. Charlie got what he was after and now he was done with her. I didn't want to say anything to make matters worse, though. "Maybe Charlie just doesn't know that you feel that way."

Linda thought about it. "No. That's not it. He knew. Because I told him. He just didn't seem to care."

"Well… maybe Charlie's just a fucking dick," I said with a shrug.

Linda broke out in a wide smile and a surprised little laugh at that. "Yeah, maybe."

I gave her a minute, letting her smile set in.

"Are you going to be all right?" I asked.

"Yes, I'll be fine," she said, wiping her eyes and smiling. "Thanks for taking Ethan out on his first date. How much do I owe you? I'm sure it cost you some money to take them out like that."

"You don't owe me anything. Don't worry about it. We had a good time."

"Are you sure?"

"Absolutely sure," I said with a smile. "I'm glad I could be there and do that for him."

Linda got a strange smile across her face right then.

"What?" I asked, noticing something new in her smile.

She said nothing, just kept on smiling.

"What?" I asked again, more demanding, but with a nervous chuckle at the end.

"For a teenage boy you're a really good man, Ronald."

Now it was my turn to be embarrassed. "It was nothing. Really."

Linda shook her head. "No, that's not true. It really is something. Thank you."

She walked me to the door, said goodnight and I heard the lock click behind me. As I walked to my car I realized she was right.

It really was something.

Chapter Nine

1. Ethan Don't Surf

School on Monday was pretty standard up until lunch.

I had a good workout in the morning, picked up Ethan and got him to class with no problems, and coasted through the first half of the day. Everything was clicking and it was easy. Ethan and I had a routine now and we were making it to his classes with time to spare.

At lunch time I helped Ethan get his tray and we were making our way to the table to eat with JK when Tabitha stopped me. Ethan kept walking, so I let him go. We could see JK from where we were, so I thought, '*Hey, what can go wrong?*'

"Hey Butcher," Tabitha said coyly, batting her eyes. "Can we talk?"

I watched over her shoulder as Ethan made his awkward way to the table. He was twisting through the grid of tables on his way and trying not to bump anyone with his swinging duffel bag.

"What do you want, Tab?" I asked. I didn't want to give her any wrong ideas, so I was being a little short with her.

"Well, uh… I was just talking with some of the girls and we were wondering… if maybe…" she said, speaking carefully and trying to be seductive. Her stammering wasn't a loss for words. She knew exactly what she was saying.

I looked back up and saw Ethan, about half way to JK's table, and then I turned back to Tabitha. "Maybe what?"

"You see, I've told some of the girls how good you are in bed and they want to try it for themselves."

She had my full attention.

"Which girls would that be?" I asked, looking back at the cheerleaders' table. I had banged most of them already, so it couldn't be that they were curious.

"A few of my friends. And a couple girls from a different school. What do you say? Are you up for it?" she said with a sly smile.

I had to admit, I was certainly up for it. Even if Tabitha was just trying a vain attempt at getting me back, I was definitely going to go for it. To anyone else it might have sounded suspicious, but I was Butcher Blake. Of course all the girls wanted to fuck me!

"When is this supposed to take place?" I asked, coolly.

"Well, I was thinking about my house right after school," Tabitha said, twirling her fingers in her hair. "You don't have practice on Monday, so you can get right over there and take care of us."

"How many girls?"

"Five. Think you can handle five hot, wet pussies that are there just for you?" Tabitha didn't usually talk like that, and it made me realize that she was up to something.

I looked up and tried to see Ethan and he was nowhere in sight. I looked at JK's table. No Ethan.

"Butcher!" Tabitha called, trying to bring my attention back to her. I stepped away from her and craned my neck around looking for Ethan.

Then I heard it. At the far end of the lunchroom, a quick triplet drumbeat being played on a table. A familiar tune being hummed.

I whirled around and saw Ethan, surfing on the conveyor belt that took our dirty trays back to the kitchen while Skyler beat out the rhythm on the table and Chewy, Shorty, and a few of the other guys from the team hummed the tune to *Wipe Out.*

Ethan had a terrified look on his face, like he was scared he was going to fall. I knew Chewy or Shorty had to have lifted him up there. With his legs the way they were there was no way he could have climbed up by himself and he sure couldn't jump down by himself. He wasn't surfing for fun, he was simply fighting his naturally poor balance to stay on his feet and not tumble to the floor and bust his head open.

"BUTCHIE! BUTCHIE!" Ethan cried out, his terror only urging Skyler and the guys on.

Suddenly *Wipe Out* stopped and a chant rose from the floor. Started, of course, by Skyler. "Teeth! Teeth! Teeth! Teeth!"

The entire lunchroom exploded in laughter once they all caught sight of what was going on. Then a few of the other students joined in the mocking cadence. "TEETH! TEETH! TEETH! TEETH!"

Setting my tray down at the first available spot I could find, I ran across the lunchroom and caught hold of Ethan and lifted him down from the conveyor belt.

"It's okay, Ethan. I've got you." I spoke calmly, hoping my calmness would keep him from spazzing out.

It didn't.

Once he was down on the floor Ethan began to cry, the fear being too much for him. He wasn't hurt, just really scared. The last time I had seen that reaction was when I caused it.

I went off.

"WHAT THE FUCK ARE YOU DOING?" I screamed in Skyler's face. I didn't have to ask whose idea it had been to put Ethan up there.

Mr. Hall, so "busy" monitoring the lunchroom that he didn't see what was going on in the lunchroom, finally took notice when he heard my raised voice and the mother of all profanities. He immediately started over toward us. Oh no, he couldn't have heard or seen anything when the football players were picking on Ethan, but now he was Johnny On The Spot. Apparently, until the threat of a fight between members of the football team arose there was no reason for him to get involved.

"What's going on over here?" Mr. Hall demanded, putting himself between Skyler and I. "Is there a problem, gentlemen?"

"No," I answered, slightly ahead of Skyler. "No problem at all."

Mr. Hall cast a look at Skyler, who just shrugged. "No problem here."

I took Ethan by the shoulder and led him over to JK's table, then I chased down his tray. It was sitting on one of the tables near the conveyor belt. A girl who had seen what was happening kept an eye on it for Ethan. I thanked her and headed back out to find my tray. No luck, though. Mine was gone. Instead of getting another tray I went out in the foyer and got a bag of Doritos and a Coke out of the vending machines.

I plopped down at the table, still angry, but trying not to show it.

"Hey man, I'm sorry I didn't see them snag Ethan. I would have stopped them." JK said.

"I know," I replied, shrugging off any implication that I thought JK was responsible for what happened. "It's my fault. I let Tabitha distract me. They used her to draw my attention away from Ethan so they could do that."

Ethan ate through his tears, but by the time he was finished his eyes were dry and he was smiling again.

On the way out of the cafeteria Skyler and his cronies, including Tabitha, waved to me mockingly, wiggling their fingers and smiling malicious smiles. JK noticed it and saw the coldness come down across my face. He knew what that meant.

"You're gonna get him, ain't ya?" he asked.

"Oh yeah," I said icily. "I'm gonna to get him."

2. The Hard Sell

When I got home from school the house was in a flurry of action. Dad was home, and for the first time in history, he was helping Mom with the housework. I could smell the apple pie baking in the kitchen and the fresh tang of the pine scented cleanser. My mother was always a conscientious housekeeper, but that day she was pulling out all the stops.

At first I didn't know why they seemed so absorbed in making sure the house gleamed, but then I remembered what was up. The guy from Penn State was coming for dinner to talk to me about attending his school. It should have been a huge deal, but I hadn't thought about it all day. I should have been excited, a college scout from a great football program coming to recruit me. It wasn't all that surprising to me, though, that I didn't give a rat's ass. I jumped in and helped get everything ready, but I wasn't thrilled about it.

My dad, on the other hand, was as nervous as a virgin on prom night. While mom vacuumed he fluffed and re-fluffed the pillows on the couch. He would fluff them up and then stand back and appraise the composition with a discerning eye and then do it again, moving the pillows around slightly. I laughed under my breath and went upstairs to my room. Not that I cared very much, but I figured I could at least straighten up my bedroom a little, considering the amount of effort Mom and Dad were making for me in the rest of the house.

I was never a slob, but I wasn't a neat freak, either. All I really had to do was to make sure that my dirty clothes were all in the hamper and that my dresser and desk were uncluttered. I didn't expect that I would be showing this scout into my room (I didn't want to go to Penn State *that* fucking bad!), but if for some reason he was brought up there, I wanted to make sure the impression my mom was going for held up. I assumed the impression was to be that we didn't actually live in the house, but that we used it strictly for entertaining. Personally, I've never had a problem with the lived-in look. Or even the extremely lived-in look. Still, if mom wanted to put forth a show home, so be it. I gave my room the once over twice and then laid down on my bad and relaxed until I was called downstairs at six when the scout arrived.

The scout was a middle-aged balding guy in a polo shirt and khaki's. He looked to be an athlete who had let himself go for a decade or so. Big, but soft. He introduced himself as Peter Kurten and shook hands with my parents, then turned to me.

"This young man needs no introduction!" he boomed, putting on the fake sincere face he would be wearing all night and shaking my hand. "Ronald 'The Butcher' Blake, the Pride of the Mims High School Mustangs! Leading the state in yards rushing *and* sacks! It is such a pleasure to meet you!"

I was taken aback, not used to this level of glad-handing. "Um… yeah. Thanks. Nice to meet you, Mr. Kurten."

"Call me Pete! Call me Pete!"

"Okay… Pete. You can call me Butcher," I said. He looked at me like the idea of calling me by a nickname made him uncomfortable, so I added. "It's either that or we do the Big Ron/Little Ron thing all night."

He laughed a big hearty laugh and said, "Butcher it is."

In a short while we were all sitting around the dining room table, eating off of the good dishes and drinking from the crystal. My parents and Good Time Pete had red wine, but I had to settle for Coke. It was okay, though. I sniffed the bouquet as I swirled the glass under my nose. It was a good year.

Mom had made a nice London Broil and roasted red potatoes with a side of asparagus that was grilled in olive oil. The dinner conversation was pleasant getting-to-know-you kind of stuff. No talking shop at the table. I could see that my dad was fighting not to wolf his food down just to get to the main event of the night. He wanted to be done with the preliminaries and niceties and get right to discussing my future.

After dinner we all went into the living room, had some coffee, and the sales pitch began in earnest. Like a good shill, he gave us the entire history of the Penn State football program. He gave us a run down of the pro players who came out of Penn State. I couldn't tell you exactly what was said, though, because I paid very little attention. Good Time Pete's Super Happy Sunshine Sermon was totally lost on me. I could tell it was a speech he had given hundreds of times before; he was merely inserting my name in place of the last kid he talked to. Granted, he did his research. He quoted my stats very accurately. The guy certainly knew every little thing about me, as far as my high school football career went.

"So, Butcher... which do you prefer, offense or defense?" Pete asked, breaking out of his preplanned litany for the first time since he initiated it.

"I never really thought about it," I replied truthfully. "I love scoring touchdowns and breaking off big runs and I love crushing quarterbacks. I can't choose."

"Well, Iron Man football is high school stuff. You won't be playing both sides in college."

I shrugged, resignedly. “I guess I would just play wherever the coach puts me. Doesn’t matter to me.”

My answer was a little too unenthused for my dad’s taste and he gave me a glowering look, as if to say, *‘You’re blowing it!’*

After a few more minutes of the hard sell, Mr. Kurten leaned back in his chair and drained the last drop of coffee from his cup. “Do you have any questions for me?”

I thought for a second, biting my upper lip with my bottom teeth. I couldn’t come up with anything I really wanted to ask. Having judged Peter Kurten as a superficial snake oil salesman just looking to pimp a football program to me, I had already decided that I wasn’t going to Penn State. I had to ask some questions, though, or my dad would be royally pissed. I thought of one.

“All right, Pete, I have a question,” I said, leaning forward into the space he had just vacated by leaning back. “If… IF… I decide to go to Penn State, can I expect to get a lot of pussy?”

There it was. The world-renowned deer in the headlights look.

Kurten looked back and forth between my parents on the couch and me in the chair. My dad’s glower grew into a full-fledged glare; my mom covered her mouth and demurely chuckled into her palm.

“Uh… ha… uh…” Kurten stammered.

“Well?” I coaxed.

“Um, okay… yeah…” he said, looking for the right way to say what he was thinking. “As an athlete at Penn State I can tell you with confidence that you won’t lack female companionship.”

"Okay. A lot of pussy. Check." I said, making a check mark in the air with my finger. Kurten was looking very ill at ease. "What about academics?"

"Excuse me?" he asked, still sweating my previous question.

"Academics," I said again, leaning deeper into his space. "You told me all about the football program, but what does the school offer in the way of academics? You didn't mention academics once."

"Well, we have strict rules on maintaining a satisfactory grade point average in order to participate in athletics."

"That's not what I asked, although that is good to know," I said, enjoying his growing discomfort. That pussy comment really threw him off his game. "What I want to know is what is the educational value of my attendance at Penn State? Am I going to come out of there as a big dumb jock with no prospects and no education to speak of?"

"Oh, no. No. Not at all. Penn State offers a fine curriculum with top-notch professors. Your education will absolutely be a priority."

"Then why didn't you mention any of that?" I said, feeling cocky. My dad looked like he wanted to jump up from the couch and strangle me.

"Well, to be honest, most of the young men I talk to never ask about anything other than the football program," Kurten admitted.

"Well, then thank you, Mr. Kurten," I began. He started to correct me and I preempted him. "Pete! Thank you, Pete. You've given me a lot to think about."

After a few more minutes of small talk and my dad desperately attempting damage control, Peter Kurten left my house and was out of my life forever. Seconds after the door closed behind the bewildered scout, my dad whirled on me in a rage.

"What the hell was that all about?" he yelled. "You blew it! You fucking blew it!"

"If Penn State really wanted me to go to their school they wouldn't have sent a plastic asshole like that to jerk me off," I said, stripping off my shirt and heading upstairs. My mom, standing beside my dad, laughed softly.

Dad shot a look at her. "What's so funny?"

"Well Ronnie is right. The guy was an ass."

"That *ass* has the power to get Mr. Funnyman here into Penn State! They have a great program there!" Dad argued.

"There are other schools," I said, leaning against the banister and putting on a serious face. "They can't all have shyster pimp recruiters, can they?"

Mom laughed a little bit and dad just shook his head. A look of pure disgust washed over his face. "You fucking dumb ass!"

Mom slapped him hard on the arm. "Don't call him that!"

"Well, he's being a fucking dumb ass!" Dad whined.

I went to my room, collapsed on my bed and fell asleep with my pants and shoes on.

It looked like Penn State was out of the question.

3. Skyler Is Meat

Skyler skipped the morning workout on Tuesday.

I was planning on confronting him then, before Coach Rollins showed up. It was the first time any of the starters had missed a morning workout and was completely unexpected. Chewy and Shorty looked lost without their fearless leader. I debated on having it out with them, but they wouldn't understand anyway. They were just Skyler's lackeys. Without his guidance it would have never even occurred to either of those big lummoxes to make Ethan surf on the conveyor belt.

I ran into Skyler in the cafeteria at lunchtime, but I couldn't get into it with him then. I wanted it to be some place where we would not be interrupted if it got physical. I desperately wanted to pound Skyler into the ground like he deserved, for more than just what he did to Ethan. He had it coming for the way he treated everyone. He had it coming for the way he treated Tabitha.

I changed my mind about Tabitha a few minutes later. After lunch I saw her leave the cheerleaders table and wrap herself around Skyler, kissing him passionately on the mouth. Even though she had helped him and the other guys by distracting me while they tormented Ethan, I never thought she would be back with the jerk. How could a guy fuck a girl and throw her out of the car with no pants and still get her to like him? No accounting for taste. Or brains.

Right then I did to Tabitha what I have always done to people. I wrote her off. The world is full of people. Why suffer the assholes when you can write them off and find the cool people? I didn't want revenge against her. I didn't want to try to make her feel bad. Nothing like that. As far as I was concerned she had just ceased to exist.

I made it through the entire day uneventfully. JK had taken to helping me get to Ethan after his classes when I had to come from one end of the school to the other, and that made everything easier. Ethan was never left in a position where the other football players could mess with him. During school hours either JK or myself was there with him when he wasn't in class.

After school I got Ethan home in record time and hurried back to practice. This was going to be it. This would be where I could get to Skyler. I wasn't exactly sure what I was going to say or do, and I hoped I could hold my temper, but something had to happen. I couldn't just let this thing with the conveyor belt situation sit inside and fester.

The team, as usual, was already out on the field when I got back from dropping Ethan off, so I dressed quickly and hit the field just in time to get in on a scrimmage. I dropped back behind the offensive line and stood to Skyler's right, waiting to hear the play. He never called it out. I looked at the positions of our receivers and guessed which play was coming. Skyler called the snap and I took my place in protecting him from the defense.

Turns out I guessed wrong. For some reason they were making this a running play, and no one told me. Skyler slammed the ball into my abdomen just about the time I was hit by our second string defensive tackle. I went down and fumbled the football.

Skyler laughed.

Mr. Walls came over and stood above me. "What the hell was that, Butcher?"

"I thought we were running a pass play for Steve!" I said, upset. I pointed at Steve Bunch and he just shrugged.

"This is a new play, to keep them on their toes," Walls said. A knowing look came over his face. "Skyler didn't tell you, did he?"

I stood up, shaking my head. "No, he didn't."

Mr. Walls showed me on the clipboard what the play was and where I was supposed to be. It was a great play and it would work, fooling everyone we played into thinking we were going with our standard slot pass. The play was perfect for a short yardage gain. It had an even better shot at working now that the running back knew the fucking play.

Walls called for us to get in formation again and we all began to quickly fall into place. I walked past Skyler on the way to my position and bumped him hard with my shoulder, knocking him back a step. "Don't fuck with me, Skyler. I've had about enough of your shit."

"Oooh, I'm so scared," Skyler mocked as he took his position in the shotgun.

He called for the snap and the formation exploded in action. I dropped out of my guard and moved behind Skyler to take the hand off, preparing to cut back to the center where Chewy and Shorty were making a hole. Skyler placed the ball firmly into my abdomen and I took hold, ready to break the line and bust out the run. But I fumbled again. Skyler, asshole that he is, held tight to the ball and pulled it from my grip, making it look like I had dropped it.

"Jesus Christ, Butcher! Hold onto the fucking ball!" Skyler shouted with a smirk. Everyone was staring at me like I was some kind of fuck-up.

I didn't say anything. I just lowered my head and tackled Skyler, driving him back and down like I had dozens of opposing quarterbacks. I heard the wind rush out of his lungs when we both hit the ground. I was on top of him, pressing hard into his abdomen and keeping him from sucking in any air. "I fucking told you, didn't I? Don't fuck with me you little bitch!"

Skyler couldn't get his breath even after I stood up off of him. Mr. Walls was on his knees beside the star quarterback hoping that he was all right. Coach Rollins was running across the field, having seen the incident from the other side of the field with Mr. Buck and the first string defense.

Myself, I was feeling really good about putting Skyler down. There was no permanent injury, I was sure, and I assumed he would have likely learned a valuable lesson about pissing me off. Even though we were on the same team, I was *still* the Butcher and Skyler was *still* made out of meat.

"Blake! Change your shoes and hit the track! Now!" Coach Rollins screamed in my face when he got there. I didn't hesitate, I just headed to the locker room to get out of my cleats to do my punitive running. I didn't mind, though. It was worth it.

Mr. Walls had gotten Skyler to his feet when I heard the bastard laugh. "Have a nice run, Butcher!"

I turned around then and saw Coach Rollins walking over to Skyler. "Are you okay?"

Skyler stretched his neck a little, "Yeah, I'm fine."

"You're sure?" Coach Rollins asked. "No damage? Nothing hurt after that hit?"

"No, I'm good," Skyler smiled.

"Great," Coach Rollins said, hooking a thumb toward me. "Then you can join him, smart ass. Change your shoes and hit the track. You've got one minute to get back out here and start running!"

"What?" Skyler whined, a look of abject shock on his face. "But I… but he… but… but… but…"

"But but but… you sound like a goddamned motorboat! Get your ass in there and get your shoes changed! You're running with Blake!"

I had turned around and was headed for the locker room again when I heard Skyler speak again.

"How many laps, Coach?" Skyler asked.

"The rest of practice. You're running until I say to quit!" Coach Rollins turned to Mr. Walls. "Mark, take my bicycle and pace them. I want them running together. And keep them quick."

Mr. Walls nodded and headed for the locker room. That's where Coach Rollins kept his bike.

For the remaining hour and forty-five minutes of practice, Skyler and I ran around the track, side by side, keeping pace with Mr. Walls, who seemed to be enjoying himself. He kept just ahead of us, making us constantly work to stay up with him.

When practice was over and we saw the team head into the locker room, Mr. Walls poured on the speed and made us run extra hard for the last stretch of the lap leading up to Coach Rollins. I was exhausted, but I think Skyler was worse off. Quarterbacks always have it a little easier than everyone else. If they want it that way, that is. For me, running was almost effortless back then. The fact that we ran for so long that day was the only thing that got to me.

Coach Rollins stood between Skyler and I as we stood there on the track, bent over and sucking air. "Are we going to have any more problems, gentlemen?"

Skyler shook his head no, still fighting for his breath. I had recovered mostly and I stood up and looked Coach Rollins in the eye. "No. It's cool."

"See that it is! I'm not a babysitter and this ain't track and field. We're going to play football. If you two don't want to play football you can run at every goddamned practice from now on! Understood?"

Skyler nodded wearily.

"Understood," I said.

"Shower up and get the hell out of here!"

4. Dinner At Ethan's House

After the debacle at practice on Tuesday, everything else went fine. I avoided Skyler and he avoided me. During school he walked on the other side of the hall when we passed and he left me, and Ethan, alone in the cafeteria. At practice on Wednesday and Thursday he kept it professional, if not a little cold.

I didn't care. I didn't need, or even want, to be his friend. We were just on the same football team and that was it. Being the statistic whore that he was, Skyler realized that he needed me, perhaps, more than anyone else on the team. I was the best running back in the state, and if not for the threat of my big run he wouldn't have anywhere near the level of success in his passing game. When they had to hold guys back on the line to stop me it opened up the receivers, allowing Skyler to burn them deep. He might have hated my guts, but he wanted to win. He would learn to tolerate me if he had to.

In just a few dry runs on Wednesday we nailed the new play that led to the trouble on Tuesday. By Thursday we had it perfected and ready to drop into a game, should the proper situation arise.

Best of all, they had left Ethan alone since Monday. We got through three whole days without one single incident of Skyler or his goons picking on Ethan.

Linda met me at the door when I dropped Ethan off after school on Thursday. "Hi, Ronald."

"Hi," I said, dodging Ethan as he nearly barreled me over running to his mother.

"Hey, I was wondering if you wanted to take me up on that dinner?" Linda asked, opening the door for Ethan and stepping onto the porch. "I'm making spaghetti and meatballs tonight. It's about the best thing I make."

"Sounds great!" I said enthusiastically. But not too enthusiastically, I hoped. I knew full well that I had a crush on Linda Miles, it just seemed really inappropriate for me to put that vibe out there, considering the situation. She was almost twice my age, she was my friend's mom, and she had a boyfriend. I had to tone it down.

"Good. How's seven o'clock?" she asked.

"Seven works for me," I said, knowing that I would have come over at three in the morning if she had asked.

Practice that afternoon seemed to drag on. I didn't want to be out their grinding out runs and working on defense. I wanted to get home and get ready for Linda.

The only thing I could do was throw myself headlong into practice and not think about it. Being in a hurry to get home wasn't going to make seven o'clock get there any quicker.

There was a certain connection between Linda and I. Both of us knew it, too. We spent any time we were near each other wordlessly denying it, but it was definitely there. It was an interesting predicament I found myself in. For the first time since I had become sexually active I was facing a woman who I just couldn't walk up and take whenever I wanted. But not only did I have to control myself, strangely enough I *wanted* to control myself. I really liked the feeling of added maturity expected from me from an older woman.

I found myself humming the tune to *Mrs. Robinson* while I jerked off in the shower before heading over to dinner.

Ethan met me at the door, looking for all the world that if he had a tail it would be wagging feverishly. "Butchie!"

"Hey Ethan!" I said, genuinely glad to see him.

The smell wafting out from the open door grabbed my nose and virtually dragged me into the house. The spaghetti sauce smelled unbelievably good. I walked in the house and followed the aroma right into the kitchen where Linda was in the process of straining the pasta in the sink.

"Hi, Ronald," she said barely looking up. "Your timing is excellent. We're just about ready."

"Is there anything I can do?" I asked, even though I was a complete waste of space when it came to kitchen work. Anything beyond microwave burritos and I was lost.

"No, I've got it. Just give me a few minutes and I'll call you guys in."

With that, I allowed Ethan to lead me back into the living room and sat down with him in front of the television. He had been watching a movie called *S-s-s-s* about a guy who was turning into a cobra. As titles went I thought it was a good one.

Soon enough, Linda was calling us back into the kitchen and Ethan clicked off the tube before heading in. I waited and followed him to the table. Linda had laid out a nice spread for us. There was a tall tapered candle burning in the center of the table and three heaping plates of spaghetti covered in sauce that was thick with meatballs. Some seriously aromatic garlic bread rested on small plates next to the spaghetti. The silverware was laid out on nicely folded cloth napkins and an empty wine glass sat near the plates on the ends of the table. Ethan's place had a large glass of chocolate *Quik* in front of it.

Linda was at the counter working a corkscrew on a bottle of red wine. "I'm having wine. Would you like some, Ronald?"

I was a little taken aback at Linda's offer of alcohol. And although I didn't really like wine, I said yes. That's what adults drank, I figured, so what better way to demonstrate my maturity. Linda poured two glasses and we had a seat.

"Everything looks great... and smells even better," I said, feeling my stomach growl. For my stomach, the smell of the food was like blood in the water and I was working up to a feeding frenzy. Back then I could seriously tear up some food. The constant working out kept me ravenous.

"Thank you, Ronald! I hope it tastes as good," Linda said, taking a seat.

"Linda?" I asked.

"Yes?"

"Could you do me a favor?"

"Sure. What is it?"

"Could you call me Butcher? I really don't like to be called Ronald."

She just smiled. "I'll try. I really don't feel comfortable calling you by a nickname, though. It seems so… impersonal. But I'll try."

"Thank you."

The spaghetti and meatballs was incredible. I had always loved my mother's cooking, but Linda's spaghetti and meatballs blew Mom's away. I'd never tell Mom that, though.

"Ethan and I have a date on Saturday," Linda announced, washing down a bite with some wine. "Don't we Ethan?"

Ethan just nodded, not looking up from his plate. He had sauce smeared all around his mouth and a huge glob of spaghetti hanging from it and down onto the plate. Ethan couldn't have cared less about Saturday night right then.

"Charlie is taking both of us out for dinner and then to a movie. Whatever Ethan wants to see."

"That's nice. So Charlie's coming around in his thinking now?" I asked, not wanting to say the wrong thing.

"Well... not exactly. But he's going to try. I talked to him about it the other night. Let him know that I wasn't totally pleased with how things went and told him what I expected in our relationship. What I needed from him."

"He was okay with it then, I assume?"

Linda shrugged, but smiled. "He said he was."

That shrug and smile didn't look good. I got the impression that Charlie was less than forthcoming with Linda. And she knew it. Still, she wanted so desperately to believe him that she was willing to give him the benefit of the doubt. All I could think to do was to say, "Good luck."

The food was excellent, the conversation was engaging, and Ethan was a mess. All too soon it was over. I offered to help Linda clear the table, but she would have none of it. She supervised Ethan as he cleaned himself up and then set to work cleaning up the rest of the kitchen. "Ethan loves spaghetti, but it always gives him trouble."

I nodded, noticing that he had a few large splashes of sauce in his eyebrows and some on his right ear.

"I need to get Ethan into the bathtub to get him ready for bed. If you have a seat in the living room we can talk a little bit while he's in the bath."

I had a seat while Linda worked on getting Ethan ready for bed. She joined me on the couch in no time. "I gave him his submarines and diver men, he'll be occupied for a while."

Linda sighed and looked at the television, even though it was turned off. She clicked it on then turned it down real low, mainly for background noise. It helped ease an uncomfortable silence. After a few long seconds she spoke. "You know, I can't tell if Charlie is serious or not. But he says he's willing to try and that's better than what I usually get."

"Maybe so. But is it good enough?" I asked. I didn't feel like I could tell her to abandon Charlie summarily when she had spent so much time being lonely. But being a guy, and a longtime asshole, I saw exactly what Charlie was doing. I thought she saw it too, she was just refusing to acknowledge it. Charlie was treating her the same way I had treated girls all through high school. He got what he was after and now the reality of dealing with her and her life was too much.

"It's good enough for now, I guess," Linda said, easing into the couch and becoming more comfortable. Her expression changed suddenly. "This really sucks!"

I simply nodded.

"Is my life really so fucking awful that no one would want to share it?" Linda asked, exasperated. She threw up her hands. "I don't think it's that bad. I mean, sure, I'm struggling financially, but I keep the bills paid. Ethan is slow, but he's a great kid. I can't figure out what is so fucking terrible about being with me!"

"There would be nothing at all terrible about being with you," I said, trying not to betray my crush. "Anyone who doesn't see it that way isn't worth being with in the first place. Charlie is the first guy you've been out with in a long time, right? Don't hang all your hopes and dreams on him. If he's not the one, turn him away and find someone else. There is someone out there who would jump at the chance to be with you. And Ethan. A lot of people. You've just got to meet them first."

At that she smiled. "You're such a sweet kid."

Kid? Fuck.

"If you were ten years older..." she said flirtatiously.

I wanted to say, "To hell with those ten years. Why not give me a shot?" Instead, I said, "Yeah, if only..."

Too soon she had to get Ethan out of the bathtub and I had to go. I hated to leave. It was torturing me, being so near someone I was so taken with and not being able to do anything about it, but I was enjoying the torment.

Linda gave me a sad-eyed kiss on the cheek as I left. "Goodnight, Ronald."

"See you in the morning."

5. Taking Out the Titans

Friday night brought another home game. We were hosting the North Ledford Titans.

The biggest threat in playing the Titans is that they had a monstrous defense. The game was going to be a matter of who broke when the irresistible force met the immovable object. We had them hands down on offense and our defense had only allowed one score all season up to that point, thanks to our third string laying down for the fucking Jaguars, but their defense was touted to be as good as ours.

Luke Staniak was their biggest weapon. Six foot six and close to three hundred pounds, so far he had proven to be a virtually unstoppable pass rusher. He was second only to myself in the state. The difference was in our styles. I was a speed rusher with some strength, and he was a power rusher with a little speed. I had him by three sacks going into the game and it would be essentially up to me to maintain my lead in that statistic. Once Staniak got past Chewy and Shorty, which he would, it was up to me to stop him long enough for Skyler to get the throw off. I would be staying back to protect Skyler throughout most of the game.

Coach Rollins walked us through the game plan in the locker room and I knew right then that I may not get the chance to score that night. The coaching staff was so concerned with Staniak that I was relegated to blocking for the most part. I was okay with that, but if the opportunity came to run the ball I wanted to ram it down their throats.

Everything would have been fine, probably just another of our average high scoring blowouts, if Skyler had just been able to keep his mouth shut until after the game. That was simply too much to ask.

Late in the third quarter, in the huddle, Skyler started his shit. Why he did it, I don't know. I was his last line of protection and I was doing a great job. Staniak had gotten past Chewy and Shorty routinely, but I stopped him every time. Staniak never even got a hand on Skyler throughout nearly three full quarters. We were up 56-0 with a little more than a minute to go in the third quarter when he started in on me.

"Butcher, keep your head in the game. Staniak is getting close," was all he said first.

He was way out of line, but I said nothing. It was just Skyler being Skyler. Staniak got some pressure on him and he hurried a pass, nearly getting it intercepted. It was totally Skyler's own fault, but taking blame wasn't his style. I didn't want to get him flustered and make him play worse, so I just shook off what he said and did my job.

The next down was almost exactly the same thing. I had Staniak stopped, but he was close, and Skyler threw another one away. Skyler came back bitching again. "Butcher, get your head out of your ass and block that sonofabitch!"

"I stopped him. Just throw the goddamned ball and quit whining!" I retorted after the second haranguing. Skyler shot me an evil look.

Third and ten, we called another pass play and Skyler hit Steve Bunch along the sideline, getting the first down and stopping the clock. However, Staniak did get a hand on him this time. Skyler went down kind of hard, but he had already gotten the pass off. Skyler called for a huddle and we huddled up.

"Blake, if you would spend as much time thinking about football as you do playing with that fucking retard then Staniak wouldn't be touching me!" Skyler bitched.

"Maybe the Gruesome Twosome could slow him down a bit before he gets to me. He's blowing right past you guys!" I said, directing the last part to Chewy and Shorty. They said nothing because I was right.

"What the fuck? Is that retard sucking your dick or something? What's the deal?" Skyler said, for no apparent reason. "Get your head back in the game! This guy is killing me out there."

Skyler and I had vastly different definitions of killing. I was holding the second best pass rusher in the league to zero sacks in three quarters almost single-handedly. Staniak only touched him once and it was too late to matter. By anyone else's definition I was doing a phenomenal job.

"Are you going to call a play or are you just going to fucking cry?" I asked, agitated. We were running out of time and all he had done was bitch and insult me.

Skyler backed off and called a play. The same play that they had just stopped us on twice in a row before the completed pass. It was a bad call. They were going to eat us up on it again.

"What about the new play?" I asked. "They're expecting the pass. We line up like that and I can break off a run and they'll never expect it."

"No," Skyler said, standing up. "I call the plays. We're passing. Break!"

We took the formation and waited for the count. Skyler called for the snap and Staniak came through the line, untouched. He was building up a head of steam coming around Chewy and when he was clear of the line he really poured it on. Staniak had the look in his eyes. I knew the look. It was the same one I got when I desperately wanted to crush a quarterback. He was snorting like a bull, his eyes red and his face flushed. Staniak wanted this sack badly. He wanted it so bad he could taste it.

So, I let him have it.

Instead of putting myself in the way, I dropped back a step and then feigned a slip on the grass.

The crash was horrendous. Staniak was almost at a full out run when he slammed into Skyler's blind side, slamming him to the ground and knocking the ball loose. The ball wobbled toward me and I picked it up, debating quickly about whether to just fall on it or try to make a play. The field looked to be fairly wide open to the right side, so I took off.

JK came and gave me a great block and I got to the sideline. I wanted to be able to step out and stop the clock if necessary. There was time for another play if they stopped me, but we had to get the clock stopped.

No one else even got close to me and I ran the ball in for a touchdown.

After the play was dead Coach Rollins and Mr. Buck ran out onto the field. Skyler hadn't gotten up. He was lying on the ground and holding his knee, rocking back and forth in pain. I trotted back to the scene of the collision with everyone else. When I got close enough I could hear Skyler. "Blake! You motherfucker! You did that on purpose! You did that on purpose!"

He kept screaming that and I walked away to let the medics come out and get him. Staniak walked past me on the field and gave me a suspicious and knowing look. He didn't know why I had let him through, but he knew that I had.

Greg Nelton, our second string quarterback, came in for the fourth quarter while Skyler was taken to the hospital for x-rays. We didn't score again, but we held the Titans scoreless and ended up with a 63-0 victory.

Myself, I had a bit of an '*oh shit, what have I done?*' moment about halfway through the fourth quarter when our offense kept going three and out. If Skyler was seriously hurt then our great run could be finished. We only had one more game in the regular season, but then the sectionals started. Then regionals and, finally, state.

Greg Nelton was a nice guy, but not much of a quarterback. If we were stuck with him in the sectionals it was going to be a very short post season.

For a second I almost regretted letting Skyler get crushed.

Almost.

Chapter Ten

1. Hillbilly Jerkatorium

For the second week in a row I skipped all the after game partying. I went right home and got right into bed.

Saturday morning I woke up before my alarm clock and got to the school well before Randy and Hub. Not that I liked cleaning the school, but I was ready to seize the day and get it over with. This week and then next week and I was done with my punishment. I could go back to enjoying our after game celebrations when we were into the post season.

Randy and Hub pulled up together, both of them looking like they had been scraped off the bottom of someone's shoe. I got out of my car and met them as they got out of Randy's car. The first thing I noticed was that they reeked of stale sweat, cigarette smoke, and last night's beer. The alcohol smell seeped through their skin and lightly stung the insides of my nostrils. They were squinting in the early rays of the morning sun.

"Morning," I called out.

Randy and Hub buried their faces in their hands and waved me off. Randy groaned and hissed, "Not so fucking loud! Dang!"

"Keep it down for a little bit. It was really drunk out last night," Hub said, smiling through a stinky burp.

In order to appease their aching heads Randy and Hub declared that I was going to have to work extra hard and take up the slack for them. When I protested Randy reminded me that I really had no choice. They were the only ones who could vouch for me that I was even there. If they said I didn't show up then Principal Greenwood would be on my ass.

They worked slowly, like zombies in coveralls, shambling from classroom to classroom. The only real effort made by either of them was when Randy would tell me to work faster or we'd never get done. I was doing four classrooms for each one they finished. This was bullshit of the highest order. I didn't mind having to work to pay off my punishment, but I was not happy about being a slave to a couple of hung over rednecks. I thought about walking out, let the chips fall where they may. But I chose to stick it out. Maybe once they got moving the hangovers would go away and they'd do their part.

At about the same time as the week before, Randy and Hub got me started cleaning the bathrooms and then they disappeared. I worked for about five minutes and I was getting madder by the second. I finally threw the mop down and stomped off looking for Randy and Hub. I was going to tell them how it was going to be and if scrawny little Randy or that fat tub of shit Hub gave me any grief I was going to pound them. I had no doubt in my mind that I could beat both of their asses at the same time.

Making me do all the work while they lounged around and nursed their hangovers was pissing me off big time.

I went looking around the school for them, particularly Randy, seeing as he was the boss, and I was going to set everything straight once and for all. I was not their damn slave and I wasn't going to allow them to treat me like one. Everywhere I looked, though, I didn't see them. I decided to look out into the parking lot to see if they were in Randy's car, or if they had maybe even left. As I turned out of the large foyer and looked down the hall by the gym, I found them.

Well, actually I found Hub's cart. It was parked outside the broom closet down by the gym. The hall was completely empty save for the custodial cart. I walked down to the broom closet and then I could see Randy's mop and bucket behind Hub's cart. I looked up and down the hallway again and saw no one. The girl's volleyball practice was over because I couldn't hear noise coming out of the gym. The doors at the end of the gym hall led out into the parking lot and I could see a lot of cars out there. The girls volleyball team was still here. I instantly put two and two together and opened the door to the broom closet.

And I was right.

Randy and Hub spun around, looks of terror on their faces. They were both kneeling on the floor in the broom closet and peering through small holes in the wall. A shared wall between the broom closet and the girls locker room.

"Shut the fuckin' door, you moron!" Hub hissed excitedly, then hurried back to putting his eye to the wall. He looked even worse than he had the week before when he come back to help me clean the bathrooms and he was flushed and sweating. Hub was breathing like he was running a marathon. Randy said nothing and went right back to peering through his hole.

Inside the broom closet I could hear the water running in the shower on the other side of the wall. Hub was wheezing and rubbing the taut crotch of his coveralls. Randy was trying to hide the fact that he had been masturbating before I came in. I turned around and walked out of the broom closet.

Those sick fucks were in there jacking off together while peeking in on the girls volleyball team while they showered. Hub looked like he was on the verge of a stroke, while he stroked. I stood on the opposite side of the hall across from the broom closet and waited for them to exit their jerkatorium.

A few minutes later, Hub and Randy came out of the closet, both of them sweating profusely and casting a glazed look in the brightness of the hall. They just looked at me, but they said nothing. So I spoke.

"I'm fucking done! I'm not cleaning another damned thing," I said angrily, leaning against the wall with my arms folded. "If you tell Greenwood that I'm not here doing my work, I'm telling him about your little peepshow."

"Ain't no way we can get done today without you helpin' us," Hub said, still breathless.

"That's your fucking problem!" I walked away, down the hall and out into the parking lot. I heard Randy telling Hub to just let me go. He knew that I had them by the balls and there was nothing they could do about it.

I could have went home and that would have been that.

But I didn't.

For some reason I felt like Randy and Hub had to be stopped. It just seemed too creepy and disgusting to let it go.

Out in the parking lot I found Betty Beatty's car and waited beside it. She was the captain of the volleyball team and I had something I thought she might want to hear. While we weren't friends, per se, we had known each other since kindergarten. She also played the snare drum in the band, so she was at all the football games. She was pretty hot. If she weren't a lesbian, as was rumored, I wouldn't have minded taking a shot at her.

Shortly, the girls began filing out of the school, laughing and playing around. Betty came out last, talking to one of the other girls. They all separated at their cars and went about their way. Betty saw me at her car and approached cautiously. "Tell me that you aren't waiting there to ask me out."

I laughed. "No, I'm not. I've got something to tell you and I think you might want to hear it."

"I'm listening."

"You know those two janitors that clean the school on Saturdays?" I asked.

"Yeah. The smelly drunks."

"That's them," I said, deciding the best way to tell her what I had to tell her was just to blurt it out. "Well, they've made holes in the wall of the broom closet outside the gym and they are watching you girls take showers after practice."

"What? WHAT?" Betty screamed. "You've got to be kidding!"

"No. I caught them doing it just a few minutes ago."

"You caught them? What happened? They wouldn't let you look, so you're telling on them?" Betty asked skeptically and very agitated.

"You know, I didn't have to tell you."

I explained my situation with having to help clean the school and everything. "While I told them I wouldn't tell Greenwood, I didn't say I wouldn't tell anybody. I just think you and the other girls need to know what's going on."

Betty was livid, pacing back and forth in front of her car. A tremor of disgust shook her body. "Ewwww! Those mother fuckers!"

"I've told you. Now I'm going to let you handle it," I said, walking away from her and heading toward my car.

"Ron!" Betty called out behind me. I turned around.

"What?"

"Thanks," she said gravely and grudgingly.

With a nod and a wave I made my way to my car.

2. Early Morning Ass Chewing

I went into the gym Monday morning knowing that there was going to be Hell to pay.

And I was quickly proven right. Coach Rollins was waiting for us when we got there. One of the janitors, not

Randy or Hub, let us in the school as usual, but when we turned on the lights to the gym, Coach Rollins was standing at parade rest in the middle of the floor. From behind his back he pulled out a newspaper. "Skyler. Blake. My office. NOW!"

The reason I knew there was going to be trouble was because my dad had thrown the newspaper in my face Sunday morning. The Saturday paper was just Bill Morgan's usual blow-by-blow account of the game, making his home team seem like white knights on the road to glory. His Sunday piece was a whole different thing.

For one thing, there usually wasn't a Sunday piece on us during the season. During the post-season tournament there was always something in the paper about the Mims Mustangs everyday, but during the season we only got the standard game rundown. Sunday's piece wasn't your typical glowing poetic prose preaching the virtues of the Almighty Mustangs. This was one large headline and all it said was "TROUBLE?"

Apparently when Skyler went down and they were carrying him off the field to the ambulance he was ranting about how I blew the block on purpose because I was jealous of him being the star. Morgan was standing there beside the medics, walking along and taking everything down. From the tone of the article I would imagine that the idea of trouble between Skyler and myself was deeply disturbing to Morgan. His words were little more than fearful doomsaying predictions about our chances if Skyler and I couldn't get our act together for the good of the team. The article stopped short of saying that I had let Staniak through on purpose, but considering that Skyler's enraged ranting was the only source for the piece it was implied that I did.

The issue wasn't whether I let Staniak through so that he could crush Skyler. I did. The real issue was that no matter what anyone said, they couldn't prove it. All I had to do was swallow a little bit of pride and just say that Staniak beat me fair and square and no one could prove otherwise.

Skyler came in limping that day, even though the x-rays came out negative. It seemed very likely that Skyler was never hurt at all, especially with the speed of which he seemed to recover that week. He was just being his usual whining, crying self when he left the game Friday night. Skyler was always a little bitch.

Coach Rollins' office was just down the hall from the gym and Skyler and I followed him there wordlessly. Skyler did begin to exaggerate his limp a little more on the way. I just shook my head and looked away from him in disgust. What a pussy! Fucking quarterbacks! Sheesh!

In his office, Coach Rollins sat behind his desk and motioned for us to take the seats in front of his desk. "This has got to stop and stop now."

I looked at Skyler and he looked at me, neither of us having anything to say. And neither of us wanting to be the first to say the wrong thing.

"Blake!" Coach Rollins said with authority. "Did you blow the block and let Skyler get sacked on purpose?"

"No, I didn't." I hated lying to Coach Rollins, but the truth just wasn't going to work.

Coach Rollins nodded his head. "Fair enough."

"Bullshit! You fucking liar, Blake!" Skyler shouted.

Before I could say anything Coach Rollins stood up and leaned over his desk. "I said 'fair enough'. It's settled! Butcher didn't do it on purpose and that's that! Understood?"

Skyler wasn't happy and he just sat back hard into his chair.

"Understood?" Coach Rollins asked again, but more forcefully.

Skyler nodded. "Understood."

"I'm not going to have this shit! Especially now!" Coach Rollins said, sitting back down. "We've had a great season. One more game and we go undefeated. You saw what happened when Skyler left the game the other night. We didn't score again. That is unacceptable!"

Coach Rollins punctuated the last word by slamming the rolled up newspaper on his desk.

"What is worse is that it is bad for morale. The team looks up to both of you and if one of you is having a bitch fit it hurts everyone. The whole town is behind us and it bothers the town when they see something like this. We've got some damage control to do."

"Like what?" I asked.

"Bill Morgan will be here after school today. Both of you are going to give him an interview and answer every question he asks. And you are going to answer him the right way, if you know what I mean. This is not the forum for you two to be sniping at each other for any reason. Not even over Tabitha Butler."

I said nothing. It wasn't about Tabitha at all. It was about what Skyler did to Ethan and the way he was such a prick to me on the field. It was easier not to go into it, so I didn't.

"You're going to be interviewed together," Coach Rollins continued. "I want Bill Morgan to think that you guys are the best of friends by the time he leaves here tonight. Am I clear?"

"Yes," Skyler and I answered in unison.

"Get back to the gym and work then. And Derek, take it easy on that leg."

"Yes Coach," Skyler said, making a show of his difficulty in rising from the chair in such pain.

I didn't wait for Skyler, I just headed back to the gym at a brisk walk. Before I entered, though, I looked down the hall and saw Skyler approaching with a spring in his step and a shit-eating grin on his face.

That hurt leg appeared to be all right to me.

3. Putting Up a Good Face

I had all day to steel myself for the interview after school, and it was a good thing. Even up to the point where I was driving back to the school after dropping Ethan off at home, I was still unsure of my ability to be civil and do what Coach Rollins had ordered.

The first order of business was the report on Skyler's health and likelihood of his playing on Friday. Bill Morgan was very happy when he learned that Skyler expected to play and thought he'd be at one hundred percent by game time. I just quietly smirked, knowing that Skyler was at one hundred percent right that very moment.

Soon enough, Morgan moved on to talking to both Skyler and I together.

All I could think about was what I *wanted* to say, and not what I *had* to say. I *wanted* to tell Bill Morgan that this whole thing got blown out of proportion because Derek Skyler was a little crybaby bitch. I *had* to say that everything was really fine and that there was no truth to the rumors that there was trouble on the team. I *wanted* to tell Bill Morgan what a whiny little prick, full of ego and entitlement Skyler was. I *had* to say that Skyler and I were good friends on and off the field. I *wanted* to punch Skyler in his smirking face right there during the interview. Instead, I *had* to smile and shake his hand.

The interview was held in Coach Rollins' office with Skyler and I sitting in the same chairs we had earlier that morning. Coach Rollins said nothing in the interview, he just hovered around us as we answered all of Morgan's questions. Truthfully, Coach Rollins' presence was probably the only thing keeping me on an even keel. Skyler said all the right things. It was just the way he said them that made me want to smash his face.

In all fairness, Skyler was also forced to say good things about me that he didn't feel. The only thing either of us had no trouble saying was that we respected each others playing ability. The more we could stay on that topic, rather than letting Morgan dig for our personal differences the better things went. It's easy when what you're saying is true, whether it is actually relevant or not. I lied to Morgan much easier than I lied to Coach Rollins that morning when I told him that Staniak just beat me that time. That was an easy lie. But everything else was completely true.

Derek Skyler was the absolute best quarterback in the state. Bar none. He had an arm that could throw through a brick wall. His ability to read defenses and call plays was unparalleled at the high school level.

About me, Skyler said that I was the best running back he had ever seen outside of the pros. He said he knew that if they needed one yard or ten yards he could give the ball to me and know that I would die, if I had to, trying to get those yards.

The final question was a good one.

"Derek, do you trust Ronald Blake to block for you now, after the big hit you took on Friday?" Morgan asked. I could see as he spoke that it was the question he had been wanting to ask since he sat down with us.

Skyler looked at me, then at Coach Rollins. He leaned forward, closer to Morgan. "I'll put it like this..."

I didn't know what he was going to say. It wouldn't have surprised me one bit to hear him tear off on a rant against me, even after our enforced mutual ego stroking.

Skyler cleared his throat, more for effect than anything I assumed. "There is no one I would rather have blocking for me in the backfield than Butcher Blake. No one."

I could see Coach Rollins quietly let out the breath he had been holding.

Morgan asked for a final statement from us to close out the interview, and we gave him one. Skyler said it and I backed him up.

"Bill, I guarantee that this game on Friday against the Eastern Giants will be our best game of the year up to this point." Skyler sat back in his chair, all his smugness showing.

Morgan looked at me and I nodded. "Best game of the year. I promise."

That made Bill Morgan smile. On one hand it was nice to have someone so interested in the Mustangs that they lived for it like Morgan did. On the other hand, it was a little pathetic that a grown man lived so vicariously through the successes and failures of a high school football team.

Skyler and I shook his hand, thanked him for the interview and exited the office when Coach Rollins opened the door for us. We kept on our phony smiles and stepped into the hall, Coach Rollins shutting the door behind us.

"Now maybe if you can get your head out of that fucking retards ass you can actually back up those big words we just gave," Skyler sneered, back to his old nasty self.

I stepped up and got in his face, keeping my voice down so as not to tip off Bill Morgan that our act in the office was just a façade. "Maybe if you would mind your own fucking business and act like a football player instead of a whiny little bitch we could back up those big words!"

"You better back up off of me, Butcher. I mean it!"

"What are you going to do about it? Your goons aren't here. You want to go? Right now?"

"This is your last warning. I…" Skyler trailed off as the door to Coach Rollins office opened and Bill Morgan began walking out. Morgan looked up and saw us, toe to toe in the hall.

I leaned in to Skyler as if telling him a secret. "Pretend I'm saying something funny to you."

Skyler laughed quietly. I continued whispering.

"Now, nod, clap me on the shoulder and walk away. Say, 'Hey, see you in the gym' or something, and smile as you walk away."

Skyler nodded, clapped me on the shoulder with a laugh and turned around to walk away. He turned back, "You gonna meet us all at Sharky's?"

I faked a smile. "Yeah, I'll see ya there."

Skyler and I walked our separate ways down the hall, and I nodded to Bill Morgan as I passed him.

Coach Rollins had a suspicious look on his face, but he said nothing.

4. The Pep Rally

Things had changed for me at school that week. People looked at me differently.

Instead of being in awe of Butcher Blake, they seemed to see me as the guy who was willing to throw away their football season over a little tiff. I was the guy who allowed Derek Skyler to take a hit that could have ended his season, thus ending the Mustangs shot at the state championship. The other students looked at me like a traitor.

I noted happily, perhaps for the first time in my life, that I truly didn't care what they thought about me. I would continue playing football, I would continue crushing quarterbacks; I just wouldn't play their damn social games. The rest of the school didn't like me over a perceived infraction, and that was fine. It actually worked out great. Being so close to the status of persona non grata,

I was free to be myself and to take care of the things that I had to take care of.

People still stared at me when we walked through the halls, but it wasn't from fear and/or admiration, or the fact that I was babysitting that freaky slow kid, Teeth. It was because I, myself, had become the freak. I was one of the cool kids who had resigned my membership in their special little club. The word was out and so was I. I had been ostracized from my team, then from the cheerleaders, and now I was being ostracized from the rest of my fellow students.

But you know, I just looked at the situation like it says in the Bible.

Fuck 'em.

It's in there somewhere. Around Deuteronomy, I think.

Everything was going fine and I didn't mind all that much that I was on the outs with everyone. They were all caught up in the final game of the season, which was coming up the next Friday. Everybody wanted to see us go undefeated and the excitement level was high, despite the cold shoulder I was getting. I had to admit that I was enjoying it a little, the fact that I was able to be *almost* just a face in the crowd. It was pretty nice.

Until Friday afternoon, that is.

We got out of class early for a pep rally, hoping to stir the student body to a fevered pitch and get them to follow us out of town to play our final regular season game against the Giants. We expected a great turnout from our students, considering all that was riding on the game. Not only was it the last game, and our chance to go undefeated, but everyone knew that Coach Rollins had a serious hate-on for the Eastern Giants coaching staff. It had been big local news when the current Eastern coaches had drummed him out in order to get his job. Everyone wanted to see us just flat out kill the Giants.

The band geeks were in the gymnasium, jamming our school fight song and marching the perimeter of the gym floor, the cheerleaders were jumping around and doing their acrobatics, and the crowd was going wild. The team was waiting in the hall with Coach Rollins, watching through the skinny windows in the doors leading into the gym. Having that many people going nuts to celebrate something that you did is very intoxicating. Having that many people behind you is a godlike feeling. Pure, unadulterated hero worship.

The band came to a thunderous close and the crowd got even louder. On cue, before they could die down, Coach Rollins stepped through the doors into the gym and they erupted into much more explosive applause and cheering. He waved to everyone as he jogged to the center of the floor and out to the solitary microphone, waiting on its stand. With an arcing swing Coach Rollins swiped the microphone from it's clip and yelled into it, "HELLO MUSTANGS!"

The pressure on our eardrums increased with the further swelling of noise. You could feel the massive gymnasium pulse, as if it were breathing heavily, in and out.

It went on for what seemed like a very long time, Coach Rollins standing in the center of the gym, hands at his sides, waiting for them to quiet down a little. When they finally did, he spoke again.

"On behalf of *your* football team, I thank you," he began, stopping to let the students cheer some more. "It's been a great season, and the support you've shown us has been a major part of that success. Give yourselves a hand!"

And they did. A very boisterous hand at that. The noise trailed off a bit quicker this time, though.

"Without further ado, let me introduce your MIMS MUSTANGS FOOTBALL TEAM!"

Coach Rollins started with the defense, the unsung heroes of the sport. The second and third stringers were the first ones introduced at every pep rally, and while they were cheered very politely, the real raving was saved for the stars, of which I was one. And as such, I was told to wait and be introduced with the offense, even though I was also the big star on the defensive side of the ball.

The first real eruptions of noise happened when Shorty was introduced with the offensive linemen. Same thing with Chewy. The crowd was building itself up to near frenzy. They knew that they were getting close to the big heroes. The ones who would be responsible for bringing a state championship home to them. JK, Skyler, and I were the only ones left in the hall, besides the assistant coaches, who would come out last, and almost as an afterthought.

"JEROME 'HAMMERHEAD' KENT!" Coach Rollins shouted, and JK trotted out into the thrumming airwaves of the gym, hands over his head and fists pumping. I looked out into the gym and I watched JK run down the line of players, slapping high fives with the rest of the team.

I was next and I was ready, the energy was coursing through me and I was primed to run into the warm adoration awaiting me in the gym.

Coach Rollins called out, "RON 'THE BUTCHER' BLAKE!" and I burst out into the gym with the same energy I used to break through the opposing lines on the field.

Almost abruptly, the cheering dropped in volume, replaced by an equally loud chorus of boos. I didn't know how to handle it. I had never been booed before. And especially not in my own school. They hated me. It was painfully obvious that our special PR interview didn't work in swaying the perception of what happened.

It was crushing.

The worst part was that I didn't expect it to be. I thought I was completely over my dependency on peer acceptance, but there I was, feeling the air go out of the room and the wind going out of my sails. I could hear that there were still quite a few people cheering for me, but the booing seemed to keep getting louder, until the people cheering me were all but drowned out. I stopped in my tracks and didn't even finish running out to meet my team in the center of the floor. I stopped and looked around, taking in all the angry faces that were booing me. I looked behind me, to the other side of the gym, and I saw the discomfort of the band. I caught sight of Betty Beatty as she stood stoically in her band uniform, her snare drum hanging at her hip, and she looked really sympathetic. Some of the teachers were moving through the crowd of booing students and trying to shut them up.

Coach Rollins began shouting through the microphone for them to quiet down. He was not happy at the outburst that they dished out to me. After shouting, "HEY!" about ten times, the crowd finally quieted a little bit.

That's when I heard it.

"YAY BUTCHIE! YAY!"

I followed the sound and quickly tracked Ethan in the crowd with the other slow kids from his class. He was standing up and cheering, waving two purple and green crepe paper streamers awkwardly over his head. "YAY BUTCHIE! YAY!"

The remaining boos and cheers all stopped as everyone turned to look at Ethan. He kept right on cheering my name, an ear-to-ear jagged smile on his face. "YAY BUTCHIE! YAY!"

I waved to Ethan, and despite the crushing feeling of being turned on by my former worshippers; I had a smile of my own. I resumed my run and trotted out to the line of players. Everyone slapped me a high five, but not all of them meant it. I heard some snickering as I went by, many of them laughing at what Ethan had called me. I couldn't tell who was saying it, but I would hear someone say, "Butchie!" and laugh at the name. Butchie is just a lot less scary than Butcher, but as you know, it stuck.

Apparently Coach Rollins decided that it was best not to dwell on the negative and so he carried on. "And last, but certainly not least, your quarterback… DEREK SKYLER!"

The cheering erupted again as Skyler trotted out, favoring his leg that I supposedly caused to be hurt. He made his limp more pronounced and went down the line, slapping hands with his underlings. When he got down to me he leaned in and whispered, "Wow! They really fucking hate you!"

He laughed, I gave him my high five, and he took his place at the head of the line, as the assistant coaches were introduced. Coach Rollins went into his planned speech, trying to put all the booing and negativity behind us, and it seemed to work very well. The crowd was right back into it.

At one of the quieter points of the pep rally, JK leaned over to me and whispered in my ear.

"I don't think they were booing," he said.

I laughed. "Oh really?"

"Yeah, they were cheering. They were saying, 'BOO-TCHER! BOO-TCHER!'"

I almost hurt myself trying not to laugh out loud.

5. The Giant Killers

To say that we beat the Eastern Giants is a huge understatement. There have been prison rapes that were far less brutal than what we did to them.

A big part of the reason was that we had permission.

Before Coach Rollins came to be the coach at Mims, he was the coach for Eastern. The current coaching staff at Eastern had undermined him and stabbed him in the back to get him fired so that they could all take over the team, and that really stuck in Coach Rollins' craw. We all knew it bothered him whenever we played the Giants, but that year was especially bad because the year before we had lost to them in overtime.

Coach Rollins came into the locker room before the game and gathered us all around. We didn't go over plays, we didn't get a further lecture on their weak spots. He said what he needed to say to us.

"I don't want to beat this team. I want to DESTROY THEM!"

A loud cheer went up. Giving killers the order to kill is like handing them a blank check.

"I want to rip off their heads and piss in their skulls!" he exclaimed, stalking around the locker room like a caged lion. "No fucking mercy!"

We were getting pumped up just from his adrenaline. Energy crackled throughout the room and sizzled along our skins. Coach Rollins was on a dizzying rant. It was so frenetic that I didn't catch half of what he was saying, and I remember much less than that. I can clearly remember the last thing he said before we charged out onto the field, though.

"MAKE THESE MOTHER FUCKERS SLEEP IN THE WET SPOT!"

All year long everyone accused of us of running up the score on these teams. While we did score a lot, it wasn't our intention to embarrass anyone. We couldn't help it if we were just so much better than everyone else that they couldn't compete. You can't get a lead on a team and then lie down, they'll come back and bite you in the ass. We never intentionally ran up the score on anyone.

Until that night.

Coach Rollins had us going for two points every time we scored a touchdown. He wanted the score to be as high as we could get it. I scored five of our eleven touchdowns, one on a pass play, and I ran in for our two extra points nine times. The great thing is that they knew I was coming and they just couldn't stop me. Four of their offensive linemen ended up being taken off the field, three of them to the hospital. I hit the line every time with the intent to kill. Anyone who got in my way did so at their own peril. I hurt two of them and Chewy hurt two more.

On the defensive side of the ball is where I did most of the real damage, though. I took out their starting quarterback in the first quarter with a devastating sack. It was my third one of the game. In the second quarter I took out their second string quarterback with my fifth sack. My sixth sack took out their third stringer late in the third quarter. After that they put in a guy who had never played quarterback in his life, simply because he was the only thing they had left. We didn't hurt him, but we knocked the shit out of him the rest of the night. The team had twelve sacks, nine of them were mine. On the last sack of the game we had the Giants pressed back on their one-yard line. I hammered their fourth stringer and knocked the ball loose. Out of the corner of my eye I saw it rolling away from him and I dove on it, giving me my fifth touchdown and ninth sack, both in the same play.

The game ended when we stopped the Giants at mid-field with a crushing blow to their wide receiver. The score was 88-0.

The rest of the Mustangs charged onto the field to celebrate with the defense and I found myself earnestly shaking hands with Derek Skyler. We both had huge smiles on our faces, and at that moment everything between us was just fine. It wouldn't, couldn't, and didn't last, but right then we were the epitome of teammates. Which worked out great, considering that was exactly when Bill Morgan decided to snap his photograph for the sports section the next day. That one picture reassured the rest of the football fanatics at home that the trouble in paradise was either not true or a thing of the past.

For the first time in three weeks I got to go to the after game celebration and dance. I knew that I didn't have to be at the school in the morning to help Randy and Hub, so I just stayed up and partied. How many times in an athletic career does a team have an undefeated season? Not very damn many. We showered, took a rowdy bus ride home and went into the dance as soon as we arrived.

The dance was already underway when we got there, so when we walked in as a team the place erupted in resounding, boisterous cheers. The deejay knew to cut the sound because the music couldn't be heard over the din anyway.

That night we weren't just heroes.

We were gods.

Chapter Eleven

1. The Victory Celebration

The dance/victory celebration on Friday night wasn't the "real" victory celebration. That came on Saturday night at a private party held at the very same pole barn as the one where those two fuck-ups got Ethan stoned.

Although I really wasn't interested in going, I showed up, hoping to show some team solidarity. To be honest, I was partied out. I was thoroughly unimpressed with how much I, or anyone else, could drink. I no longer cared to be around the majority of the people who were there, players and cheerleaders and the other popular kids. I felt the way that I imagined old men must feel when witnessing the impetuousness of youth. I remembered feeling the same way as all the drunken kids, but it seemed so long ago.

I was just completely over it.

But still I went. I showed up late and left early, but everyone knew I was there, so my expected appearance was granted.

JK's brother's band was playing again, minus the mohawked bass player and his nagging girlfriend. The new bass player had a skinny tie and sunglasses, totally out of place with the rest of the band. He danced around like he thought he was in *The Breakfast Club* or something.

At a couch in the corner I saw Tabitha sitting astride Skyler's lap and they were making out. I breezed through the mingling, dancing guests, looking for JK, the only person there I was really interested in talking to. I finally found him in the back room with a couple other people and he was hitting the cobra bong with the skinny guy who had gotten Ethan all messed up. The skinny guy nodded as I walked up and gestured to the bong, offering me the next hit. I declined politely with a small wave.

JK held his smoke a long time and then finally exhaled, coughing a little. "Butcher! You gotta hit this shit! My man…"

Losing his recollection of the skinny guy's name he just pointed to him.

"Call me Cal," the skinny guy said, sticking his hand out and we shook.

JK nodded. "My man Cal got some wicked weed!"

I declined again. Weed was just never my thing. "Nah, I'm good."

One of the other guys sitting around the table graciously stepped up and took my hit.

"Oh! Did you hear what happened at the school today?" JK asked excitedly.

"No. What?" I asked, not all that interested.

"That fat fuckin' hillbilly janitor fuckin' died!" JK exclaimed.

"What? Hub died?" I was shocked.

"I don't know his name. That fat one that was always sweating all over the place."

"Shit! What happened?"

"Betty Beatty and a bunch of the girls caught him and the little weasel-lookin' janitor guy peeking on them through a hole in the shower room wall," JK explained, and I knew exactly what he was going to say. "The volleyball team went in to take their showers and a few of the girls went outside and opened up the broom closet and those two rednecks were in their jacking off. The fat one freaked out, had a massive heart attack and dropped dead right there in the hall outside the gym!"

"No fucking way!"

"Still had his dick out!"

Damn! I didn't know Hub was going to keel over. I felt horrible right then, knowing that I may have been responsible for his death. I wondered if maybe I handled the whole thing wrong. Maybe I should have gone to Principal Greenwood about it instead of telling Betty Beatty. Maybe Hub would still be alive.

What little part of me still felt like partying flooded out of my system and I stood there in the haze of marijuana smoke feeling cold. "What happened to the girls?"

"Nothing," JK replied, reaching for the bong again. "They didn't do anything but open the door and yell at them. The guy must have just had a bad heart."

I hung around a few more minutes, but it got to be too much. I just wanted to leave. I wanted to go home and be alone. Alone with my guilt. I could only imagine how Betty and the other girls must have felt, watching a hugely fat man die of a heart attack with his dick in his hand while they were yelling at him. I said my goodbyes and turned to head back to my car and off for home. To everyone else it was kind of a joke, but to me it really hit home. Intentional or not I had taken a direct action that resulted in a man's death. A party just wasn't the place for me.

I was just outside the pole barn's big doors when Stacy Lampley caught up to me. She wanted to talk on and on about really boring mundane stuff and all I wanted to do was get to my car and get the hell out of there. If she'd had something important to say, fine. I could hang around all day and talk to her. If all she was going to do was hem and haw about the weather and the football games, I would just as soon stop talking and leave. She was just sort of rattling, her words coming nine miles a minute, but saying nothing.

"Stacy, I really need to go. I have to get home," I said politely, stopping her rambling in its tracks.

A stricken look crossed her face briefly and then disappeared. She went back to being her bubbly cheerleader self. "Okay. Maybe I'll call you later and we can talk more."

"Sure," I said noncommittally, already walking toward my car and leaving her standing by herself in the big open doorway.

I drove home slowly, soothed by the sound of the engine. Mom and Dad were out when I got there, but they came home shortly after I arrived and went right to bed. I stayed up and watched Saturday Night Live for a little while, drinking beer after beer and staring at the screen more than actually watching it, though. Matthew Broderick was the host, which was okay, but I just couldn't get into the musical guest. The Sugarcubes just didn't do it for me.

About one o'clock in the morning the phone rang and I had to go out. Linda Miles was crying. I could tell she had been drinking and she said she needed to talk to me.

I told her I would be right there.

2. Charlie Whitman is a Pigless Dick

Normally I wouldn't have driven after killing a six-pack, but I knew that Linda needed me or she wouldn't have called.

She was waiting on the front porch for me when I pulled up, the porch light shining out into the darkness of the sleeping neighborhood. A wine bottle hung at her side, mascara trails streaking down her face, smudged where she had tried to wipe away her tears. She was still dressed for her date, and it would have been really hot if not for the disheveled appearance her emotions had wrought.

Linda seemed to be holding things together pretty well until the very second I stepped up on the first porch step. Then the waterworks started anew.

"Thanks for coming, Ronald," she whined, slumping back against the side of her house.

"What's wrong?"

"That… that… mother fucker!" she hissed through a heavy slur, spitting a little bit on the hard F. Wobbling to her full height she stood up from her resting place on the siding. Then she got loud. "That mother fucker fucked me! And I'm a mother! Charles is a mother fucker!"

She laughed at her own joke.

I looked around the still and peaceful neighborhood and wondered how long it would remain still and peaceful with Linda swearing loudly into the night. "Why don't we go inside? You're going to wake up your neighbors."

Linda's face grew serious and she tottered. She brought a finger to her lips. "Oh! Shhhhhhhhhhh!"

With a hand on her elbow I opened the door and helped her stagger into the house and guided her to the couch, where she plopped down gracelessly. She handed the wine bottle to me and I took a big drink and handed it back. It was almost full, so I surmised that it was the second bottle of the night for Linda.

"Charlie is a pigless dick!" she half shouted, suddenly remembering that Ethan was asleep in the next room and quieting herself.

Pigless dick? Oh well. Not important.

"That asshole dumped me tonight!" she exclaimed, her eyes tearing up again. "He said we couldn't work out because of Ethan. He couldn't handle the responsibility of taking care of Ethan, and so he couldn't stay with me. He sure didn't have a problem with sticking his dick in me the other night, though!"

Linda burst out into a whole new level of crying, her chest heaving with wracking sobs. "He… he… he said… he said… he said he loved me!"

I sat down on the couch beside Linda and put my arm around her, pulling her close and letting her cry her eyes out. Charles Whitman was a piece of shit. Sure, it was exactly the kind of thing I would have done a few weeks prior, but that was history. I was shocked at how deeply offended I was at how Linda had been treated.

My old theory was that whatever you had to do to get the pussy, it was all fair game. That kind of thinking was foreign to the new me at that very second, though. I was thoroughly disgusted with the actions of Charlie Whitman. I pondered the variables of going to his house and pounding his face in. He definitely had an ass-kicking coming and it was well deserved.

"He said it right in front of Ethan, too!" Linda said, wiping her eyes again. "He said that Ethan was the reason we couldn't be together, and Ethan understood what was happening. He might not understand much, but he understood that! Ethan cried all the way home because Charlie didn't like him."

Through drunken chronology I gathered a logical scenario of what had likely happened. Charlie had been taking Ethan out on their dates a couple times in the last two weeks, making nice with the potential future stepson. He acted like everything was just fine, playing with Ethan and treating him like gold. The trouble started after Linda decided to go to bed with Charlie. Once Charlie got what he was after he began losing interest. Ethan was way too much of a burden just for some steady pussy. The problem was really that Charlie tried to play it off like everything was great, when the whole time he was looking for a way to get away from Linda and the retarded albatross around her neck.

The date earlier that night had been to a rather nice restaurant, and Ethan and Linda had dressed up for the special occasion. Linda had thought that maybe Charlie was going to announce his intentions to take their relationship further and he wanted to do it with Ethan present. That would have been a really sweet gesture.

Instead, after placing their orders, Charlie announced that the relationship was over. Linda cried harder when she told me about the pure shock that washed over her with his hurtful words. She had thought that things were going extremely well and it blind-sided her when Charlie informed her that things weren't what they seemed.

"Ethan is far too fucking great a fucking responsibility for me to fucking take on at this fucking point in my fucking life. I'm sure you fucking understand," is what Charles said, according to Linda. The accuracy of that statement, though, may have been altered due to an alcohol induced paraphrasing impairment.

Charles ate in silence while Linda and Ethan absently picked at their food, and then he loaded them into his car for the last drive he'd be taking to the Miles home. Ethan cried all the way home, but Charles stared stoically out the windshield, never acknowledging the crying boy in his backseat. Linda, however, kept it together pretty well. At least until she got Ethan put to bed.

"It was horrible, Ronald," Linda sniffled as she recounted talking to Ethan before bed. "He was distraught. He kept saying, 'Mom, I'm sorry! I'm sorry I'm a stupid head'. Over and over. Then he started hitting himself in the face. Hard! I had to hold him down to get him to quit. He gave himself a bloody nose."

I held her and we talked and drank the wine, for how long I don't know.

The last thing I remember was Linda leaning in with her eyes closed and kissing me.

3. The Wake-Up Call

Sunday morning arrived, screaming at me from all sides.

"Get up, Ronald! Get up!" Linda whispered, but wanting to shout. I don't know how long she had been trying to wake me up, but apparently it had taken quite some time. My head throbbed and my stomach felt as if it were going to crawl up my throat and punch me in the face for pouring so much alcohol into it the night before.

I groaned and opened my eyes to a room lit far too brightly with sunlight. "Awww, fuck!"

"Be quiet!" she whispered frantically. "Ethan is awake."

That's when I heard the incessant tattoo on the door and the mantra of "Mom. Mom. Mom. Mom," coming from the other side of it. My eyes snapped open and I shot up in the bed, immediately wishing that I hadn't. My headache surged forward and brought my stomach with it, a small bit of vile tasting vomit reaching the back of my tongue. I clamped my hand over my mouth and took a huge disgusting gulp. I squeezed my eyes shut and let the wave of revulsion run its course as quietly as possible, hoping that swallowing that small amount of booze puke wasn't going to bring more with it on a return trip. Slowly I realized that I wasn't going to throw up again. At least not right away.

Linda was standing at the foot of the bed and holding my clothes out to me. The look on her face told me to get them on and get the fuck out. I stood up cautiously and took the clothes from her, slipping into my briefs and jeans first. As I was putting the shirt on she grabbed me and pulled me close to her, giving me one last kiss on the lips before pushing me away.

"You'll have to go out the window," she said as she tightened the belt on her robe. I nodded slightly, doing what I could to allow my headache a peaceful place to reside. "Call me tonight. We need to talk."

"I will," I said, scanning the bedroom floor for my shoes. I didn't see them. I leaned over carefully to look under the bed and then I remembered where they were. "Uh-oh."

"Uh-oh what?" Linda asked, looking worried.

"My shoes are in the living room. I took them off in there and left them by the coffee table."

"Okay… go out the window and run around to the front. I'll get Ethan's breakfast ready and when he's distracted I'll put them on the porch."

It sounded like a good plan, so with one more quick peck on the lips she pushed me toward the window. I unlocked the window and slid it up as quietly as I could and swung my right leg out. Linda grabbed my ass playfully as I pulled my left leg through and then dropped to the ground. I headed around to the front of the house as I heard the window sliding closed behind me.

At the side of the house I waited until I heard the screen door open and close, then I ran to the porch and grabbed my shoes, with the socks stuffed down inside them. I walked carefully but quickly to my car, since I have incredibly tender feet. A big, tough guy like me and I can't even walk on a bed of pebbles without wincing.

I threw my shoes onto the passenger seat, fired the ignition, without revving the engine unnecessarily just this once, and pulled away from the curb. As I got down the block I breathed a little easier. If Ethan had found me there it would have been very bad. After what Charlie had just done to Ethan he wouldn't have handled it very well.

For one thing, I was his friend. To find out your friend is fucking your mom would be disturbing to most guys. Ethan wasn't like most guys. He would have been very confused, and that's a best case scenario. Ethan was retarded, but he was no dummy. He would have known if he had caught me in his mom's bedroom that something was going on. More than anything in the world, I didn't want to hurt him.

Linda and I had an unspoken understanding. We both knew that nothing was going to come of our night together. Ethan wouldn't understand that. If he learned of it and then realized that I wasn't going to be with Linda I was worried that he would think that I was abandoning his mom because of him, just like Charlie did.

The smart thing to do would have been to leave. Things would have been far less complicated if Linda and I hadn't ended up in bed. There is always that one person that you really shouldn't sleep with, regardless of attraction, and Linda Miles was that one person for me. She was almost twice my age. I was just barely on the wrong side of legal. She was my friend's mother. She was only having sex with me because of her emotional distress and the alcohol.

Still, I couldn't say I regretted it. It was what it was. And it's not like it was ever going to happen again anyway.

Dad was sitting across from Mom at the kitchen table reading the paper and sipping his coffee when I came in. He was in his Sunday Going To Meeting clothes; Mom was still in her nightgown and robe. Dad went to church every Sunday by himself and always thought of that as a reason to look down on Mom and I, at least a little bit. I had been forced to go to church with him every Sunday until I was thirteen, but then my mom stepped in and said I could decide for myself if I still wanted to go. I didn't.

Dad saw my haggard look and let the newspaper fall to the table. "Well, well, well. Look who finally found his way home!"

"I stayed with JK last night. He called after you guys went to bed," I lied, knowing the truth was no good.

Dad shook his head in disapproval. "You know I don't like you staying in that part of town."

"What part of town is that, Dad?" I asked, knowing what he was going to say. As soon as he said it I knew that the pressure would be off of me because my mom would be on his ass.

"Nigger Town! I don't like you staying in Nigger Town!" Dad yelled. He sensed the bait, he knew it was a trap, and yet his bigotry was so strong that he couldn't just keep his mouth shut.

A large portion of my hometown was, and still is to some extent, segregated. Not through any laws or economic necessity, just through the natural attraction of like being drawn to like. The fact that the majority of the black people in my town lived in this certain eight or nine block area earned it the derogatory name of Nigger Town. I have no idea why the remaining area within the city limits wasn't referred to as Ignorant White Trashville.

"Ron! That's enough!" Mom shouted at Dad, incensed once again by his unabashed racism.

"Hey! I'm just concerned about his welfare!" Dad argued defensively, hands in the air. "You think it's all right for our boy to stay in a place full of drug dealers and thieves, by all means, let him stay."

I got a drink of water from the tap and headed up to my room while Mom read Dad the standard riot act to his bigotry.

Just like that, I was in the clear.

4. Attempted Hatchet Burial

I only slept for a few more hours and then I got up to meet the team at Sharky's.

Everyone tended to gather there during the pro football season and watch the games together. Considering that I hadn't spent much time with the team, outside of practice and games, I thought it might be a good idea to go down there and try to mend fences. Try to show that I was still a part of the team. Besides, the Bears were playing and I could go down to Sharky's and watch Walter Payton run all over the hated Dallas Cowboys.

When I walked into Sharky's the acrid smoke of a freshly burnt pizza hung thick in the air. The game hadn't started yet, so everyone was just milling around and making small talk. Some of the guys were at the video games along the wall playing Tempest, Sinistar and Joust, trying as hard as they could to get the high scores so they could put their initials in the Hall of Fame. It seemed like ASS, FUK, DIK, COK, and CUM were all really good at those video games. Their initials filled up a lot of the spaces on each game. SUK, _MY, and DIK held the top three spots on Sinistar's top ten players.

Skyler, book-ended by Chewy and Shorty, gave me much the same welcome in Sharky's as my dad had given me at home that morning, in attitude if not in words. "Butcher Blake! To what do we owe the honor?"

"Give it a rest, Skyler. I just came to watch the game with my team."

JK kicked out an empty chair across from him and motioned for me to sit down. With a wave of his hand he offered me some Cajun style pizza. There were no exotic New Orleans toppings or spices, it was just burnt all to hell.

"Are you sure you're on this team? I mean, I see you on the field, but you're never around anymore. What's up with that?" Skyler asked mockingly.

"I'm here now," I said, speaking up so that everyone could hear me. Some of the other guys began to move in around the table. "It's time to bury whatever fucking hatchet we've been grinding away on. The sectionals start Friday and we're going to have to play tough to win this. We can't beat the best in the state if we're at each other's throats."

Skyler weighed my words. The light went on in his eyes and everyone knew that he had some other smart-ass comment to make. He was cut short by Donnie Marks, who stepped to my side and clapped me on the shoulder. "Good to have you back, Butcher."

From the reaction of the rest of the team I assumed that Donnie was the only one who felt that way. He looked around at everyone and noticed that he was the only one who had come to my side and he quietly sat back down.

"So..." Skyler started, dragging the word out for a long time. "...Are you or are you not fucking that retard's mom? I told the guys you had to be or you would be down with the team still. Are you?"

The truth would have made me a hero in their eyes. But I was past wanting to be anyone's hero. "No. It's not like that."

"You mean to tell me you've been blowing off your team so you can hang out with a retard?"

"Skyler, I didn't come here to do this. I came here to try to set things right going into this post season. We've got the best chance ever to win the whole fucking thing and I don't want any of this bullshit to get in the way."

All eyes were glued on Skyler and I, everyone spinelessly waiting to hear what their fearless leader would say. Skyler had those guys eating out of his hand and thinking he was the Second Coming.

"What makes you think that you can just walk back in here and make everything right after how you've treated this team all season? Ever since you took up with your little retard boyfriend." Skyler spat the words with venom. Shorty chortled at his master's insult.

"Okay," I said, throwing my hands up in the air. "I tried."

I got up and moved to another table, JK immediately joining me. Sometime in the first quarter of the game Donnie Marks and Steve Bunch came over and sat at the table with JK and I, earning a baleful glare from Skyler. We watched the game, keeping to ourselves and ignoring the cold stares from Skyler and his minions.

The looks on the faces of my other teammates, the ones from Skyler's table, seemed to say that they just wished that we could have settled everything between us, but barring that, they were obligated to side with Skyler.

The Bears ended up beating the Cowboys 17-7 and the party broke up shortly after that. As Steve and Donnie got up to leave I shook their hands.

"You guys know that you just brought Skyler's wrath down on yourselves as well, don't you?"

Steve laughed. "Screw him. Who else is he going to throw to?"

"Yeah. What he said," Donnie added wryly. They both walked out together.

"I guess we're not the only ones on the Shit List now," I said to JK.

"Fuck it, man. Steve's right. Without the four of us, Skyler is going to be standing back there holding the ball all day. What else can he do?"

The idea was to get Skyler back into a position to unite the team again. That wasn't going to happen any time soon it seemed. But maybe by having every weapon in Skyler's arsenal - JK, Bunch, Marks, and myself - on the same page it would bring the other guys around.

We'd just have to see.

JK and I walked out of Sharky's and I leaned against my car to talk to him about something serious. I didn't want to bring it up in front of the other guys.

"I... uh... I..." drooled lazily out of my mouth. Even though I knew I could trust him completely I didn't want to say anything to JK just yet, but I had to say something to someone. "I did something kind of stupid last night."

JK laughed. "No shit. You left the party too early. It got pretty wild. Two fights broke out after you left and a couple junior chicks got drunk and made out."

"Damn, I miss everything," I said dryly. "No, I really messed up last night, I think."

"What happened?"

Just then another group of guys walked out of Sharky's and right past us. Since Skyler wasn't there breathing directly down their necks they waved and said goodbye.

JK lowered his voice to a stage whisper. "What happened?"

"I... uh... I... fucked Linda Miles last night."

"All right!" JK exclaimed, raising his hand for a high five.

I grabbed his wrist and pulled his hand down. "Hell no, it's not all right."

"She's smokin' hot! What's the problem?"

"She's Ethan's mom, dude!"

"And?"

"And nothing. That's enough." I couldn't believe JK didn't get it.

"You worry too much," JK said, leaning beside me against my front fender. "Don't think I wouldn't fuck her if I got the chance."

I laughed and then he did. "Oh, I fucking know you would!"

After a few seconds of silence JK asked the question I'd been asking myself ever since I woke up that morning. "So, are you going to do it again?"

"Hell, I don't know." I shook my head, but that didn't necessarily mean no. Knowing I shouldn't and knowing that I wasn't going to were two completely different things. "I have to call her tonight. She wants to talk about it."

"About doing it again?" JK asked with a raised eyebrow.

"About last night. We need to discuss… things."

"You're going to fuck her tonight," JK said matter-of-factly.

"No, I'm not. We're just going to talk."

"Naw, man. She's going to call you up and you're going to end up going over there and doing it again."

"I'm telling you, it's not happening. I'm a man of principles. I can't let that happen again. Not without getting everything worked out."

JK smiled. "Okay."

"Seriously."

JK smiled and nodded. "I know. I hear ya."

"Fucking quit it! I'm not kidding. Nothing's going to happen." I jabbed an elbow into his ribs.

"Mm-hmm. I believe you. Really."

I shook my head and gave up. There was no convincing JK that I was merely going to talk to Linda, but he was wrong. There was no way in hell I was going to have sex with her again. Not after how bad I felt about Ethan that morning. This was far too important to let hormones dictate the course of events.

It simply could not and would not be allowed to happen.

5. Principles Schminciples

So there I was, eleven thirty Sunday night, balls deep in Linda Miles.

I don't know how it happened. I was so intent on not letting things get that far ever again. I kept thinking *'This cannot happen! This cannot happen!'*

I was even thinking those exact words as I put her ankles over my shoulders and pounded into her like a defensive line.

It all started out so innocent. She sounded like a shy high school girl on the phone when she called me that night. We danced around the subject, talking about Ethan and school and football. Anything but what we really needed to talk about. After almost an hour of doing the avoidance two-step Linda abruptly cut to the chase.

"I don't want to talk about last night over the phone," she said, her tone growing serious. "Ethan's in bed. Can you just come over?"

I wasn't supposed to go out that late on a school night, but Mom and Dad were in bed and had been fast asleep for over an hour. My dad slept like the dead and Mom was virtually oblivious when she was tired. "I'll be right over."

When Linda answered the door she grabbed two handfuls of my shirt and dragged me into the house and straight to her bedroom.

Eventually, though, we did have our talk. Lying there in the dark, her curled up to my chest, the words we struggled over earlier came easy.

"I feel like what we're doing is wrong," Linda said with a long sigh.

"Yeah. Me, too." She didn't seem to hear me.

"I mean… I'm old enough to be your… much older sister. You're barely eighteen. Not much older than my son."

"I agree." I wasn't eighteen yet, but I saw no harm in letting her think so.

"You're Ethan's friend," she continued, pulling away from me and sitting up in bed. She brought the sheet up to cover her breasts. "It's just not right that we should be doing this when Ethan could react like he did with… whats-his-name."

"Pigless Dick?"

Linda laughed. "Yeah, that guy."

"Linda, I think you are absolutely right about all of this."

"You do?" She seemed genuinely surprised to hear me say that.

"Yes, I do. I've been thinking about it since last night and I totally agree with you. We shouldn't be doing this. Not anymore. I don't want to hurt Ethan."

She gave me a smile that seemed to say *'Oh, you're so sweet'*, but she said nothing. For a long time. Long enough that it became awkward.

"Well… uh… I should probably go," I said, tossing back the sheet and standing up. My clothes were at the foot of the bed in a hastily discarded pile.

"I think that would be best," Linda said. I looked at her on the bed and saw her appraising my body. She dropped the sheet from her breasts and lay back on the bed, propping herself up on a stack of pillows.

Feeling a little self-conscious before the eyes of this woman, who seemed to be enjoying the sight of me, all I could think to say was, "What?"

"Just enjoying the view one final time," Linda said, a lascivious smile on her face.

That was all it took. Little Butchie decided it was time for the second performance of the night, right then and there. It went from fully soft to fully hard so quickly that it must have looked cartoonish.

"Oh my!" Linda exclaimed with a pleased look. Then a look of concern crossed her face. "Well, I just can't let you go home in that condition, now can I?" She flung the sheets back exposing her incredible body to me. "Come here!"

I dropped my underwear back on top of the pile and went to her, all my earlier objections melting away to nothing.

That night I learned some very important lessons about women. Linda taught me that there are some occasions when pounding through all obstacles isn't necessarily the best way to go. Power and force are nice options to have on the table, but there is room for subtlety and finesse.

That night John Riggins played like Walter Payton.

Chapter Twelve

1. Ass Men Revisited

Picking Ethan up for school on Monday morning was very awkward for me. I was sure that he had no idea what had happened between his mother and I, and likely wouldn't comprehend it even if he did know, but the fact of the matter was that I knew and it felt very strange.

Being absorbed with thoughts of Ethan and Linda helped me to tune out Skyler and the Goon Squad in the gym early that morning. As was to be expected, Skyler had something to say to everyone about me. JK was giving me a spot and I was trying to bench press another personal best lift, four hundred pounds, when Skyler and his court circled the bench I was working on.

"Whoa! Look at all the weight Mr. One Man Team is pressing here!" Skyler mocked.

The weight had been slowly lowering to my chest and I was running out of steam, but when Skyler said that I felt a surge of energy as anger flushed through my body. I had been ignoring his snide comments and his dirty looks all morning, but now he was standing right over me, taunting me.

The bar stopped its downward fall and I pushed it up, a painfully slow climb toward the ceiling. My anger at Skyler fueling the lift, like a slow motion launch of an Apollo rocket. Slow, controlled power. My chest was burning and the pressure was intense as my muscles strained to give me what I was asking of them.

Much easier than I expected, though, I hit the peak and finished the lift. Then I did something dumb.

I went for a second lift.

In one smooth motion I let the weight start to drop back to my chest, maintaining full control all the way.

"Holy shit! He's going for two! The One Man Team is going for two! He won't need any of us if he can pull this off!" Skyler continued.

JK had his hands under the bar, ready to give me a nudge, or to pull the bar off of me, should I lose the strength to finish. At first I thought that I was doing fine. The weight reached the bottom of the motion, about four inches above my chest, and immediately started moving back up when I pushed. I hit a stop about four inches into the lift. The weight wasn't going back down, but it wasn't moving up any more at all. Every ounce of my strength was wrapped up in simply holding the weight in exactly that position.

"PUSH IT, BUTCHER! PUSH!" JK shouted, looking down at my straining face. "DON'T QUIT! GET IT! FUCKIN' GET IT, MAN!"

The weight held firm about eight inches from my chest. My arms were trembling with the effort, my face a mask of reddened pain. Even my anger at Skyler wasn't enough fuel for the lift. I quite simply had found my limit.

Then the chorus erupted around me, started by Skyler and joined by everyone except for JK. "ONE MAN TEAM! ONE MAN TEAM! ONE MAN TEAM!"

I heard someone laughing.

The bar went up another inch or so.

"ONE MAN TEAM! ONE MAN TEAM! ONE MAN TEAM!"

Cocksuckers, I thought. *Fuck you all.*

I pushed the bar up another two inches, a loud grunt escaping my throat.

JK tried to be heard over the chant, but it was hard to hear him. "PUSH! PUSH! PUSH!"

"ONE MAN TEAM!"

"PUSH!"

"ONE MAN TEAM!"

"PUSH IT!"

I was almost there. Just a little more and I could lock my elbows and drop the weight back on the bench.

Then I hit the second stop.

I gave it all I could; I just didn't have anything left. I was toast.

JK saw me losing it and he grabbed the bar and helped me set it down.

My disappointed audience groaned when I gave up.

I let my arms drop and hang from the sides of the bench, a strong tingle running from my hands to my elbows, my pulse hammering inside my head, fast and hard. My chest hurt to let my arms hang there like that, but it hurt more to try to lift them up.

"Awww, that's too bad!" Skyler said, leaning down over my face. "I really thought you were going to make it. Guess you're not as strong as you thought, hmm?"

Through my panting I tried to speak, but all that came out was, "Stronger than you."

"Yeah, well… if I need to lift four hundred pounds I'll just make Chewy do it."

The King and his court walked away from the bench, laughing at my "weakness".

I just laid there for a few minutes, until I had enough strength to get up and get ready to pick up Ethan.

Linda was waiting at the door with Ethan when I arrived and she played it far cooler than I could have hoped to do. Once I realized I was staring at her I made a conscious decision not to even look at her again. Of course, Ethan was oblivious, lost in the retelling of the *Thundercats* episode from the day before. I had no idea what he was talking about, other than recognizing a few of the characters names, but he rattled all the way to the car.

Once I got him in the front seat I went around to the drivers side and established my stare again. Ethan couldn't see me looking at his mother so lasciviously with the roof of the car in his way. Linda Miles always went to work dressed to kill, the hotness seeping right through the business suits she wore. When she turned and went back into the house she gave me an extra little wiggle of her ass in the navy pinstriped skirt.

All the way to school Ethan continued his tale of the latest adventures of the *Thundercats*. I didn't even pay any attention to what he was saying until he spouted off with, "Mumm-ra is a sonofabitch!"

I laughed, shocked at Ethan using that language. His eyes went wide and fearful.

"I'm sorry! I didn't mean to say that!" Ethan said, worry etched into his simple face. "Don't tell my mom, okay?"

"Don't worry, Ethan," I said, nudging him with my elbow. "I've seen a couple episodes of the show. Mumm-ra is a sonofabitch. I won't tell on you."

"Oh, thank you, Butchie! Thank you!"

"Ethan, it's okay. Don't worry about it. That Cheetara sure is hot, hmm?"

"What's hot mean?" Ethan asked.

"You know... sexy." I was thinking, *You know... like your mom.*

"Oh..." Ethan's face went instantly red.

"Like Miranda Lewis," I teased.

Ethan's face then went ten deeper shades of red. "Stop it, Butchie! You're embarrassing me!"

"Okay, okay," I said, reaching up to turn on the radio. "Cheetara is hot, though. Right?"

Ethan gave an embarrassed laugh. "Yeah. She's got a pretty butt."

"Whatever happened to Miranda? Are you two going to go out again?"

Silence clamped down over Ethan.

"What's wrong?"

"No. No." Ethan said, his face solemn.

"Didn't both of you have a good time?"

"Yeah. Yeah," Ethan said, nodding. Then he shook it once and said, "No."

"I really thought your date went well. She seemed to dig you. You put out the old vibe like a major stud. What's wrong?"

"She told everyone that I touched her butt," Ethan was getting upset.

"Maybe she told them because she liked it?" I offered.

"Everyone laughed at me because I touched her butt."

"Hey, there is nothing wrong with touching a girl's butt. I do it all the time."

"Really?" Ethan asked, in awe.

"Hell yeah. All the time. I like touching girls butts." *Like your mom's.*

"It doesn't make me weird?"

"Ethan, you'd be weird if you didn't like touching girls butts. You're perfectly normal."

We rode in silence for a minute or two, and then Ethan perked up again. He held his hands in front of his face, as if he were holding a cantaloupe in each hand and raising them slightly, one at a time.

"I like it when their butts go like this when they walk," Ethan cackled, a dirty and conspiratorial laugh.

"You're preaching to the choir, man," I said through a huge grin.

"I like it when you see one and it's shaped like this." Ethan made a tight half circle in the air with his cupped hand.

"Tell it, brother man!"

Ethan cackled maniacally, his wrecked grill of teeth taking up a large portion of his face.

"You know what else, Butchie?"

"What?"

"I want to bite a girl's butt!" He yelled it. And just as we were pulling into the parking lot. With the windows halfway down.

A group of girls hanging out at a car and smoking cigarettes shot a nasty look our way. I just waved. Ethan was oblivious.

"Is that weird?" he asked again, his smile slipping.

"No. Not really. You're fine, Ethan. If a girl wants you to bite her butt, and you want to bite her butt, there is nothing wrong with it. I've bitten a butt or two in my day."

We walked through the halls without incident, as was becoming more and more common. We stopped at our lockers and made our way to class without one single problem.

The problem came just as Ethan was walking into class.

Miranda Lewis was just ahead of Ethan. I was turning to head to my class when I caught the look in Ethan's eyes, and I knew exactly what he was going to do.

"No! Ethan!" I yelled. But it was too late.

With a reserve of hidden agility somewhere in his body Ethan lunged at Miranda's backside. He grabbed a hip in each hand. He opened his mouth wide and reared his head back. And he bit her square on the ass.

Miranda squealed in shock, and maybe pain, and ran straight ahead into the class, never even looking back. Ethan wasn't gentle. He bit her kind of hard.

Ethan turned to me and smiled, very pleased with himself. The smile dropped from his face quickly when he saw the look of shock on mine.

One thing for sure, Mrs. Rickman was not amused.

2. Ethan Miles: Ass Biter

Mrs. Rickman wasn't amused, but Principal Greenwood sure was.

Maybe the innocent goofy look on Ethan's face just seemed too endearing to him, I don't know, but I could tell that the principal was fighting back a smile. Once he found out that Miranda wasn't injured he loosened up quite a bit.

Principal Greenwood stepped out of his office and left Ethan and I sitting there in front of his desk. Ethan was holding his ear. It was red and puffy from where Mrs. Rickman grabbed it and half dragged him down to the office, his toes seeming to barely keep purchase on the floor. I followed along behind the raging shrew who was trying tug my friend's ear off, trying to get her to let him go. Ethan was crying and yelling all the way down to the office.

"Why did you do that?" I whispered, leaning over closer to him so they wouldn't hear us talking through the open door.

"You said it was okay to bite a girl's butt!" Ethan didn't whisper. He almost shouted it.

I shot a quick look over my shoulder to see if anyone out in the foyer had heard what he said. It seemed that no one did, but I wasn't sure.

"Keep your voice down, Ethan."

Unnecessarily, he whispered, "You said it was okay to bite a girl's butt."

"I know what I said. But you can't just do it any damn time you want to!"

Ethan had a puzzled look on his face. "Why would I bite a girl's butt when I didn't want to?"

"That's not what I'm saying," I said, trying to figure out how to make him understand. "You have to know that the girl wants you to do it."

"Oh, I see." Ethan said, but the look on his face told me that he still wasn't getting it.

"You do? What am I saying then?"

Ethan was quiet for some time. "I should… ask her if she would like me to bite her butt."

"Well, I guess you could do that. But you'd be better off just letting nature take its course and see what happens, I think."

"Maybe I could send her a card?" Ethan's eyes lit up with the idea.

"I don't think Hallmark makes an '*I want to bite your ass*' card, Ethan."

Ethan cackled again like he had done in my car. I looked back out into the foyer, hoping that no one heard him laughing. We weren't supposed to be having a good time in there.

Eventually Ethan's cackling died down and he whined to a halt, and we sat in silence for several seconds. I was reliving my trip to the principal's office from the day

I had been caught picking on Ethan. Who could have guessed that I'd be where I was right then, sitting next to Ethan in the same office, as his friend.

"Butchie?"

"What?"

"I'm in a lot of trouble, am I? I mean, aren't I?" he asked, looking nervous again.

"You might be in a little trouble, but I think it will all be okay." I didn't want to tell him that if they really wanted to they could kick him out of school and send him back to the school for the slow kids. He would have been heart broken. Ethan was so proud of the fact that he got to go to a regular high school, sending him back to the other school would have devastated him. I didn't think they would do that, but they could have.

Ethan started crying again.

"Relax, it won't be that bad. We'll get it all straightened out."

"They're going to send me back to my old school!" he whined.

"I don't think they will. Just be sure to tell Miranda you're sorry and let Principal Greenwood know that it won't happen again."

Ethan nodded his head, but he looked sad.

"What's wrong with that?" I asked.

"I'll say I'm sorry. But then I'll never get to bite a girl's butt."

I couldn't help but laugh. "At least not in school, okay?"

That brought a wan smile to his face. "Okay. No butt biting in school."

Principal Greenwood left us alone in his office for a long time. I was beginning to wonder if they were starting the paper work to send Ethan back to the slow school.

Finally, the principal came back into the office and took a seat behind the desk. Ethan went ramrod straight in his seat, barely breathing.

"I've talked to Miranda Lewis. I've talked to her mother," Principal Greenwood said gravely, steepling his fingers beneath his chin and shooting a look at Ethan. "And I've talked to your mother."

Ethan swallowed hard. Principal Greenwood remained quiet for a long time, primarily for dramatic effect, I believe. When Ethan started looking like he was going to cry again, Principal Greenwood let the serious pretense drop.

"If you will agree to apologize to Miranda and promise not to engage in this kind of behavior anymore, we will let it drop right there. Is that fair enough?" The amused look was still under the principal's serious visage.

Ethan nodded his head so hard that his whole body moved back and forth in the chair. "I will 'pologize to Miranda!"

"And promise not to do it again?" Principal Greenwood coaxed.

Ethan balked and gave me a worried look.

"Ethan, do you promise not to do it again when she doesn't want you to do it?" I clarified.

Again, Ethan nodded his torso.

"And not in school?"

More torso nodding.

"Then get out of here and get to class," Principal Greenwood ordered, his smile slipping through as we stood to leave.

Miranda was in the foyer as we stepped from the outer office, looking none the worse for wear.

Ethan ran up to her. "Miranda, I am sorry I bited your butt and I will not do it again unless you tell me to!"

After stopping to get a pass to get me into my first period class without a tardy I walked Ethan and Miranda back to Mrs. Rickman's class. I assumed everything was going to be all right between them. They were holding hands.

The rest of the day there were two stories circulating around the school. The one about Hub dying while spying on the volleyball team, and the one about Teeth's ass chomping.

3. Working My Ass Off

Coach Rollins hammered us relentlessly for the rest of the week.

We had the King Aztecs at home for the first round of the sectionals and he wanted to be sure that we had something to offer that they hadn't seen before. A lot of the pressure fell to me, as their weakness was stopping the run, and Coach Rollins told me before practice on Tuesday that he was going to work my ass off. Of course, I welcomed it. When your coach tells you that he is going to make you the centerpiece you give him what he wants.

We started out with a few run-throughs of our tried and true plays, which we nailed like clockwork. And then it got tough. Mr. Walls ran a lot of the new plays as Coach Rollins observed and made suggestions. Mr. Buck told the defense nothing about how to defend what we were attempting on the offensive side. He wanted to see how well the defense could adapt to use as a gauge as to how the Aztecs defense might adapt.

Needless to say, the first few attempts were rough. They always are. By the time we got the play into some semblance of workability the defense was starting to catch on to the formations and were adjusting accordingly. About half way through the practice I was feeling like one giant bruise. Even though the hits we gave at practice weren't full force, it was still painful to get pounded constantly by defenders who are sometimes trying to make the first string. Hitting me at practice is often their only way to show the coaches what they've got, so while they weren't looking to injure me, they weren't treating me with kid gloves either.

Skyler was getting a kick out of watching me take my beating. He was the only guy at practice who never took a hit. You just don't tackle your own quarterback, they're too valuable. Especially going into the sectionals. Every time I took a hit that put me on my ass I heard Skyler's braying laugh, followed by Chewy and Shorty. Once they heard their fearless leader sound off they knew that they'd have permission to laugh as well.

Toward the end of the day Mr. Walls called us into the huddle and showed us a new play we had never even considered. He pointed it out on his clipboard with his middle finger, having lost the index finger some time during his almost twenty years of teaching woodshop. The play was genius, and I was absolutely sure that it would work to stymie the defense one hundred percent of the time.

Provided I could pull it off.

Coach Rollins wasn't kidding when he said that he was going to work my ass off. For the first time in my life I was being called upon to throw the ball in a game. And not only was I being called upon to throw the ball, it was an extremely difficult throw to make. One that Skyler should have to make, but he couldn't or the play wouldn't work.

We set up in formation for our famous stretch play, with one exception. The tight end, JK, set to the left when we were set to pull right. At the snap we would go into the full motion of the stretch play, the receivers cutting to the right to draw their defenders with them. I would take the handoff, as usual. The teams we played saw this dozens of times. We burned them on it several times. We knew that their defenses were practicing their hearts out trying to defend against the stretch play. Our own practice defense had seen it coming and adjusted for it. They were all in place and ready to hit me when I ran the ball toward the right sideline.

So, when I stopped, spun, and threw the ball all the way back across to the left side of the field to JK everyone stopped and stared. There was no one even close to him. With a catch he had a straight run to the end zone.

Unfortunately I threw the ball away, behind him and out of bounds. From the heavy bench-pressing on Monday I felt something pull in my chest and pain shot from my sternum all the way to my right elbow. I pulled my arm into my chest and hugged it to me, wincing as my shoulder moved inward.

Skyler, as expected, was the first to comment. "Nice throw! I guess I better watch my back or you're going to have my job."

"Shut up, Derek," Coach Rollins said calmly as he walked up to me. "How's the arm?"

"I think it will be okay. I maxxed out on the bench yesterday and I wasn't ready for the throw."

Coach Rollins nodded. "All right! That's it for today gentlemen. Have a good evening."

While everyone else turned and ran off the field I walked off slowly, still cradling my arm.

"Rest that arm, Butcher. Nothing says we have to run this play on Friday. You tell me when you're ready to try it again. I want to have it in the repertoire for the sectionals if at all possible, but not at the expense of my star running back."

I nodded and grunted. Perfectly acceptable communication while in a football uniform.

"See a doctor if you have to, but take care of that arm."

Another nod and a grunt and our conversation was over. Coach Rollins walked off toward the coaching office and I headed to the locker room.

On Wednesday I had a light practice at Coach Rollins insistence. I was willing to give it all I had, but my arm was still a little sore, so he asked me to take it easy. Of course, this made me a huge pussy in the eyes of my enemies on the team. Todd Ebert, the second string running back, tried to fill my shoes and it didn't quite work. I know it sounds arrogant, but he just wasn't as good as I was. On any other team he would have probably been a starter, but for the Mustangs that year he couldn't cut it. Todd didn't have the speed for the stretch play. The defense ate him up every time. He didn't have the power to break the line. When they sent him up the middle it was like hitting a brick wall. Without the speed and the perception to find the holes he had no choice but to try to physically bust through. He just wasn't capable of doing it.

The meat of my job on Wednesday was to help Todd adapt to the offense. I was fully expected to play on Friday, but in order for the rest of the team to have a meaningful practice the running back had to be right on it.

After about fifteen or twenty plays Todd Ebert had just about had enough. The hits, comparatively light as they were, took a toll on someone who wasn't used to taking so many of them. Jim Dole, the third stringer who had yet to get in a game, came in and did okay. In my opinion he did better than Ebert, but it was probably just because he wanted it more. He was a sophomore and was looking to the future, while Ebert was a senior. With me on the team Todd Ebert knew he wasn't going to be a starter. Jim Dole knew that the next year was going to be his and was itching to show his stuff.

Thursday saw me back in the mix and it was a great practice. We didn't attempt the sneaky pass play again, but we got some of the new running plays up to game speed. My arm felt good and I could tell there was no damage done, but Coach decided to give it a longer rest anyway. I was to start practicing my throwing at home after the game on Friday. I'd have to drag my dad out in the backyard and have him play catch with me like when

I was a kid. We hadn't done that in a long time, and to tell you the truth, I was looking forward to it.

For the first time all week I stepped onto the defensive side of the ball and ran a few plays just to keep my tackling chops up. Defense always felt natural for me, as I *really* liked to make hits. Learning the new offensive plays was more important than making sure that I still knew how to tackle. All the adulation about my running game was great, but what I really loved was hitting people. I was pretty sure I could still crush a quarterback at will.

All in all we were more than ready for the Aztecs, who had improved dramatically since we faced them in the regular season. But so had we. There was no doubt in the mind of any Mustang that we were going to dominate the game. Everything was looking as close to perfect as it ever had and we were running like a well-oiled machine. There was an unspoken harmony that had developed between teammates over the rough week and we knew we were a united force to be reckoned with, more than ever.

That's what made it so bad the next day when I had to kick Jim Dole's ass.

4. Beating Dole's Ass

By Friday the talk of Hub's death had died down considerably. A fat janitor dying with a hard-on in the school hallway after spying on the girls volleyball team was hardly news anymore when you had the top ranked Mims Mustangs going up against the King Aztecs in the first game of the sectionals.

The buzz was amazing. I had been through sectionals before and it is always an exciting time, but the 1988 season was different. It felt like destiny was pulling us toward the state championship and the whole town was going to follow us to glory. A pep rally was being held after school out by the football field, instead of in the gymnasium where we usually had them, in order for the public to be able to come and participate. It was being said that a lot of people were leaving work early just to be there to cheer us on.

Walking through the hallways in our game jerseys was another big deal. Like always, the crowds parted when any player passed, but that day was different. It wasn't just Game Day. It was *the* Game Day. Several times that morning cheers erupted in the halls when a group of players made The Walk. Myself, I didn't participate in The Walk anymore, not since the one where I humiliated Ethan, but a lot of players still did it. Especially the younger ones. Some of them were getting their first taste of hero worship.

JK, Ethan and I were standing in the hallway by my locker between third and fourth period when one of the loud cheers erupted. Everyone in the hall began to push up against the walls and make way for the players strutting down the corridor. Ethan, a look of fear on his face, hugged his duffel bag to his chest and tried to squeeze himself into the wall. A sharp twinge of guilt poked at me. I knew that what I had done to him was the cause of his persistent fear. Even though he was perfectly comfortable with me now, the fear of that day had made a permanent scar on his mind.

"Don't worry, Ethan. They won't do anything to you," I assured. The look on his face said that he really wanted to believe me, but somehow he just knew better. "I won't let them if they try."

Even telling him that didn't seem to help, so I just made sure to put myself between him and whatever group of players was getting ready to come around the corner. JK saw what I was doing and he stepped up close on the other side of Ethan and gave him a nod and a smile. We had the kid blocked in pretty well. Nothing could get to him through us.

Finally, the group of players doing The Walk strutted proudly around the corner and down the hall where we stood. Skyler was in the lead, flanked by Chewy and Shorty. On the outside ends of the line were Todd Ebert and Jim Dole.

I just started to laugh.

Skyler was so obvious. He was walking with my back-ups instead of me. Somehow that was supposed to make me feel… what? Jealous? Angry?

What I felt was… free. I felt so much better about myself, knowing that I wasn't basing my self-worth on the worship of the school. Knowing that Skyler's little digs and his slights, like this, were the best that he could do to get to me. Most of all, I felt good that I wasn't one of those overbearing pricks who pushed people around with my fleeting high school celebrity anymore.

Because I was blocking Ethan I wasn't really close enough to the wall to let the line of strutting cocks pass unimpeded, so when they got to me Jim Dole, who was on our side of the hall, had to drop back and wait for the rest of the line to pass first so that he could get by me.

Unlike how they/we used to do it, no one tried to push past me or make threats. Dole just dropped back and went around me.

A few snickers were stifled as people watched the sophomore running back break the formation. Dole's face went instantly red the second he realized the laughter was directed at him.

After Skyler and his cronies were by us JK nudged me in the ribs. "Damn, man! We done been replaced by second stringers!"

Both of us broke out laughing at that. Since we stopped doing the weekly Walk with Skyler back when the Ethan incident happened Skyler had continued making his rounds with other players. But never second stringers! Steve Bunch and Donnie Marks walked with them for a little while after JK and I stopped, but now the two receivers were on the outs with Skyler and Company as well.

"Skyler keeps his shit up and pretty soon he'll be forced to do The Walk with the JV squad," I said.

JK and I were still laughing when we parted ways to get to class.

The next time I saw Jim Dole was at lunch and that's when the shit hit the fan.

I'm not exactly sure of the motivation for what Dole did at lunch that day. I don't know whether it was his own ego making him want to do something toward me for not getting out of his way during The Walk or if Skyler put him up to it. It didn't matter either way, really. What mattered was that he went after Ethan.

JK, Ethan and I were making our way to our table, meeting up with Bunch and Marks who had also started sitting with us since being excommunicated from the Players Table. Due to the position of the Players Table pretty much everyone had to walk by it to get anywhere in the lunchroom. As we were walking by, Ethan in the lead, I saw Jim Dole, who was sitting on the end and facing us, smile at me. Then lightning fast, his foot shot out in front of Ethan.

There was no time to say or do anything to stop it. Ethan went sprawling, his chest landing square in his tray. Dole and everyone else at the Players Table burst out into cruel laughter. Jim Dole had the cackling little laughter of a toady, overjoyed at his master's pleasure.

I felt a burning rage boiling inside me. I knew it was going to bubble over if I didn't get it under control. And Jim Dole was going to get himself burned.

As angry as I was I still had the presence of mind to see where Mr. Hall, the lunchroom monitor was. He was looking right at me, watching the situation. Our eyes met and he turned around and walked away, like he hadn't seen anything. That was all I needed. I took it as permission.

The laughter died and the smile dropped off of Dole's face instantly when I grabbed a handful of his hair and dragged him off of his chair.

Dole was almost as big as I was, and I'm sure he could have put up a better fight, but I never let him get to his feet. I dragged him the by the hair out of the lunchroom and down the hall to the bathroom, kicking and screaming all the way. There were two of the known hoods of the school hanging out in there and smoking cigarettes, but they cleared out quickly when I tossed Dole at their feet and jumped on him.

I wasn't just issuing punishment to Dole, I realized later. I was making an example of him. I beat the shit out him. Literally. "Butcher! Stop! Stop!" Dole begged. "Stop it! I shit myself!"

I had hit him so hard in the stomach that he shit his pants.

If I hadn't been so angry I would have laughed.

I stood up over Dole's prone form, the smell from the back of his pants rather pronounced. He had two quickly blackening eyes and blood trailing from his nose and into his ears. Probably broken, I thought. I turned around and walked out, going back to check on Ethan. I knew he would be okay. I knew JK would be looking out for him. I just felt like I had to check on him, too. After all, it *was* my job.

Back in the lunch room things were calm. JK and Ethan were sitting at our usual table and talking to Mr. Hall when I walked up.

"Ronald, here's a pass," Mr. Hall said, handing me a small green slip of paper. "You need to take Ethan home and let him change clothes. Do I need to check on Mr. Dole?"

"Yeah, you might. He'll need to go home and change clothes, too."

I took the pass and walked Ethan out of the lunchroom, right past the Players Table. I was glaring at them, daring one of them to open their mouths. I was perfectly willing to dish out a little more of what I'd given Dole in the restroom. Hell, how much more trouble could I possibly get in?

The Players Table was silent as we walked by.

5. Hand Me Down Sweetness

Ethan didn't carry a set of house keys, so I took him to my house to get him a different shirt to wear.

My clothes were way too big for Ethan, but it was better to have an ill-fitting, baggy shirt than to walk around covered in instant potatoes and a gray meatloaf-like substance. Fortunately, not much got on his pants. He would have been out of luck trying to fit into even the tightest pair of my pants. One of my thighs was about the same size as his waist.

"Shit," I said under my breath as we pulled into the driveway.

"Shit what?" Ethan said, quickly clamping a hand over his mouth when he realized that he'd said a bad word.

I pointed to the truck in the driveway. "My dad's home."

I led Ethan around to the backdoor, preferring to go in through the kitchen, just in case any of the food we hadn't been able to scrape from his shirt happened to fall off. It would be easier to clean up, and easier to keep my mother from having a fit, if it fell on the linoleum rather than the carpet.

Dad was standing at the kitchen sink, spooning Spaghetti-O's into his mouth right from the can. He always said they were already cooked, so he didn't need to bother heating them up, even though it drove Mom nuts to see him do that. "What are you doing home?"

Then he saw Ethan coming through the door behind me. A look of disgust crossed his face briefly, then he hid it away like it was never there.

"Ethan had an accident at lunch and got food all over him. He needs a new shirt, but he can't get into his house, so I'm going to let him wear one of mine."

Dad just grunted when Ethan said hello and gave a little self-conscious wave.

I gave Ethan an old Chicago Bears jersey that I couldn't wear anymore. It fit him better than it did me. I should have thrown it out years ago, but I couldn't. It had *PAYTON* and the number *34* on the back of it. Ethan's food stained shirt went into a sink full of cold water in the upstairs bathroom. I didn't know if it would help keep the shirt from staining, but Mom always did that when something was spilled on clothes, so it made sense to me that I should do it.

The phone rang as Ethan and I were coming down the stairs and I heard Dad answer it. As we stepped into the kitchen Dad was hanging up the phone. He gave me a suspicious scowl.

"What?"

"When you get back to school they said you are to take Ethan to class and report to the principal's office immediately. Is there something you need to tell me?"

"No."

"You're sure."

"No. There's nothing."

"Don't you fuck this up now! The sectionals start tonight!"

"Dad, there's no problem! I don't know what they want."

I know he didn't believe me, but he let it drop and I was glad. I didn't want to keep lying to him and I certainly didn't want him going into the school with me.

If there was going to be a problem I was absolutely sure it would be easier to handle without my dad there.

6. A Perfectly Good Lie

"Mr. Blake, we have a bit of a problem here." Principal Greenwood leaned back in his chair, rocking it back against the wall behind him.

I let my face go blank, not putting on any kind of front. I was trying very hard to make it look like I wasn't trying very hard to hide something. My constant theory on life applied then as it does now. If the cop didn't see it, I didn't do it. Principal Greenwood was, for all intents and purposes, the cop who didn't see anything. I knew that if he had anything on me he would have come right out and said it.

"What kind of problem?" I asked, looking as innocent as possible.

"It seems that Jim Dole was hurt in an altercation today during lunch. The only name that has come up when we asked who might have hurt him has been Butcher Blake. What do you know about that?"

"I don't know anything about that. I went home for lunch today. Can't Jim tell you who did it?"

Principal Greenwood stifled a bemused chuckle. "Mr. Dole says that he doesn't know who it was. However, a witness has claimed to have seen you dragging Mr. Dole out of the lunchroom shortly before the beating occurred."

"That's ridiculous. Jim is on my team. He's my back-up. I need him ready to play."

Principal Greenwood sighed. "Yeah… yeah."

"Is he hurt bad? Will he be able to play tonight?" The faux concern was dripping from my voice.

"He says he's fine. He told Coach Rollins that he would be ready to play tonight. We sent him home to get cleaned up."

"Good," I said, acting like it was the best news I could imagine getting. "Jim is a good running back. The team needs him."

"So… why do you think someone would come and tell me that you were involved in a situation with Mr. Dole when you weren't?" The principal leaned up, putting his elbows on the desk and steepling his fingers beneath his chin. His signature move. "Would anyone have a reason to try to get you in trouble?"

"Not that I'm aware of. But as a popular football player I can sometimes be a target by someone who is jealous of the attention we get for being on the team. I find it very disturbing that someone would say something like this about me. How many people told you that I was fighting with Jim?"

"Just one. You know I can't tell you who it was, so don't ask."

"Well, that should you tell you that your witness is lying. If this happened in the lunchroom then a lot of people would have seen it. The monitors would have seen it. Did you ask Mr. Hall?"

That was a gamble. I was fairly certain that Mr. Hall and the other staff in the lunchroom would have been asked about the incident well before Principal Greenwood called me to his office. If one of them had told him that I was guilty of dragging Dole out of the lunchroom he wouldn't have bothered asking. He would just started dishing out punishment. The risk was calculated, but it was still a risk.

"According to the lunchroom staff no one saw anything," Principal Greenwood said with a shrug. "You understand, I have to follow up on any leads when something like this happens."

"Of course. Of course," I said, nodding in understanding. "I'm sorry I couldn't be more help. And I'm glad Jim's going to be okay."

I could see in his eyes that there was more that he wanted to say, but Principal Greenwood let the subject drop. He knew he wasn't going to get anywhere. "Have a good game tonight, Mr. Blake."

"Thank you. I intend to, sir."

7. The Aztecs Return

The King Aztecs played a lot tougher game the second time around. We still beat them 48-0, but their defense did hold us to field goals twice.

Maybe it was my ego, but I felt like they wouldn't have been able to keep us from the end zone if Skyler had given the ball to me. I scored four or our six touchdowns simply by plowing through the defensive line. For some reason, though, Skyler decided to throw the ball on the two times we were stopped. The only thing I can figure is that he was chasing stats. Quarterbacks are often looking for touchdown passes much more than handing the ball off and letting someone else get the glory. If we'd lost the game Coach Rollins would have ripped his ass for that shit, but the game was so well in hand by the time they stopped us that nothing was brought up about it.

JK got a touchdown that game as well, catching a pass right up the middle. He took a hit, but stayed on his feet and broke off a thirty-five yard run for the score. Steve Bunch caught a pass in the end zone for the other TD.

I ended the game with four touchdowns and three sacks, but the true highlights for me were the three interceptions that Skyler threw. The fact that he was picked three times when he should have been concentrating on the running game made my night. Touchdown passes sure look great on a quarterback's stat sheet, but getting intercepted is an inherent danger in going for the big pass.

One of the interceptions came when he was trying to hit Donnie Marks in the end zone. Marks was covered heavily and there was really no shot at getting the ball to him, but Skyler made the decision to throw to him anyway. JK was getting open in the middle and the double coverage that the Aztecs had on our receivers had left the line weak. A simple hand off and I could have gotten a first down, if not the score, but Skyler had to make sure everyone knew he was the star of the team.

I made the tackle at our forty-five yard line to stop the defender from running the ball all the way back for a touchdown. Skyler stomped off the field in a huff. Chewy came up and clapped him on the shoulder and Skyler roughly pushed his hand away. Unfortunately there was no time for me to enjoy the dissention in the ranks of Skyler and his Goon Squad, I had to stay in and play defense.

On the first play after the interception the Aztecs quarterback dropped back to pass and I hammered him. The ball came loose and I dove on it, recovering the ball and giving Skyler a chance to redeem himself.

Coach Rollins brought me out for a quick rest and put Jim Dole in for a little while since I had been on the field for most of the game up to that point. To Skyler's credit, he did try to re-establish the running game with Dole in there, indicating that maybe he had learned from his mistake. He even went to Dole twice in a row. The problem was that Dole was hit behind the line both times and brought down for a loss each time.

On the third down Skyler went deep again and was intercepted again. It was picked at the goal line, intended for Bunch, and ran back to the twenty before JK made the stop. Skyler stormed off the field again, this time yelling at Steve Bunch for not being open.

Coach Rollins heard Skyler yelling at Bunch and stepped in for the receiver. "Hey Showboat, you shouldn't have thrown the fucking ball to the guy who was covered! Marks was wide open! Hammerhead was wide open!"

Skyler was steaming. For one thing, he wasn't used to getting his ass jumped for anything. For another thing, the coach called him Showboat and he hated that name. But when the coach says it you just have to take it.

Skyler ended the third quarter with another interception and he came out in the fourth. It was partly to keep from running up the score unnecessarily, partly to lower the risk of injury to the QB, and partly to give Greg Nelton a chance to play and get some game speed experience. I also thought that partly it was to punish Skyler for being an ass, and I know Skyler felt that, too.

Most of the first string offense came out in the fourth, though. We never scored again, but the second and third stringers got some valuable experience in moving the ball and they didn't screw up. I only played defense in the fourth quarter. Even though we had the game well in hand they kept the first string defense intact. We still didn't want to let anyone else score on us.

When the game was over the hometown crowd went nuts, and once again, we were the big heroes. As we were running into the locker room after the game, the Mustangs fans formed a gauntlet and cheered as we walked among them. We made our way through the tunnel of people, shaking hands and passing out high fives.

Ethan and Linda were there and when I passed her she grabbed me and hugged me. Ethan was jumping up and down and hugging me.

"Great game, Butcher!" Linda screamed over the din.

"Thanks!" I shouted, finally getting congratulations I truly appreciated. I pulled away to head into the locker room and Linda held on a little longer, giving me an electric look. There was no mistaking it. Anyone who saw the look knew what it meant.

When I looked across the crowd, scanning for my parents, I quickly found my mother. I could tell from the look on her face that she had caught Linda's look.

And I could tell that she knew what it meant.

Chapter Thirteen

1. Hero Of The Moment

When celebrating a victory every member of the team is required to make an appearance at the after game dance.

So I did.

I didn't want to be there, but I showed up just the same. There was a smoking hot full-grown adult woman with electric eyes waiting for me not far from where I stood and I intended to ditch the dance as soon as possible and get to her. Being one of the big stars of the game I, of course, had a lot of female attention at the dance. I just wasn't interested in mere girls any longer.

Linda would need a little time to get Ethan into bed, a few minutes to let him get to sleep, and then I could feel safe in sneaking over to her house. All I had to do was make sure I was at the dance long enough for the coaches to see that I showed up, which should have been about the same amount of time Linda would need.

Coach Rollins and Coach Walls were standing with the other chaperones along the wall, as far away from the deejay's speakers as possible while still being able to actually see the students on the floor. I decided to walk over and say something to Coach Rollins, just so he'd know I was there and I could get the hell out. I'd just tell him that I had things to do in the morning and I was going to take off if he didn't mind.

"Hey Coach! I think I'm going to..."

"Butcher Blake!" Coach Rollins shouted, still up from the victory. "I'm glad you came over. Help me collect the team. I spoke to the deejay and he's going to let me make an announcement and introduce the team. Talk about the game a little bit."

Shit.

I didn't like it, but I did as I was asked. In all honesty it probably didn't take me that long to round up the team. It only seemed like it. Every minute I was there was another minute I wasn't driving over to see Linda. It probably took less than ten minutes, but it felt like a half hour. We all gathered around Coach Rollins and he led us to the small stage where the deejay had his gear set up. Coach Rollins took the stage as the inane little dance song ended and the deejay handed him the microphone.

"HELLO MUSTANGS FANS!" Coach Rollins shouted into the microphone, feedback piercing eardrums throughout the crowded dance floor. No one let that stop their boisterous cheering. Everyone was really pumped. After all, we had just soundly trounced a team in the first game of the sectionals.

I fidgeted the whole time I was on the stage with Coach Rollins. It wouldn't have been so bad, but there was a clock on the wall directly across from us and I could do nothing but stare at it as the hands moved around the dial. When Coach Rollins got on a roll there was no telling how long he would talk. At the five-minute mark he finally got around to introducing the team. Scrubs first, but he even said a few good things about them. Nice work ethic, ready to step in when called upon. All that bullshit that you tell the guys who will never get in a game barring the death of several players.

Five more minutes and he was starting to talk about the second string players, some of whom participated in the win, so it took a lot longer. Almost ten minutes.

Sonofabitch! Come on, Coach! I need to go!

Surprisingly, no one seemed to be getting bored listening to the coach go on and on about the team. Well, I was getting bored, but no one else appeared to be.

Once he got to the first stringers, Coach Rollins really let it loose.

The cheers for those of us on the starting squad were deafening.

On the wall across from us the clock mocked me, burning away the minutes. It was getting later and later. How long would Linda wait up for me? If Coach Rollins kept going, inciting more and more hero worship, how long until I could get away?

Coach Rollins talked about the awesome play of the offensive and defensive lines and our great pass coverage in the secondary. He talked about JK's touchdown. He talked about Steve Bunch's touchdown. He talked about Skyler's two touchdown passes, casually glossing over Skyler's bonehead interceptions.

That's when I knew there was going to be trouble.

Coach Rollins broke with protocol and an evil look passed over Skyler's face. Skyler, as the quarterback, and as such *the* star of the team, was used to being introduced last. Not this time, though.

"I think it goes without saying who the most valuable player in the game tonight was," Coach Rollins teased. The students went nuts.

"BUTCHER! BUTCHER! BUTCHER!" the crowd began chanting. Coach Rollins signaled for the crowd to quiet down so he could speak. "Four rushing touchdowns! Three sacks, including one that forced a turnover, and more huge stops than I can even remember right now… BUTCHER BLAKE!"

The chant went up again. "BUTCHER! BUTCHER!"

Not to seem ungrateful for their adulation I stepped up and raised my hands in the air, basking in the glow. I didn't feel it, but I knew what they wanted to see. And I also knew that every time they said my name it drove an ice pick of rage through Skyler's brain. Most of the team slapped me on the back in congratulations, but not Skyler. He crossed his arms in a huff and threw glaring looks at me the whole time I was standing there with my arms raised.

The team walked off the stage and the deejay put on another stupid ass dance song. I made my move to start heading to the parking lot. The bad part was that I had to walk through the clamoring throng of Butcher Blake idolaters to get to my car.

Several minutes later I had made my way through the biggest crush of fans and well-wishers and I reached the door, which was a larger victory in my mind than the one on the field.

I had taken about ten steps out the door when I heard a girl's voice call out behind me. "Butcher!"

Turning around, I saw Stacy Lampley following me out. I stopped and waited for her to get to me. When she got to me, though, she didn't say anything. I gave her a look that said, '*What do you want?*'

"Uh… hi…" she said.

"Hi," I said back, waiting for what was so important as to chase me down.

"Are you leaving?"

I held up my car keys and jingled them. "Yeah. I'm outta here."

"Can I come with you?"

"Well… I… no. I have to be somewhere."

A morose disappointment spread across her face. "Will you give me a call then?"

"Yeah, sure. I'll call you," I said, having no intention of doing it. Stacy was a great girl, but that was just it. She was only a girl. I had a woman and she simply couldn't compete with that.

I watched her turn and walk slowly back into the school for a few seconds before sprinting to my car. I was hoping that Linda would still be up and waiting for me as I smoked the tires leaving the parking lot.

2. The Second Most Important Lesson I Ever Learned

I needn't have worried. Linda was still waiting on me.

No sooner had I stepped from my car then the front door to her house flew open, and there she stood, looking very anxious in a fuzzy pink robe, which I suspected to be all she had on.

Seconds later I found out that my suspicions were right, sliding my hands inside her robe and running them along her naked sides, down her legs and back. Her kisses were frenzied as she dragged me by the belt into the bedroom and closed the door behind us.

With the slightest of effort, Linda directed me to the bed and gave a little push, sprawling me backwards onto the mattress. If the Aztecs had seen how easy it was to take me down I'm sure they would have altered their game plan a little.

Faster than I could have imagined my pants were splayed wide open and my cock was in Linda's voracious mouth. She was a woman on fire and I wasn't about to do anything to quell the flames. I kept my mouth shut, laid back and let her do her worst. Even being so young I recognized the fact that it wasn't my place to make any decisions right then. Not that entire night. My sole purpose in her bed that night was to bring the hard-on and do whatever I was told.

After a few minutes it began to feel good. Really good. I reached up and stroked Linda's hair as her head bobbed up and down. All I received for my attempt at tenderness was an angry grunt and my hand slapped away. I pressed both hands against the mattress and held on for dear life, my body as rigid as a piece of oak, eyes wide in shock and awe. Years later the U.S. military would use the term "shock and awe" to describe their tactics.

They had no fucking idea.

My orgasm began to build, swelling in my lower belly and moving in tingles down my legs. My toes spread out and stretched, clenching spasmodically from the intensity of the pleasure. My breath came in hitching gasps and a slight trembling moved throughout my frame. This was it. I was going to erupt like Mount Vesuvius. And I actually felt like I could wipe out a city with what was soon to happen.

Ready to tumble over the edge I let out a little groan and a sound that came out like, "Gah –ah-hah-ah-ga."

Suddenly it stopped.

I opened my eyes and looked down, just as Linda angrily seized my shaft and squeezed. Hard. It looked like she was attempting to wring the neck of a chicken she absolutely hated. She snarled. "Don't you dare fucking come yet! I'm just getting started!"

Oh…

…Shit.

I was in serious trouble. You just don't get that close to an orgasm and back off like nothing happened. I had to focus. I took my attention completely off of what was going on below my waist. I tightened my abdominal muscles as tight as I could get them and squeezed, concentrating on the burn. I paid close attention to my breathing, calming it and making it as shallow as possible. For what seemed an eternity I was balanced on the edge of the orgasm receding and of it spewing like a geyser.

Eventually I regained my composure and let out a long, low sigh.

"Are you okay now?" Linda asked, still squeezing me.

"Yeah. I think so."

"You'd better do more than think so!" She squeezed even tighter.

"Yeah, yeah! I'm all right!"

"Good," she cooed playfully, dropping the strict demeanor almost instantly. "You don't get to come until I say you can."

I just nodded.

Linda released her grip and moved on top of me in one fluid motion, straddling my waist, taking me in to the hilt. I grabbed her hips and held her still for a second. If she moved at all right at that moment my best intentions weren't going to matter much. I had my eyes closed, trying to put my mind somewhere else.

It worked.

When I opened my eyes Linda was looking into them. She must have read something in my face because she knocked my hands away from her hips and began to move, slowly but deliberately. The sensation was on the verge of being too much, but I didn't want to stop her. I pushed my mind away again.

I'd heard all the jokes about guys having to think about baseball in order to put off their orgasm. I'd never had occasion to worry about putting off an orgasm before because I simply never cared if the girl got off or not. I wondered if it would work. In my head I started to recall the infield line-up of the Chicago Cubs.

It was working. Kind of.

I moved to the outfield.

So far, so good.

Batting order.

I was stuck. I couldn't think of the batting order. That's when the physical sensations began to creep in again. Baseball wasn't working.

What else could I concentrate on? Anything to keep my mind from realizing that I was having sex. As soon as I was fully in the moment I knew the moment would be gone. I had to think of something. Quick.

Video games!

I was relatively bored by video games, but I knew a lot about them. I could think about playing video games and that would keep my mind too busy to focus on Linda and her torturous ministrations.

I thought of *Pac-Man* for a little while. Nothing to it. In my head I watched the little yellow ball move around and eat up dots, and I was completely in control. For a while.

So then I thought of *Joust*. I was flying my ostrich all over the screen, trying to knock the other ostrich rider off with my lance. The symbolic sexual overtones were far too close to home. I had to think of a different game.

Linda let loose some guttural moans as her first orgasm washed over her. A wave of relief washed over me at the same time. Surely the torture was almost over. She had hers, now she would let me have mine. I picked up speed, trying to catch up to her.

With her internal muscles she clamped down on me, stopping my motion. "Don't even think about it!"

Linda leapt off of me and stood beside the bed. She slowly bent over, wiggling her ass lasciviously in invitation. She didn't have to tell me twice. I stood up and moved behind her, letting her help guide me inside. With slow, agonizing strokes I set a dangerous pace. I was going too fast to last long and too slow to reduce my speed without stopping.

I needed another game.

Pole Position?

No. The words "pole" and "position" weren't working for me right then. My pole was in the wrong position to be thinking that way.

Defender?

No. It wouldn't work. The spaceship firing lasers looked way too much like something else. Something that I was trying to avoid.

Punch Out?

Yeah. *Punch Out* would work.

I worked through the game in my mind, facing off against Glass Joe. He was always the punk of the game. Of course, he was a white guy. The announcer's voice called out each punch as I threw it.

"*Right hook. Right hook.*"

It didn't take long. Glass Joe went down like a hooker late on her rent. In my head my little green framework guy raised his hands in victory as the announcer yelled, "*Knock out!*"

It was working quite well. I decided to stick with the game. Hopefully Linda wouldn't pull the trick that women are famous for and ask me what I was thinking. I was too intent on my façade to have a good lie prepared, and I didn't think she'd want to know what I was really thinking about.

I looked down and saw the fleshy white globes of her ass cheeks in my hands. I was sawing into her steadily, my fingers denting her skin where I gripped her so firmly. The view was so hot that I...

Had to go back to thinking about *Punch Out*. And fast!

Shit! Who was next? Who was it? Glass Joe and… damn. Who?

BALD BULL! I almost shouted.

I could see him and it helped. A hulking, bald black man with red trunks. He was faster and stronger than Glass Joe. Bald Bull would move in, throw some punches and jump back out. Then he'd crouch down and taunt my green guy. Patience was all you needed. When Bald Bull moved in, dodge to the side and throw a punch from the opposite direction.

"*Right hook. Right hook.*" The announcer said lifelessly. I saw Bald Bull rocking from my strikes. I had to get more aggressive, more punches.

Linda moaned louder and hammered her hips backward into my body, taking me as deep inside of her as the position would allow, over and over. She forced her face into her pillow and screamed.

Sonofabitch, I hissed under my breath. She sure as hell wasn't making it easy on me. I redoubled my efforts to think about the game.

I was fine until the announcer went into his typical phrase when the player is beating up on the computer opponent.

"*Mighty blow! Mighty blow! Mighty blow!*" the announcer boomed.

Awww, damn it!

I had gotten carried away with those mighty blows and the festivities were going to be coming to a close very soon. I didn't want to disappoint Linda, but there was simply no turning back. She was going to think that I was just some two-pump chump high school boy. Which I kind of was, I just didn't want her to think it.

"Come for me!" Linda hissed back over her shoulder. "Come for me!"

Cha-ching!

Saved by the... bell?

With massive relief I gave up any pretense of holding out any longer and let my orgasm go. I instantly felt lighter, as if I was about to float up off of the floor. That feeling progressed to a sensation of being totally insubstantial. I was only vaguely aware of Linda's trembling body against mine. I was so caught up in the moment of weightlessness, basking in the glorious nothingness of my being, as incorporeal as a spirit. Lighter than a feather I felt myself poised to rise into heaven, and perhaps beyond. There were no coherent thoughts, other than the impulses streaming through my consciousness, unbidden, telling me that I was nothing more than drifting, crackling energy, unbound by the rules of physics and the laws of nature.

And then, suddenly, all my weight came back to me in a rush. My knees buckled, I fell backwards and hit my head on the dresser.

It hurt, but I couldn't have cared less. Time seemed to stand still.

"Damn..." I muttered.

I realized that Linda was standing over me, trying to help me up. "Are you okay?"

All I could do was laugh a tired little laugh.

I was so far beyond okay that I had no idea how to tell her.

3. Wasted Weekend

Saturday was kind of a wasted day for me.

I didn't get home until almost four a.m. and I was completely wrung out when I got there. I had just played an intense football game and then participated in more than three hours of sexual acrobatics. All I wanted to do was collapse into bed and wake up... whenever.

That's not how it went, though.

At seven o'clock my dad decided it was time for everyone to be up. He was awake, so everyone else in the house should be, too. The pounding at my bedroom door jarred me out of a deep sleep.

"Daylight is burning!" Dad bellowed from the other side of the door. It was one of his favorite up-and-at-em' phrases, right next to 'drop your cocks and grab your socks'.

"Let it burn," I groaned. It would have been fine with me if I missed every second of daylight that day.

"Get your ass out of bed and seize the day, Junior!"

"Seize this, Honkus." I rasped under my breath.

"What? Honkus?"

Dad never watched *History of the World Part One*. For JK and I it was the ultimate movie. I bet we watched it a hundred times. For a long time whenever JK was getting ready to leave I would say, "The jig is up!" His reply: "And gone!"

Dad pounded on the door, harder this time. "Get up!"

"Leave me alone. I'm tired."

"You wouldn't be if you'd come home at a decent hour."

"Jesus!" What the hell was wrong with sleeping past seven on a Saturday?

Fortunately, there was a way out of it. I knew how to get him to leave me alone. Throwing back the covers I stumbled out of bed and made my way clumsily to the door. I unlocked it and opened it wide. "I would like to rest up as much as I can today, please. I played a tough game last night. And then I spent the rest of the night banging not one, but two cheerleaders. I'm a little tired. Okay?"

My dad just shrugged and stepped back away from my door, a satisfied look on his face. "Okay."

I shut the door and heard him walk down the hallway. My mom yelled something to him, but I couldn't tell exactly what it was. Dad answered back, "No, he played a tough game yesterday. I'm just going to let him sleep."

A few seconds later I was sawing logs.

I slept through all the college games that I had wanted to see that day. There was no team playing that was worth missing out on sleep for. I never remembered my mattress being *that* comfortable, but I just slid down into it like a second womb. I didn't wake up until well after six p.m.

Sunday was equally wasted, however, I did get up and watch the NFL games with Dad. At halftime I made the food run to the kitchen, and that is where my mom cornered me about Linda.

"So, Ronald," she began, like she was trying to decide which way to go with it. "Is there anything you should tell me about that older woman at the game on Friday?"

Play it dumb, I thought. I continued making sandwiches. “Older woman?”

“After the game. The slow boys mother.”

“Lin…” I started, almost messing up. “Mrs. Miles?”

“Yes. Mrs. Miles. Is there something going on?”

“No,” I laughed. “She’s Ethan’s mom.”

Mom seemed satisfied with my response. “All right. Well, you just watch yourself around her.”

“Why?” If you’re going to play it dumb, play it real dumb.

“I saw the way she was looking at you and how she acted toward you. That woman has bad intentions, Ronald.”

“Oh, come on!” I laughed again to show her how silly the notion was. “You’ve got to be kidding!”

“I’m serious. You just watch yourself. She’s too old for you.”

“Yeah, no shit! She’s Ethan’s mother.”

I grabbed the sandwiches and another bag of chips and headed back into the living room to the game, shaking my head to let my mother know that I thought she was way off base.

Inside I was going, ‘*Oh shit! Busted*!’

Considering that I did so much with Ethan I had an out anytime I wanted to see Linda, but I was going to have to be careful. Sure, I was almost eighteen and could do what I wanted, but it just seemed like a better idea to keep as much secret as I could. It suddenly occurred to me that the best cover would be to act offended. I turned and went back into the kitchen.

"Mom, Mrs. Miles asked me if I could take Ethan trick-or-treating next week. She is going to have to work late. Is it okay if I do that, or do you think I'm going to be having sex with her?" I put on my haughtiest, most self-righteous voice I could muster.

I knew it worked. She looked almost apologetic. "It's not like that, Ronald! I wasn't accusing you of anything. I was just asking. I have a right to be concerned. I'm your mother. That woman isn't much younger than I am."

"Hey, it's fine if you don't trust me. I'll understand. I'll tell Ethan that he has to stay home because my mom thinks I'm screwing his mom!"

"Ronald!" I was getting the look.

"I might have to tell him what screwing means, but I think he'll get it. Is that what I should tell him?"

Mom pursed her lips and glared at me. "Forget I even said anything. I was just looking out for you."

I put down the bag of chips on the counter and gave her a strong one-armed squeeze. "I know. Don't worry."

Just like that the issue was closed.

Linda had, in fact, asked me to take Ethan trick-or-treating for her because she did have to work late. Halloween, being the last day of the month, just happened to land at a very busy time when her boss wanted the months business completely wrapped up before anyone went home.

If I stayed a little late that night to get a treat of my own from Linda, who would be the wiser?

Chapter Fourteen

1. The Butcher Blake Hall of Fame

I went through the motions on Monday.

It was the gym early in the morning, school all day, and then home. Simple, to the point, and boring. I was invited over to watch Monday Night Football at JK's, but I thought I was going to give it a pass. Not that it wouldn't be fun to watch the game with JK, but I wanted to be able to leave at a moments notice if Linda should happen to call and there was a chance for more mind blowing, life altering sex.

A lot of the players were going to watch the game at Sharky's and I definitely knew that I didn't want to be there. I could deal with Skyler and his goons at practice, at games, and even at the victory dances. When I was on my own time I wanted nothing to do with them. I just couldn't relax around the team anymore. You always had to be watching your back to see what was coming next. Being that I was Skyler's current favorite target I saw no point in hanging out with the team. Sure, it made Skyler's argument that I thought I was too good for the team look like it was an actual fact, but there was nothing I could do about that. I didn't have the inclination or the energy to waste on defending myself to the players who would believe his bullshit.

Having dropped Ethan off at home and having an afternoon to myself I found the inspiration I had needed to do some of the chores my dad was always after me to get done. It was a crisp and cool day. A good day to clean out the garage. I put on some clothes that I didn't mind messing up and went out to the disaster that Dad called a garage.

We hadn't been able to keep a car in there for quite a few years. The whole space was filled with boxes and other items of unknown origin. Unknown to me, at least. I was certain that Dad knew exactly what everything was, where it came from, and how long he'd had it. Why it was up to me to clean up his mess I had no idea. I didn't worry about that, though. I dove right in and started trying to make headway.

Being a contractor, Dad had boxes upon boxes of old and broken power tools. Circular saws that had long since burned up their motors, drills that smoked when you used them. I tested them and discarded them into a different area of the garage for removal if they didn't work. I sorted and neatly stacked the left over wood trim from when Dad remodeled the living room several years before.

After that I stopped and looked around at the huge job that still awaited me. The only way to truly get the garage cleaned out would be to rent a dumpster and just throw it all out. I had no idea where to put some things,

I didn't know if Dad wanted to keep some of the things that I was sure was junk. I began poking around, more to put off doing any more work than actually looking for anything.

That is when I found the goldmine.

In a large box marked "IMPORTANT", I found the key to my Dad's attitude toward me.

The box was packed with albums of photographs of me playing football from all the way back when I was seven years old in the local youth league up until my junior year. There was an album of newspaper clippings of everything I had ever done on the football field. I found the clipping in it from when my first team, the Beecher Tool and Die Steelers, defeated the Dennings Construction Dolphins for the city championship. I was eight years old and that was the first year I got to play very much. They always let all the kids get in the game, but of course, some played more than others. When I was ten I had to become a lineman instead of a running back. They had a rule to keep the big kids from crushing the little kids, so anyone over one hundred forty pounds couldn't carry the ball. It didn't feel exactly fair, but it made good sense. Plus, it taught me how to play defensive tackle, which I loved.

Turning more pages I got into my junior high school years. My school was extremely politically incorrect back in those days. Our mascot was a Native American warrior and we were known as the Cutler Park Savages. They've since changed the team name to the Cutler Park Tigers and replaced the mascot with a Tony the Tiger clone. A group of concerned citizens protested until the changes were made. The town took part in renaming the team through a contest in the local paper. If the protesters had known the names that were suggested they would have felt lucky that we had gone with the Savages to start with. My mother had a friend at the paper and she told us some of the names that were suggested. The Drunken Injuns was the most popular submission. Racial insensitivity was a repetitive theme throughout the contest, it seemed. The Sweaty Mexicans, the Greedy Jews, the Cheap Scotsmen, the Angry Germans, the Hairy Wops. Other names included the Cretins, the Assholes, the Pig Fuckers. You get the picture. It's no wonder they went with the Tigers.

Even in junior high I was the star. The clippings from Bill Morgan sang my praises back then just like they always had. In seventh grade he did a long piece on me, saying that I was not just a future NFL star, but a definite Hall of Famer. I had to laugh. It was flattering as hell, but it was no wonder I was the kind of asshole that I had become in high school. For as long as I could remember everyone had been telling me how great I was, simply because I could play a game well. It takes the reality right out of real life.

Besides Bill Morgan's bootlicking articles Dad had cut out letters that people had written in to the paper that mentioned me. One guy went so far, during my freshman season, as to call me the Second Coming. That was just unreal. I had never seen that particular piece before and I had to admit, it freaked me out a little bit. What kind of damn town was I living in where people wrote things like that to the paper? About a high school freshman no less!

Under the books I found my old Steelers helmet from our championship year. Inside the helmet there was a football. I took the ball out and looked at it. Dad had written on the side of the ball, in magic marker, "Ronald's First Touchdown" and then a date that had been smeared and wasn't legible.

They didn't give us our first touchdown ball or our helmets. The league couldn't afford to give that stuff away. Dad must have bought them from the league. I had no idea. Under the helmet there were plastic bags with my old jerseys in them.

The box was almost a shrine unto me. I was humbled. I never knew that my dad had kept all of that stuff and that he had all of those pictures of me. In a lot of ways I still thought that he was living through me and wanting my success as a testament to him, but after finding the box I realized that there was more to it than that. His constant bitching and all the pressure he was putting on me to succeed was something he was doing because he wanted that success for me.

Well, mostly.

"I see you found the box," Dad said from behind me. I didn't hear him walk up. I hadn't even heard his truck pulling into the drive.

"I didn't know you had all this stuff!"

"That's not all of it. There's another box in my bedroom. The more recent stuff."

"Wow! I haven't even seen some of this. Those letters people wrote and all that kind of thing!"

Dad leaned against the doorjamb and sighed. "You didn't realize how big of a hero you are to some of these people around here, did you?"

I knew I was very popular, but being called the Second Coming was new to me. "No. I had no idea."

"That's why I push you so hard. You have something that millions of people would give anything to have. I see it as my job to make sure that you don't squander it. It's not everyday that a kid comes along who can play *one* position like you do, much less *two* positions."

I stood there and thought about what he was saying for a second. I knew he was right and I felt like a damn ingrate, taking my talent for granted all those years.

"Don't forget, you've got a guy from Iowa coming to the game on Friday night. That's a good football school. Show him something out there."

I nodded and held up my first touchdown ball. "Want to throw it around a little bit?"

Dad smiled and nodded, "Yeah, we can throw the ball a little bit. But not that one."

Dad grabbed a ball off the shelf by the door and we threw it back and forth until Mom called us in for dinner. It was good, throwing that ball and talking to my dad. Almost the same as it was when I was a kid and he was just teaching me how to throw it. I think he always wanted me to be a quarterback anyway, but that's not the direction my talent took me. We had a great time.

It was actually one of the last good days I had with him.

2. When Retards Attack

At practice on Tuesday I nailed our trick passing play.

I think it was probably the extra practice of throwing the ball with my dad that did it. We ran the stretch play like always and then I stopped, turned, and threw across the field to JK who was standing there all by himself. By the time the defense caught onto the play he was crossing over the goal line. And our own defense should have known it would eventually be coming at them. I hoped we would get the opportunity to run that play. If it worked it was going to be beautiful and I really wanted to try to make that throw.

Wednesday I concentrated more on working with the defense. I pushed the tackling sled around the field for a little bit and worked on speed drills. The Moore Mavericks would likely double team me like they did the first time, so I wanted to be fast enough to go around the outside if I had to and still get pressure on the quarterback. Moore was a good team. We beat them 50-0 the first time we faced them, but they had gotten better over the season and we expected a much better game from them this time around.

Chewy missed practice on Thursday, and I found it hilarious. He missed practice because of Ethan.

For some reason Mrs. Rickman allowed Ethan to leave class early to go to the bathroom down the hall. Maybe she thought he'd be back before the bell rang, I don't know. When I got to the class to pick him up and take him to his next class she let me know that he wasn't there. She had let him go to the bathroom and he hadn't come back. I immediately knew that something was wrong and I took off at a dead run to get there.

As I was nearing the bathroom I saw a lot of underclassmen hurrying out of the bathroom with fearful looks on their faces. It made me think of rats abandoning a sinking ship. Whatever was happening in the bathroom wasn't good and they wanted to be long gone before it happened to one of them. I didn't even slow down as I burst through the door.

The first thing I saw was that Skyler and Chewy had a small kid down on his knees and I could hear the sounds of crying. They weren't doing anything, just standing there and laughing. I didn't know if they had done anything physical to the kid on the floor, but I knew it was Ethan and I knew that if they had I was going to be in some serious trouble for what I would do to them.

"Skyler, leave him the fuck alone!" I commanded.

"Lighten up, Butcher," Skyler began, his normal cocky attitude seeping through his words. "We haven't touched him."

"Ethan, what did they do to you?" I asked, finally seeing his tear streaked face. "Did they hurt you?"

He shook his head without ever taking his eyes off of Chewy. Ethan tried to talk, but his lower lip was quivering so much that nothing came out.

"Calm down, Ethan. What did they do?"

"I told you we didn't do anything to him! Jesus, Butcher! Why don't you two just get fucking married?" Skyler leaned against the tiled wall.

"I didn't ask you a damn thing, did I?" I yelled at Skyler, pushing him in the chest and pointing my finger right in his face.

"Don't fucking push me, Blake," Skyler said, a hint of fear in his voice. Chewy stood there, dumbstruck. He normally would have gone after anyone who touched Skyler, but since it was me he was unsure of what to do.

I pushed him again. "What did they do to you, Ethan?"

This time Ethan found his voice. "They... they... yelled at me. And called me names. I tried to leave and they wouldn't let me!"

"Shut the fuck up, Teeth!" Skyler shouted. "We didn't touch you!"

I pushed him again. "You shut the fuck up!"

Skyler nodded to his bodyguard. "Kick his ass, Chewy!"

I knew that a big, meaty fist would be coming my way as I turned around, so I was prepared to take the hit if I couldn't dodge it. It was going to hurt like a mother fucker, too. Chewy was as strong as an ox and almost as smart.

The blow never landed. I had gotten myself turned in time to see the massive fist coming for my head, but suddenly it stopped in mid-swing and dropped. I wasn't sure why Chewy would have held back his punch. That is, until I saw Ethan.

When Chewy tried to sucker punch me from behind, Ethan launched himself from off of his knees and seized Chewy by his quite substantial groin area with both hands. Vicious snarls were issuing from Ethan, who held on like a pitbull. Drool trailed from Ethan's mouth and the fire that burned in his eyes was rather scary. Ethan growled, "Don't hit Butchie! Don't hit Butchie! Don't hit Butchie!"

Ethan's grip and momentum combined to drive Chewy backwards and off of his feet, slamming full force into the stall partitions and breaking them, and then down to the floor. Chewy hit with a heavy thud and the air rushed out of his lungs. He was gasping for air and

Ethan still held on, both hands packed full of the big man's crotch.

"GET HIM OFF ME! GET HIM OFF ME, BUTCHER!" Chewy screamed when he got enough air back into his lungs, his voice higher than normal. He was panicked and in serious pain. Chewy reached down and tried to push Ethan away, but Ethan held on even tighter. Then he began to twist. "STOP HIM, BUTCHER! PLEASE!"

Skyler looked down and saw Chewy in trouble and he did exactly what I expected him to do.

He ran.

"Don't hit Butchie! Don't hit Butchie!" Ethan continued to chant gutturally, still squeezing.

Chewy tried to yell something else, but when he opened his mouth all that came out was a geyser of vomit. I jumped out of the way when it headed toward me.

"Ethan! Let him go!" I said.

"Don't hit Butchie! Don't hit Butchie!" More crotch twisting.

Chewy puked again.

"ETHAN! LET HIM GO! HE'S HAD ENOUGH!"

Ethan quit his growling chant, but he didn't release his grip. He looked up at me and began to cry all over again.

"Come on, Ethan. Let him go," I said calmly.

Ethan broke down in tears and let go of Chewy's twisted crotch. Chewy just lay there on the floor, breathing heavy and squeezing his eyes tightly shut. A few dry heaves wracked his body. I helped Ethan to his feet and then leaned down over Chewy.

"You got what you had coming. Let's leave this here. All right?"

Chewy groaned and nodded.

"Don't mess with Ethan anymore."

Chewy groaned and nodded again.

I helped Ethan clean himself up and dry his eyes and then we walked out of the bathroom together, heading to his next class.

"Thanks for helping me back there, Ethan. You did good. Chewy would have crushed my skull." I said, reaching out to shake his hand. He went from tears to smiles in no time flat.

"You wouldn't let people pick on me. I won't let them pick on you, either. You're my best friend, Butchie."

"You're my best friend, too, Ethan."

Ethan smiled even more broadly and then his face grew dark. "What about JK? Isn't he you're best friend?"

"Yeah. He is, too."

That answer seemed to be good enough for him.

3. The Mother Fucking Butcher Blake Power Hour

The bus ride to the Mavericks game was a tense one.

Skyler and his cronies had taken it upon themselves to segregate the bus, trying to separate me, and anyone who would sit with me, from the rest of the team. I realized from all the snide sarcasm that I was supposed to be bothered by it, but I wasn't. In fact, I rather enjoyed having a peaceful ride to the game. JK, Bunch and Marks sat with me and we had a good, productive conversation on the way. Sure, we briefly spoke about the game, but we eventually got down to the really important issues. You know, like which cartoon character would you most like to have sex with and why, or what two celebrities would you like to see in a knife fight to death and who would win. Those kinds of important issues.

For the record, I said Betty Rubble because I like her laugh and a knife fight between any two New Kids On The Block. I didn't care who won.

Nothing was said about Ethan taking Chewy down in the bathroom. I assumed Skyler and the Goon Squad wanted it kept quiet and I would oblige. The fastest way to get Ethan messed with some more would be to antagonize the big oaf about it.

Despite the animosity on the bus we played well. The Mavericks had gotten a lot better over the season, so we only beat them 21-0 this time. They nearly scored a couple times, though. If not for two huge goal line stands by our defense they would have gotten into the end zone on us. And if not for two huge plays by yours truly they would have most likely kicked a field goal.

We drew first blood with my forty-yard run for a touchdown on our first possession. On the first kick off to the Mavericks our special teams folded and let them run it all the way back to the one-yard line. Coach Rollins was furious. I was very glad that I wasn't playing special teams. On the other hand, a defensive player doesn't like to take the field for the first time while being asked to not allow even one single yard.

The Mavericks first play was a very predictable, very telegraphed run, right up the middle. We stopped him for a yard loss. The next play they tried to get sneaky and set up in the same formation, with the exception of pulling their wide receivers slightly farther outside. We picked up on that and expected a pass play, but we still had to defend the run just as tough. They faked the hand off and the receivers tried to get open. Todd Benson, their quarterback, had nowhere to throw and I could see the panic on his face as I crushed him into the turf on the six-yard line. I think I hurt his shoulder a little from the way he was moving it when he got to his feet.

On the third down we expected another run attempt. They were going to play it safe, not wanting their quarterback hit again and not wanting to risk turning the ball over. They'd give it one more shot and then bring out the kicker. Our special teams had virtually assured the Mavericks a minimum of three points, so we were just doing what we could to make sure that was all they got.

Their running back, I think his name was Davis, took the hand off and went for a hole. He was hit at the line of scrimmage by Brad "Tank" Sherman, who drove his helmet into the ball and popped it loose. The ball almost seemed to hover in the air between Benson and myself, two steps away from me and three steps away from him. I snagged the ball and less than a second later Benson tried to tackle me.

I promptly knocked him down and ran his ass over. When he went down it was all open field from there on out and I was gone. I scored my longest touchdown run ever, ninety-four yards.

Less than three minutes into the game and I had already scored twice. Bill Morgan was definitely going to have something to write about in Saturday's paper.

Benson went out of the game at that point and they brought in their back up for the rest of the quarter. He returned in the second. I don't think I hurt him with the sack, I think he hurt himself trying to tackle me.

The Mavericks secondary coverage was excellent and Skyler had a hell of a time trying to find an open receiver throughout the rest of the first half, forcing us to go to the run more than we expected. We had limited success with the stretch play, but the Mavs always stopped us, forcing us to punt our way to half time.

In the locker room at half time Coach Rollins demanded that we score on our first possession of the second half. His contention was that fourteen points was a long way from enough to guarantee we beat the Mavericks, and he was right. We had beaten them pretty badly early in the season and they absolutely knew they were a better team than they had shown us the first time. They weren't going to quit. They wanted us bad.

We kicked off to them, stopped them three and out, and returned their punt to the fifty. I got seven yards on our first down with the stretch play, and that was all we got. Skyler threw an incomplete pass, followed by an interception that was run back to the ten yard-line before JK took him down.

On the Mavericks first play I put the pressure on Benson and he made an ill-advised throw, trying to avoid the sack. He had a man in the end zone, somewhere in that general direction, but the receiver was swamped in purple and green jerseys. Mike Emmons, our top cornerback, stepped up and picked it out of the air as if it were intended for him. They brought him down just outside of the end zone, not even to the one.

Skyler passed Emmons as he was taking the field with the offense and Emmons held up a hand for a high five. Skyler coldly ignored the gesture. Emmons just shrugged and said, "You're fucking welcome!"

To get us out of their end zone Skyler called a pass play. And, to stick with the theme for the night, it didn't work. Incomplete pass to Marks in the slot. Skyler threw it behind him and then yelled at Donnie for missing his shitty throw. Skyler called another pass play and he actually hit Steve Bunch along the sideline, but the throw was high and when Steve came down his right foot was out of bounds. Of course, that wasn't Skyler's fault, either. In the huddle before the third down Skyler called another pass play. I had to say something.

"Let's try the stretch. I bet it will at least get us out of the end zone." I offered. The team was in my heart and I honestly wasn't looking for personal glory. Skyler didn't see it that way. He blew up at me.

"I CALL THE PLAYS, GODAMMIT!" Spittle dripped from his enraged mouth. "THIS AIN'T THE MOTHER FUCKING BUTCHER BLAKE POWER HOUR"

"It's not the Derek Skyler All-Star Showboat, either," I said calmly. I wanted to settle him down, but still get him to see reason. "Their pass coverage is too good. These guys are no joke. We've had some success with the stretch."

"Give him the fucking ball, man." I didn't know who said it, but when I followed the voice I was looking at Chewy. "We'll make sure he gets the yards."

More voices chimed in, echoing the same sentiments. All the linemen, including Shorty, wanted to go for it.

Skyler grudgingly conceded and called the stretch. "If it doesn't work this shit is on you fucking assholes!"

To Skyler's dismay I got twenty-one yards on the play.

We went to the run exclusively for the next seven plays, taking us down to their forty-yard line.

Skyler's ego was aching, so he insisted on another pass play, and it was nearly intercepted. That was when Coach Rollins gave us the sign. He wanted us to try the trick play. Skyler didn't like it, but he knew better than to ignore the sign. We set up in the trick formation. If they didn't catch the fact that JK was in a different position we knew we had a chance to pull it off.

They didn't catch it.

Skyler called for the snap and we all swept to the right. The Mavericks all followed us, knowing that they had to stop the stretch again. Skyler got the ball into my hands and I stopped on a dime. The play continued moving right.

When I turned I saw JK standing way off on the other side of the field, all by himself. It was just like playing catch with my dad in the backyard. I threw the hardest pass I could and hit him dead in the numbers. JK could have walked it in, no one was close enough to have a shot at catching him.

I expected Brent Patton to hustle out onto the field to kick the extra point, but when I noticed no one was moving I looked back to the field.

There was Skyler, lying on the ground and holding his shoulder. To this day no one can remember anyone touching him, but he insisted that he took a hit while blocking for me. We all know what really happened.

Skyler couldn't get it going and so he quit. He just plain quit on us.

The extra point made it 21-0 and that is where the score stayed. Greg Nelton took over for Skyler and had no better luck with the pass than Skyler did. We moved the ball, we just never got in scoring position again. More importantly, neither did the Mavericks. I ended the game with three sacks, two touchdowns and a touchdown pass.

Once again, Derek Skyler was wrong, and he knew it.

That night it was, in point of fact, the Mother Fucking Butcher Blake Power Hour.

Chapter Fifteen

1. Halloween With Ethan

After a great weekend, Monday came too fast.

Friday after the game I talked to Henry Landru, the scout from Iowa, and he said that he wanted to come to my house to speak to me sometime. Dad invited him for dinner on Saturday and he accepted, so I didn't have to bother with making any plans for Saturday night. Not that I was planning much. I figured that after Ethan went to bed I would sneak over and visit Linda. That was pretty much the extent of my social life anyway.

Saturday's dinner was pleasant enough. Mr. Landru impressed me with his sincerity and he answered all my questions. Even the ones that weren't about football. When he left he told me that he would be following up on me and that he personally thought I would make an excellent Hawkeye. That wasn't a guarantee, but it sounded damn good. I didn't know if I wanted to go to Iowa for sure, but it was a good school with a good football program, so it was nice to have someone on the inside wanting me. I had plenty of time to make a decision. At least Landru wasn't a plastic jerkoff like Peter Kurten had been.

Once Mr. Landru left I excused myself for the evening and went to hang out with JK until it was time to go see Linda. JK had a date with a cheerleader from DeMille, so he had to kick me out a little early. I spent a few hours driving around just to kill time.

Finally, I got over to see Linda, and once again, she tore my ass up. She made me wait in the living room while she did something in the bedroom, the anticipation nearly killing me. I had no idea what was going on, but I was pretty sure I was going to like it.

And I did.

When Linda called for me to come into the bedroom I was met with quite a sight. She was in her old cheerleader outfit, her hair pulled back into a ponytail and purple and green pom-poms going nuts. She did a few high kicks and whispered a couple of "Yay's", so as not to wake Ethan up. I thought I'd seen a glimpse of pink when she did the kicks and I turned out to be correct. Linda stopped and thrust out her hip, tilting her head down and raising her eyes to mine. She tossed the pom-poms aside and grabbed the front of her skirt, raising it slowly to show me what was underneath. "Butcher…"

"Y-yes," I stammered.

"Come here and give me an 'F'."

And boy did I.

Sunday was more football at home with the old man. We just sat there and watched the games, not really talking about anything except what was happening on the field. Even when we had nothing else to talk about, Dad and I could always talk about football. The conversation could realistically go:

"You're a dick!"

"You're lazy! Do your damn chores!"

"How about those Bears?"

"Payton is God."

Argument over.

The only thing out of the ordinary that happened all day Sunday was that we kept getting phone calls, but the caller would hang up before saying anything. You have to remember, this was back in the days before everyone had Caller ID on their home phones. I answered the phone once and someone started to speak, and then seemed to think better of it and they hung up in a hurry. It was getting pretty frustrating. For all I knew it was Skyler or one of his toadies messing with me. I wouldn't give them the satisfaction of getting angry and yelling over the phone. I spent most of the day just politely listening to the caller hang up.

Finally on Monday, school was a breeze. Skyler was still pissed at me for doing my job and playing well, but instead of doing anything or saying anything directly to me, he just left me alone. In the gym that morning he totally ignored me, which was actually about the best I could hope for.

After school I took Ethan back to his house, and using the key that Linda gave me, we went in and I helped him get into his Halloween costume. He was almost bouncing off the walls in his excitement to go trick-or-treating. There was a Polaroid camera on the kitchen table with a note that instructed me to be sure to get a picture of Ethan in his costume, there were Cokes in the fridge, and she would be home a little after eight or nine unless something went wrong.

Linda had made Ethan's costume. He was Liono from the *Thundercats*. The costume looked to be pretty authentic, but Ethan just didn't fill it out properly. Liono was a walking muscle with a mane of flowing red hair. Ethan, in the costume, looked like a Liono stick figure with an orange Q-tip on his head. That didn't matter, though. He seemed to be incredibly happy in the outfit. I took his picture, we each drank a Coke, and we headed out to start the pillaging.

In his own neighborhood Ethan did very well. Everyone recognized him and gave him a little extra. He made out like a bandit in the three square blocks surrounding his house. When we got beyond that things started to dry up for him. A lot of people didn't want to give him any candy because of his age, but they still did, albeit grudgingly. When the people started in with their attitudes I decided to tell Ethan trick-or-treating was over and we had to head home. Ethan was upset, having just found his groove, yelling, "Thunder! Thunder! Thundercats!" as we approached every house. It was still early when we got back to his house, his *Thundercats* pillowcase only half full of candy.

With shoulders dropped and shuffling feet, Ethan began the long slow walk to his bedroom to get out of the costume. It was pitiful and I hated watching him slink off like that. I had an idea that might perk him up.

"Ethan, don't change just yet. I have somewhere else we can go."

Ethan's face lit up like a small sun. "Really?"

"Yeah. Let's get in the car and I'll take you out to Rambling Hills. They really do it up big for Halloween out there." I expected that he would more than double his haul out at Rambling Hills, so I had him dump his pillowcase into a big mixing bowl for later. "You're going to need the whole bag."

We drove out there, pulled through the big open gates and parked in front of the first house on the right. There was nothing on the left except for a big, man-made lake anyway. I got Ethan out of the car and he froze, staring up at the house.

The place was huge, for one thing. I could see where that could be kind of intimidating to Ethan. The other thing, though, was the elaborate decorations. There was a fairly reasonable facsimile of a blood-soaked operating room on the front lawn, complete with a mad scientist in medical scrubs and a blood encrusted scalpel. Body parts littered the yard. There were small speakers near the garage pumping out spooky Halloween sounds. Ethan seemed to want nothing to do with going up to the house and getting some candy.

"Well, are you going up?"

Ethan shook his head no, fear lining his face.

"Come on, Ethan. It's just pretend. They give good candy out here. Sometimes you might even get a full size candy bar."

His interest was piqued, but he still wasn't moving.

I had been waiting back on the sidewalk and letting him walk to the doors by himself earlier in the night. Of course, there was nothing in his neighborhood like that display, or any of the others we could see down the block. "Would you go up if I went with you?"

Ethan looked relieved and nodded a yes.

"Okay, come on." I clapped him on the shoulder and we made our way up the driveway and onto the front step. "Go ahead. Ring the bell."

Ethan put his finger out to ring the bell and pulled it away. He put it out again and jerked it away at the last second. A third time he pulled his finger back and I reached up and rang the bell for him. He gave me a panicked look that seemed to say, *'I can't fucking believe you did that!'* He held his ground, though. I saw him steeling himself as we heard the footsteps from inside the house coming to the front door.

A middle-aged man in a pastel orange sweater answered the door, and he was holding a martini glass. Ethan opened his mouth to say something and nothing came out for a few seconds. He finally blurted out, a little too loud, "TRICK-OR-TREAT!"

The man jumped back at Ethan's shout, spilling his martini on his sweater. "Damn it! Look what you did!"

"I'm sorry, mister!" Ethan was horrified that he had made the man spill his drink on himself. "I didn't mean to yell."

The man was holding the sweater away from his body and looking at it with disgust. "It's not mister. It's doctor. And sorry doesn't fix my sweater!"

"But I'm REALLY sorry!" Ethan said, almost pleading for the man's forgiveness. "REALLY, REALLY."

I was about to step in and try to defuse the situation, but I didn't get a chance. The man shifted his disgusted look from his supposedly ruined sweater and cast a baleful glare on Ethan.

"Don't you think you're a little old to be out trick-or-treating?" the man asked.

Ethan didn't respond. He didn't know how to respond to the hostility he was getting from the man.

"You're too old. I'm not giving you anything. Get out of here," the man ordered with a sneer of derision. Ethan began to tear up, his eyes brimming.

I leaned in to whisper something to the man, so that Ethan wouldn't hear it. I didn't want him to feel any worse. "Mister, he's... slow. In his mind he's still a kid. Couldn't you just give him some candy and we'll be on our way?"

The man's face screwed up in rage. "IT'S NOT MISTER! IT'S DOCTOR! I DIDN'T GO TO MEDICAL SCHOOL SO THAT I COULD BE CALLED MISTER BY A COUPLE OF PUNKS WHO THINK THEY'RE STILL EIGHT YEARS OLD!"

I grabbed Ethan by the shoulder and turned him away from the raging asshole in front of him. "Hey... MISTER! Fuck you!" I extended my middle finger and put it a couple of inches in front of his face.

"GET OFF OF MY PROPERTY! RIGHT NOW! TAKE YOUR RETARDED FRIEND WITH YOU!"

The man was coming out of the house, so I guided Ethan away from him, putting myself between him and the man. "We're going. We're going."

"YOU'RE DAMN RIGHT YOU'RE GOING! YOU'RE GOING TO JUVENILE HALL IF YOU DON'T GET THE HELL OUT OF HERE!"

When I got Ethan halfway down the driveway the man stopped and watched us go. I heard a woman's voice from inside the house say, "Wayne, just give them some candy, for Christ's sake!"

He spun on his heel and stomped back into the house, looking like his anger had just found a new focus. I felt bad for the woman, but I had to get Ethan out of there. Tears were streaming down his cheeks and he was sobbing as he got him into the car and then ran around to jump in the other side.

"Butchie... why does everybody hate me?" he whined, a snot bubble expanding and bursting out of his nose.

"Oh, come on," I said, softening my voice for him. "That guy is a dick. And he was mad at me for cussing at him. He wasn't mad at you."

"Oh yes he was! I made him spill his drink on his sweater. I'm so stupid!"

Ethan's torso was heaving with giant hitching sobs and he was sucking in quivering gulps of air through his trembling lips.

"Ethan, stop it! You're not stupid! You're just different. If everyone was the same, wouldn't this be a boring world?"

I started the car and turned around in the first driveway I came to and headed out of Rambling Hills. "Don't let what that piece of shit said make you feel bad. He's just a mean old bastard. I should have had you twist his nuts like you did to Chewy."

Ethan let out a small burst of laughter, bracketed by louder sobs. "It's not just him. Everyone hates me at school, too. I'm good! They should like me. I'm good!"

"You are good, Ethan! You are! If someone picks on you that means that there is something wrong with them, not you. Do you remember when I picked on you?"

He nodded, and turned his head to me. The tears were still streaming, but the heaving had stopped.

"Well, that had nothing to do with you. It was a problem with me. There was something wrong with me that made me do that to you. When people pick on you they are unhappy with a part of them. It's not your fault. It's never your fault! If these people could get to know you they'd love you!"

"Because I'm good?" Ethan asked hopefully.

I had to laugh. "Yes, because you're good."

Ethan smiled a sad smile through his tears. "I just wish people weren't so mean to me."

"Me too. It's not fair. But you know, it happens to everyone."

Ethan didn't look convinced. "Even to you."

"Yeah. There are people who don't like me. Quite a few actually."

"Why don't they like you?" Ethan looked personally offended that someone wouldn't like me.

"That's not important. What is important is that you know that what has happened to you also happens to everyone else at some point. You're just a normal kid and this is a normal kid thing."

I could tell that nothing could have made him happier than to be told that he was a normal kid. He wiped his eyes and dried the tears from the backs of his hands on his silver Liono suit.

"That guy back there was just a real bastard and he was mean and rude. But there is one good thing to think about." I reached up and took off the orange wig that was starting to slide over Ethan's face.

"What's good to think about?"

"Well, people like that always get what's coming to them. It might not be now, or even in a year, but sooner or later they get what they deserve."

Ethan didn't really understand what I was talking about, but the tears had stopped and he was somewhat back to normal.

"Butchie, let's go home and eat my candy. You can have the candy corn. I don't like it."

"I want that little Snickers bar you got."

"Nooooo," he giggled. "I love Snickers!"

"Then how about the Milky Way?"

"Nooooo! I love Milky Way!" He was giggling even more, the crying jag of a moment before now nothing more than ancient history to him. "Just kidding! You can have it!"

Ethan was laughing again and I was glad to see it.

If you'd told me a few months before that seeing a retarded kid laugh would have made my day I would have thought you were crazy.

2. A Big Gulp Of Pride

When I walked into the locker room before practice on Tuesday I was greeted with cold stares and dead silence.

I had no idea what I had done, but I was pretty damn sure that Skyler had something to do with it. One minute the locker room was a virtual riot and the next a hatchet of silence slammed down, cutting off the noise.

"What?" I asked. No one said anything. "What?"

Soon enough I got my answer.

Someone had taped an article from Bill Morgan on my locker door. I hadn't read it, didn't even know it existed, but I knew it wasn't good. Morgan had given us a great write-up in Saturday's paper, yet for some reason he felt the need to add to it. The entire story was on me and how great I was. What was worse was that it mentioned specifically how poorly Skyler performed against the Mavericks on Friday night.

Morgan's story gushed embarrassingly about my exploits in the game. The hero worship got to the point where I wished that I hadn't done so well. It talked about how I completed the only touchdown pass of the game, something that "not even Derek Skyler could do". And there, in a nutshell, was the source of the problem.

"Hey Mr. Superstar! Thanks for letting us mere mortals play with you." I turned to see Skyler standing among his court, all of them glaring at me.

"Fuck off, Skyler," I said, tearing the clipping from my locker and wadding it up.

"The only reason you threw that touchdown pass is because of the trick play," Skyler almost whined.

"Yeah. No shit."

Did he honestly think that there was any question of that?

"You think you're a better quarterback than I am?"

I shook my head in mild disgust and frustration at having to placate his delicate ego. "No. And I never said I was."

"Well, Bill Morgan sure thinks so. He..."

"Skyler, will you shut the fuck up? Bill Morgan gets paid to write this shit for the paper. If there is nothing to write he still has to write something. I had a good game on Friday, so he wrote about me."

"That's right, the mighty Butcher Blake. He wrote about you." Skyler was looking to all of his followers for their support, and of course they gave it to him.

"Jesus, you guys are weak!" I exploded at my teammates who were kissing Skyler's ass. "Are you going to buy into everything he says?"

Everyone was quiet. I suspected they were waiting for their fearless leader to say something else, but he didn't.

"Yeah, I got the stats Friday night. Fine. But I didn't do it on my own and you all know that, no matter what Morgan says. Without the offensive line I don't get those rushing yards. Without the good coverage in the secondary I don't get those sacks." The part that I hated the most had to be said next. "Without the perfect execution of that trick play I don't get the touchdown pass. The Mavs were good! You can't take that away from them. They had our number in the passing game and they stopped us. Skyler, you're the best in the state. You know it, I know it. Everyone knows it. But they set up to defend against you. That's why I carried the load on Friday night. They took the risk of letting me have a big game to stop you."

It was the truth, but it still sucked having to say it. The first time we played the Moore Mavericks they couldn't defend against the pass and Skyler burned them on it for the whole game. Of course they were going to prepare better for the pass the next time they faced us. The strength of the Mustangs that year, though, was that we had too many weapons. If they took one weapon out of the arsenal, like they did, we just burned them with the other ones.

I could see that what I had said had begun to win some of them back to my way of thinking. They weren't all the way there, though. "Look in the scorebook. Does it say Blake 21 – Moore 0, or does it say Mustangs 21 – Moore 0?"

Skyler walked out onto the practice field, knowing that he'd lost them that time. I didn't have them, either, but at least they weren't siding directly with him right then. I could deal with that.

The next game was going to be very important to us. Yes, in the post season it's win or go home, but this game was even more important than that. Our next opponent was the Central Jaguars, the only team to score on us all year. We wanted some payback. I'd like to act like I was above such pettiness, like I had grown beyond those kinds of desires, but it would be a lie. I wanted to annihilate the Jaguars as bad as anyone. I wanted to exact a vengeance on them just as much as Skyler and the rest of the Mustangs. If all I had to do to make that happen was swallow a little pride to help unite the team and make it happen, that was a small price to pay.

I spent practice making sure that I didn't outshine anyone. I did my job and nothing more, working hard at making it look like I was working hard. All in all it was a good practice, though. The other guys seemed to enjoy playing at the same level with me for once. JK gave me a few strange looks, knowing that I was sandbagging, but he didn't say anything.

At the end of practice I was back on the same footing with the team that I had been. Not good, but nowhere near as bad as Skyler had hoped.

3. Guess Who's Coming To Dinner

Even though it stood to further damage my relationship with the team I elected not to join them at Sharky's after practice on Thursday.

Skyler went around the locker room after we'd showered and tried to make sure that everyone would be there. He wanted the entire team to show up and hang out, to really get psyched up for beating the hell out of the Jaguars. I just didn't want to do it. The stress level of having to be "on" all the time was just too much to worry about, so I told the team that I was going to have to pass. It was exactly what Skyler wanted, and I served it up on a silver platter. It gave him more time to run me down and turn any players who were on the fence against me.

I didn't care. It was worth it not to have to hang out with some of those classless wastes of space. I was just going to go home and relax.

Around six o'clock JK showed up unexpectedly at my house. He'd gone to Sharky's with the rest of the team and I didn't figure on seeing him until school on Friday. He had a very grave look on his face

"What's up?" I asked, letting him in the back door, into the kitchen.

"We're going to have a serious problem."

I walked to the fridge and took out two cans of Coke and handed him one. He took it and then we sat down at the kitchen table. "What else is new?"

"No, Butcher, man. I really don't want to be a part of this shit if it goes down."

"What's going on?" JK was dead serious.

"The team is going to do some bad shit at the game. Skyler is hyping everyone up and trying to get us all to go out and intentionally hurt the Central players."

"Are you fucking kidding?" I was shocked. This was low even for Skyler.

"No, I'm not! He's putting a point system in place and he's giving out prizes for Mustangs players who injure Central players!" JK was fidgeting. This was really bothering him. And I couldn't blame him. It bothered me, too. "I ain't going out there to try and hurt nobody!"

I knew he wasn't. And I wasn't about to do it, either. But I was positive that quite a few of the other guys would. "So... what are we looking at here? Who's in on it?"

"It could have just been talk, but I think everyone is in... except for you and me, and maybe Bunch and Marks. I'm not even sure about them, you know?"

"We gotta tell Coach Rollins," I said, wracking my brain to think of a way to stop the plan from being set in motion.

"I thought of that, but that could ruin everything for us. I still want to win. Just not this way." JK took a long drink of his Coke and let out an equally long burp. "This sucks, man! Coach Rollins will bench everyone involved and we'll lose."

JK was absolutely right. Coach Rollins wouldn't sit still for that bullshit. Even if it meant losing the game he would pull every single player that went headhunting and all those years of work leading up to a shot at the state championship would be wasted.

"The only other thing we can do is to try to talk some sense into the guys who are going along with it. I'm not going to share the field with those assholes if they are going to play that way."

"We've got the day at school tomorrow to change minds. That's it. Skyler has these guys screaming for blood." JK said, still looking very worried.

"We'll just have to do what we can to try to convince them to play clean. That's all we can do. No matter what they decide I'm not playing dirty. And if it gets real bad I'll take myself out of the game."

I was getting angrier the more I thought about it. Because the Central Jaguars had had the nerve to attempt to beat us in a football game and the further audacity to actually score, the scumbag element of my team was going to play thug ball. I didn't want to hurt a single Jaguars player, but I could think of quite a few Mustangs players I wouldn't have minded hurting right then.

The sound of mom's car pulling into the driveway brought the conversation to a close and we waited quietly as Mom and Dad made their way into the house. They were carrying grocery bags and Dad had a case of beer.

"Hello Jerome," Mom said, setting the bags down. "It's nice to see you."

"It's nice to see you, too, Mrs. Blake," JK said, not seeming Eddie Haskell-ish at all.

Dad just grunted.

"How are your parents?" Mom asked, as she always did.

"Oh, they're doing great. How are things with you?"

"It's good, Jerome. It's good." Mom said, reaching under the counter to pull out her frying pan. "Would you like to stay for dinner?"

My dad's spine seemed to stiffen when he heard the question.

"What are you having?" JK asked.

"Fried chicken," Mom replied, pulling a whole chicken from one of the grocery bags.

"Sure, I'd like to stay for dinner. I love fried chicken," JK said with a huge smile.

"That's a fucking shock," Dad snapped sarcastically.

"Ron! That's enough of that!" Mom scolded. Dad and JK had gotten into it so many times that she was no longer horrified by Dad's open racism, merely ashamed of it.

JK winked at me. "Matter of fact, the only thing better than fried chicken is fried chicken fixed for you by a pretty white woman."

Dad didn't say a word. He just took his last cold beer out of the refrigerator, slid the new case in on the bottom shelf, and walked out of the kitchen to the living room and his precious television.

Mom stifled a laugh. "That was bad!"

We all laughed quietly until we heard the news blaring from the other room.

While Mom made dinner and Dad watched the news JK and I killed time by playing football on my old Atari 2600 game system. Sure, the graphics and the realism of the new video games are impressive, but with the old Atari football game you could throw a curveball to your receiver. I'd take that option any day.

Mom called us for dinner just after I intercepted one of JK's passes that could have won the game for me. I was still ten yards from the end zone when he flicked the switch and turned the game off. "Dinner time. I win."

"Like Hell you win!" I laughed, pushing him. "I was going to score!"

"Maybe. But you know the rules. I win."

He was technically right. When we were younger and spent long portions of our weekends and summer nights playing that game my mother had established a rule concerning the game. No matter where we were in the game, when she called us for dinner the game was over and whoever was in the lead was the winner. She got tired of yelling for us to come and eat only to be told, "Just a second! We're almost done!"

Mom had the table set and her and Dad had taken up seats at each end. JK and I took our seats and my dad started to pray. Mom and I nearly killed JK right then. He looked like he was going to rupture something internal in trying not to laugh out loud as we made our traditional goofy faces at each other. He was hardly breathing at one point, little squeaks coming out from between his tightly clenched lips. Tears were pooling in the corners of his eyes. Dad prayed on, oblivious to our jolly good time. Mom rolled her eyes back in her head and stuck out her tongue, wiggling her head and torso like Katherine Hepburn on cocaine, and JK let out a sound that was a cross between a grunt and a squeal. Dad stopped praying, right in the middle of his usual litany of blessings.

"What the hell is going on?" he demanded angrily. He was looking right at JK, who was struggling mightily to keep what composure he could muster. He looked at all of us then, knowing that something had been going on between everyone else at the table while his eyes were closed. "I won't have this! Not at my dinner table, goddammit!"

Mom stepped in. "Ron, it's nothing. Don't worry about it."

"You are all so disrespectful! And ungrateful! I'm thanking the Lord for what He's given us… and you're having a fucking laugh riot! Jesus Christ!" Dad fumed.

"Ron! There's no need to use the F-word at the table," Mom chided him, but not too sternly.

"Well, damn it, I'm over here showing my reverence for the Creator and my gratitude for the great life I've been given and you guys can't even shut up for those few minutes! I'm down here talking heart to heart with the fucking Lord and you can't even respect that!"

That was it. I burst out in full belly laughs and JK followed, unable to hold it in any longer. Mom knew that she would be the one to handle the brunt of Dad's anger and frustration, so she continued to keep a straight face and try to calm the situation.

"Okay boys, that's enough! We've all had our laugh, now settle down," she coaxed. We could hear the laugh trying to escape as she spoke. Eventually it all died down.

"Okay. Are you done now?" Dad asked everyone. We all nodded and he closed his eyes. "Amen."

That brought fresh peals of laughter, even from Mom.

"You didn't let me finish!" Dad said incredulously, shocked at our laughter. "How is God going to know I'm done praying if I don't say 'Amen'?"

I laughed a little, but pushed it down quickly.

"Laugh all you want, but when I'm in Heaven and you're all burning in Hell, let's see who's laughing then!" Dad said seriously.

Dinner went quietly after that. JK was obviously uncomfortable, being in the middle of the situation Mom and I had caused. There was virtually no conversation throughout the meal. During dessert is when my dad really started to shine, though.

It started out seeming innocent enough.

"So, Jerome," Dad began, taking a bite of chocolate pudding. "What schools are you looking at?"

JK, stunned at the civility of the question, wasn't sure he heard him correctly. "Excuse me?"

"Schools! Schools! Which ones are you looking at?" Dad condescended.

JK took it in stride, as he did with everything my dad said to him. "I've talked to Michigan. They might be good. Ohio State came to the house. USC might be interested. I don't know what I'm going to do. There are a few others I like. Purdue. Georgia."

"Which way are you leaning right now?" Dad asked.

"I kind of like USC. They've got a good program," JK replied. "I wouldn't mind staying closer to home, though."

"Hell, I guess it doesn't matter where you go, as long as you go somewhere. Either that or welfare, right?"

JK let a broad smile stretch across his face. This was what he was used to from my dad. "Lawdy no, Massa Blake! I ain't goin' on no welfare! No gub'mint cheese for this darkie! I's got me some pride. I's gone sell drugs!"

Mom got up from the table and walked away.

"I'll probably go to USC. They got a lot of blondes out there in Cali. I like blondes. They'd love a brotha like me," JK taunted.

"I've been wondering something, Jerome. Maybe you could help me out here?" Dad asked.

JK gave me the here-it-comes look. "Sure. What is it?"

"What's the deal with black guys always going after white girls? I mean, aren't black women good enough for you? Don't any black guys like black women anymore? That's all you see these days. It is unusual to even see a black couple when you're out."

"I love black women! My mom's a black woman. A strong black woman! There are a lot of strong, beautiful black women out there," JK said earnestly, leaning in towards my dad. "But here's the thing… do you white guys get mad when you see a black man with a black woman?"

Dad shook his head. "No. Not at all."

"There you go," JK said with a smile.

"So, you're telling me that black guys only want white women just to piss off white guys? That's all?"

"Yeah. Pretty much."

"That's what I thought! I've got a black guy who works for me sometimes and he's married to a white woman. He said he loves her, but I figured it had to be more about sticking it to whitey!"

"Absolutely," JK said, mock seriousness etched on his face. "Don't go and believe any of that crap. Love a white woman? Hell no. We just hate you white devils so bad that we take your women to get back at you. Ain't nothing makes me happier than to have a white woman on one arm and a watermelon in the other. Drives you honkies insane to see that!"

"The jokes on you then, boy," Dad said. I was unsure of whether he meant "boy" as in a racist remark or the fact that JK was in fact an adolescent male. I knew how JK took it. "See, we don't care when we see you black boys with white girls. It doesn't bother us."

"Then why'd you ask?"

"I just wanted to know what's wrong with black women that you feel the need to go after white girls. That's all."

"Ah, I see."

"Besides, you're only getting the white girls who are willing to dirty themselves with black boys, so why would we care?"

"You should care because almost all white women secretly want a black man. It's the black sexual power." JK was having fun.

"I've heard of that!" I said, throwing JK a bone and receiving a nasty look from my dad. "Didn't they have an after school special about that?"

"Oh bullshit! That's not true!" Dad exclaimed, throwing his hands up in the air.

"Yes it is! Black sexual power is no myth. White women are especially susceptible to black sexual power. I don't even approach white girls. They come to me."

JK usually dated black girls, but there was no sense in letting Dad know that.

"I don't buy that. It's unnatural for races to mix. There can't be *that* many white women who want black men. That's not true." Dad seemed fairly certain.

"You said it yourself. You see more black men with white women than black couples these days. You know it's true."

Dad looked less certain. Maybe even a little concerned. He was a bit intimidated by the idea of black sexual power.

I had to help him out somehow.

"Dad, if you want I'll start dating black girls."

Dad didn't say a word. He just stared daggers at me.

I took that as a no.

4. Payback Is A Bitch

There was no way of knowing how effective our campaign to thwart Skyler's headhunting excursion was going to be.

Even in the locker room before the game neither JK nor I could tell if we had gotten through to anyone. The only ones we were certain of, after coming right out and asking them, were Steve Bunch and Donnie Marks. They wanted no part of the dirty play. As wide receivers they wouldn't have many, if any, opportunities to put a hit on anyone anyway, but at least they were on our side. We spoke to them during lunch and they both agreed to try to talk the others out of their sinister mission.

With everyone else we spoke to all we got were half-hearted assurances that they were going to play a clean game. We didn't believe them for a second. As a last ditch effort I talked directly to Skyler. I passed him in the hall while walking Ethan to class after lunch and I cornered him without his goons.

"Hey, you've got to call that shit off," I said firmly.

"What are you talking about?" he asked, playing dumb and scowling at Ethan. Ethan was oblivious to Skyler's dirty look and just kept staring down the hall to the classroom I was taking him to.

"This whole thing about intentionally taking out Jaguars. That's some bush league bullshit and we're better than that!"

"I think you're imagining things. I don't know what you're talking about." Skyler was as easy to read as a picture book.

I pulled out the big guns. The bell was going to ring and time was of the essence. "Do I have to go to Coach Rollins about this?"

A look of consternation passed over Skyler's face. He was trying to determine if I was bluffing or not. He decided that I wasn't. "You don't need to go to Coach Rollins. I'll talk to the guys and see if I can settle them down."

"Good," I said, still not believing him one hundred percent. "We don't need to do that to beat these guys. Let's show some class when we do it. They only scored against our third string anyway. It's no big deal."

Skyler just nodded and turned away and I hurried to get Ethan to class on time.

We were already in our locker room that night when the Central Jaguars pulled into our parking lot in their bus with a long caravan of honking cars behind them. Looks of hate crossed the faces of several of the players when the sounds of the horns reached their ears. I knew right then that Skyler either hadn't said anything about stopping the plan or that they just weren't listening. The game was going to be ugly and there was nothing I could do about it. I should have gone to Coach Rollins right then and told him what was going on, but I didn't. Instead, I went to Skyler.

"Did you call it off?" I asked, a tone of seriousness in my voice.

"Yeah. I called it off."

The look I gave Skyler showed him that I wasn't fucking around and that he had better have called it off. He picked up on that.

"Seriously! I called it off!" he said.

We'd just have to see. If things got bad I'd go to Coach Rollins and tell him what was happening. Even if he pulled the starters or made us forfeit the game I was going to tell him.

As it turned out, I drew first blood myself.

It was completely unintentional, and it was the worst thing that could have happened. I took out their quarterback on the first play from scrimmage.

The Jags won the coin toss and elected to receive the ball first. We took their kick returner down at the seventeen yard-line and their offense trotted out onto the field, looking very ready to go to work. Their quarterback, Trent Morris, was very good and he could dump the ball pretty fast. I knew I had to get to him quick.

Morris called for the snap and I was around the offensive line in no time. They didn't even get a hand on me. Morris was looking for someone and not seeing anyone open. He also didn't see me barreling up behind him with a full head of steam. I hit him hard from behind just as he was getting ready to pass. The ball went flying backwards and he went down, unmoving.

I heard something crunch, either in his back or his neck, and I knew it wasn't good. I didn't even try to recover the fumble. They recovered the fumble and I called for the refs to get the medics on the field.

"Fuck! Fuck! Fuck! Fuck! Fuck!" I hissed under my breath. I didn't even have to look at the exultant faces of the rest of the Mustangs to see that they just took my unintentional wounding of the quarterback as their permission to destroy the Jaguars. I walked back to my team, who were keeping a respectable distance from the injured player.

Tank Sherman raised his hand for a high five. "Fuck yeah, Butcher! Get some!"

The rest of the defense echoed his sentiments.

"That was not intentional! Don't do this, guys! We don't need to win that way!" I pleaded. They weren't listening to a word I said. They were hearing me, but they weren't listening.

Morris was taken off the field in an ambulance and eventually the game was back on and their second string quarterback, almost shaking in his cleats, took the field. I couldn't blame him after what he just saw me do to the first stringer. I really hoped that Trent Morris wasn't as seriously hurt as I thought he was, but I tried to shake it off and get back in the mindset to play.

The Jaguars tried a few running plays up the middle and it didn't work. Tank Sherman made the tackles with the intent to kill, hitting far harder than necessary, and driving the running back into the ground like he was trying to plant him. They were forced to punt and we took over on their forty-nine yard line.

On our first play we set up showing the run, but it was a ruse, and they bought it. Skyler was going deep. I stayed back to protect him and he connected with Bunch at about the five-yard line. Steve ran it on into the end zone for the touchdown. Instead of kicking the extra point we went for two and got it.

On the next kick off the Jaguars kick returner called for the fair catch, but our guy, Fred Clark, leveled him anyway. It was so blatant that there was no warning. The referee immediately threw Clark out of the game. The Jaguars lost another guy, but he left the field on his own two feet. They helped him hobble off and I knew he wasn't coming back.

Coach Rollins was pissed and yelling in Clark's face as I was putting on my helmet to head out to defend. I caught sight of Skyler clapping Clark on the shoulder pads in congratulations as Clark went to the showers.

The Jaguars, fifteen yards further down the field due to the penalty, tried a short screen on their first play and we broke it up. On the second down they tried a run to my side and I took their man down behind the line. On third and long they tried a big pass and Mike Emmons snatched it out of the air, and ran it back to their ten-yard line before being brought down.

Our offense quickly took the field and on first down we went with a running play. Me right up the middle. I came out of the backfield like a runaway truck, heading for the hole that my line made for me. Before I could reach it, though, the hole started to close, so I tucked my shoulder and slammed into their defender, hoping to drive him back and get some positive yards before he stopped me. Unfortunately, he went down hard. From my momentum I stumbled into the end zone before I even knew what had happened.

When I looked back to celebrate with my team I saw the Jaguar player on the ground, writhing in pain. I just let the ball fall from my hands. "Sonofabitch!"

The medics were on the field again and another Jaguar ended up leaving in the second ambulance. And this one was my fault, too. The first ambulance wasn't even back from taking Morris to the hospital yet.

While we were waiting for the medics to get the guy off the field, Skyler came up to me and patted the top of my helmet. "Goddamn Butcher! You're fucking brutal! You don't even want the prize and you're dropping these fuckers like flies!"

"Fuck off, Skyler. I didn't mean to hurt that guy," I argued.

"Two guys leaving on stretchers in the first quarter? I don't buy it. You're headhunting, too."

"You better call this shit off! I'll go to the coach. I mean it!"

Skyler mocked me with a whiny nasally voice. "I'll go to the coach. I mean it!"

I started to walk toward our sidelines and Skyler jogged over and stopped me. "What are you going to tell him? That the rest of us are trying to hurt Jaguars players, but you, the guy who just sent two of them to the hospital in the first quarter, aren't in on it? Yeah, he'll buy that. Go tell him."

Skyler had me there. It was going to look like I was part of the whole deal considering that two of the three injuries were caused by me. "Just make sure this shit is clean. Okay?"

Skyler shrugged off my words. "Line up and play ball, Killer. We're going for two again."

As we lined up we could hear Coach Rollins yelling at us. He wanted us to kick the extra point and get off the field, but Skyler commanded the attention of the team, so we all lined up and went for it. A quick drop to JK in the back of the end zone and it was 16-0.

While our special teams prepared to kick off for the third time I stood at a distance and listened to Coach Rollins chew Skyler's ass for not listening to him.

"What's wrong with going for two. They can't stop us?" Skyler asked.

"When I say kick the extra point, we're kicking the damn extra point! That's it! End of discussion!" Coach Rollins bellowed.

"It was okay to run up the score against the Eastern Giants. Why not now?"

Coach Rollins was being hypocritical, but that wasn't the important thing. He did instruct us to run up the score on the Giants, but he was the coach and what he said went. "Because I fucking said no, goddammit! Now drop it or you're on the bench!"

Skyler wisely said nothing more and let Coach Rollins stomp back to the sideline.

We kicked off and it was a good, deep kick. The second string kick returner fielded the ball badly, dropping it when he took his first steps. By the time he picked it up our guys were all over him. He went down and fumbled the ball backwards, towards our goal line, and we picked it up and casually trotted it into the end zone. Skyler stayed on the sidelines and we kicked the extra point, bringing it up to 23-0.

Personally, I was just glad to see that their kick returner wasn't hurt on the play.

At the end of the first quarter it was 30-0. Three Jaguars were out of the game, two of them at the local hospital.

By half time we had them down 58-0 and two more of their players were out of the game. Thankfully, I had nothing to do with either of those injuries. Coach Rollins gave us a cursory talk in the locker room, urging us to keep up the intensity. Not much of a pep talk is needed when you've scored almost sixty unanswered points in the first half.

At the beginning of the third the Jaguars had to kick off to us for the first time. We called for the fair catch and started on the twenty yard line with our second string offense in the game. I was the only starter staying in on a regular basis, and that was only on defense. Todd Ebert took over for me on the offensive side of the ball and Greg Nelton gave him a workout, actually preferring the running plays to the pass. Which goes to show you why Nelton was second string and Skyler was The Man.

The Mustangs second-string offense ate seven minutes off the clock with a long, grinding drive. Ebert pounded it out on the ground pretty admirably I had to admit. When we scored next it was with Ebert pounding through the line for a six-yard run.

With the extra point it was 65-0 and the Jaguars were thoroughly demoralized. Not only were we beating them embarrassingly, we were hurting them badly. Even when players weren't taken off the field they were slow getting up. The second-string was definitely in on the conspiracy to injure Jaguars players. They just weren't as good at it.

By the end of the third quarter we had them down a whopping 80-0. Two more players had been taken out of the game. At least they didn't leave in ambulances this time. One of their receivers got crushed in the middle of the field, but he did catch the pass for the first down. Tank Sherman finally succeeded in taking out their running back, slamming him so hard into the ground that we could hear the ribs breaking with sick wet pops. He was going to the hospital, too.

In the fourth quarter I came out for good and the scrubs took over. The first and second string had done so much damage to the Jaguars that our third stringers actually scored on them. And they looked really good doing it. We ended the game 87-0, with no further injuries. We took seven of their players out of the game and sent three of them to the hospital.

It was a victory, but it tasted like ashes in my mouth.

Chapter Sixteen

I. Telling The Hard Truth

I finally got to Linda's house around eleven o'clock.

Most of the time I spent driving around waiting for Ethan to get to bed. When I called her from a payphone she told me to come over. But she heard something in my voice that concerned her.

"What's wrong?" Linda asked sympathetically. "You don't sound happy about the win."

"Yeah. I'll tell you when I get there."

I drove over and Linda took me to the bedroom, but not for the usual reason. We just talked and I told her the whole story.

After the game the team charged in through the gauntlet of fans that lined the path to our locker room, slapping high fives and shaking hands. I was the last one in, almost dragging my feet. I felt like the lowest piece of shit on the face of the earth. If I hadn't hurt Trent Morris on the first play the bloodbath might have been avoided. I knew I had hurt him very badly, too. It was the worst hit I had ever put on anyone and I was kicking myself for it. It kept running through my mind that I could have hit him a different way and he wouldn't have been hurt. Or at least not so bad.

After I had showered and was getting dressed, Coach Rollins came out of his office with an announcement. He'd been on the phone with the coach of the Jaguars. "LISTEN UP!"

The room went silent in a hurry.

"I just talked to the coach of the Jags out at the hospital. Trent Morris is wiggling his toes and his fingers. It looks like he's going to recover at this point. His other guy, Thomas… uh…"

"Lake," Mr. Walls filled in.

"Thomas Lake, the middle linebacker, just had some broken ribs. Good news about Morris, though." Coach Rollins went back in his office with Mr. Walls and left us alone again.

Knowing that Morris would recover made me feel a little bit better. But not completely. What if the best he ever got back was wiggling his fingers and toes? I was shutting my locker and grabbing my bag when Skyler came up to me.

"Butcher," he said, holding a small manila envelope out to me. "Here. You earned these tonight. Even though you weren't 'in on it'."

I set my bag down and took the envelope. Inside it was ten Polaroids. I couldn't tell what they were when I first pulled them out, as I had the backside facing me. When I flipped them over an instant rage boiled up in me. I punched Skyler right in the face and knocked him down. The locker room exploded in chaos and Coach Rollins came running back out of his office just as Shorty tackled me against the lockers to keep me off of his master.

Coach Rollins pulled Shorty off of me. "What the fuck is going on out here?"

Before anyone could answer Coach Rollins looked down and caught Skyler trying to conceal the scattered Polaroids on the ground beside him. "What have you got there, Derek?"

Caught red-handed Skyler didn't try to hide them and handed the pictures over. Coach Rollins took one look and said one word: "Office!"

In the office it all came out.

"Who's the girl?" Coach Rollins asked. "Is she a student here?"

Skyler said nothing.

"Jesus Christ! Is she at least eighteen?" Mr. Walls asked.

Skyler nodded. Mr. Buck was going through the pictures again and shaking his head. "I don't think she's a student. She looks older than eighteen."

The pictures were close-ups of a nude female with "GO MUSTANGS" painted all over her body. And she was a student. It was Tabitha Butler. Even though her face was hidden in every shot I knew her body anywhere. I didn't volunteer that information to the coaches, though.

"So… who started it?" Coach Rollins asked coolly. He seemed relieved by the idea of the girl being over eighteen, whether it was true or not.

No one said anything at first. Then I found my balls and stepped up. Whatever was going to happen to me was going to happen. "I did. I hit Skyler."

"Over these pictures? You hit him over these?" Coach Rollins seemed puzzled.

It was true. I had hit him over those pictures. But only partly because of them. I wasn't going to get Tabitha in any more trouble, though, so I only had one other thing I could tell him. I told him as much of the truth as I felt necessary.

"I hit Skyler because those pictures were payment for hurting Jaguars players."

"What? What did you just say?" Coach Rollins was boiling just under the surface. Skyler and Shorty lowered their faces.

"Skyler put out hits on Jaguars players to punish them for scoring on us during the season. Anyone who hurt a Jaguar got a prize. I didn't know what the prize was, and I wasn't in on it, but that's why I hit him."

"GODDAMMIT, BUTCHER! YOU COULD HAVE PARALYZED THAT FUCKING KID TONIGHT!" Coach Rollins roared.

"I wasn't in on it! I swear! I was trying to talk all the guys out of it!" I argued.

"YOU DID THE MOST DAMAGE!"

"I didn't mean to hurt him! I really didn't! I spent all day trying to talk the guys into not doing it!"

"IS THIS TRUE?" Coach Rollins shouted in Skyler's face. Skyler just looked away. "IS THIS FUCKING TRUE?"

Skyler looked back up, his face stony. "Yeah, it's true. Except Butcher is lying. He was in on it. He's just trying to cover his ass."

"You lying cocksucker!" I yelled, punching Skyler in the face again. Mr. Buck and Mr. Walls broke us apart.

"Wait here!" Coach Rollins ordered, striding out of his office. From right outside the door we heard him talking to the rest of the team. "Nobody leaves this locker room. Team meeting, right now!"

I didn't think anyone was planning on leaving anyway. They all wanted to see what was going to happen with Skyler and I.

When we had left the office and the whole team was gathered around, Coach Rollins broke out his clipboard and went down the list. "When I say your name come up and stand right here in front of me."

"Ronald Blake. Brad Sherman. Fred Clark. Mike Emmons. Mike Short."

The five of us went up and stood in front of Coach Rollins. "Turn around. Turn around and face your team."

We turned around.

"There were seven Jaguars players seriously injured and taken out of the game tonight by these five players. They did it on purpose."

No one said anything. They just stared at Coach Rollins and at us.

"Derek Skyler. Come up here."

Skyler came up and stood with the five of us.

"Derek Skyler paid them with… well, he paid them… to intentionally hurt Jaguars players."

Still, no one said a word.

"Is that what I've taught you? Is that what you've taken from me? That it's okay to play dirty?"

"No," was the general mumble.

"What was that?"

"NO, COACH!" came back the much stronger reply.

Coach Rollins started to pace and he looked like he had a lot to say, but he bit his lower lip and didn't say it. Finally, he walked around and stood in front of us, looking us all in the eye in turn. Everyone except me turned away from his gaze. Coach Rollins spoke calmly. "You're all benched for the regional game."

A huge ruckus erupted at that point. The other players were yelling their disagreement loudly and angrily. Coach Rollins remained quiet and held up his hand. The room went to dead silence.

"One more fucking word and I'll call the athletic director and tell him that we forfeit the game."

We all knew that he meant it.

JK, knowing that any word would make Coach Rollins do exactly as he threatened, held up his hand and waited to be called on.

"What is it, JK?"

"Coach, Butcher wasn't in on this. We were trying to get the team not to go along with Skyler."

Coach Rollins thought for a second. "So, you all knew about this?"

Everyone nodded.

"Did Butcher and JK talk to all of you about not doing this?"

Everyone nodded. Someone else said, "And Bunch and Marks, too. They were out against it."

Coach Rollins gathered Mr. Buck and Mr. Walls and they went into his office and shut the door. The team remained absolutely still in icy silence the whole time they were in there. They seemed to be in there forever, but it was only a few minutes. When they came out the fact that they had made a decision showed on their faces.

"Butcher. Go over there," Coach Rollins said, and Mr. Buck grabbed my arm and directed me toward the rest of the team. It appeared as though I was out of the woods.

"Clark, Emmons, Sherman, Short, and Skyler are all benched for the regional game. If we win, we win without them." Coach Rollins faced the team, daring us to groan or whine about it. No one did. "Since the rest of you knew about it, there will be a practice on Monday. It's mandatory. If you miss it you don't play again this year. Bring your running shoes, boys."

Linda sat with her arm around my shoulders the whole time, as far as she could reach anyway, and listened as I told her the story. "You did what you could. You can't make people do what you want."

I sighed and kissed her on the forehead. "I should have went to Coach Rollins before the game and told him."

"You were trying to protect your teammates. And your season. It's okay."

"No. It's not. I didn't mean to hurt the two kids I hurt tonight, but all seven of those injured players are on my hands."

"Ronald, you're being too hard on yourself. You're a good kid and you did what you could to make things better. You 'fessed up when you could have lied. You protected that girl's identity. You tried to keep the team from going along with Skyler. You…"

"But it didn't work!" I interrupted.

"That doesn't matter! You tried to do the right thing by everyone. You can't always do that. But you tried."

She pushed me back on her bed and we lay there, wrapped in each other's arms, for hours. That was all we did that night.

It was the best sex I never had.

2. Hell Week

The shit hit the fan almost immediately.

Bill Morgan's story in the Saturday morning sports section told of the suspensions going into the regional championship game and from there it quickly got out of hand. Those who called in to the local radio sports shows were calling for Coach Rollins to resign or be fired. True, they didn't know why the five players were suspended, the story only cited "behavioral issues", but that wouldn't have mattered. All that mattered was that our shot at the state championship was virtually gone with Derek Skyler on the bench, not to mention the other starters, and the town was not happy at all. Sometime on Saturday night Coach Rollins was awakened by a loud crash. Some brave soul had anonymously and under the cover of darkness taken a sledgehammer to his car out in the driveway.

Every player on the team received a phone call from Bill Morgan over the weekend. He was hoping someone would tell him what the suspensions were specifically about. Oh so conveniently, none of us knew, and the ones who were suspended knew better than to talk about it if they wanted a chance to play later. When Coach Rollins said we were handling it in house he absolutely meant it.

By Monday the uproar might have quieted down if it weren't for Derek Skyler's dad coming to the school with a squad of sign toting protesters. Before the first period bell rang Skyler's dad led his small band of merry slogan shouters into the foyer and took up residence, demanding to speak to Coach Rollins before he would leave. Apparently Skyler's dad was under the mistaken impression that Coach Rollins was afraid to face him. In the middle of their first chant of "LET THEM PLAY! LET THEM PLAY!" Coach Rollins stepped up and offered his hand to shake. "Mr. Skyler, I'm glad you came in to talk to me."

"Oh, I just bet you are!" Mr. Skyler said sarcastically, puffing out his chest.

"Actually, I am," Coach Rollins said calmly, withdrawing his unshaken hand. "If you'd just returned my calls this whole scene could have been avoided."

"Well, well, well… you're worried about a 'scene'! We haven't even made a scene yet!" As his father spoke I caught a glimpse of Derek Skyler slinking away from the foyer, extremely embarrassed.

"Mr. Skyler, there is an issue I need to talk to you about concerning this matter and I think it would be best for all involved if we did it in private."

"What's the matter? Are you scared to tell everyone why you benched my son and threw away the state championship?" The protesters roared as if on cue.

"I'll tell you what, sir," Coach Rollins said, beginning to get a little angry. "If you'll step into the office with me I will tell you exactly why your son and the other players were suspended. And then you can decide if you want to have your people chant about it."

Mr. Skyler thought on it for a second and then followed Coach Rollins across the foyer and into an empty office. The protesters waited in uncomfortable silence for the few minutes that their fearless leader was away from them.

When the two men finally emerged from the office the chant began again.

"LET THEM PLAY! LET THEM PLAY! LET THEM PLAY!"

Mr. Skyler walked slowly over to the group and waved them silent. "Let's get out of here."

The protesters didn't like hearing that. They'd come all this way. They got up early and organized. They'd made signs. A few of them tried to keep the chant going, but they quickly gave up.

"It's all right. Coach Rollins is doing the right thing." Mr. Skyler looked very defeated right then as he turned to walk out, not waiting on his gaggle of supporters.

After that it was a little smoother sailing. No one was happy, but the issue was pretty much laid to rest. Skyler and his five co-conspirators were going to ride the pine for the next game and that was final. The rest of the week everyone tried to rally behind those of us still playing, hoping against hope that something could be done to pull off a win.

Monday night's punitive "practice" was hell on earth. No one kept track of the miles, but we ran until we fell out. And then we ran some more. Coach Rollins ran with us the whole time, hardly looking winded even toward the end. It showed us what big pussies some of us really were. Many of the guys had to stop to puke from the exertion.

Skyler took full advantage of the situation to turn more of the guys against me. If that was even possible.

"You know boys," Skyler wheezed between sucking breaths. "We wouldn't even be out here if it wasn't for Butcher."

Everyone groaned, whether in agreement or dissent I couldn't tell for sure. I surmised it was in agreement.

I replied, "Well, guys, if Skyler had any faith in your abilities he wouldn't have felt the need to bribe you to hurt the other team. Be mad if you want, but I did the right thing." Then I picked up the pace and trotted to the head of the pack.

Tuesday brought our first actual post-suspension practice. And it also brought Bill Morgan out to the practice field to see what we were going to have to take to the regional game. I could safely say from seeing his face that he was less than impressed.

Greg Nelton and I worked and worked on the stretch play, but he just wasn't getting it. He wasn't as fast as Skyler and it was slowing the play down too much to be very effective.

With Shorty missing from the offensive line the defenders were coming through almost at will. Unless it was a run I stayed back to help block and ended up handling the major part of the pass protection. Even then, though, it was too much and Nelton was getting sacked. Well, touching him with two hands equals a sack at practice, but the point was still made. If our weakened defensive line was getting through to Nelton so easily what was going to happen when we played a team that was the real deal? We were facing the Westlake Wolves and they were no joke. Like us, they were undefeated.

Unlike us, they were bringing their full team. No doubt about it, at full strength we were a far better team. We were just going to be so far from full strength as to be laughable.

The story in Wednesday's paper didn't reflect the practice that Bill Morgan had really seen. He gave a glowing report of how well we executed the plays and said that there was still a great chance for us to pull out the win. It was purely fiction, but it did the trick. It boosted the morale of the team and we started to get things moving in the right direction. We were still a long way from where we needed to be, but by Thursday's practice we were feeling like we just might have a shot.

Nelton had found an extra burst of speed and we were beginning to pull off the stretch play. Albeit not the way that Skyler and I could do it, but it was working. The offensive line had found a way to compensate somewhat for Shorty's absence, and they cut the number of defenders getting through in half.

The real key to our success, even more than the ego stroke by Bill Morgan, was that four of the five suspended players came around and actively started to help out in practice. They had to be there anyway, so they eventually decided to help. Sure, a lot of it was selfishness, wanting to still get to state, but they did step up and do what they could. Skyler got his panties out of his crack by Wednesday and worked with Nelton on the plays and some of the mechanics that he'd need to pull off the more difficult maneuvers. Shorty worked with his replacement on the line and taught him a few tricks of the trade.

Emmons did the same with his second string counterpart, as well as with Jim Dole who was going to be switching to back-up cornerback for the game. He was fast enough to cover a receiver, he just needed to learn the position and a few of the tricks. Tank Sherman helped his replacement at middle linebacker learn to pick up and stop the run.

The only one who refused to help was Fred Clark. He did the bare minimum of what he had to do to stay on the team and that was it. I think Coach Rollins would have probably kicked him off the team if not for the fact that he needed Clark to keep his mouth shut concerning the reason for the suspensions. Clark's replacement was having a little trouble making it down the field and making the stop on the kick off, so I went to Coach Rollins and volunteered to play special teams, too.

Coach Rollins laughed. "Offense, defense *and* special teams… I don't know about that."

"I don't know either," I said honestly. "Maybe it's too much and I won't be able to do it. But if you need me to do it I will."

Coach Rollins put his hand on my shoulder. "Okay. I'll try not to need you, but if I do I'll call on you."

When I walked off the practice field on Thursday evening I would have legitimately given us a fifty percent chance of beating Westlake.

3. Guess Who's Coming To Dinner, Part 2

Dinner at my house on Thursday night was interesting.

I couldn't park in my usual spot in front of the house when I got home from practice that night because Linda's car was parked there. I was more than a little surprised, to tell you the truth. In fact, it was almost a minor "oh shit" moment. As I was thinking of the reasons that Linda might be at my house the first several were bad ones. For no real reason I just assumed that something had to be wrong.

The second I stepped through the front door everything seemed off. I recognized immediately what the problem was. I didn't hear the news coming from the television. Dad religiously watched the news every night and I had no frame of reference to know what it was like to come home from practice and not have the news on.

Instead I heard the *Thundercats*.

I stepped into the living room to see what was up and there was my dad, in his chair, shoes off, feet up, smoking his pipe. Instead of lusting after Rebecca Wayne on the channel 8 news, he now had that same burning gaze focused on Cheetara.

Ethan sat on the couch intently staring at the screen. He didn't even notice that I had walked in.

"Hey, Ethan!" I called, smiling down at him on the couch.

Ethan looked away from the screen and his beloved *Thundercats* and saw me. His face lit up and he launched himself off of the couch and wrapped his arms around me. "BUTCHIE!"

"I'm glad to see you… but what are you doing here?" I asked.

"Watching the Thundercats," he replied, gesturing toward the screen.

Well, ask a silly question…

"Your mother invited Ethan and his mother over for dinner. She wanted to get to know the people you're spending so much time with." Dad looked less than thrilled about the idea of having them over. Of course, my mom had made the call and he knew that he had no say in the matter, so he kept his mouth shut about it.

My mother was up to something. She was suspicious of Linda and she was trying to find out whatever she could find out. I was going to have to be on my toes or else I was going to slip up and Mom's wrath was going to come down. Linda being not all that much younger than she was really bugged my mother. I thought I had convinced Mom that nothing was going on, but apparently I wasn't as good an actor as I had given myself credit for.

I heard Mom and Linda talking in the kitchen, where the smell of meatloaf was originating. Ethan had gone back to watching the television screen, impersonating a catatonic. It was as if he hadn't just jumped up and hugged me, overjoyed. Those quick turnarounds were always something that threw me off about Ethan. He still does it.

Saying nothing, I walked into the kitchen and let my presence be known.

"Ronald, I thought it would be nice to invite your new friends over and get to know them," Mom said.

"Cool," I said, putting one arm around my mother and hugging her with it. "Hi, Mrs. Miles."

It was freaky weird calling her Mrs. Miles after the things we had done. What should have been an everyday term of common respect for an elder just felt completely awkward to me. It tumbled around my mouth like a marble until it finally came out.

"Hello Ronald," Linda said with a friendly smile. "How was practice? Are the Mustangs going to beat the Wolves?"

I gave a small laugh. "You know, we just might! We looked pretty good today."

"Great! I was just telling your mother that I used to be a Mustangs cheerleader. You just can't quit rooting for your home team."

Mom hugged me back with one arm and looked up at me, giving me a smile that said she knew something that I didn't know she knew. "Yes, Linda only missed me by a couple of years or we would have been in high school at the same time."

I wanted to say, "Yes, Mother Dear, I realize that my friend's mother, who I am having sex with, is only a few years younger than you are."

Instead I said, "How long until dinner? I'm starving! Coach Rollins worked us to death!"

"Just a few more minutes," Mom said, breaking out of my hug.

"So, Ronald," Linda began, gesturing to the kitchen walls. "Your mother tells me that you helped hang the wallpaper in here."

"Yeah, I did. I helped with most of the house."

"It looks lovely. You did a wonderful job."

"Thank you," Mom and I said simultaneously.

"I was wondering, Ronald… I have my parents coming over to my house for Thanksgiving dinner. Do you think you could find the time to help me hang some wallpaper in my kitchen before then?"

"Sure. I don't see why not."

What a great alibi!

"I'd love to help you, Linda. Doing home improvement projects is a favorite hobby of mine," Mom said, turning from the steaming stovetop.

Shit.

Linda didn't miss a beat. "Thank you so much! You two did such a lovely job on your home! Thank you."

"I'm happy to help. Ronald is a great assistant and he can help us old girls out." Mom laughed, turning back to the stove. Linda shot me a raised eyebrow shrug with a hint of caution.

"Well, we can certainly put him to work reaching the high spots," Linda said, laughing along with my mother.

"He's good at that. I like to keep him around to get things off the high shelves for me… and to open jars."

They both laughed at that and I excused myself until I was called for dinner. I had to get the hell out of the room before my mom took another opportunity to remind me that Linda was nearly as old as she was.

At the dinner table Mom and I made a wordless agreement not to make faces at each other during Dad's prayer. I think we both knew what might happen if Ethan saw us doing it and it was just easier to let Dad have his superstition unfettered of our mockery for one evening.

"The meatloaf looks really good… uh… Mrs. Butchie," Ethan said very politely, carefully enunciating his words.

Mom smiled and just as politely corrected him. "Thank you, Ethan. I hope you like it. And my name is Mrs. Blake."

"Oh! I'm sorry!" Ethan was mortified. "I knew that! I knew that! I'm sorry!"

"It's okay! It's okay! I know you did. It's no big deal," Mom assured Ethan. She was smiling. Dad was stone-faced. Dad hardly said a word throughout the entire meal.

My mom dominated the dinner conversation. Every single thing she said seemed to have a hidden agenda. Her primary focus was on her concern with me over how I was handling my break-up with Tabitha.

"Mom! I'm fine!" I argued, raising my voice slightly.

"You've quit dating since she left you. And that's been quite some time now. You need to get back on the horse. There are lots of girls at school you could be going out with." Mom was talking to me, but looking at Linda. Linda, for her part, just nodded.

"I go out. I go out all the time. We have the dances after the game and sometimes there are parties. I go out a lot."

"Well, why haven't I met a new young lady?"

"There just hasn't been anyone I've been serious about for a while. I don't want to force it," I said, trying to think of a way out of the topic. Suddenly, it came to me. "Besides, I realized that I needed to concentrate more on football getting this late in my senior year. This is my last chance to impress the college scouts."

Dad grunted and nodded as he worked on swallowing a mouthful of food. "Leave the boy alone. He's got bigger things on his mind than girls."

Then Dad went back to his silence.

"Linda, help me out here," Mom said, leaning toward Linda. "Don't you think that Ronald should find a girlfriend before he lets the break-up stop him for good?"

"Your mother is right, Ronald. At your age if you let something like this break-up stop you it could cause you problems relating to women for the rest of your life."

"See?" Mom said triumphantly. "You should listen to me. And to Linda. We're older and we've been around. We know these things."

I sprang to my feet and threw up my hands. "JESUS CHRIST, MOM! I'VE BEEN FUCKING LINDA FOR A WHILE NOW! OKAY? WE FUCK ALL THE TIME! IS THAT WHAT YOU WANTED TO HEAR? SHE MAKES ME COME SO HARD THAT I GET STUPID AND DROOL! BEST PUSSY I'VE EVER HAD!"

Just kidding.

What I really said was, "All right. I'll think about it. I know a couple nice girls at school."

Linda and Ethan hung around after dinner long enough to be polite. We had coffee and, thankfully, talked about other things besides my social life, and then Linda excused herself.

"Thank you for the lovely dinner and inviting us into your beautiful home! We had a wonderful time, didn't we Ethan?"

Ethan nodded his head and said, "Yes. Dinner was really good, Mrs. Blake. Thank you."

"You're quite welcome. It was nice to get to know both of you." Mom said, her arm around Dad's waist. She gave him a perceptible squeeze and Dad let out a little grunt. Then he took his cue.

"Um… yes. It was nice to have you over." You could still tell that he could have cared less.

"Thank you for watching *Thundercats* with me, Mr. Blake."

Dad just grunted again and Mom squeezed him again. "Uh… you're welcome… Ethan."

Mom and Dad stood on the porch and I walked Linda and Ethan to their car. I helped Ethan into the front seat. "I'll see you in the morning."

"Okay," Ethan said, looking straight ahead as if the car were already moving down the street and he was the driver. "Your dad is really nice, Butchie."

"You think so?" I asked incredulously.

"Yeah. He watched *Thundercats* with me. I don't even have a dad."

The kid had a point. Linda looked pained when she heard him say it, though.

"Goodnight, Ronald," Linda said as she fired the engine.

"Goodnight, Mrs. Miles," I said with a smile and a wink as I closed Ethan's door and stepped back up onto the curb.

I went back in the house, more exhausted from mentally sparring with my mother than I had been from football practice.

4. Wolves At The Door

The sense of doom that crashed down upon us early in the week was completely gone by the time of the pep rally on Friday afternoon.

The school was up and it took the team to the next level. To know that so many people were behind us, even with so many of the "stars" out, really boosted our fragile morale. Even on the bus ride to the game, over an hour away, the team was roaring like a chainsaw. The second stringers who would be starting the game for once couldn't wait to get their chance to shine. That night we took the field with something to prove.

I had originally thought that we had a fifty percent shot at winning, but when Steve Bunch ran the opening kickoff back for a touchdown I increased our odds quite a bit. It was a beautiful run. The blocking was perfect and they just couldn't get a hand on him. You could tell from the reactions of the Wolves players and the fans that they weren't used to that sort of thing.

When we kicked off to them our special teams downed the ball on the three-yard line. We were really going to make them work for it. Their fans were really loud and ready for some payback. They just knew their Wolves were going to take it to us.

On the first play they tried a run to the right side and got stopped at the line of scrimmage. On the second play they went up the middle and lost a yard. At third and eleven they were going for a short screen pass, but I got the quarterback first, sacking him almost on our goal line.

Their fans got really quiet at that point.

They punted and we took the ball near midfield. Greg Nelton was so nervous he was shaking when he took the field for the first time.

"Relax," I said, clapping him hard on the shoulder pads. "Just like practice."

He nodded, but said nothing.

The first play was a pass play, and I knew it was a mistake. I just didn't want to say anything to shake his confidence. As our quarterback he needed to know that we were behind him. Even when he stayed with the pass as the defenders lined up ready for it. With a run we would have stood to gain at least five yards, maybe more. Skyler would have switched the play at the line, but Nelton didn't do that. On his first pass he was almost intercepted.

"Shake it off," JK said as he walked past Nelton, who was grimacing at the bad pass. "We ain't hurt."

Maybe it was for his own confidence or maybe he really thought he could pull it off, but Nelton called another pass play. Marks and Bunch deep, JK in the slot. The Wolves lined up, showing blitz. They were going to see how well Nelton could handle pressure.

As it turned out, not well. The Wolves came through our line like it wasn't even there. I pushed two rushers away from Nelton, but it wasn't enough and he went down hard. Fortunately, he popped right back up, unhurt.

We moved to huddle and Nelton waved us back up to the line. "Let's go! Let's go!"

The Wolves defense had trouble getting set in time and when we snapped the ball they were in chaos. Nelton made his first complete pass. It barely got back the yards we lost with the sack and we still had to punt, but the importance of that completion was immeasurable. It let Greg know that he could do it.

There were no more scores in the entire first half. The game became a defensive battle. It was pretty impressive, if you like to watch good defense. I was certain it would have been a different story had we been at full strength, but as it was, both teams really ground it out. They actually took us three and out for the next four possessions.

Right before half time they got within field goal range and it was looking like they were going to be the second team that season to score on us. Not much we could do about it. We were going to try to block the kick, but that's much easier said than done. I resigned myself to the fact that they would score. And then we dodged a bullet. Their kicker pulled it too far left and missed by inches. We took over from the spot and knelt it out, going into half time.

I fully expected Coach Rollins to yell at us when we were in the locker room, but to my surprise, he was pretty happy with our performance. We only had seven points, but we'd held them to nothing. We'd stopped the Wolves every time we'd had to. It was something we hadn't experienced that entire year. We were in a football game with a team that was virtually our equal.

"THIS IS WHAT IT'S ALL ABOUT, GENTLEMEN!" Coach Rollins bellowed, silencing us as we jabbered away on the benches. He was extremely excited. "THIS IS FOOTBALL!"

The plan for the rest of the game was a simple one. Coach Rollins laid it out for us. "Try to score. Don't let them score. That's all. Same game. Keep up the pressure and see if they break."

That's just what we did.

Throughout the third quarter we went back and forth with the Wolves just as we had in the first half. We moved the ball, but not enough. We couldn't sustain a drive to save our asses. Their offense continued to struggle even worse than ours. Without Nelton's arm being a big enough threat the Wolves concentrated on stopping me. I was hit behind the line more times that game than I ever had been. Somehow I managed positive yardage, even dragging the Wolves defenders with me. They were willing to give up the short pass, but they were scared of giving up the big run, so they congregated at the line and held me to less than two rushing yards per run, on average. It was frustrating, to say the least.

The fourth quarter was yet more of the same. No scoring, just some serious hard-nosed defensive play. Nelton was getting very upset and down on himself, but surprise of all surprises, Skyler took it upon himself to encourage his replacement. Skyler actually said, "Shit, you're doing as good as I could in the situation! Just keep it up! You can win this!"

Of course, it wasn't true. Skyler would have done much better in every facet of the game than Nelton was doing, but it was very cool of him to tell Greg that. And the truth was that Greg wasn't doing such a bad job. Their defense was, on that day at least, as good as ours.

With a minute left to go in the game we thought we had it in the bag. The Wolves had the ball, but we were going to stop them again like we had the whole game. We had them pressed back to their fifteen yard-line. It was third and twenty-two. One more play and it was over. We'd be able to kneel out this brutal damn game and go home with a win.

The Wolves weren't reading from our script, though. With absolutely nothing to lose their quarterback put up this long bomb. I'd never seen a high school kid throw a pass that long and that sharp. Not even Skyler, who had an arm like a bazooka.

Still, if our defender could bat the pass away it was over for them. I was pretty sure that Jim Dole was going to get a hand on it. He'd played excellent coverage throughout the game and he was right on the receiver all the way down the field. All he had to do was reach out and smack the ball away when it got there.

Instead, he pushed the receiver away from the ball and drew a pass interference call.

When they placed the ball at the spot of the foul the Wolves had the first down on our thirty-nine yard line. Pulling a trick from our own book they hustled to the line, no huddle, and they burned us for a huge run while we scrambled around like chickens with our heads cut off. I made it through the line easily, but they handed off to the other side and the play was out of my hands. I could see the game going into overtime as I watched their running back hauling ass toward the goal line with no one stop him. If we went into overtime I wasn't so sure we had it in us to pull out the win. We were all just about dead on our feet. And we sure didn't have enough time to score again unless we ran back another kickoff. I stomped the ground in frustration, sending up a clump of dirt and grass.

Then, from out of nowhere, Jim Dole blasted their running back and took him down. I didn't even see him coming. I was so certain that it was over that I guess I wasn't paying enough attention. When I saw the runner go down before he hit the line I sprinted my ass down the field to get in position to defend. We didn't have any timeouts left and the Wolves were sure to pull another no huddle run and try to keep us just as scrambled. I had some time, though. There was an automatic timeout on the field because Dole had injured the running back with his brutal tackle. Forgetting myself, and just being happy to still have a chance to pull out the win, I found myself quietly celebrating their player's injury. It wasn't that I was glad he was hurt, we just really needed the timeout to collect ourselves.

"All right, guys! This is it! One last goal line stand and we go home with a win!" I said as I gathered the defense around me. "Watch the pass, but it's most likely going to be a run. No matter what... THEY GET NOTHING!"

The referee placed the ball at the two yard-line. They had about thirty seconds and four downs to try and tie this game and we had no choice but to stop them. Our crowd was screaming like crazy as the Wolves took their formation. They were going to run, I just knew it. Their receivers were making such a big show of being out on the corners that I was absolutely positive that they were coming up the middle.

And they did.

The hole they needed was full of our middle linebacker, a kid who played great the whole game, but whose name I can't remember. I saw that he had it covered as I broke the line. One step and I was going to take their running back down behind the line. Then it would only be three more chances for them to push the game into overtime. I spread my arms, ready to wrap the runner up and bring him down. At the last second our no name middle linebacker knocked the ball loose. He drove his helmet into the ball and it sprung out of the running back's hands and hit me in the chest.

I'm not sure how I got my arms closed in enough time, but somehow I held onto the ball and took off at a dead run. I had been facing the sideline when the ball came to me, so I ran hard that direction to get away from anyone who would have a chance at tackling me. Their quarterback was the only one who had any idea what was happening and he tried to make the tackle.

By that time in the season I didn't feel like I was particularly ego driven, but one thought went through my mind as I saw the quarterback coming after me. I said it in my mind. "There is no way some fucking quarterback is going to tackle Butcher Blake!"

I put my shoulder into him, but he held on. He couldn't bring me down, but he could slow me down enough for someone else to help him. I dragged him with me for five yards before he lost his grip and fell off.

And then I was gone. I ran like I knew that I was never going to run again. Ninety-eight yards later I crossed the goal line and collapsed.

The fatigue was just too much and my legs completely gave out on me. I was fine while I was pouring on the speed, but once I slowed down the muscles just let go and my legs felt like rubber. As I was lying there in the end zone, looking up into the night sky, the cramps came full force. My hamstrings seized, drawing my feet up. I squeezed my eyes tightly shut and let out a strangled scream. The pain was excruciating. My biggest hope was that it was just a cramp and that I hadn't done any real damage.

When I opened my eyes Coach Rollins was standing over me, along with the team trainer, and they were pushing my celebrating teammates away from me.

"Let him breathe! Back the fuck up! Let him breathe!" Coach Rollins told the players.

The trainer checked me out and straightened my legs, which hurt almost as much as the initial cramps. He determined that it was likely nothing serious, and they helped me off the field to the wildest cheers I have ever heard in my life. The suspended players, even Skyler and Shorty, were going nuts on the sideline. I sat on the bench and watched as we kicked the extra point and then kicked off to the Wolves for the last time. Time ran out while their kick returner made his last ditch effort to achieve *anything*.

14-0 is not the impressive score we were known for, but I am certain that we never played a more impressive game that whole year.

Chapter Seventeen

1. Wiped Out

I remember pulling out of the parking lot in the bus, but after that I don't know what happened.

I slept through the entire celebration on the way home from the regional championship. We were going to the semi-state championship, and I was excited, certainly, I was just way too exhausted to do anything else. I had played all but a few plays in the game. I was off the field for the kickoffs, punts, and that last extra point. Other than that I was in on every play.

JK woke me up in the Mims High School parking lot and I just went home to crash. The rest of the team was planning on having a party and they insisted that I come along, but all I wanted was to go home and get in bed.

My parents pulled into the lot after us, part of the caravan of Mustangs fans that made the long trip to support us. I talked to them briefly in the lot and told them I was heading for home, and then hobbled to my car on pain-wracked legs, waving to well-wishers who called out, "BUTCHER!" and " WOOOO!" and other such cheers.

At the end of the parking lot where my car was I could see the outline of someone waiting beside it. It was dark down there and I wasn't sure who it was at first, but as I got closer I could see that it was Stacy Lampley. I maintained my limping pace, hobbling unhurriedly on my way.

"Great game, Butcher," Stacy said, a noticeable lack of excitement in her voice.

"Thanks," I said, equally enthused. She was leaning against the driver's side door and made no attempt to step aside as I got closer. But she said nothing else. She just stood there.

"Stacy, I am dead tired and my legs are killing me. I'd really like to go home."

"I just wandered if you, maybe, wanted some company," she said, sounding nervous. There was obviously something on her mind, something bothering her. And I didn't want to hear about it for anything in the world right then.

"Not tonight, Stacy. Sorry," I said, trying to sound like I really was sorry. I don't think I quite pulled it off. If Stacy had come looking for sex she was barking up the wrong tree. I was so tired that I doubted my own ability to even get it up.

"I really need to talk to you," she said, imploringly.

A long sigh made it's way out of me from somewhere down near my feet. I sounded totally exasperated and put out. "Can it wait? I am mentally and physically wrung out and I can't handle anything else tonight."

"It's really important."

I gave another sigh, but a shorter, less exaggerated one. "What is it?"

Stacy lowered her eyes and seemed to be thinking of what she wanted to say to me and exactly how to say it. I think she almost had it when a car pulled up beside us.

"BUTCHIE!" came the cry from my left and Ethan came bounding from Linda's car toward me. He hugged me and jumped up and down at the same time. With the short little jumps that his legs were barely capable of I imagine it looked like he was trying to hump my leg like a dog. "YOU WERE GREAT!"

I caught Linda looking back and forth between Stacy and I, a questioning look on her face. Not an accusing look, just sort of a bemused, quizzical expression.

"Thanks, Ethan," I said, trying to calm him down and get him to step back off of me a couple of paces. I had my eyes glued to Linda's face, though. She gave me a wan smile.

"Come on, Ethan. Let's get you home," Linda called out from the car. "We drove up to see you play and he was dying to tell you how well you did."

Ethan let me go and started walking back to the car. I walked him part way over and Linda pointed behind me. "Your friend is walking away."

I looked back over my shoulder and saw Stacy winding her way through the other cars.

"She said she wanted to talk about something. Must not have been all that important."

"Really? I thought maybe you were taking your mother's advice." Linda said, a touch of jealousy in her voice.

I laughed. "No. It's nothing like that. I don't even know what she wanted."

Then it was Linda's turn to laugh. "I do. And I know why." She said the last bit very flirtatiously.

When Ethan was on the other side of the car and I was right by the driver's window Linda whispered, "Call me later."

I nodded and went around to help Ethan into the front seat. He was having a little trouble, as usual. We said our goodbyes and Ethan and Linda drove away, Ethan grinning ear to ear.

Suddenly I didn't feel quite as bad as I had. Something about being around Ethan and his persistent happiness just picked me up, I guess. I was smiling when I walked back to my car. I was wondering what Stacy was going to say, but I wasn't overly curious. Not enough to track her down. I was going to head home and that was that. I'd stay up long enough to call Linda after she'd had time to get Ethan in bed, and not a second longer. Stacy could wait.

By the time I made it home Mom and Dad had already gotten there and were getting ready to go to bed. Dad gave me a pat on the back and a "Good game" and followed Mom into the bedroom. I pulled the phone over by the chair and sat down to watch television until Linda called. I snatched the phone up before the first ring ended about twenty minutes later.

"Hello," I said into the receiver, my voice cracking with fatigue.

"Ethan's asleep. He barely made it through the door. Want to come over?"

The heart and the penis were willing, but the rest of the body issued an instant protest. I groaned. "I really want to. I just don't think I can."

When I heard Linda's light laugh I was glad to hear that she wasn't disappointed. If she had been I would have mustered up whatever strength I had left and headed my ass right over to her house. "I guess you really did leave it all on the field tonight then, hmm?"

"You could say that," I said, feeling the fatigue pull my weight down heavier into the chair even as my cock began to harden. I thought I was too completely drained for that, but that just goes to show you: Never under estimate the power of teenage hormones.

"When do your parents go to bed?"

"They're in bed right now."

"Are they heavy sleepers?"

I knew what she was thinking and I wasn't so sure I wanted to try it. My mom would go ballistic if she woke up and caught Linda in the house with me. Even if she didn't catch us in the act. I couldn't risk it. I had to tell her not to even try to come over.

"Yeah. They're heavy sleepers," I said, betraying my own best interests. "Come on over."

"I'm on my way."

"You can't just leave Ethan, can you?"

"My neighbor is still up. She said she'd stay here if I ever needed to run out to meet you in the middle of the night. I'll ask her and be right over."

"Your neighbor knows about me?" I asked, shocked.

"Well, she saw you sneaking out of the house carrying your clothes. She figured things out," Linda gave a small laugh. "She doesn't know you're in high school, but she thinks it's great that I have a younger man."

Before I could say anything else, even if I'd been inclined to protest, she hung up. Fifteen minutes later she pulled up three houses down from me and walked to the house. I met her at the back door and we both crept quietly through the kitchen and toward the stairs. My heart was hammering and I was holding my breath until we were safely in my bedroom with the lock thrown on the door.

Linda told me a good bedtime story. It was the one where the Fairy Princess sucks every drop of Prince Charming's energy out through his dick.

I love that story.

The next thing I knew it was late Saturday afternoon.

2. Who Wants To Be A Hero?

I staggered down the stairs on still wobbly and painful legs at around four in the afternoon on Saturday.

The leg pain was of much less concern to me at that point because I recognized that it was only cramps. A little rest and I would be as good as new and ready to play in the semi-state by Friday. It wouldn't hurt to load up on fluids, either, so I made my way into the kitchen. I violated another one of my mother's cardinal rules by drinking milk right out of the carton, receiving a sharp smack to the back of my head when she walked up behind me. Cold milk splashed out of the carton and ran down my chin.

"Thanks! I needed a milk bath," I said, wiping the milk off of my face and chest.

"Ronald, how many times have I got to tell you not to drink out of the carton? I mean, now really? What are you, five years old?" Mom sighed in exasperation. "You need to make a phone call ASAP."

"To who?"

"Bill Morgan has been calling here all day. He wants to talk to you before they run his story. The number is by the phone."

I didn't really feel like talking, but if I didn't call him back he would just continue to call until he absolutely had to go to press with whatever he had, so I grabbed the phone and sat on the stairs and dialed his number. I tended to do all my business on the stairs, it seemed.

"Morgan. Sports desk," came the terse answer from the other end of the line.

"Bill, this is Ronald Blake."

"Butcher! Glad you called! I was hoping to ask you some questions for the story."

"Sure. Let's do it."

He didn't beat around the bush. The first question wasn't a softball pitch. I instantly knew I was going to have to be careful in how I answered his leading questions.

"You were in on every single play from scrimmage, offense and defense. You scored both touchdowns. You led the defense. Did it even matter that so many starters were out?"

I had to laugh at the ridiculous question. Where the hell did sports writers come up with that shit? "Well, sure it mattered. It was a rough game, but we got it done. The benched players actually contributed a lot to this game.

Derek Skyler was on the sidelines giving advice to Greg Nelton. Mike Short was encouraging the offensive line. It wasn't like they just hung us out to dry. They were very important to this win."

I waited patiently for the next question. Bill Morgan was a quick scribbler and I let him get his notes down.

"There's been some word that you were responsible for getting the starters suspended. Were you regretting that out there on the field last night?"

This wasn't the usual Bill Morgan ego stroke. I used to make fun of his fluff writing, but I realized right then that I would have preferred the fluff as to having to answer that question.

"I don't think you've got the story right, Bill," I said, trying to play it off and sound convincing. "Whatever happened with those suspensions had nothing to do with me."

"That's not how I hear it. I hear that you called certain members of the team out because of a plan devised to go headhunting for the Central Jaguars. Coach Rollins got wind of it and suspended the guilty players."

"I don't know what you're talking about or who you're getting this from, but that's totally wrong."

"My source is very reliable."

Well, that was certainly true. I wasn't about to confirm it, but the source was, in fact, very reliable. Someone was talking and they should have kept their mouth shut.

"Your source is wrong. You should probably find a new source."

"That's what I'm trying to do right now."

I wanted to hang up and end the interview. I knew if I did it would only look bad on me and would help to confirm his allegations. "Bill, are we going to talk about last night's game or last week's?"

"See, right there! That's the catch! Last night's game was so directly impacted by last week's shenanigans that it is *still* the story. What I want to do is show the town who the real hero is. This is a great story on sportsmanship and I can show the town what a brave thing it is that you did. The whole town was so upset about the suspensions, but now that we won the game they can know the real story. It's not going to go away. You should tell your side before someone else does."

And there was the old trademarked Bill Morgan ego stroke I was missing.

I was careful not to sigh out loud or give away any sign of what I was thinking. As soon as I was off the phone with Bill Morgan I was going to call Coach Rollins and warn him. "The story would go away if you'd just drop it and let us get on with the season. Whatever happened that got the players suspended was kept private for a reason. It had nothing to do with me, and furthermore, I don't care to know what happened. We beat Westlake, even without the suspended players and that's all that matters. I'll answer anything you want to know about last night's game and I'll even speculate on next week's game, but I won't comment any further on last week. That's history, not news."

"It's still news if no one knows the truth," Morgan countered.

I sat there on the stairs, dead silent. If I didn't say anything I figured he would see my side and change the subject. And I was right. He did change the subject. To something I wanted to talk about even less.

"All right. I'll leave it at that. For now. Let's talk about Ethan Miles," Morgan segued with all the finesse of a screeching stop.

"Bill, you are aware that I played a good football game last night, aren't you?"

"You played an excellent game last night! I loved it!"

"It's your job to write about that game, right?"

"It sure is."

"Then couldn't we just talk about the game?" I pleaded.

"I've already written the story about the game. Now I'm working on the... um... human-interest angle. People want to read about heroes and from what I've heard you fit the bill. You're a star on the field, but you were willing to sacrifice a chance at the state championship to do the right thing. You have taken a mentally challenged kid under your wing as a mentor. These are noble qualities and I'd like to show that side of Butcher Blake to the town."

Oh, fucking please!

I was not about to fall for that crap. He figured that if he gave me an emotional handjob over the phone I'd spill my guts. I had to get off the phone, and soon.

"Bill, I'm still very tired from running up and down that field all night. My legs hurt... but they'll be fine for the game next week... and if you're not going to talk about the game I'd just as soon get off the phone and get more rest. Okay?"

Morgan was silent for a few seconds and then I heard him smack his desk. "Okay. I guess if you don't want to be a hero..."

He had that much right. I didn't want to be a hero. I remained silent.

"All right then. Good luck against Barrington next week," Bill said. I didn't know that we were playing Barrington yet, but I took his word for it.

"Thanks. I'll talk to you later, Bill."

I hung the phone up with my finger, keeping the receiver to my ear, and immediately dialed Coach Rollins' phone number. Bill Morgan's tone was different and I didn't like the way that conversation had gone. It could turn out badly. After three rings Coach Rollins picked up.

"Rollins. Go."

"Coach, this is Blake. I think we might have a problem."

3. The Triumphant Hero Who Sucked

I probably should have just talked to Bill Morgan. I should have just answered his questions. It sure as Hell wouldn't have made me look any worse in the eyes of my team compared to what he ended up writing.

My legs were still sore on Monday, so I broke with tradition and skipped the gym that morning. If I had gone to the gym, though, the confrontation could have happened in private instead of in front of the whole school, and I would have much preferred that.

Ethan and I had no sooner walked through the door and into the main foyer when the other football players swarmed us. Some of them had copies of Sunday's sports page and were waving them like those crazy Arab terrorists waved burning American flags. The tone of their behavior wasn't all that different, either. They had lain in wait for me just inside the doors they knew I always entered the school through and they were primed and ready to pounce. The ringleader was…

Anyone?

Anyone?

Correct. Very good.

Derek Skyler.

When I read the paper Sunday morning I expected a bit of grief over the article, but I hadn't expected a lynch mob. These guys were mad, and I could completely understand it. Morgan had pulled a real job on me. He took one quote out of context and made it sound like I was self-aggrandizing throughout the entire interview. The rest of the story he had written using his reliable source. And since he was correct it did look to the rest of the team as if I was the one who had squealed.

Morgan had three stories on the front page. All of them starring Butcher Blake, front and center. The story on the game was a continuation of what he had written for Saturday morning, highlighting my contributions to the win and no one else's. That wasn't good.

The next story was written as speculative about how I was responsible for insuring fair play and true sportsmanship, according to the source he'd spoken to. He did at least admit that I had denied the allegations made against my teammates. The damage was done, though. My denial was a short little line toward the end of the story, and mentioned only after laying out the many correct details of what had happened, including the confrontation in the locker room. Why someone on the team was trying to submarine the whole thing for us was beyond me, but that was the only thing they could have been hoping to achieve.

The last story was about how I had befriended Ethan and about how I was a perfect role model for the youth of the town. There was no mention of the fact that I had only started taking care of Ethan because they made me or that I had picked on him to bring it on myself. By the end of that first page you wouldn't have thought I was a sex obsessed, slightly neurotic high school senior with severe questions about my future. As far as Bill Morgan was concerned I was Saint Butcher and the sun rose and set on my ass.

"Three cheers for Butcher Blake! He won that game all by himself!" Skyler taunted. There was a rousing, yet morose, chorus of "Hip hip hooray" three times.

None of the good things I'd said about him or the other suspended players made the paper. The one actual quote from me came out of context when he "asked" if we missed having the suspended players on the field. At this point he quoted me as saying, " We beat Westlake, even without the suspended players and that's all that matters."

Not a single word about how I defended Skyler and the others and told about how much they actually helped in winning the game. Nothing like that. The quote seemed to be placed there just to damage my reputation and I had no idea why Bill Morgan would do that. Or why he would do any of it. He was a huge Mustangs fan, and historically a huge Butcher Blake fan, and he had to know that the team would turn against me with the things he wrote.

"Calm the hell down!" I shouted over the din. No one did. A couple teachers noticed the disturbance and walked on. They probably thought there was nothing wrong and that people were really celebrating my entrance to the school as the conquering hero.

"Tell us how you did it, Butcher! How did you beat that whole Westlake team by yourself?" Skyler asked condescendingly.

I looked at Ethan and could see that he was getting scared.

"Guys, this isn't the time for this. Let's talk after school and I'll explain everything."

Shorty stepped up and got right in my face, inches from my nose. "Fuck that! We're going to settle it now!"

"What the hell, Shorty? Are you trying to kiss me? I don't dig you that way, man. Back off!" I said, pushing him away. A few people laughed and that made him mad. Before he could step back up to me Skyler called him off. "Morgan wrote what he wanted. He didn't write what I said. I never said anything about why players were suspended. He got that from someone else."

"Bullshit! You told him all that to make yourself look good, you fucking liar!" Skyler snarled. Chewy and Shorty were encroaching upon me again. They looked like they were both ready to pound me into the ground. Ethan started to cry, quietly.

Skyler shot a look at Ethan and then back at me. "You better get your girlfriend to class. He's getting all emotional. Must be that time of the month."

Laughter circled us, interrupted by the first bell of the morning. We had five minutes to get to class.

I grabbed Ethan's arm and led him down the hall to his first class, both of us walking a gauntlet of distrustful and dirty looks.

"Butchie, were they going to beat us up?" Ethan asked in a tiny voice.

"They were thinking about it, but no, they wouldn't do it. They were just mad at me because they think I did something wrong."

"Did you?"

"No. I actually did everything right this time. I guess that doesn't pay either."

"Why do they think you did something wrong?"

"Well, because someone lied about me, Ethan. Someone who is going to pay for it after school."

"Really? How much are they going to pay?"

"Never mind. It's not important."

"Could you make them pay me a dime? I'm collecting dimes."

4. Diplomacy In Action

After school I dropped Ethan off at home and then went straight to the newspaper office to have it out with Bill Morgan.

School had been pure hell the rest of the day. The morning attack was just the beginning of the festivities.

It seemed like a different player harangued me before, during, and after every class. And my other classmates who didn't play football just stared me down with contemptuous looks. Ethan was even getting picked on more than usual. After second period a couple guys took his duffel bag and threw it in the girl's restroom before I got to his class to pick him up. Fortunately two girls went in and got it for him. I could handle the heat, if I had to, but Ethan didn't deserve any of that. I simply was not going to let Bill Morgan get away with what he was trying to do.

The worst part was the feeling of betrayal. I knew that Bill Morgan was a big Mustangs fan and that he wanted what was best for us. Could he have possibly been so angry about being kept out of the loop concerning the suspensions that he was willing to write these stories as a kind of passive/aggressive swipe at the team? He'd always been very favorable toward me in his writing, but he had to have understood what the things he wrote would do to the team. The more I thought about it the angrier I became.

At the newspaper office I walked right past the front desk and back to the sports department. I was carrying a rolled up newspaper in my hand. No one said anything to me as I moved through the smattering of desks as if I belonged there. Morgan had his own office and an assistant stationed outside it. The door was closed.

I approached his assistant, a squat middle-aged woman with bulldog jowls. "I need to see Bill Morgan right now."

She wasn't the slightest bit taken aback at my curtness. "Mr. Morgan is in a meeting and he can't be disturbed. Can I take a message and have him get back to you?"

"No. I'm going to talk to him. Right now!"

With that, I stepped around her desk and headed for his door. The assistant tried to get to me quick enough to stop me from going in, but she wasn't even close.

"Sir! You can't go in there!"

Proving that I could, in fact, go in there, I threw the door open and stepped inside the office. Bill Morgan was sitting behind his desk and two other men were sitting in the chairs in front of the desk. They had cups of coffee in their hands and almost spilled the steaming liquid as they looked up at me in surprise.

"YOU MOTHER FUCKER!" I yelled, dropping the newspaper and lunging across his desk and grabbing him by the tie and the hair. The tie tightened around his neck, giving me a lot of leverage and control of him. The hair, however, came off in my hand. I threw it hard against the window behind Morgan's big, cushy leather chair and it smacked and stuck a little before sliding down the window, looking like a tarantula that had been shot out of cannon. I dragged him across the desk, spilling his coffee and scattering his papers everywhere. "WHAT THE FUCK ARE YOU TRYING TO DO TO ME?"

Morgan couldn't answer because he was choking from the tie strangling him. The two men stood up and skirted the edges of the office, trying to stay away from the big crazy guy choking their colleague. They ran out of the office and I got down to business.

When I dropped the newspaper it had landed on the corner of the desk and I snatched it back up. Rolling it tightly in my right hand I proceeded to spank Bill

Morgan with it like a badly behaved dog. He was trying to pull away from me and stand up, but I was far too strong for him. And at that moment I was even stronger because of my anger.

"WHAT THE FUCK DO YOU GET IN TRYING TO RUIN ME?"

"ARRRRGGGGHHHHH!" Morgan countered succinctly. I smacked his bald head with the newspaper. He was starting to go unconscious from the strangling. I would have choked him out, too, if it hadn't been for the huge rush of people swarming me at that point.

I went down under an avalanche of human flesh, Morgan's tie instantly ripped from my hand. People were punching me and kicking me, but it didn't hurt. I was too angry to feel the pain. I punched and kicked back as best as I could from my prone position on the office floor. They had the advantage, though. They had numbers and more guys kept jumping on me until I couldn't do anything.

I fought futilely for several minutes, hoping against hope that I could land a blow against someone who would slip up and let me escape the crush. I didn't want to flee, though. I just wanted to take more swats at Morgan.

"STOP IT! STOP IT!" someone was saying. "DON'T HURT HIM!"

I finally recognized the voice as Morgan's.

"LET HIM UP! COME ON! LET HIM UP!" Morgan was shouting.

"YEAH, LET ME UP! SO I CAN BEAT THAT COCKSUCKER'S BRAINS OUT!"

To my surprise, they didn't let me up. Hmmm?

I was finally giving up my useless struggles about the time the two cops walked into the office. They immediately joined in the fun and flipped me over on my belly, handcuffing me behind my back. The police station was two buildings down from the newspaper office, so I probably should have counted on a pretty good response time. The cops hauled me to my feet by my cuffed wrists. Pain screamed through both of my shoulders.

"You have the right to remain silent. Anything you say…" one of the cops began, but he was interrupted by Morgan.

"Officer, I don't think we need to press charges," he said, his face still red from the good sound choking I'd dished out. "It's just a misunderstanding that I think we can work out."

The cop looked disgusted. "Are you sure?"

Morgan looked me up and down and then turned back to the cop. "Yeah, I'm sure. We're just going to talk things out. Right, Butcher?"

I was still glaring at him.

"Right, Butcher?" Morgan said again, coaxing me. His tone told me to either say yes or go to jail.

"Yeah, that's right. We're just going to talk."

"Butcher?" The other cop recognized me then, and he beamed like he'd just met a movie star. "Butcher Blake! Man, I love watching you play!"

"Um… thanks," I said, more like a grunt.

The first cop wasn't as impressed with me. He pulled me roughly toward him and said clearly into my ear, "When I take these handcuffs off you are going to sit down in that chair and not move. Understand?"

I nodded.

"Understand?" he asked again, a little louder.

"Yes, I understand."

"Good. Because if you don't we're going to take you down. Hard. And you're going to jail."

He took off the handcuffs and I sat right down in one of the chairs vacated by the coffee-drinking guys.

The cops stood there watching me for a few seconds, until Morgan told them it was okay to leave the office.

"We'll be right outside if you need us," the first cop said.

"Thank you, but that won't be necessary. We're old friends. We'll be all right."

The first cop was looking at me and I nodded to him. "It's cool. Nothing's going to happen."

Reluctantly the cops left the office. Morgan let them get a little distance between them and the door before he said anything.

"I didn't press charges because I deserved that. I'm sorry, Butcher," he began, taking his seat behind his desk once again. His remaining hair jutted out at odd angles around his almost glowing bald head.

"Why did you do that?" I asked in lieu of accepting his apology. "Why would you try to turn the team against me?"

"I had no choice. I was being blackmailed."

"Blackmailed?" I repeated incredulously. Someone would blackmail a man to get at me? It sounded crazy. "Blackmailed how?"

Morgan's hands were shaking a little bit as he brought them to his face and rested his head in them. "Butcher... um... Butcher... I'm..."

The silence hung tangibly in the air for several long seconds. I wasn't sure what he was going to say, but he was having a very hard time of saying it.

"Butcher, I'm gay."

It wasn't a huge shock. For a sports writer Bill Morgan always came off as a little effeminate to me. I still wasn't sure what it had to do with anything.

"And?"

Bill leaned way back in his chair and looked me in the eye. "I was down in Fillmore Johnson Park. I did something stupid. I let someone lure me into a trap. A bunch of… boys… smacked me around a little bit, until one of them made them stop. He knew who I was and he wanted me to write those stories about you. To make it seem like you felt like you were above your teammates. I didn't want to do it. I had no choice. He was going to tell my wife."

"Who was it?"

"I'd rather not say," Morgan said, looking down at the floor.

"You don't have to. I know who it was." There was only one person it could have been, as far as I was concerned. "It was Derek Skyler, wasn't it?"

Morgan nodded a little bit, but then quickly shook his head and said, "No. No."

That was a big ass yes.

"He was going to ruin me. Ruin my life. If I didn't do what he said he was going to go to my wife. He's got… evidence. If it came out that I was gay, not only would I lose my wife, I'd probably lose this job. He told me about what happened with the suspensions and wanted me to print it. He was even willing to take some of the heat to make you look bad."

I didn't say anything. Any anger I'd had at Bill Morgan had completely drained away. Skyler had really outdone himself this time. He found a way to get two victims at once. Bill Morgan and I.

"I'm very sorry, Butcher. You know how much I respect you. I've been following your football career since youth league for Christ's sake. I have always expected to follow it right into the NFL. I feel terrible about what I did."

Morgan apologized and it seemed the least I could do. "Don't worry about it. I understand. I'm sorry I choked you. And ripped off your toupee. And spanked you like a dog." It sounded really bad when I recited it in a list like that.

Morgan put his hand on his head in a panic. In all the commotion he hadn't realized that I had ripped the toupee off. He began looking around for it in a panic.

"It's over by the trash can," I said, pointing toward the corner of the window.

In a flash he jumped up and ran to it, picking it up like an injured animal. He turned it a few times trying to figure out which way it went on his head. From the look on his face I thought that ripping his camouflage off hurt him worse than the choking or the spanking. He finally just shrugged and threw it down on the desk and tried to smooth down the hair on his head. "I guess I won't be needing that anymore."

We sat there quietly for several long seconds. I think maybe we were observing a moment of silence for his fallen hairpiece. Finally Morgan spoke. "What can I do to make it up to you?"

After I'd physically assaulted him he was still trying to make amends to me. He would have been completely in the right to press charges against me, but he didn't.

If he was willing to let that go then I was willing to call things even.

"Skyler got us both. We're even, if that's okay with you," I said, extending my hand for a handshake.

Morgan took my hand in an overly firm grip. I felt like he was overcompensating for the fact that I now knew he was gay. "Fair enough."

"I'm not going to tell anyone that you're gay," I said as I let go of his hand.

"I knew you wouldn't," he said with a wan smile.

"How did you know that?"

"Butcher, I've followed every aspect of your life since you were six or seven years old. I know you. I realize that those good things I said about you in those stories caused you some trouble, but the simple fact is that they're all true." Bill was smiling broadly now. "You're an honorable person and it's been a great joy in my life to see you grow into such a fine young man."

I squirmed a little. "Bill, are you hitting on me?"

Morgan jerked back like he had been smacked. "Um... no... I..."

"Sorry," I said, putting a hand on his shoulder. "I was just kidding. I'm sorry."

Morgan relaxed a little then and gave a sad smile.

"Why does Derek Skyler hate you so bad?" he asked, leaning back against his desk.

"Because if he's the only star that makes him the biggest star. He can't stand someone else making plays and winning games. You know... typical quarterback bullshit."

I walked out of the office trying to think of some way to get back at Skyler.

5. Going To State

My hands were tied.

Without risking Bill Morgan's secret getting out there was nothing I could do. I decided, for once, to do nothing. I was just going to go out and do my job. Nothing more, nothing less. I went to practice all week and did my job to the best of my ability. And then I went home and forgot about football.

On Thursday night Skyler called a "mandatory" team party. Of course, I skipped it. And of course, I had to deal with it the next day. On the bus ride to the game JK and I rode in the front of the bus, just the two of us. We left the back to the "in" crowd. They were mostly talking about me anyway, so it would have ruined their fun if I'd ridden back there with them.

That night we beat the Barrington Huskies 45-0.

Skyler had a plan that he used throughout the entire game, and fortunately for him, it worked. The plan was to keep the ball out of my hands as much as possible. The only time I got the ball was on short yardage situations where there was no chance that I was going to score. If he needed two yards for a first down, he'd come to me for it. Other than that my job all night was to block for him.

Giving credit where it's due, Skyler was definitely on his game that night. It seemed like he could do no wrong. Every pass hit the intended receiver right in the numbers. He was threading the needle all night, throwing successfully into double coverage like it was the easiest thing in the world.

During a timeout while we were both on the sidelines I heard Coach Rollins getting in Skyler's ass about not using running plays when they were the best option. Skyler, of course, had an answer.

"They're giving me a lot to work with out there. I can throw all day on these guys."

"I bet we can run on them, too," Coach Rollins countered. He didn't have a lot of arguing room considering the great job that Skyler was doing. By halftime he had completed thirty-nine passes out of forty-four attempts, with no interceptions. He was flat kicking ass.

Skyler was going to make damn sure that I wasn't the star of the show again that week, and I was fine with it. On the offensive side of the ball I was a virtual non-entity. Skyler even called some plays that likely ended up holding us to a field goal once rather than give me a chance to shine. I participated in the win by blocking well for him, but that isn't the kind of thing that is often recognized. My offensive rushing yards for the game totaled eleven.

Less than impressive, to be sure.

However, on the defensive side of the ball I was once again The Man. I had six sacks, including one that caused a fumble near our goal line that I recovered and ran in for a touchdown. I didn't need Derek Skyler to feed me the ball to make me a good player. I just came out like I had all week and did my job.

The Barrington Huskies were a good team, but we made them look really bad. Walking off the field that night everyone just knew that the state championship was ours for the taking.

I knew it, too.

I just didn't really care.

Chapter Eighteen

1. There's No "I" In Team

Following the game I took the opportunity to make even more enmity among my teammates.

On the bus ride home Skyler made the official invitations with one sweeping statement. "Party at my place after the dance! Everybody be there! Everything is on me!"

A cheer went up that shook the bus. At the front of the bus where I was riding by myself, not far from the coaches, I could feel the shout reverberating through the shell of the bus. I didn't shout along, I just stared straight ahead as the highway unfolded before the bus. I didn't want to go to the dance; I didn't want to go to the party. I just wanted to go see Linda and get my usual after game treat. I wasn't even paying attention to what was going on in the back. I drowned them out with my thoughts.

We rode along for several miles before I felt a hand clap on my shoulder. "Hey, Butcher! Good game! You coming to the party?"

It was Skyler, perhaps offering an olive branch of sorts.

"No. I'm just going home."

A disgusted look crossed over his face. "What the fuck is it with you? You really do think you are too good for the team, don't you?"

At Skyler's words all the coaches turned to see what was going on.

"Actually, yes. I do." There it was. Out there and hanging in the air.

"WELL, WELL, WELL GUYS! IT FINALLY COMES OUT!" Skyler shouted as he stood up and turned to the back of the bus.

The ruckus from the back stopped and they were all ears.

"BUTCHER JUST ADMITTED THAT HE DOES THINK HE'S BETTER THAN ALL OF US!"

The team started shuffling forward down the aisle. JK, who had been talking with Bunch and Marks, just leaned his head back against the window with a sigh and the look of a man accepting the inevitable. He'd known it was coming for a while. I can only keep my mouth shut for so long.

Coach Rollins stood up in the aisle. "Everyone just settle down. You've all just played a hard game and we don't need to be butting heads with each other."

"But Coach! He's been like this all year! If he thinks he's better than us how can we be expected to play with him?" Skyler was getting very animated, but trying to look calm.

"Skyler, I wouldn't worry about how I can play with you this year. I've never fucking liked you and we've played pretty well together over the years." I enjoyed watching Skyler's jaw drop. "You're upset because I'm not going to your party. Well, I'm not going because I just plain don't like most of you."

A look of triumph slid across Skyler's face. "Butcher, there's no 'I' in 'team'."

"Yeah, but there is a 'U' in 'Fuck off'."

"I'll play football with you guys. I'll workout in the gym with you guys. I'll practice every night with you guys. But I don't want to go to your stupid party… because I don't like you. It's amazing to me how such a bunch of fucking losers can make up a winning team like this."

That got them riled. I heard a few cries of, "Fuck you, Butcher!" and of course, the obligatory, "Fag!"

Coach Rollins turned to me. "Butcher, that's enough! You guys are a team! Act like one!"

"Sorry, Coach. Just telling them how it is."

"What the hell did we do?" someone shouted from the throng choking the aisle.

"I'll tell you what you've done. You went along with Skyler when he wanted to hurt the Jaguars. Only five got suspended, but except for me, JK, Bunch, and Marks, the rest of you were in on it. You just didn't get the opportunity to hurt anyone or you would have done it.

"The sense of entitlement you walk around the school flaunting just pisses me off. You can play football. So fucking what? Why does that give you the right to push everyone else around? That's bullshit! We shouldn't be doing that kind of shit. Even though we can get away with it, we shouldn't be doing it. People don't deserve to be treated like that."

"Ah, how sensitive! Read that off a Hallmark card?" Skyler asked, turning to his admiring throng for their approval, which came in waves of laughter. "Coach, I think Butcher should probably have the trainer check him out for an injury. It sounds like he might have hurt his pussy."

The laughter swelled and rolled over me like a hot wave. Coach Rollins walked across the aisle and grabbed Skyler, pulling him up to the front seat, across the aisle from me. The crowd went silent when they saw how hard the coach had jerked on Skyler's arm.

"Hey! He fucking started it! I just invited him to a party and he insulted me!" Skyler whined.

Coach Rollins turned to the hovering crowd. "Go back and sit down. Now!" Then he turned toward us and took a seat behind Skyler.

"Coach, he started it! I don't know why I'm in trouble!" Skyler whined some more.

"Jesus Christ, Derek! Shut the fuck up for a second, would ya?" Coach Rollins spat.

Derek shut the fuck up for a second.

"This is not going to happen. Not this year," Coach Rollins said looking back and forth between Skyler and I. "This team is just too damn good to let this petty bickering tear it down. Because it will.

"You two have played together for four years. We're going to the state championship and that's what we've been working for all this time. There has never been a better team on a high school football field than this year's Mustangs. We need to do this, men. You'll remember it forever."

Skyler was looking at me as if he was perfectly willing to let bygones be bygones. I knew he wasn't, but he wanted to give Coach Rollins what he wanted to see. I wasn't giving an inch. I extended my middle finger firmly in Skyler's direction.

Coach Rollins let out an exasperated sigh. "Fix it! That's an order! I don't care what agreement you have to come to, fix this!"

With that Coach Rollins got up and went back to sitting with the other coaches. After a few awkward moments Skyler slid over toward the aisle and leaned over my seat to talk to me.

"Butcher, you heard the man. We've got to fix this. We owe it to everyone on the team. We owe it to the Coach. Hell, we owe it to the whole town."

"Hey, I will go out there every day and do my job. I'll practice as hard as ever. I'll play to the absolute best of my ability every time I touch the football. If you don't want to let me run I'll just block for you all fucking day. I don't care. But I'm not coming to your fucking party because I hate your arrogant, self-obsessed guts. I hate your fucking goons, Chewy and Shorty. I hate it that we've cheated to win every game this year."

A panicked look streaked over Skyler's features, but disappeared as quickly as it came. He shot a glance toward the coaches sitting not all that far away. Skyler hissed under his breath, "We didn't cheat!"

"Like Hell we didn't cheat! What do you call that shit Chewy and Shorty shoot up all the fucking time? That's cheating. We don't deserve what we've got. We don't deserve to be where we are. We cheated!"

"You better keep your mouth shut about that shit, Butcher, if you know what's good for you! I'm not playing with you!"

"Skyler… you're a bitch. I've already smacked you down like a bitch and I'll do it again. Pull your John Wayne act somewhere else, I ain't buying it."

"I swear to God if you let that out and they take this season away from this team, I'll… I'll…" Skyler stuttered in a growing rage. He brought himself under control and leaned even closer to me, mere inches from my shoulder. "If you tell anyone about that and they take this season away I will have you killed!"

I'm sure he meant it, in his own little way. That could be the only reason he looked so shocked when I laughed in his face. I said dryly, "Oh, stop it, Showboat. You're scaring me."

"I mean it! I can have that done!" His face was red with anger and it only got worse when I laughed again.

"You want to see how scared I am, Showboat?" I said with a broad smile.

Then I brought my right elbow up into his chin and knocked him away from me. He lost his balance trying to scramble back into his seat and I was on him. I grabbed him around the throat and squeezed, leaning in close to his ear. I whispered, "You ever threaten me again and I'll kill you myself. I don't have to have it done for me, you fucking pussy!"

Coach Rollins was on me then, trying to pull me away from Skyler. I wasn't letting go and Skyler's red face was turning purple.

"I didn't say anything all year and I don't intend to," I whispered. Then I let go and allowed Coach Rollins to pull me away. "But don't you ever make the mistake of thinking I'm scared of you. You're a little punk bitch and everyone knows it."

Coach Rollins worked his way between Skyler and I. "Butcher, why don't you just come back here and sit with me."

I cast a smile into Skyler's scared and embarrassed face.

"Sure, Coach."

I enjoyed watching Skyler sweat when he saw me talking to Coach Rollins and he didn't know what I was saying. I didn't tell on Chewy and Shorty and I meant it when I said I never intended to. I really wasn't lying.

But Skyler didn't need to know that.

2. MVP – Most Vilified Player

By practice on Tuesday I was just about fed up with the team and I was ready to walk.

It had been a pretty decent weekend, due in large part that I had nothing to do with any of the Mustangs, except for JK. I spent Friday night with Linda until almost 4 a.m. and she kept my mind off of my issues. The only sign that anything was bothering me was that I was a little more aggressive than usual. Linda seemed to like that, though, so we just ran with it.

As it turned out, she wasn't just making small talk when she'd told my mom that she wanted to enlist my help in doing her wallpaper in her kitchen. I was leaving that morning when she asked me if I would come over after practice on Wednesday and help her hang her new wallpaper. Hanging wallpaper isn't my idea of fun, but after the treat she had just given me how could I possibly say no?

On Saturday afternoon JK and I went to the movies. I know when people say that they generally mean that they paid their admission and watched one movie. That wasn't our style. When we paid our admission we were in for the long haul. We saw three movies for one price that day just by hanging out in the bathroom between showings. We watched *They Live*, *High Spirits*, and *Child's Play*. We almost stayed for *Oliver And Company*, just because we could, but we just decided to leave and hang out for a while. We went to JK's house and played *Pitfall* on his Atari. And we didn't talk about football even once. Of that I was glad.

My dad was a little surprised that I skipped watching college football with him on Saturday and he was even more surprised when I skipped watching the pro games on Sunday. He asked me why I wasn't watching the games and I just shrugged and said that I wasn't interested. He seemed kind of alarmed at that, but said nothing. I'm sure he was hoping that it was just a phase and didn't want to compound any problems by talking about it. It was because I was quiet instead of wanting to argue about why I wasn't interested that gave him cause for concern. If I had been my usual loudmouth self he would have just chalked it up to rebellion.

Throughout the weekend, mostly while I was gone, we received dozens of crank phone calls. People calling and hanging up, people saying very rude, nasty things to my mother about me. When she asked me about the calls I told her that I didn't know why anyone would be calling.

Thankfully she let it drop, even though she knew I wasn't being completely truthful. I didn't want to bring it up to her and then have to get into it with my dad about what I had said to the team.

In the gym on Monday morning I was constantly being stared at by my teammates while I did my leg workout. None of them said anything at all. They just glared at me. I ignored them and did my workout. I had a job to do and I was there to do it, not kiss and make up with those bastards.

All day Monday, as Ethan and I walked through the halls between classes, I heard the whispers and saw the nasty looks. The story of what happened on the bus had made significant rounds, and by nature, it was already blown out of proportion to what really happened. I kept hearing about how I had said, "Fuck the school! Fuck the town! I'm Butcher Blake! I do what I want!" I was not well liked that day, even by some of the staff it seemed. Teachers were cold toward me. The cafeteria ladies seemed to serve my food to me under protest. They'd all heard about the vile things I had said about the school and the town.

Never mind that it wasn't true. That wasn't important.

I did notice that no one was talking about the fact that I had busted Skyler in the face with my elbow. That part seemed to be conveniently left out.

I'd been waiting on it and it finally came. Chewy tried to corner me in the hallway after fifth period, using his considerable bulk to press me into the corner. Some of the other players had run interference down the hall, keeping the teachers attention diverted from what was going on between me and the goon.

"Butcher, you had better not tell anyone about the steroids," he whispered. "If you do we'll tell them that you take them, too."

He looked very satisfied with himself, proud that he may have finally outsmarted someone.

I leaned in closer to Chewy's ear. "Hey dipshit! They can test for steroids. I will test clean. You, on the other hand..."

The wind went out of his sails. Big dumb ox.

"I told Skyler I wasn't going to say anything. If my word isn't good enough than you guys can just sweat it." I pushed past Chewy, collected Ethan, and made my way to my next class.

It was more of the same on Tuesday during school, but things really heated up at practice that afternoon.

The defensive players we were scrimmaging against were honestly trying to hurt me on every tackle. Every time we ran a running play my blockers were blowing their assignments and letting the defender hit me. And they were hitting hard. JK was the only one actually trying to block for me, but the other players were ganging up on me.

Tank Sherman laid a crushing tackle on me when Skyler sent me up the middle. He put everything he had into it and drove me backwards and into the ground. The air rushed out of my lungs and for a long time I couldn't catch my breath.

"Fucking little bitch!" Tank hissed into my face, lying on top of me. "You're going to pay for what you said!"

Tank got off of me and I stood up a few seconds later. I looked over and saw the coaches all turn their backs on the field. I took it that they were giving me permission to retaliate.

Tank was standing at the line, hands on his hips and braying like the jackass he was. Everyone else was laughing right along with him. He had his head turned and didn't see me until it was too late. With three big, momentum building strides, I kicked him right in the nuts. A sound like a firecracker exploded on the field as his athletic cup shattered from the force of my kick.

Tank went down and the laughing chorus stopped dead.

Eventually he hobbled off the field and took a seat on the bench. I saw Coach Rollins talking to him and Tank was shaking his head. I assumed he was telling Coach Rollins that it was a clean hit that took him to the sidelines.

After the timely kick in the nuts, I really got my mean on. I hit the line every time like I was trying to kill the defenders. Anyone who got in my way went down hard. I wasn't going to be the punching bag for these pricks. Not without punching back. Chewy intentionally dropped his block and let a defender into my lane. So I switched my angle and plowed full force into Chewy's back, knocking him to the ground and knocking the wind out of him.

I knew that Coach Rollins was letting a lot of this go on because he wanted us to fix it ourselves. It didn't take him long to realize that nothing was being settled, though. The practice field had turned into a free-for-all, with everyone trying to get me and me trying to get them back.

We lined up for the stretch play and Coach Rollins blew his whistle, killing the play. "Over here! Take a knee!"

We all did as we were told.

"THIS SHIT STOPS NOW!" He threw his clipboard hard into the ground right in front of us. Some of the guys jumped.

Coach Rollins was pacing back and forth, the assistant coaches standing firm right behind him. His face was contorted in rage and he was fighting to calm himself down enough to talk.

"All right! I know what Butcher said on the bus. I know how it pissed you guys off. But Butcher has been true to his word. He has come out here to do his job, just like he said he would."

Everyone turned and shot evil glares at me.

"Next time someone drops a block for him I will call the High School Sports Association and forfeit the game."

A shocked gasp went up.

"Yeah, that's right! I will forfeit the state championship if you don't knock this shit off!" Coach Rollins spat.

Everyone cast more of their evil glares at me.

"Go ahead. Get all your shitty looks in at Butcher now. Get it out of your system. Because when you go back out on that field, if he gets hit like that one more fucking time, one more dropped block, your season is over."

To no one's surprise, I didn't get touched behind the line again throughout the rest of the practice.

3. The Last Straw

Wednesday was the day that it all finally came down.

It was the last day before our four-day weekend for Thanksgiving, so things were a little erratic compared to our normally regimented week of practice. There was a major pep rally in the gym right after lunch, the whole school wishing us their best in the loudest terms possible. We had been conquering heroes all year, but this was what it was all about for the Mustangs fans. For the first time in almost twenty years we had a chance to bring home the title of state champions to Mims, and these people wanted it. Bad.

The big surprise was that we were released from school early, right after the pep rally. No one had any idea that an early release was coming, but they sure dug it. The gym emptied out in record time at the end of the rally.

It was a different story for the football team. We got the opportunity to practice extra long that day, since we weren't going to be practicing on Thanksgiving. I took Ethan home and hurried back for the extended practice session.

I had never really thought the day would take the turn it ended up taking. School went fine. Practice went fine. I had no more problems at all from anyone. They were still very unhappy with me, but they knew better than to say anything and test Coach Rollins' resolve about making us forfeit.

No, the day was as good as could be expected when you're a high school pariah. The trouble came that evening at a hardware store.

I was helping Linda hang her wallpaper in the kitchen, as I'd promised. She was more watching me do it than helping, but that was okay. Ethan wanted to help, so I let him hand me things. Hanging wallpaper has a trick to it, especially when you have to match patterns, so I didn't want to have him hang a piece sideways or something.

We were almost done when Ethan tore the last strip that was large enough to work with. He was trying to help me take it out of the water and he dropped one end and stepped on it, tearing the strip.

"Shit!" Ethan and I said at the same time. Then he slapped his hand over his mouth.

Linda had stepped into the living room for a few minutes and she heard our exclamation and came back into the kitchen. "Shit what? What happened?"

"Ethan… uh… we tore the last piece." I didn't want to put it all on Ethan, he felt bad enough for messing up anyway.

Linda didn't get angry, but she looked disappointed. "Do we have any other pieces?"

"Just scraps. Nothing big enough to cover this last spot," I said, pointing to the gap in the country flower print paper we'd been hanging.

She looked at her watch. "DeWalt's is still open if you'd go down there and pick up another roll of paper for me."

"Sure." Like I was going to refuse the woman who gave me the most meaningful experiences of my young life.

Ethan gave a little awkward jump. "Oh! Can I go with you Butcher?"

"If it's okay with your mom it's okay with me."

Linda looked at me questioningly. I nodded. She smiled and said, "Be careful, guys."

Ethan cackled and shook his fists close to his chest.

Linda was handing me some money from her purse when she said, "Are you sure you don't mind taking him with you? Ethan can get a little… excited in stores."

"Oh, he'll be fine. We're only going to be in there for a second. What could happen?"

"I'm just letting you know. He likes to wander off and look at everything. Touch everything. Especially in DeWalt's. I'll keep him home if you would rather not have to deal with him there."

I let out a little laugh. "No, he'll be good. Besides, he'd be crushed if you didn't let him go now."

On the way out the door I grabbed a sample scrap of wallpaper, just to be sure we got the right stuff, while Linda smoothed down Ethan's major cowlick as best she could. "Now Ethan, you listen to Ronald. Do whatever he says. Okay?"

"Okay," Ethan nodded absently. Then he added with a puzzled look, "Who's Ronald?"

"Listen to Butchie," Linda clarified.

"Okay. I will."

I drove Ethan and I over to DeWalt's at a fairly good clip. It was close to seven and I was sure he'd be closing by then. Especially on a night before a holiday.

DeWalt's Hardware and Home Improvement was located in a small storefront just down from Sharky's, so I knew the area well. It took no time at all to get there and for me to parallel park the Trans Am in one of the many open spaces on the street in front of the store. From the outside there didn't appear to be anyone else in the store. I helped Ethan out of the car and we hurried up to the door. I half expected to find it locked, but it came right open when I pulled on it, a jingle of bells sounding from the string hanging from the inside of the door.

The store was narrow but long and that made it easy to find everything, so I just walked right to the back of the store where the big sign that said "WALLPAPER" hung from the ceiling. Somewhere along the line Ethan became fascinated with some shiny object or another and he broke away from me and went off on his own. Not a big deal, I figured. The place was about as empty as it could get.

The racks in the back of the store that held the wallpaper weren't exceptionally well stocked, and as such it didn't take me very long to match my sample to the sample on the middle rack.

The empty middle rack.

Shit! They were out.

As I was standing there stewing over the missing wallpaper a little bald man in a buttoned down green cardigan came around the corner of the aisle. He had a DeWalt's Hardware and Home Improvement nametag on his sweater that told me he was STANLEY.

"Can I help you?"

"Um… yeah," I said, holding up the scrap with one hand and pointing to the empty rack with the other. "I need another roll of this kind of wallpaper and you appear to be out of stock."

Stanley reached up and took the scrap from my hand and looked at it intently. "I think… now don't quote me on this…"

I heard the bells ring at the front door.

"But I think…"

Did Ethan walk out? Out into the street? Shit!

"I think we have another case of this particular wallpaper in the back room. Let me check on that for ya."

As Stanley walked away I went looking for Ethan. I let out a sigh of relief when I found him quickly. He was about six rows over in the paint department playing with the stir sticks, acting like he was playing drums in the air. I felt better knowing that someone had come in instead of Ethan going out and I headed back to the wallpaper area.

Stanley seemed to be taking quite a while looking for that roll of wallpaper, but I waited patiently. Then all of a sudden I got the feeling that something was wrong. I had no basis for the feeling, but I was sure that there was something bad about to happen. I had to find Ethan. Even if I was wrong and just being paranoid I needed to put my mind at ease. I'd never had that kind of feeling before, but I didn't want to ignore it.

I looked down the aisle where Ethan had stood before and he wasn't there. I went to the next aisle and he wasn't there either. As soon as I stepped into the last aisle of the paint department I realized why I had felt the knot in my gut. I didn't see Ethan.

I saw Chewy, Shorty, and Skyler.

The sight of them huddled down like they were didn't register for a second and then I saw what they were huddled around. Ethan was on his hands and knees, facing the wall. I started walking down the aisle toward them and I heard Skyler say quietly, "Don't worry. This will be fun."

That's when I saw what they were doing and I went off. They had Ethan's head duct taped to the paint can shaker and Skyler was getting ready to turn it on.

In just a few steps I hit Skyler at a dead run and knocked him into a display of spray paint. "YOU MOTHER FUCKER!"

This wasn't just a prank. I don't know if they realized it or not, but if they had turned that paint can shaker on it would have broken Ethan's neck.

I turned away from Skyler's sprawling body to head back to Ethan and Shorty caught me on the chin with a solid, steroid fueled jab and I went down. I wasn't out, but I couldn't stand up to such a solid hit when I wasn't expecting it.

I heard Ethan cry out in terror, "BUTCHIE! BUTCHIE!"

When I tried to stand up to go to him Shorty shoved me back to the floor. Chewy was advancing on me as well. From the ground I had nothing I could really do, so I went with my tried and true maneuver that I had used on Tank Sherman. I kicked up with all my might and drove my foot hard into Shorty's crotch. He came up off the floor about two feet and landed with a dull thud on his back. I had just squat lifted his nuts for him.

Once again I tried to get to my feet, but this time Chewy was on me. He pushed me while I was off balance and I went sprawling toward Skyler, who had just stood up. I hit him and we both went down in the clatter and scatter of spray paint cans.

While on the floor I took the opportunity to grab Skyler by the hair and grind his face into the linoleum floor. I snarled gutturally, "You fucking sonofabitch!"

With a big heave I pulled Skyler's head up from the floor and I was getting ready to slam his face into it as hard as I could. My maneuver was cut short, though, by a very intense pain in my right knee. It felt like it was crushed. I let go of Skyler and tried to roll to the side and I felt another crushing blow land on my knee at a different angle.

Chewy was standing over me and stomping on my knee. He looked insane with an angry, knitted brow and a big, goofy grin on his face.

I curled up on the floor and grabbed my knee, grimacing in pain. I didn't cry out. I wouldn't give them the satisfaction. But it hurt like a bastard.

Ethan was still crying out, "BUTCHIE! BUTCHIE!"

On the floor I tried to cover up, awaiting the next blow to my injured knee from the stupid-faced giant standing above me. But the blow didn't come. Instead I heard a loud slap.

"You fucking moron! Not his knees!" Skyler screamed in the face that he had just slapped.

"Hey! What's going on here?" Stanley demanded from the end of the aisle.

Skyler and the goons hauled ass out of the store. Chewy was kind of helping Shorty along, who was still rubbing his nuts and looking a bit green.

"Oh my God! Are you boys all right?"

Stanley helped me to my feet and I tentatively put pressure on my knee. It hurt, but not nearly as badly as I had expected. From the initial pain I was sure that something had been seriously damaged.

"BUTCHIE! BUTCHIE!"

"I'm coming Ethan!" I said, hobbling over to him. Stanley helped me extricate Ethan from his duct tape headlock. He was crying.

"They said it would be fun. It just shaked a little is all they said. I'm sorry, Butchie!"

"Ethan, it's not your fault."

"I'm sorry! I'm sorry!"

"Ethan! Listen to me! It's not your fault! You don't have to be sorry for anything!"

"Ethan?" Stanley asked, looking down at the crying kid on the floor. "Are you Ethan Miles? Linda's boy?"

Even with snot bubbling in his nose and tears streaming down his face, Ethan tried to remember his well-practiced social action move. He extended his hand and said, "Yes sir. My name is Ethan Gabriel Miles. I'm happy to meet you. I go to high school."

"Are you hurt?" I asked Ethan.

He was shaking. And he shook his head. "I don't think so."

Stanley helped me bring Ethan to his feet and then he looked at me. "Did you know those boys?"

I have no idea why I said it, and I probably should have told the truth and pressed charges.

Instead I said, "I have no idea who they were."

Ethan and I made our way back to his house with a complimentary roll of wallpaper. Stanley got a dreamy look on his face and refused payment once he found out it was for Linda.

It looked like I had some competition.

Short, bald, old, paunchy competition.

Nice enough guy, though.

4. The Death Of My Dad's Dream

Linda just about had a fit when we came back to her house, Ethan crying and me limping.

"What happened?" she asked, almost in a panic. She went immediately to Ethan. "Are you hurt?"

Ethan shook his head no, but continued to let out quiet little sobs. His red-rimmed eyes still had a look of fear in them.

"What the hell happened?" Linda demanded of me, her voice a mix of anger and concern.

I told her the whole story, apologizing for not keeping a better eye on Ethan. She didn't say anything for a while and then she resolutely picked up the telephone.

"What are you doing?" I asked, knowing damn well what she meant to do.

"I'm calling the police. This is assault. They're going to jail!"

"I think you should reconsider," I said, not making a move to stop her.

"Reconsider? Hell no! I don't think so! They could have killed Ethan! They hurt your leg! I'm calling the police!" Linda was fuming.

"Linda, it won't help. It might make things much worse on Ethan later, though."

Linda still looked intent upon making the call, the handset held to her ear, but she wasn't dialing yet. "What do you mean?"

"The police aren't about to do anything to a Mims football player right before we go to state. It's just not going to happen."

"They have to! I want to press charges!" Linda yelled, her anger rising. "They could have broken my son's neck!"

"But they didn't. And because they didn't, even though they surely would have, the police will do everything in their power to keep this quiet and not rock the boat going into the state championship. Remember Jeff Dennings?"

Linda and Ethan had followed Mustang football for a long time, so I was sure they remembered our star player from the 1987 season. Linda thought for a second and nodded.

"Well, last year, right after our first sectional victory, Jeff Dennings basically raped a girl at a party the team had. His girlfriend missed the party and Jeff decided that he was going to get laid whether she was there or not. He got very rough with a girl at the party and forced her into the bedroom. We thought they were just playing around. A few minutes later she came running out of the bedroom, holding her clothes around her and crying. She ran into the bathroom with a few of her friends and got dressed and then they left.

"Not long after that the police showed up. The girl had reported that Jeff had raped her. While they took her to the hospital to get checked out a couple of the cops came to talk to Jeff. He admitted to having sex with her, but said that it was consensual. They left it at that, his word was good enough. We were all standing around, underage, and drinking beer with the cops while they took his statement. They wished us good luck and told us not to drive.

"The thing was, we found out later what kind of damage Jeff had done to that girl. She had vaginal tearing and fist sized bruises on her ribs. There was no doubt he'd raped her when that came out. But nothing was ever done about it. The girl's parents tried to pursue it legally and they kept hitting a brick wall with the cops. They eventually left town because some of the players and other Mustangs supporters harassed them until they left."

Linda pulled the phone away from her ear, but she didn't put it down. She looked stunned. "Oh my god… is that true?"

"Yeah, it's true! I never participated in any of it, but I know who did. They were punishing that girl and her family for trying to stand up for themselves, and the police did nothing."

Linda held the handset above the cradle. Her anger hadn't ebbed, but she had absorbed the depth of what I'd told her. "They can't get away with this!"

"They're not going to," I said, putting my hand on hers and hanging up the phone. "But the police won't help."

"What are we going to do?" Linda asked. It felt odd, a full-grown woman looking up to me as an authority on anything. "What can we do?"

"I'm going to take care of it. One at a time. I'll get them alone and beat the fuck out of them."

"But then you'll get in trouble!"

"No, I won't."

"You won't?"

"No, I won't. I play football for the Mustangs. Mustangs don't break laws. They don't apply to us. I'll take care of this when the season is over."

Ethan's sobs had gone away since he'd gotten home to his mother and he realized that we were all right. My knee was really starting to hurt, though. When I first stood up after Chewy had stomped on it I expected a lot of pain and damage. It didn't really hurt that bad, but since I had been up on it, walking and standing, the slight pain was getting persistent. I could tell, even through my jeans, that it was a little swollen.

I broke the long silence. "Hey, let's get this last strip of wallpaper up. I want to go home and ice down my knee for a while."

I dug in my pocket and handed Linda's money back to her. She held it in her hand and just looked at it, and then at me. "What's this?"

"Stanley said it's on the house. When I told him it was for you he refused to take the money."

"Oh," Linda said flatly. "That was really sweet of him."

I didn't say anything else. I just went to work on the wallpaper. Ethan came to help with the last strip and he was being extra careful this time. I think it made him feel good that I let him try again after he'd messed up the last piece.

I stepped up on a kitchen chair to get the paper up near the ceiling and make sure that I was lining up the pattern all the way down. After smoothing out all the wrinkles at the top I stepped down off of the chair to get the middle and the bottom.

That's when the *real* pain hit. My right leg buckled when I tried to put pressure on it.

"Ow, Shit!" I exclaimed, hitting the kitchen floor hard on my back. "Shit! Shit! Shit!"

My shouting scared Ethan, who was finishing smoothing out the middle when I fell. He began to tremble in fear and parrot what I was saying. "Shit! Shit! Shit!"

"Don't move! I'm calling your parents! We're going to the hospital!"

Linda was dialing the phone and Ethan was still shaking in the corner, looking down at me and saying, "Shit! Shit! Shit!"

With the phone to her ear Linda looked down at me holding my knee on her kitchen floor. "It's ringing. It's ringing. Ethan. Quit saying 'Shit!' all right?"

Ethan did as he was told.

"Mr. Blake, there's been an… accident," Linda said, trying to sound calm. "I'm getting ready to take Ronald to the hospital."

I heard my dad yell something unintelligible from the other end of the phone. As loud as he said it I figured I would have been able to hear him without a phone from all the way over at my house.

"He's hurt his knee and he needs to have it looked at by a doctor. It's not life threatening," Linda said.

I heard my dad again, louder this time. And it was no longer unintelligible. I clearly heard, "Oh, Jesus Christ! No! Not his knee!"

He said some other things, but I couldn't hear them. I wasn't the least surprised that my dad was crushed when he heard it was my knee. But I got the impression that if it were something that didn't threaten my game he couldn't have cared less.

"We're on the way. I'll meet you there!"

For once, instead of me helping Ethan into the car, it was the other way around. He helped me out of the car at the hospital, too, and helped me walk into the emergency room. Just as we were entering the doors my dad's pickup truck came screaming into the parking lot, almost taking the turn on two wheels. Dad was alone in the truck.

"Where's Mom?" I asked, as he approached Ethan, Linda, and I at the door.

"What happened to your damn knee?" Dad demanded, ignoring my question.

"I fell off a chair while I was helping hang wallpaper," I lied. There was just enough of the truth in it to make it seem almost legitimate.

Dad went off on a long, loud, tirade at the stupidity of me being up on a chair with the state championship coming up. I yelled over him until he stopped to listen to me.

"Dad! Where is Mom?" I asked again, loud and slow, as if talking to a child.

"Oh shit! I forgot to tell her! I just ran out of the house when I heard!" Dad was looking down at my right leg. "Not your knee! Not your knee!"

The three of them got me inside and Dad signed me in while Linda called my mother to let her know what was going on. It was hard to believe that my Dad could be so selfishly worried about my potential career that he didn't even think to tell my mother that I was in the ER.

Linda and Ethan took seats in the lobby and Dad went back with me to see the doctor. That was good. I didn't want him out there screaming at them about how they might have just ruined my life. And I certainly didn't want to tell him the truth.

After a couple X-rays and some intense examination the doctor determined that I had no serious injury. Mostly just swelling and pain, which would go away on it's own. He instructed me to go home, stay off of it, elevate it and keep it on ice to get the swelling down. Except for the X-rays that was pretty much my plan anyway. That little bit of medical attention cost my dad's insurance nearly a grand. At least with the X-rays they could be pretty sure that nothing was damaged.

"Will he be able to play football on Friday?" Dad asked gravely.

"If the swelling is down and the pain is gone, I would say he probably could. But you need to follow up with your family physician and let him make that decision."

Being Thanksgiving weekend we were pretty sure that our family doctor wasn't going to be in the office until Monday. There was no way I was going to get a clearance from my family doctor before Friday night's game. The ER doctor said his goodbyes and went back to the main desk with his charts.

"You take care of this damn knee and get it in shape. Even if it hurts a little bit, you can still play!"

My dad was going to be so disappointed when I didn't play. Whether I was better or not, I had decided that I wasn't playing in the game. I was not about to help those bastards become state champs. I would have to call Coach Rollins as soon as I got home. He would be upset, too, but I got the feeling more from Coach Rollins than from my own father that he was actually concerned about my wellbeing.

When Dad and I came out into the lobby, Mom was sitting there talking to Linda. Ethan was asleep with his head on his mother's lap and stretched out across the too small couch. They all stood up to come see me as I hobbled out on my brand new crutches. My leg was wrapped in a brace-like bandage to limit my motion until I got home and got it iced down.

I saw my dad rearing up to start yelling at Linda and I stepped in front of him, cutting him off. "Thanks for bringing me to the hospital, Mrs. Miles."

"You just get better, okay?" Linda said, sounding motherly toward me. "Thanks for your help, but I would have rather done it myself than to have you get hurt."

"These things happen," I said with a shrug. "I'll be okay."

I was glad that Linda was going to go along with my lie. It would make things a little easier.

Mom grabbed Dad by the arm and guided him toward the door, and then she took up on my left side. Ethan was on my right. They couldn't really help if I fell, but they were there anyway.

Dad turned around and shot an evil look at Linda and then stomped out the door.

Things were going to suck at home for a while.

Chapter Nineteen

1. Dad's Last Ditch Effort

I woke up Thanksgiving morning with the sound of the Macy's Thanksgiving Day Parade broadcast coming from the living room and a dull pain in my knee.

The knee felt much better than it had the night before when I was talking to Coach Rollins on the phone. When I had been talking to him it still hurt a lot and I didn't think there would have been any chance that I could have played, but the way it felt that morning I wouldn't have been surprised to find it healed enough to play by Friday evening. Of course, I still wasn't going to play, even if it was perfect, but I felt like I would have been able to.

Coach Rollins had been upset by my news, but he seemed more genuinely concerned about how I was doing than my own father did. Instead of finding that weird, I found it to be par for the course.

"Coach, this is Blake. I've got some bad news," I said when he answered the phone.

"What's wrong, Butcher?" Coach Rollins asked, trepidation in his voice.

"I don't think I'm going to be able to play in the state championship. I hurt my knee really bad last night."

"Shit!" Coach Rollins exclaimed. "How bad is it?"

"It's pretty bad. Hurts like hell and it's swollen about twice the normal size. They said I need a doctor's clearance before I can even think about playing. As bad as it is I just don't see it getting better in enough time."

From there I went on to tell him the established lie about falling off the chair. Maybe I should have told him about the fight and all the things that Chewy and Shorty were up to. In fact, I know now that I should have told him. But the "no-I-in-team" philosophy dies hard when it's been ingrained in a person from almost the point of birth. I wasn't going to help the team by playing hurt for them, but I saw no reason to destroy the hopes and dreams of everyone in town over those three. It was bad enough that I was endangering the dream by refusing to play even if I could. I'd get my revenge off the field in it's own time.

"Well, Butcher, I hate to hear that. But more importantly… how's it going to heal? No permanent damage?" Coach Rollins asked.

"I don't think so. The X-ray didn't show anything damaged. Just a lot of pain and swelling as far as they could tell."

"Damn it, Butcher! I hate to lose you! You are the biggest part of what got us to the championship. You deserve to take the field and bring it the rest of the way home. I feel horrible for you. Is there no chance you could play at all?"

"I really don't think so," I said, looking down at my heavily bandaged knee, surprised that I couldn't actually see the pulses of pain that I was feeling. "This is a bad one."

Coach Rollins sighed. "I'm so sorry, Butcher. We'll try to win this one for you. You just get better. Okay?"

"Yeah, I will." At that moment it was hugely difficult not to just tell him that I would try to play. If he'd asked me to play hurt I know I would have. Coach Rollins felt bad for me not being able to play, but I felt bad for him, taking the team that he'd built into the championship game without, all modesty aside, one of the biggest weapons he had.

I sat up in bed then and heard my dad calling to my mom, who was in her traditional haven for Thanksgiving morning, the kitchen. He wanted her to come see this "amazing float". That was another Thanksgiving tradition. Dad and I watching television while Mom worked her ass off. I rubbed my knee through the bandage a little and it wasn't as tender as it had been the night before. I carefully swung my right leg out of bed and put my foot on the floor.

So far, not much pain. Just a soft, dull ache.

Curiosity got the best of me and I decided to unwrap the bandage and look at my knee. It wasn't hurting very badly at all and I found that strange, considering how painful it had been when I went to bed.

The Velcro straps made hideous ripping sounds as I pulled them apart and spread the padded cloth open, revealing my horribly savaged knee.

It least that was what I'd expected to see.

My knee looked almost normal. There was barely any swelling and no discoloration at all. I was amazed to think that I could have healed so much over night. I decided to take the bandage the rest of the way off and stand up on it, just to see what would happen. Slowly I rose to my feet and I stood there for a few seconds, waiting for the sharp stabbing pains of last night to return.

They didn't.

I took a step.

No pain. Well, none but the previously mentioned dull ache. It didn't hurt to step down on the right foot. I bent the leg up. There was a little twinge of something, but it disappeared as quickly as it came. I straightened my leg out slowly and bent it again. This time there was nothing. It didn't hurt to bend it at all. I knew, absolutely knew, that with another day of rest I would be able to play if I wanted to. If I didn't do anything to aggravate the knee it would be good enough to play on by Friday night.

I put the bandage back on, grabbed my crutches and walked to the door carrying them. I didn't need them, but I was going to have to sell the injury to keep myself off the field tomorrow. I scooted down the stairs on my ass because the bandage held my leg too straight to step down.

In the living room I collapsed heavily onto the couch and settled in to watch the parade with my dad.

"How's the knee?" Dad asked.

"Still hurts like Hell," I lied.

"Well, I've got a doctor coming at eleven to take a look at it and see if we can get you cleared to play."

I didn't say anything. I just nodded and went back to half-assed watching the parade.

At eleven o'clock on the nose there was a doctor standing in our living room. My dad had been pacing for the last few minutes before the doctor arrived. It wasn't our family doctor, but he looked somewhat familiar. I wasn't sure where I'd seen him before, I just knew that I had. Maybe he was one of the doctors who shared an office with Dr. Woodruff, our family doctor.

"Hello Ronald, I'm Dr. Stevens," the man said, extending his hand. At the sound of his voice I recognized him. It was the sonofabitch who yelled at Ethan and I when I took him trick-or-treating in Rambling Hills. "Let's have a look at that knee."

"Why don't you go fuck yourself?" I said angrily, and the doctor recoiled.

"What? WHAT?" he bellowed. The doctor, who had unbuttoned his coat, began buttoning it back up. "I'm leaving. I don't need this. On a holiday no less. Enjoy your pain, young man."

"Wait! Dr. Stevens! Wait!" My dad cried, following him out of the living room. "He's in pain, he doesn't know what he's saying! Come back and just look at his knee! Please?"

"I will not be spoken to like that! Goodbye!" Dr. Stevens said, opening the door and stepping out onto the porch.

Before the door could close Dad yelled out, "I'll double it."

The door stayed open for a few seconds, closed a little bit, paused, and then opened all the way up. Dr. Stevens stepped back inside.

"Thank you! Thank you! I couldn't find another doctor who would make a house call. Especially on Thanksgiving. Thank you so much!"

'*Jesus, Dad! Why don't you just blow him while you're at it,*' I thought.

Dr. Stevens took the bandage off of me and examined my knee. "It doesn't look bad at all."

Dad was looking over his shoulder and his expression became very pleased when he saw how good my knee looked as compared to last night. "No. It doesn't! I bet he'll be able to play!"

Dr. Stevens let a look of mild annoyance cross his face. I got the feeling that he didn't like someone else playing doctor for him. "Don't get ahead of yourself, Mr. Blake. Just because it doesn't look bad doesn't mean there isn't a problem. Let me finish my examination and I'll tell you if he can play or not."

Dr. Stevens had me stand up, which I did very gingerly, really playing it up as if I were in agony. He felt around my knee and looked at it from every angle. "Can you walk across the room?"

"I don't know," I said, an exaggerated grimace on my face.

"Well… could you try?" Dr. Stevens said, obviously unhappy with my attitude.

Without further ado I began to hobble delicately across the living room, wincing with imaginary pain every time I stepped down on my right foot. After a few steps the doctor stopped me.

"Bend it for me," he ordered.

I leaned against the couch and bent my knee up, slowly and with great determination. Dr. Stevens was feeling my knee as I bent it and straightened it repeatedly. "Everything feels all right in there. I saw the X-rays at the hospital and it all looks clear."

There was no way he could see me in that much pain and still clear me to play. Could he?

"Aside from the reported pain I see no reason that you couldn't play. I'll clear you."

I wanted to scream, "WHAT? YOU'RE CLEARING ME!" But I didn't. I just gave a smile as false as the pain I had just faked.

"If it gets to where you can handle the pain I think the knee is in good enough shape to handle playing. I can give you some painkillers if you think they'd help you get through the game."

I shook my head no. I wasn't about to take painkillers I didn't need. I didn't like taking them when I did need them. They made me feel horrible when I was coming off of them.

Dr. Stevens signed a paper and handed it to my dad. "Well, then… stay off of it as much as possible. Get plenty of rest. If the swelling starts to come back get some ice on it. If it feels good enough to play on tomorrow night you're cleared. Go Mustangs."

My dad shook Dr. Stevens hand and showed him to the door. When he came back into the living room he was beaming.

"You're cleared! You can play! Call Coach Rollins and tell him!"

"Dad, if this still hurts like this I won't be able to play," I explained.

Dad got quiet and I could see his look of exasperation on his face. "Ronald, you've been cleared to play. That means nothing is wrong with you. You're going to play tomorrow night."

"The doctor just said that if the pain went away I was free to play. If the pain doesn't go away I'm not playing!"

"A champion plays with pain, son. A champion… plays with pain."

Dad picked up the phone and handed it to me. "Call him. Now."

There was no arguing with him, so I did as he ordered and called Coach Rollins.

"Coach, this is Blake," I began, looking at my dad as he stared at me. "I've got some good news."

"Let's hear it," Coach Rollins said. He sounded very pleasantly surprised.

"Yeah. I've been cleared to play tomorrow. If I can get the pain under control."

When I said the part about the pain Dad shot me a disgusted look.

"Are you still in a lot of pain?" Coach Rollins asked.

"Yeah, it's pretty bad. But according to the doctor who just left here, and my X-rays, there is no real damage. If the pain lets up he said I can play."

Coach Rollins got quiet on the other end of the line. "Blake, it's good that you've been cleared, but if you're in a lot of pain I don't want you to go out there and hurt yourself even worse. Don't push it. If it hurts too much you let me know and we'll stay with Ebert and Dole."

Right then I knew for a fact what I had only suspected. Coach Rollins really did care more about me than my own dad did.

"I'll let you know, Coach," I said.

"Let me know before the game and we'll decide who starts. If you're up to it the spot is yours. Just don't tell me you're up to it if you're not."

"I won't. I'll tell you if it hurts too much to play."

"Have a good Thanksgiving, Blake."

"You too, Coach."

From the look on Dad's face he wasn't having as happy a Thanksgiving as he'd expected. I could tell he was upset that I had told Coach Rollins about the pain and that I still might not play. Especially after he paid some doctor a bunch of money to make a house call on Thanksgiving to clear me.

A few minutes later Dad had his first of many beers of that day.

2. Thankful? For What?

The parade of losers that passes for my family began trickling in around noon. At least it was a relatively short parade.

Uncle Jimmy, Dad's older brother, was already blitzed when he got there. Not just on alcohol, either. There was a little white powder on his nose and I think the alcohol he had obviously drank only helped to level his coked up jitters out a bit. His girlfriend, a big haired truck stop bimbo, bounced in after him, the same telltale powder on her nose. Uncle Jimmy was a long haul trucker, so it was pretty apparent that he just snagged a lot lizard for his Thanksgiving dinner date and brought her over with him. Uncle Jimmy was proud white trash until the day he died, which was only a few months later. One night at his monthly Klan meeting his robes caught fire as he lit the cross. Ironically, Uncle Jimmy ended up dying blacker than the people he'd spent his life hating.

"Hey, Little Ronnie! How's it hanging?" Uncle Jimmy shouted, grabbing me in a headlock and twisting me to my knees. He still called me Little Ronnie even though I towered over him by almost a foot.

Dad freaked out. "Jimmy! No! He's got a bad knee!"

I guess the huge padded bandage wasn't a big enough clue for Uncle Genius.

"Oh! Fuckin' shit! I'm sorry, man! Dang!" Uncle Jimmy let me go and half-ass helped me to my feet.

"I'm okay, Uncle Jimmy. No harm done," I said, even though I knew I should have really put on a serious stabbing knee pain right then.

"Hell, I knew you were a tough guy!" Uncle Jimmy said, stretching up to put me in another headlock, but not twisting me down to his level this time. Abruptly, he changed subjects, just as he had my head pointed straight into the chest of his lady friend. "Little Ronnie, what do you think of them funbags? Huh?"

They were huge and barely constrained behind the skintight pink polyester blouse she had on. A dainty hand with nicotine stained fingers and long 'fuck me red' nails extended toward my face. "Hi. I'm Bambi. Nice to meet ya."

Uncle Jimmy let go and I politely shook Bambi's hand. She had a voice like a strangled airhorn, but she might have been pretty at one time. "Pleased to meet you, Bambi."

Uncle Jimmy took Bambi by the arm and escorted her into the kitchen and ditched her with my mom before joining Dad in the living room. Dad had a cooler by the chair and he tossed a beer to Uncle Jimmy. I knew Mom would just love being saddled with a drunk and coked up truck stop prostitute, so of course, I had to go observe.

Grandma and Grandpa, my mom's parents, got there about twenty minutes after Uncle Jimmy. Grandpa was a retired minister, and I know his heart was always in the right place, but he just wasn't very big on approval. No one was Christian enough for Grandpa. When I met them inside the door he didn't even say hello. I said, "Hi Grandpa" and he didn't bat an eye before saying, "What have you done for the Lord today, Ronald?"

"Uh… nothing," I answered, taken aback even though I shouldn't have been.

"That's what I thought," He said accusingly and dropped his coat into my arms. He turned to Grandma, "Come on."

She obediently followed him into the kitchen, Grandpa delivering her to her place.

Aunt Polly, Dad's younger sister, showed up shortly after Grandma and Grandpa, her two illegitimate half-breed kids right behind her. Aunt Polly had a huge ass and JK had told me that a huge ass was like catnip to a black guy, which explained the dark kids trailing her blonde head. As you can imagine Dad and Uncle Jimmy had no use for their little sister, the "nigger lover". Besides having two half black bastards, Aunt Polly was a thief and a pillhead, so we had to keep an eye on anything that wasn't nailed down. Mom had already locked up the contents of the medicine cabinet the night before.

Aunt Polly put the kids, Andre and Shanay, in the living room with her drunken racist brothers and took her place in the kitchen as well. I have to give Dad and Uncle Jimmy some credit, though. At least they had the decency not to pick on the kids. Of course, a big part of that, I'm sure, was fear of my mother.

Not long before dinner there was a huge crash and screams from the kitchen and my mother started yelling, "Ron! Jimmy! Get in here!"

My dad and my uncle hauled ass into the kitchen and I followed along, Grandpa not far behind me.

In the kitchen Bambi had Aunt Polly down on the floor and was hitting her. Aunt Polly covered her face and tried to weather the blows, screaming her head off the whole time. Uncle Jimmy grabbed Bambi around the waist and pulled her up and off of his little sister.

I'd seen enough. I turned around and went to the stairs, heading to my room. The last thing I heard was my mom telling Uncle Jimmy to get that crazy bitch out of her house.

Two hours later dinner was ready and I poked my head out of my room, however reluctantly, and headed downstairs, playing up the pain even more than I had in the morning. I sat down at the table just as Dad was relinquishing the prayer duties to my Grandpa. I tried to tune everyone out and just eat my damn turkey. Nothing but bitching, whining, and preaching went on at that table. Uncle Jimmy had come back without Bambi, having dropped her off at a nearby truck stop.

I was casually aloof and happy not to be included in any of the conversations, until Uncle Jimmy opened his big mouth. "So, Little Ronnie… ready for the big game tomorrow?"

I looked down the table at my dad who was staring at me. "I might not be able to play, Uncle Jimmy. This knee is really killing me."

Dad, fueled by Budweiser, began to steam. "God… God… God…"

He was trying very hard not to say it.

"God damn it! You've been cleared! You're fine! You're playing!" he yelled.

"Dad, I'm hurt! How can I play when I can barely walk?"

"A champion…" Dad began condescendingly.

"Plays hurt," I interrupted. "Yeah, I know. But I can't do it. My knee is hurt too bad."

"You fucking pussy!" Dad hissed, a slight slur to his words. "Jimmy… Jimmy… what do you think about a kid who is the star player on the football… um… team… and he doesn't want to play?"

Uncle Jimmy didn't say anything, wisely not wanting to get in the middle of it.

"Ron! That's enough!" My mother said from the other end of the table. "Stop it! Now!"

Dad, of course, let the alcohol keep talking and ignored her. "Jimmy… what do you think about a kid who is the star player on the football team and he's only got two friends… a nigger and a retard!"

I looked at Mom, eyebrows raised as if asking, "What do I do?"

"RON! YOU'RE DRUNK! SHUT UP!"

"Hell, Jimmy! He ain't even got a girlfriend. Could be a faggot for all I know!"

At that point even Uncle Jimmy felt like he had to say something. "Ron, come on. Let's not do this. Not today. All right?"

There is something seriously wrong when the guy who paid a hooker to accompany him to Thanksgiving dinner with his family becomes the voice of reason.

"That's what it is! You're a damn faggot, ain't ya? That's why you don't wanna play. What? Are you scared you're going to break a nail?"

Andre and Shanay were about to start crying and Aunt Polly was trying to comfort them.

"I just paid a doctor a lot of money to come clear you so you could play. You are playing tomorrow. And that is final!"

That was it. I could take no more.

"You know what, Dad? It's not final! I'm not fucking playing tomorrow! At all! Go fuck yourself!"

"Young man, you need to watch that language! Jesus doesn't like to hear that sort of talk." Grandpa scolded.

"Fuck you, Grandpa!" I said, standing up and not bothering to fake the pain. I didn't need to say that to him, but I was too mad to focus my anger where it needed to go. I turned to leave amid the gasps of surprise and shock.

"Where do you think you're going?" Dad asked, a tone of challenge in his voice.

"I'm leaving. I don't need this shit," I said, heading for the door.

Dad dropped his fork and hurried to block my way. "You're not going anywhere! You sit back down there and you apologize to your grandfather!"

"Not a chance! I'm out of here!"

Dad grabbed me and pushed me backwards, trying to keep me in the room. I pushed back and sent him hard against the wall.

"OH! YOU THINK YOU CAN TAKE THE OLD MAN NOW! IS THAT IT? WELL, COME ON AND TRY ME!"

I had no intention of fighting my dad, even when he put his fists up in a fighting stance.

"RON! DON"T YOU DARE HIT HIM!" Mom roared.

I left my hands at my side and tried to walk through the door, right past my dad who was bobbing and weaving like he was a boxer. I never expected him to sucker punch me in the side of the head, which he did. I fell against the wall, but I didn't go down. Apparently Dad thought it hurt more than it did. Before I recovered all the way Mom was at my side.

"WANT SOME MORE? OR DO YOU WANT TO SIT DOWN, APOLOGIZE TO YOUR GRANDPA AND EAT YOUR DINNER?" Dad yelled crazily, his eyes wild.

I stood as straight as I could and walked forward again. Dad moved to hit me again and I sidestepped the blow and threw a punch back at him. It connected, but I didn't think it was a good solid punch. It must have been, though, because Dad dropped like a stone. He was out cold. I turned to look at my mom and she had her hand over her mouth in disbelief.

"Sorry… I'm sorry!" I said through a haze. "I'm sorry I ruined dinner."

"Ronald, just get out of here for now. I'll handle your father, but you need to get out of here for a little while."

I stepped over my dad's prone form and headed for the hall closet to get my coat. I stuck my head back in the dining room before I left and wished everyone a Happy Thanksgiving.

No one wished me one in return.

3. Letting It Go

I was far from ready for Friday night's game by the time we were loading into the bus.

My knee didn't hurt at all, but I was still walking with a limp. My biggest problem was the hangover that was kicking my ass. After I left the house the night before I had nowhere I wanted to be. I sneaked back into my dad's garage and stole a twelve pack of his beer and went driving around the whole night. I drove by Linda's and thought about stopping in, but she was entertaining for the holiday and I didn't want to intrude. Same thing at JK's house, even though I know I would have been welcome there. I just really needed to be alone and work things through in my head. I had no idea if I was ever going to be allowed in the house again as long as my dad was alive, and I had no idea where I might go if I needed a place to stay on a more permanent basis.

I slept in my car in the parking lot beside the playground in Fillmore Johnson Park, letting it idle all night to keep the heater going. The Midwest in November is no time or place to be sleeping in a car. When Dad went to work the next morning I returned home, grabbed some fresh clothes and my sports bag and headed back out. I hung out with JK until it was time to head to the school for our little warm-up practice.

When JK first saw me come walking up to his front steps he knew something was wrong. I didn't have to say anything, but he just picked up on it. After I told him the whole story and that I wasn't playing he surprised me. He didn't try to talk me out of it. He understood completely.

"Man, they've been busting your balls all season. I can't blame you for not wanting to play their game. But I'm playing."

"I wouldn't expect you to sit out on account of me," I said.

"Well, there are going to be scouts there and this is my last chance to show 'em what I got. If I don't get a scholarship I can't go to college," JK said, shaking his head. "I have got to get my black ass into a good program, and unlike you they haven't exactly been beating down my door."

"You've had some schools talk to you," I offered.

"Not the ones I want. Not like what you've got. I mean, shit, I'd love to sit this one out in support for you, but I have to make a statement in this game. You're already in. Hell, you can write your own ticket."

He was right and it made me feel kind of guilty and selfish.

"Well, look at it this way… with me out the running game is probably not going to work as well and Skyler will have to throw more. A few of those passes will surely be meant for a tight end."

I rode to practice with JK, leaving my car in front of his house. I didn't participate, but I sat on the sidelines with the coaches and watched.

After the warm-up, Coach Rollins gathered the team in the locker room before we climbed aboard the purple and green monstrosity we call the team bus and he announced that Todd Ebert would be starting at my position. There was a palpable sense of disappointment, even though no one said anything. I think that maybe the deafening silence let Ebert know that his team had no faith in him. The team we were playing, the Douglas Atoms, had a very strong run defense, and the team didn't feel comfortable without me doing the running. It was hard not to tell Coach Rollins that I would play right then and there, but I stuck to my guns. I was willing to dress for the game, but I had no intention of stepping foot on the field. Fuck the Mustangs. They didn't deserve to win and I wasn't about to help them become champions.

The drive there was another exercise in the silent treatment from the team. But Skyler and his goons didn't say anything. They knew it was their fault that I had gotten hurt and they didn't want me to announce it to the team. I didn't say a word. I just slept all the way there.

In the locker room Coach Rollins gave us the rundown on the Atoms, but I didn't pay attention. Normally I would have been riveted on every single word he said, but I figured I didn't need to listen. After his talk Coach Rollins gave us a few minutes while he and the other coaches met in the office. I took the opportunity to slink off and wrestle with my decision some more. This was going to be it. If the team took the field and I wasn't with them there was no going back. I was letting my entire high school dream fall by the wayside. I was letting Coach Rollins down. I was letting the town down. I didn't want to do that.

But I wanted to help Skyler and Company win the state championship even less.

JK came around the corner just as I was making up my mind to stay on the bench and he asked me one question. "Are you sure this is what you want to do?"

I nodded.

JK nodded back.

From the front of the locker room we heard Coach Rollins calling us all front and center.

"Take it to 'em, Hammerhead!" I said, clapping JK on the shoulder pads and following him to where the team was gathered.

Coach Rollins was pacing in front of the team, the other coaches standing silently behind him, as he waited for everyone to get in position and quiet down. When you could hear a pin drop he began.

"Tonight will be the last night that you will play together as a team. After tonight some of you seniors may never step onto a football field again. But that's all right. We don't have to worry about the future. We have Right Now.

"Let me tell you about Right Now. Right Now… is the most important time in your life. Right Now… you are the best high school football team walking the planet. Right Now… you are preparing for what may be the biggest game of your life. Right Now… I am very proud to take the field with you, as a team… as this team… one last time."

Coach Rollins started a steady clap, his expression deadly serious. Everyone joined in and clapped along with him. The clapping was echoing off of the tile walls, an insistent tattoo that physically displaced the air in the room. I could feel the pressure in my ears with every clap. I was getting caught up in it and I had to fight myself back down.

"RIGHT NOW!" Coach Rollins yelled.

"RIGHT NOW!" the entire team yelled back.

"RIGHT NOW YOU ARE IN CHARGE OF YOUR DESTINY!"

A loud "Hell yeah" came from somewhere in the back.

"RIGHT NOW!" Coach Rollins roared again.

"RIGHT NOW!" we roared right back. I was as into it as anyone.

"RIGHT NOW THERE IS ONLY ONE TEAM THAT STANDS IN YOUR WAY!"

"PUSSIES!" Chewy called out.

"RIGHT NOW!" Coach Rollins shouted, stopping his clapping and dropping his hands to his side.

"RIGHT NOW!" the team shouted back, still clapping.

"RIGHT NOW LET'S GO KICK SOME ASS!" Coach Rollins snarled, and turned to lead us out of the locker room.

The Mustangs roared with unbridled intensity. I roared with them.

Goddamn I wanted to play!

I mean I *really, really, really* wanted to play.

But I wasn't going to.

4. The State Championship

For the first time during the entire season the Mims Mustangs were in a real fight.

The Douglas Atoms won the coin toss and came out gunning from the start, scoring on their first possession. Jim Dole was trying to fill my spot on the defense, and he just wasn't up to it. Their running back, a monster named Lewiston, ran right over Dole like he wasn't even there. I have to admit I took a bit of smug satisfaction from knowing that they couldn't do it without me. I had every confidence in the world that I could have stopped Lewiston, and that would have changed Douglas's approach. Dole was not only missing the run coverage on his side of the line, but he was getting zero pressure on their quarterback, a rocket-armed kid named Kyle Hunt. Hunt was only a junior, so they'd have him for another year, and he was already about as good as Skyler.

After our first possession, a three and out, my teammates on the bench started looking at me with a curious expression. They still didn't seem to like me, but I could tell that they were hoping that I'd step in and save their collective ass. Todd Ebert wasn't cutting it on the offensive side of the ball, equally as bad as Dole on the defense. On the first down they ran the stretch play and he fumbled the hand off. Fortunately he fell on the ball and retained possession with only a one-yard loss. The next play was a run up the middle and he screwed that up, too. The line made him a hole, but he hesitated too long and was crushed at the line of scrimmage as the hole collapsed on him. On third and eleven Skyler was looking for a pass, and he might have gotten it off if Ebert had blocked for him. Skyler was hit as he threw and the ball dropped incomplete at Steve Bunch's feet.

The Mustangs offense came off the field bewildered as the punting team prepared to kick it away. It was a strange feeling for me, sitting there on the bench and seeing all the things that could have been done differently. The stretch play, had Ebert held on to the ball, would have worked because the defense wasn't pulling quick enough to the outside. It's pure speculation, but I probably would have gotten at least ten yards out of the play. The run up the middle would have worked with me in there, too. I saw the hole open up from the sideline and I was reacting to it long before Ebert did. The pass play, had it even been necessary at that point with me in the game, would have worked because I saw the rusher who was going to get through the line before the ball was even snapped. I knew that if I had played everything would have been different. I just knew it.

And so did the rest of the Mustangs.

Derek Skyler sidled up to me on the bench, sipping from a cup of Gatorade. "So, have you proven your point yet?"

"What point is that?" I asked obliviously.

"That we need you on the field for us to win this game."

"I don't need to prove anything. Everyone already knows you need me on the field to win this game. If you fucking assholes hadn't attacked Ethan and then stomped on my knee we'd be up 7-0 right about now," I said, rubbing my knee to accentuate my point.

"Cut the shit, Butcher! Your knee is fine. I saw you walking around on it in the locker room. Get your ass in there and do your fucking job!" Skyler hissed in a whisper right by my ear.

"My season ended in the paint aisle at the hardware store. I'm not playing in this game. You superstars will have to do this one on your own."

Skyler leapt to his feet and stomped off.

The first quarter ended 7-0 and Ebert was limping already. He wasn't running smart, just hard. Unfortunately for him, he wasn't big enough to play the game he was attempting. Every time he tried to overpower the defenders at the line it looked like he was hitting a brick wall. And he wasn't fast enough to pull off the speed plays. Ebert got hit hard at the line or behind it every single time he got his hands on the ball.

Early in the second the chant started coming up from our fans, all of them having traveled a long way to see us win. They didn't come expecting the showing they were getting. The chant was, "BUTCHER! BUTCHER! BUTCHER!" I turned around and looked into the stands, giving them a pathetic shrug. I had another mental debate then, wondering if I could bring myself to tell Coach Rollins I would play. I wanted to go out and play for the fans as much as I had wanted to play for Coach Rollins. The key was still that I didn't want to play for me. Or for Ethan. I sat there on the bench and tried to tune them out. The crowd got louder every time Ebert fucked up a play, so I stood up and faced them, motioning with my arms for them to keep it down.

I'm not sure how I did it, but somehow I zoomed in right on my dad's face, sitting there with a sour look amid the throng of purple and green. He was glaring at me, and I could tell he was barely controlling a desire to come out on the field and hit me, but one thing still remained true. He was there. While our eyes were in contact I gave him a nod of acknowledgment, which he returned. Then his face grew sterner and he pointed out onto the field, mouthing the word, "Play."

I shook my head, turned my back to the crowd and sat down.

Ebert found a way to break the line late in the second quarter and he ended up with a positive gain of six yards. The bad news was that he went down hard on the knee of the leg he'd been limping on since the first quarter. Ebert got up slowly and limped back to the huddle where Skyler was already sending the offense to their places. It was a pass play, mainly to give Ebert a chance to recuperate a little. The Atoms showed blitz and they brought it hard and heavy, crashing into the line. One guy made it through the line and was hauling balls toward Skyler, who had his back turned to the rush. He was getting ready to launch a big one down field and the defender was going to slam him from the back. Ebert surprised me because this one time he actually picked up the coverage and blocked the guy.

Skyler's pass was long and beautiful, right into Donnie Marks' arms. Marks went down nineteen yards from our goal line, the Atoms piling on unnecessarily, but there was no foul whistled. The team charged down the field to get in position for the next play and that is when Ebert went down. I was watching him trot down the field and I saw his knee give out. The whole leg just collapsed under him. He had to come out, and after a quick check by the trainer it was determined that he was leaving the game for good.

Coach Rollins decided to let Jim Dole try to play some Iron Man football the way I did it, and Dole charged onto the field full of fire. Three plays later he walked off the field looking like a book of wet matches. The Atoms absolutely crushed him on his three running plays. Brent Patton did kick the field goal, though, and got us on the board.

At halftime we went into the locker room down by four, 7-3.

Coach Rollins didn't say anything about putting me in during his little pep talk in the locker room. He wasn't too upset that we were down, he just wanted the team to start executing. Four points is nothing at halftime, he was careful not to let the players get down on themselves more than they already were. It was a balancing act between wanting to yell at them for screwing up and wanting to keep from destroying their egos so they'd be able to find what they needed to win.

I followed the team out of the locker room, but before I could fall into line and walk to the field with them I felt a hand grab my arm. I turned around and it was my dad.

"You either get your ass in there and play or you find another place to live! I'm not kidding a bit," Dad said gravely. Mom wasn't with him. She was apparently still up in the stands. I knew he wasn't echoing her sentiments. "If you sit that bench the rest of this game you can just go live with that nigger friend of yours for all I care."

I didn't say anything to him, I just tried to pull away. He jerked back on my arm hard. It pulled me off balance and I almost fell. Coach Rollins was walking up behind me and he helped steady me. Then he looked my dad in the eye and pried his fingers from my arm. "I know he's your son, but he's mine until the end of this game."

I walked to the field with Coach Rollins and took my place on the bench. The second half started almost exactly the way the first half went, except we got the ball first. Our offense went three and out, and then the Douglas Atoms scored again, a seventy-yard touchdown pass. After the extra point it was 14-3.

Dole's ineffectiveness forced Skyler's hand and he ended up making some passing plays that he normally wouldn't have had to attempt. He pulled off enough of them to get us in position for two more field goals in the third quarter, but we still couldn't find the end zone. JK took a hard shot from behind when Skyler dropped him one right in the middle of the field. JK held on, despite getting hit so hard his helmet flew off. His catch allowed us to make the second field goal of the quarter, bringing the score to 14-9.

On our first possession of the fourth quarter, Dole got crushed coming across the line and I heard something pop all the way over on the sideline. His heel had gotten stuck in the turf and as the defensive linemen drove him backwards his knee snapped the wrong way. It was a sickening sound, one that you never get used to hearing. And as always, it was followed by a lot of screaming. Deep, manly screaming. The worst kind.

All eyes turned to me as Dole was taken from the field on a stretcher and into the ambulance. The chant of "BUTCHER! BUTCHER!" grew even more insistent. I looked at Coach Rollins and shook my head, mouthing the word, "No". I could see his frustration, but he let it pass and went on scanning the bench.

"Templin! Get in there for Dole!" Coach Rollins yelled.

Rob Templin looked stricken. "Me? Coach, you want me to go in?"

"Yes! Get your ass in there! Now!"

Rob Templin grabbed his helmet and charged onto the field for the first time since early in the season when Coach Rollins let him play a few downs after we had the game in the bag. He'd never been allowed to do anything important, and of course, he didn't know the plays.

At the line Skyler pointed Templin where to stand and block for him, and went with a short pass up the middle to JK. It was complete, but once again JK got his bell rung. The ball was short of a first down by inches, so it was going to be a run.

Skyler handed off to Templin who drilled it right up the middle. He got the first down and a few more yards. Then he went down under a barrage of tackles and he didn't get back up. The stretcher carried him off as well. We lost two running backs in three plays.

Coach Rollins sent in David Jenkins to replace Templin, and Jenkins only lasted for about eight plays before he came out with a shoulder injury from being slammed to the ground. Mustangs were dropping like flies. Toby Killian, normally a third string defensive lineman, got his chance to get in and be a running back. He actually did pretty good in moving the ball, but they still couldn't score.

The Atoms didn't score again either, so that was a small miracle, considering the number of Mustangs out of the line up. The Mustangs played very good defense in the fourth quarter to keep the Atoms out of field goal range, but the offense was just so ineffective that it didn't seem to matter.

After a final stop the Mustangs got the ball back with just under two minutes left to play. Skyler took the ball at the one after the punt and worked his way down field. He hit JK up the middle again, but this time JK shrugged the tackle and broke off a big run that took them almost to midfield. If there were scouts in the crowd, and I was sure there was, then JK had just increased the value of his stock. That was a huge play.

Killian pushed the ball another nine yards on the first down, but they stopped him on the next two plays to get that last yard. With third and one Skyler called for the stretch play formation instead of just trying to pound it up the middle. It was a feint and it worked. The Atoms bit on the stretch play and Skyler sneaked the ball, barely, across the first down marker. They brought out the chains to measure and just the tip of the ball had made it.

In an attempt to control the clock Skyler began passing to the sidelines, but with little success. The Atoms were all over Bunch and Marks and didn't let them get out of bounds. On third down, with about two yards to go and forty-four seconds left, Skyler sent Killian up the middle, and he got the first down.

He also got knocked the fuck out.

The Atoms hit him so hard that he went down on his helmet and didn't move for a long time. When he finally did it was slow and sluggish, but the trainers were on him and took him back to the ground. He left the field on a stretcher as well.

Five running backs taken out of the game in one night. It was ridiculous.

As they were getting Killian squared away Coach Rollins came to talk to me. He leaned in and said earnestly, "Butcher… we need you. Can you play? We can still win this."

I hated to do it, but I had to. I told him no. "I'm not going to win this game for these sons of bitches. Don't put me in."

There was a war going on in Coach Rollins head. "I've got no one else. They're killing the new guys! If you've got anything… anything at all… I'd like to have you in there."

"Coach, I'm not playing in this game because Skyler, Chewy and Shorty tried to duct tape Ethan's head to a paint can shaker at the hardware store the other night. When I tried to stop them Chewy stomped on my knee. This team has been against me since I was shackled with Ethan and I've had it. I'm not going to give them a championship. They don't deserve it and I'm not doing it."

"Butcher… I've got no one. Can you play?"

"I'm not…" I started.

"I'm not asking if you will. I'm asking if you can." Coach Rollins interrupted.

"Yes. I am capable of playing."

"Then get on the field. Get out there now."

"Don't give the ball to me. I'm not going to win this game for these pieces of shit. I mean it."

"Just get your ass out on that field!" he bellowed.

I grabbed my helmet and slowly put it on as I moseyed out to meet up with the team on the thirty-six yard line. Strangely enough there was also thirty-six seconds left in the game. I casually walked out to the huddle and stood there outside it. It seemed like where I belonged.

Skyler grabbed my arm and tried to pull me into the huddle, but I pulled away.

"It's about fucking time!"

"I'm not playing. I'm just filling up space. Don't give me the ball." I said stonily.

"Fuck this shit!" Chewy roared, pushing me in the chest and mashing his facemask into mine. "I shoulda broke your goddamned leg!"

Skyler put a hand on Chewy's chest and his pet goon backed off of me. "We'll go with pass plays. Don't worry about it. We can still win this without his pussy ass!"

I walked away from the huddle as Skyler was still talking and watched as Killian finally left the field. The crowd cheered for him until the cheer blended into the chant of "BUTCHER! BUTCHER! BUTCHER!" again. I ignored the crowd and took my place next to Skyler, who was in the shotgun, even though I had no intention of blocking for him. The Atoms were showing blitz, and so far they had brought it every single time they lined up for it.

Skyler called for the snap and the blitz came full force. I was prepared to step aside and let them plow his ass into the ground when the unexpected happened. Skyler slammed the ball into my chest with three rushers bearing down on me. The fucker changed the play after I left the huddle. He was either trying to see me get crushed or trying to force my hand and make me run the ball. So I made my decision in a split second.

I tucked the ball and ran for the line, ducking and slipping tackles as I fought my way to the line of scrimmage. One of the Atoms got a grip on me, but I pounded him loose and broke away. No sooner had I broken his tackle than I felt another set of hands tugging at my jersey. It slowed me down enough for the third rusher to get his hands on me and I was coming to a dead stop. That's when Chewy and Shorty came back and leveled the guys trying to bring me down. That broke the tackle and I finally made it to the line.

Every defender on the field was sweeping my way and every Mustang was scrambling to block for me. I know they could all taste the victory when they saw me break the line. Every time an Atoms defender got near me another Mustang came out of nowhere and put them down.

I crossed the twenty-yard line with a relatively clear shot at the end zone. Only a few more defenders stood in my way and they were hopelessly outnumbered by the swarming Mustangs who were buzzing around me like soldier bees just looking for something to sting.

By the time I reached the ten-yard line I was almost at the sideline and there was not one single Douglas player near me. It was going to be nothing to slow down and strut across the goal line for the biggest victory of my football career. I was going to be the biggest hero in Mims High School football history with only about four more steps.

Instead I cut hard to the right and charged across the field, right on the ten-yard line, straight back into the meat of the Atoms defense. I had no idea how many seconds were left on the clock, but I was determined to stay on my feet and to make slow, but continuous forward progress so that the clock could not be stopped. An Atoms player tried to tackle me, but I sidestepped him back toward the twelve-yard line and then swerved back onto the ten, running a straight line, like a high-speed sobriety test.

It was about this time that the Mustangs figured out what was going on and they joined the Atoms in trying to tackle me. In fact, my own teammates were trying to tackle me even more intensely than the Douglas Atoms were. I slipped between an Atoms player and a Mustang who were both trying to bring me down as I was nearing the opposite sideline. With my patented turn on a dime maneuver I spun and ran back across the field.

The first tackler approaching me was none other than Derek Skyler. I took great pleasure in grabbing his facemask and dragging him across the field with me for a few steps before dropping him on his ass. However, my effort in dragging him by the facemask slowed me down enough for Chewy and Shorty to make it across the field. They both hit me as I sped along the nine-yard line and they were trying to drive me into the end zone. Their momentum moved me all the way to the two before I got traction and drove back against them. I could feel the strain on the knee that Chewy had stomped on and it felt like it was going to break, but I held my ground and pushed back with all of my might. Being smaller than either of them I utilized my slight advantage at having a lower center of gravity and held fast to my patch of ground.

The referee's starter pistol fired, signaling that time expired, at just about the same time that my knee gave out. I did my best to fall straight to the ground and not allow them to push me into the end zone before I could down the ball. I could feel myself moving toward the goal line, though. Despite my best efforts I felt like I was going to fall over the goal and accidentally win the damn game.

I landed flat on my back and came to a dead stop and the world went silent. I looked up and could see the referee standing above me and the two goons piled on top of me. He was waving his arms, almost like a baseball umpire calling a runner safe.

No touchdown.

The Douglas Atoms and their fans began to celebrate. They were the 1988 State Champions. The players on the field celebrated in a more subdued fashion than they normally would have. They were still a bit befuddled about what had just happened. All that really mattered, though, was that the Douglas Atoms won and the Mims Mustangs lost.

My knee was killing me, but I was smiling, very satisfied with myself. I got to my feet and saw the other Mustangs stomping angrily around the field. They were roaring and yelling at the sidelines in their bewilderment. I looked over and saw Coach Rollins standing there, staring at me with a blank expression. I could get no reading at all from him as to what was going on in his head. The Mustangs fans were booing me even more loudly than they had cheered.

I didn't care. I felt, and still do feel, that what I did was justified.

The unmistakable roar of a bull moose brought me back to the situation on the field. Chewy was bearing down on me, his typical roid rage increased tenfold, fueled by the royal screwing I had just given my bastard teammates. His eyes were red and tears were streaming down his face from the incredibly intense anger rippling through him. I took off my helmet and held it by the facemask, letting it dangle at my side. Chewy saw this and took off his own helmet and threw it across the field, never once slowing down his angry approach toward me.

"CHEWY! THAT WAS FUCKING STUPID!" I yelled.

He slowed down a bit, the familiar dumbstruck look gliding over his contorted features. "Huh? What?"

"THAT WAS DUMB! YOU JUST THREW YOUR HELMET! WHY DID YOU DO THAT?"

He stopped and gave me his typical idiot look. He was still mad, but you just can't counteract stupidity.

"YOU SHOULD HAVE NEVER THROWN YOUR HELMET! NEVER!" I shouted.

"Why not?" he hissed through his teeth.

In one lightning fast, whistling arc I swung my helmet by the facemask and brought it down across his big stupid face. I heard his nose crunch and he began to fall backwards. In one fluid move I brought the helmet across with a back swing and caught him in the nose again. He crashed to the ground as if his big ass had just fallen from a beanstalk. I stood over him and pounded his face repeatedly with my helmet. His eyes rolled over white and he lost consciousness.

Too late I realized that Shorty was coming up behind me. I knew I wouldn't be able to turn in time to keep him from crushing me, so I braced for whatever impact might come.

But none did.

JK had flown across the field and tackled Shorty about the knees, dropping him to the ground. I took the opportunity to kick him as hard as I could in the ribs about ten times as he struggled to get to his feet. When he was on his hands and knees I used my free left hand to strip his helmet from him and I pummeled his head with his helmet and mine. Blood began streaking in huge arcs behind my swings, flinging ropes of gore everywhere. I busted his head wide open and Shorty dropped to the ground, unconscious.

With the same sense that told me where a tackle was coming from during a game, I realized that someone was coming up behind me. I whirled and came face to face with my entire team, minus Skyler and his goons. Skyler was on a stretcher, being hauled off the field. I had done some damage to his neck with my brutal facemasking.

I stood my ground, a blood drenched football helmet in each hand. "Who's next?"

That stopped their approach.

"WHO IS FUCKING NEXT?" I raged. Still no one moved. I held my ground and waited for someone to find their balls and charge me. But it never happened.

Coach Rollins stepped around the side of the lynch mob and addressed them forcefully. "HIT THE SHOWERS! NOW!"

No one moved and he grabbed one of the guys by the jersey and pulled the player face to face with him. "I SAID HIT THE SHOWERS! DO IT NOW!"

The team slowly broke away and left me standing there. I thought I was alone, facing Coach Rollins, but then JK stepped out from behind me.

"I had your back," he said, and then charged off to the showers.

"You better try to find your own ride home, Blake," Coach Rollins said before turning away and walking to the locker room. He didn't seem angry, but I couldn't imagine that he wasn't disappointed.

I dropped the bloody helmets and limped off the field to find my parents for a ride home. I turned and watched the other coaches helping Chewy and Shorty sit up.

I didn't care about the state championship. I didn't care about all the people who hated me.

As far as I was concerned, I had won.

Epilogue

Well, as you have probably surmised, considering you know that I bounce in a titty bar, I never made it to the NFL. As soon as word got out about what I did the colleges pulled every scholarship offer from the table.

After that loss in the championship game my dad grudgingly gave me a ride home. For two hours we rode in dead silence, his eyes glued to the road and his knuckles white on the wheel. It must have taken titanic effort for him not to jump in the backseat and attempt to throttle me.

For a few weeks after I lost the game for the Mustangs, I found myself fighting at the drop of a hat. Some adults even picked fights with me. I had upset the entire town and I was the local pariah. Until years later when Lenny Kapowski and his huge lottery windfall of "fuck you money" came along I was the most hated man in town.

Like all things, though, eventually it died down. It went from fistfights to name calling to dirty looks and then it all just sort of went away. Soon enough my antics were only mentioned during the post season if the Mustangs were making a run for it again.

Coach Rollins called me down to his office the following Monday and we made our peace. He didn't like what I did, but he understood. We shook hands and never spoke about it again. In 1991, 1992, and 1993 his teams won the state championship. Even after the impressive three-peat, he would still tell you that his 1988 team was the best team ever.

For those of you who follow pro sports, you know what happened with Derek Skyler. He had a stellar college career, followed by a lackluster pro career. All the talent in the world and the attitude of a prima donna. He played in the NFL for nine years, eventually ending his career with the Raiders. He had become too much of a behavior problem for anyone else to deal with him. After two seasons even the Raiders cut him. When your behavior is too bad for even the Raiders you might determine that you have a problem. He's still a spoiled millionaire, though. There is no justice.

Mitchell "Chewy" Gumm would have made it to the NFL, too, except he is in prison in Georgia. His senior year in college he flipped out in another of his famous roid rages and killed a guy in a bar fight. He's due for release pretty soon, but what can he really do? The guy proved to be the total waste that I always knew he was. I predict he'll get out of prison and go right back in.

Mike "Shorty" Short never made it to the pros either. He flunked out of college and came back home. He drives a delivery route for a package service and he's a fat, bitter, drunken, regular at Gazonga's. The idiot seems to think we're friends because we played on the same team. If you keep an eye on our local paper you'll read about Shorty fairly often. He's usually listed in the police blotter for everything from public intoxication to domestic violence. His wife stays with him even though he beats her. Sooner or later he'll kill her and he'll be in prison like his fellow goon.

Jerome "JK/Hammerhead" Kent, like Chewy, is also in prison. Except JK is a corrections officer for the state of Ohio. He was injured in college and even though he healed up perfectly fine, it scared off the pro scouts and he was never drafted into the NFL. However, the CFL gave him a shot and JK ended up playing three seasons in Canada for the Toronto Argonauts. An injury ended his career there and he moved back home. Shortly after he was hired on at the prison he took up playing semi-pro football in the Cleveland area. He just gave it up last year. It sucks to get old.

I never played football again after that last game for Mims.

But I did go to college.

My grades were good enough and I qualified for some financial help, so I put myself through school. My dad refused to help me. In fact we barely spoke ten words to each other right up until he died two years ago. He never forgave me for crushing his dream. I did forgive him for usurping all of mine, though.

I went to Ball State University and got a degree in Special Education. I work at a school for developmentally challenged kids. It doesn't pay a lot, so I bounce at Gazonga's as many nights per week as I can. The real reward I get for teaching these kids is not financial, but they are infinitely worth it. Even though I haven't played football in years, my athleticism hasn't gone to waste. I'm a coach and trainer for the Special Olympics. A couple years ago I got a new assistant to help me out. Coach Rollins retired from Mims and now he helps me out with the kids.

Besides my job at the school I work with developmentally challenged adults as they try to make their way in the world. We get them jobs and train them for participating in the workforce in whatever capacity they can. Because of the extra effort I gave him, Ethan has really learned to shine at his jobs. Sometimes he screws up, but for the most part he does very well. He was being treated poorly at the restaurant job I had gotten him before he came to work at Gazonga's with me, so I got him out of there. He really seems to enjoy spinning records for the dancers. And he still fondly remembers Darlene Fish, who dances as China Doll. She has no idea who he is, but Ethan is never without two packs of cigarettes. Just in case.

Ethan doesn't get paid a lot at any of the jobs he has had, however he does have quite a sizable bank account. He is still hoarding dimes. Seriously, he could probably buy himself a house with nothing but dimes if he were so inclined.

It wasn't long after the state championship fiasco that I found out what was so damned important that Stacy Lampley wanted to talk to me about. Our little one night stand connected us for life. She was pregnant. As of this writing our son, David, is seventeen years old, and he loves his Uncle Ethan. I refused to have a Ronald Blake III. Stacy and I never got together. She married a really good guy who has always treated my boy as if he were his own. I can't complain about that.

Linda and I saw each other secretly throughout the rest of the 1988-1989 school year and the following summer. When I went away for school she ended up dating Stanley DeWalt from the hardware store. They were married and Ethan inherited a stepbrother and sister. They're still happily married and it is only mildly awkward when I am around their family. I figure Stanley probably knows about Linda and I from way back when, but it never comes up. If he doesn't know, I hope he doesn't read this.

I've never been married, and I rarely have time to date. The girls at Gazonga's take care of me, though. Bouncer pay isn't all that great, but there are incredible fringe benefits. I look at bouncing in a strip club like working at a video store. I need to sleep with as many dancers as I can, so that if someone asks me what is good I can tell them.

I will admit that I sometimes find myself wondering how my life might have turned out differently. Sometimes when it's late at night and I'm sitting at the kitchen table trying to figure out my bills and who gets paid this month, I entertain the occasional "what-if" fantasy. What if I had won that game? What if the college scouts hadn't pulled their offers from me after I tanked the game? There are just so many questions that can't be answered.

Where would I be if things had worked out differently?

I had to think about that. If I had never met Ethan, never picked on him. If I had never been shackled with taking care of him. The likely scenario was that we would have won the state championship. I would have gone on to play college ball, and the smart money would suggest

I would have made it into the NFL. You know, barring injury and such. Instead of working myself to death with two jobs I could be living the high life in a huge mansion with girls on each arm and a fleet of sports cars in my giant garage. Instead of trying to figure out if I could afford cable television I could be buying property in Hawaii for my offseason home.

When I find myself thinking like that it doesn't last long. I usually sigh and smile. I realize quickly that I had asked myself the wrong question. It's not about where I might be.

The real question always brings me back to reality.

Brings me to the one true question that makes it all worth it.

Where would Ethan be?

April 9, 2006

Afterword

Did anyone notice the date at the end of the story?

I finished the first draft of this book on that day, almost four years ago.

I never planned on taking so long to follow up Mr. Undesirable, but sometimes things just don't work out within the lines you draw. I thought I'd have Picking On Retards out by June of 2006, but something major got in the way.

My band, Fetish, made the Grammy ballot.

(www.myspace.com/fetishrock for those of you playing at home.)

Two days after I decided that I was going to put music on the back burner and concentrate on writing I got the call that our album, Triple X, was being considered for a spot on the Grammy ballot, so I called the other guys and we decided to get serious about music again. For the next few years, with twists and turns, Fetish hacked it out on the live scene. We missed a nomination in 2006, but we began writing better music and really came into our own as musicians. It was really getting good.

Then on December 18, 2009 we called it a day. We played our last live show and went our separate ways.

I had been running so hard doing band things that I hadn't written in a long time. I finally got the opportunity to reopen the file languishing on my hard drive and read it again. Seeing it with new eyes was just what I needed.

I loved this story all over again.

Some of the parts in here I had totally forgotten about, and as I read it for the final edit I found myself thinking, "Wow! How does this part come out?" I didn't even remember the part about headhunting the Central Jaguars until I started to read it again. At times it was like reading someone else's writing. I'm not the same writer I was then. (But I do still kind of like that guy who wrote this book.)

Now, I figure out where to go next. I have about half a children's novel finished that I was really getting into when I skidded to a halt on my writing. (Yes, a children's book. No swearing at all!) I have music that I still want to do. I have a wife and four kids to take care of. I have a day job. (And I can't get Lenny Kapowski to give me any money so I can quit punching the time clock. Fucking prick.)

For those who have asked and were wondering... there you go. This second book has been done for a while, I just got lost on the way to publish it. Now that it is here, and I'm assuming you read it before you got to this part, I hope it was worth the wait. As one of my proofreaders said when I asked him if it was funny:

"Yeah, but it's bad funny."

I can live with that.

Thanks,

Scott Carpenter

3-10-10

LaVergne, TN USA
21 June 2010
186817LV00001B/2/P